PRIVATE LESSONS

ALSO BY BERNARD O'KEEFFE

No Regrets
10 Things To Do Before You Leave School
The Final Round: A Garibaldi Novel

For my daughter, Caitlin
(1988 – 2020)

Prologue

It was unusual to see anyone in the overgrown, derelict cemetery. That's why they went there whenever they could, armed with booze from the supermarket. That's why, as they sat on the grass between the headstones that afternoon, drinking from their cans and talking about what was going on in their lives, they were surprised to see a boy moving towards them.

He stopped a few yards away, looking at them with wild, staring eyes.

He wasn't much older than them but his clothes, his haircut, everything about him, proclaimed his difference. Different background. Different class.

'Get your money out,' said the boy.

They said nothing.

'I know you've got money. Get it out!'

They looked at each other, not sure what to do.

Then one of them got to his feet. As he did, the boy pulled out a knife and held it in front of him.

'Your money!'

Maybe he did it because he was drunk. Maybe he did it because he found the idea of handing over his money intolerable. Whatever the reason, the one who had stood up moved towards the boy, grabbed the wrist that held the knife, pushed back the arm and kicked the boy in the groin.

The boy fell and the knife flew to the ground.

He kicked the boy again, this time in the head.

Then he was on him, kicking and punching, raining blows on his face and body.

He looked back at his friends and invited them to join him.

1

Simon Mulholland closed the front door behind him, breathed in the morning air, did a few muscle stretches and set off at a gentle pace down Cleveland Gardens. He jogged through the narrow passage that led to The Terrace, crossed the road in front of Barnes Bridge, and joined the path that ran beside the river.

This was how he began each Sunday – with an early morning run beside the Thames. It would usually clear his mind and set him up for the day ahead, but today, as he ran along the towpath looking at the river glistening in the September sunshine, the exercise was struggling to work its magic.

He knew exactly why.

Another dinner party. Another night sat round a Barnes table with other young professional parents talking about the usual stuff. Where to shop. Where to dine. Where to holiday. Where to ski. The best schools for your kids. How to get your kids into them. How to keep them there.

And all with that horrible competitive edge that made any encounter with friends nowadays like a parents' race at sports day. He couldn't remember when he started to hate these occasions so much that getting drunk became the only sensible response, but he knew that last night he had needed to drink more than usual to get through. And it was the drink, together with the hostess's spicy Indian food, that was making this morning's jog so difficult.

He struggled towards Hammersmith Bridge, and carried on along the towpath until he was opposite Fulham Football Club, where he took a right, heading back to Barnes on a path that ran beside the playing fields. This morning's run, far from making him feel better, had made him feel considerably worse. His head had not cleared – it was fuzzy and aching – and his stomach felt as if something was wriggling inside it trying to escape.

He cut across the common and joined the path that ran beside the Rocks Lane tennis courts. As he did, he slowed down almost to a walk in the hope that gentler movement might make him feel better.

As he jogged past the courts, his stomach cramped.

He stopped by the couples playing early morning doubles and crouched down. He knew what was coming, and he knew it was coming quickly. He looked to his left and saw a path leading into a clump of trees. That would have to do.

He got to his feet and, unable to move freely and still clutching his stomach, hobbled his way into the trees, hoping to find somewhere out of sight of the tennis players or of anyone walking along the path.

Focused on what he needed to do, he didn't notice what was around him. He saw none of the headstones, none of the statues, none of the broken monuments. All he saw was trees, plants and foliage. All he saw was cover.

He headed in further, desperate to do what he needed to, but anxious for privacy. He found a small space between two stones, and, giving a final look around to check that no-one was in sight, dropped his shorts and pants, lifted his runner's shirt and squatted.

Out it came.

He gasped with relief as everything loosened and what had become of Alice's Indian food spattered onto the leaves below him.

It squirted onto the ground with a terrible force and his nostrils filled with an acrid stench. He glanced around again, anxious that someone might have seen him, but no-one was in sight.

He lifted himself up and examined the brown pool he had deposited, wondering how best to cover it up.

He shifted some leaves towards it with his trainers and, as he did, his eye caught something on the ground.

A hand.

A hand lying, palm-down, beside a headstone.

Simon pulled up his pants and shorts and then, eyes fixed on the hand, he moved closer to the stone. He peered over.

The body lay on its front, one leg raised, one arm stretched out behind, the other reaching round the side of the stone. Jeans, trainers, fleece – and a pool of blood spread on the ground beneath.

He bent down further to make sure. It was as he feared.

His stomach tightened again and he felt another uncontrollable convulsion in his body.

He turned away from the stone and emptied himself again.

This time through his mouth.

2

Garibaldi stood on stage beside John Prine, holding a guitar he couldn't play. He looked out at the audience and then turned to the singer, hoping he would give him some tips. But John Prine was lost in his song – 'Speed of the Sound of Loneliness'. His head was tilted upwards, his eyes half-closed, his brow furrowed with intensity.

Sweat ran down Garibaldi's back as he gazed into the auditorium. The lights dazzled but he could make out faces, most of which were looking in his direction. Puzzled faces. Questioning faces. Faces that asked Garibaldi what right he had to be up there beside the great American singer-songwriter.

Garibaldi looked down at the guitar. His hands felt its corpse-like coldness. The chorus was coming and any second now he would have to join in. He had to make sure he hit the right note. He had to harmonise.

He took a breath, shot a sideways look at John Prine, leaned into the mike and opened his mouth.

A loud bell rang. So loud that Garibaldi couldn't hear his own voice, so loud that no music at all could be heard. The bell's shrill ring filled the whole of the Shepherds Bush Empire auditorium. The house lights came on and the crowd, holding their hands to their ears, headed for the fire exits.

Garibaldi turned to John Prine. He wanted to apologise for screwing up – for not being able to play the guitar and for missing the chorus – but Prine was still singing, as if nothing had happened. The fire alarm still rang, but the singer was in his own world. 'You're travelling at the speed and the sound of loneliness,' he sang, as the crowd rushed away.

The alarm was now even louder and right next to Garibaldi's head.

He reached for it, scrabbling to find the button that would stop it, and realised that it wasn't an alarm at all.

It was his phone, ringing and vibrating on the bedside table.

He looked at the screen. Deighton.

He looked at the time. 9.00 am.

'Garibaldi.'

'Jim. Haven't woken you, have I?'

'Not at all. I've been up for hours.'

'We've got a body. In the cemetery.'

Garibaldi furrowed his brow and screwed up his eyes. A body in the cemetery. So what was new?

'The cemetery?'

'Yeah. Barnes Old Cemetery.'

Garibaldi tried to place it.

'The one near Rocks Lane,' said Deighton. 'You need to get there.'

'OK. I'm on it.'

Garibaldi yawned, stretched and hauled himself up to sit on the side of the bed.

Another anxiety dream. Another impostor syndrome nightmare.

And now a body in the cemetery.

Deciding to wake Rachel with a cup of tea before telling her he had to go, he went into the kitchen, trying to remember where, exactly, Barnes Old Cemetery was, and what he'd heard about it.

He brought two mugs of tea into the bedroom and placed one on Rachel's bedside table. Standing by the bed, he looked at her as she slept, her dark hair spread on the pillow. Who would have thought when they spent that first night together a couple of years ago, that it would lead to this? Living together. Bringing each other cups of tea in the morning.

Rachel stirred. 'What's the time?'

'Nine o'clock.'

'And it's Sunday, right?'

'Sunday. All day. No school.'

'I heard the alarm, but I dropped off again.'

'Why don't you go back to sleep?'

'Why?'

'Something's cropped up.'

'Work?'

Garibaldi nodded. 'Yeah. But there is a bright side.'

'What's that?'

'Gives you a chance to get on top of your marking.'

Rachel sighed, shut her eyes, raised a half-hearted hand in farewell, and turned onto her side.

Garibaldi unlocked his bike from the railings of Rutland Court and cycled into the High Street. Barnes was up and about, enjoying the crisp September morning. He passed the Sun Inn flower stall and glanced to his right where, beside the pond, loud young parents with loud young kids were feeding the ducks and the swans. He winced. Whenever he heard the young bankers or accountants or lawyers with their braying wives and their children, whenever his ears were assaulted by their high-volume public-parenting, he always asked himself the same question – was he just getting old and grumpy, or were they prats?

He always reached the same conclusion.

He cycled on, checking out the posters outside The Olympic and the window display of Barnes Books, took a right at the lights opposite The Red Lion and headed down Rocks Lane.

He wheeled his bike towards the police cars and the forensic van parked in the car park, locked it to a stand and walked to the taped cordon and the tent. An information board mounted on a wooden stand caught his eye and he paused to look at it. *Welcome to Barnes Common Old Cemetery.* He glanced at the pictures and the map, surprised by how he could have lived so close to the place for so long and know so little about it.

'Sir?'

Garibaldi turned to see DS Gardner in a forensic suit walking through the cordon past a uniformed officer.

'Morning, Milly. What have we got?'

Gardner stood beside him and looked at the board. 'Male youth. Twenties.'

'Any ID?'

Gardner shook her head.

'Phone?'

She shook her head again.

'What's it look like?'

'Stabbing.'

Garibaldi pointed at the information board. 'You know much about this place?'

'Not a lot. Pretty spooky, isn't it?'

'Most cemeteries are.'

'Yeah, but this one's a different kind of spooky.'

Garibaldi walked with his sergeant towards the police tape.

'And what have you been dragged away from on this bright Sunday morning?' said Garibaldi.

'Nothing much. Only Tim.'

Gardner had been with her new partner for a couple of months. Still early days, still plenty for her to worry about.

'And you?'

'Nothing much. Only Rachel.'

He knew as he spoke the words how little he believed them.

Garibaldi showed his card and nodded to the uniform at the cordon, pulled on a forensic suit hood, shoes and gloves and walked along the gravel path.

Light from above filtered through the branches and the leaves. To his left the ping and thwack of balls on rackets came from the tennis courts. To the right gravestones and memorials were dotted and scattered with no sense of order or regularity amongst low-lying shrubs, bushes and foliage. Some were broken, some had sunk into the ground and leaned at an angle, many were green and lichened. The place reeked of abandonment and decay.

Garibaldi had seen many dead bodies, but the mixture of emotions he felt when he was about to see a new one always surprised him. Fear at confronting more evidence of man's inhumanity to man, his capacity for savagery and cruelty. Fear that there but for the grace of God went us all. Fear that whoever killed might kill again. And pity. Pity for the life cut short. Pity for those who would mourn.

But there was also excitement. Not at the thought of what he was about to see, but at the thought of what he was about to engage in. Another puzzle. Another challenge. Another chance to bring whoever did it to justice and bring even a tiny amount of comfort to those who grieved.

The fear others might understand, but the excitement he kept quiet about. It might make him seem weird. Or strangely old-fashioned, like he was on some kind of moral crusade, desperate to restore order to a broken world. Both, he knew, were a long way from the truth. It was a lot more complicated than that.

Ahead, Garibaldi saw a large monument. He walked towards it, catching sight on his left of a statue of an angel. It stopped him in his tracks, making him look again to check that he was seeing things correctly.

He was. Above the wings was the trunk of a neck but the angel's head was missing.

'See what I mean?' said Gardner. 'Weird.'

Garibaldi opened the flap of the forensic tent erected next to the monument and followed Gardner in.

The SOCOs were at work, taking swabs and samples.

The body lay on its front, its head close to a gravestone, the left arm stretched out at right angles, the other arm reaching round the edge of the stone, the right leg raised and bent at the knee. The clothes – jeans, trainers, top – were the clothes of any young man. He looked to be in his twenties, but it was difficult to tell from what was visible. Not much older than Alfie, perhaps. Garibaldi shivered.

He looked up at the trees. Sunlight trickled through the branches, dappling the broken headstones and the back of the corpse and falling on the dark pool of blood.

The Crime Scene Manager came up to him. 'A couple of things to be aware of,' he said, pointing at two areas of the ground identified by crime scene markers on the other side of the stone from the body. 'Vomit and faeces.'

'And is it as obvious as it looks?' said Garibaldi, pointing at the body.

'There's a lot of blood. On him, on his clothes, on the ground, and there's some on the stone. Probably his own, but you never know.'

'And the faeces and vomit?'

'From the bloke who found him, apparently,' said Gardner.

'Shit scared was he?'

'Taken short on his run.'

'So he came in here, took a dump and vomited?'

'Says he relieved himself and then, after he found the body, he threw up.'

'Sounds like our number one suspect. Or maybe that should be our number two suspect.' The Crime Scene Manager looked baffled. 'Any sign of the weapon?'

'Nothing so far.'

'Shame. A bloodstained knife would be handy.'

'What have we here?'

Garibaldi turned to the voice and saw Martin Stevenson walking through the tent flap in a forensic suit.

'Another round of golf cancelled,' said the pathologist. 'I sometimes think they do it just to fuck up my weekends.'

Garibaldi smiled. He liked the pathologist's sense of humour. Irreverent. Ironic. Intelligent. His favourite 'I' words.

Another cry of 'Out' came from the tennis courts.

'Should have brought your racket,' said Garibaldi.

The pathologist crouched down beside the body. 'Oh dear, oh dear,' he said. He looked around at the broken headstones. 'What kind of cemetery is this?'

'An overgrown abandoned one,' said Garibaldi.

'Very Gothic.'

Garibaldi nodded his agreement. Gothic was the word. 'You should see the decapitated angel.'

Stevenson looked up. 'The what?'

'A statue of an angel with its head chopped off.'

'Fascinating. You must show me.'

'It's not the only one sir.' Gardner's voice came from behind them. 'There's another headless angel and a headless human.'

'A headless human?' said Stevenson, as if the idea held some appeal.

'A statue, that is. I looked around while I was waiting for you.'

'OK,' said Garibaldi, 'I'll have a look when—'

'When we've dealt with this,' said Martin Stevenson as he bent down to look more closely at the body.

Garibaldi looked on as the pathologist set to work. Forensics were busy searching the ground. Photos were being taken, a video camera was recording and one officer was dictating into his phone. 'Vomit located five metres south of body. Faeces five metres west.'

The pathologist went over to the officer and looked down at the vomit. 'Chicken curry, I'd say.' He moved towards the faeces. 'And this shit looks pretty human as well.' He sniffed. 'If I were a gambling man I'd put my money on it being chicken curry as well.'

The sound of the tennis players carried from the courts, a reminder that, only yards away from where a life had been brutally ended and a dead body was being subjected to the probing indignities of forensic examination, Sunday morning life was carrying on as usual.

Garibaldi looked around the cemetery and then down at the victim, wondering what had brought him here.

Sex? A creepy place for it, unless you got your kicks

from having it off on gravestones or among dead bodies and headless angels. But it wouldn't surprise him. He'd learned over the years that there was no accounting for the range of sexual appetites.

Drugs? Areas of leafy affluence like Barnes were plagued by them as much as areas of inner-city deprivation. Just different drugs and more money to pay for them.

Stevenson stood up. 'Looks pretty straightforward but can't be certain yet.'

He beckoned a couple of SOCOs and instructed them.

Garibaldi looked down on the body as they turned it. It was not quite the final indignity – that would come when it was subjected to post-mortem – but it was a step on the way. The face was now on full display, exposed to the morning light, blank and lifeless, eyes and mouth shut, a far cry from the smiling photo that would accompany the next day's news report.

The pathologist bent over the body.

'I'll leave you to it,' said Garibaldi.

He bent down to look at the face and the gravestone beside it. He tried to make out the name on the stone but the covering of moss and lichen made it impossible. All he could see was the date – 1848.

'Want to see the headless angels?' said Gardner.

'Headless angels?' Garibaldi got up and brushed himself down. 'What better way to start the weekend?'

Gardner walked into the bushes and Garibaldi followed her into the heart of Barnes Old Cemetery, leaving the SOCOs to their work and the pathologist to a closer examination.

3

'Apostrophe. Yes or no?'

In the long silence that followed, Giles Gallen wondered whether his pupil had forgotten what an apostrophe was or, more worryingly, whether he had ever known.

'What do you reckon, Paolo? Do you think that needs an apostrophe?'

Under a Mediterranean sun, apostrophes had hardly mattered. Now, on a Saturday afternoon in a London autumn, with the leaves starting to fall and the nights drawing in, the villa and the yacht and the events of the summer were behind them and apostrophes had taken on renewed significance.

Paolo looked at the sheet in front of him and tilted his head to one side. In recent years Giles had become adept at reading the backs of heads, and he knew what this one was saying. *I don't want to do this. I know my parents want to get me into a good school and I wouldn't mind going to one either but if I'm honest right now I'd rather be in the basement playroom or chilling out in the home cinema – anywhere in this multi-million-pound mansion rather than at this desk with you.*

Giles knew exactly how his student felt. Right now he'd rather be anywhere else as well.

This wasn't how he'd thought it would turn out. He'd

always imagined that when he graduated he would embark on an exciting new life – an interesting job in something (he'd never been clear exactly what), a flat in an edgy area of East London, and a continuation of the independence he had enjoyed during his time at Cambridge, this time with more money in his pocket and without the obligation to write essays and pass exams.

He'd never thought that, four years after graduating, he would still be living with his parents in Barnes and reading the backs of reluctant students' heads.

Nor that he would have got himself into such a horrendous mess.

He checked his watch while Paolo continued to ponder the unfathomable mystery of the apostrophe. Fifteen minutes to go. Time to set a little exercise and think about the evening ahead.

'OK. Paolo, here are ten sentences,' he said, reaching for a sheet and placing it in front of his student, 'but the apostrophes are missing. What I'd like you to do is copy them out and put in apostrophes where you think they should go.'

'Do I have to?'

'What do you think?'

Giles knew exactly what Paolo thought. He had to. Having a guess at where to put a few apostrophes was a better option than his mum going nuclear.

Paolo took the sheet and Giles sat back in his chair.

The door opened and Mrs Rivetti came in. Petite and lithe, with raven shoulder-length hair framing a high-cheekboned face, she radiated energy. Her dark eyes were bright and piercing. Giles sensed she was always on the brink of explosion and knew from what he had seen in the summer how true this was – like Vesuvius, she might erupt at any moment.

'How's he doing?'

Giles nodded. As parents' questions went, 'how's he doing' was no more than a loosener, the equivalent of hello or a handshake.

'Could I have a word?'

'Sure.'

'In private?'

More serious now. 'In private' had shifted it up a level.

'Of course,' said Giles, getting up from his chair.

Mrs Rivetti led him into the kitchen, or at least what the Rivettis liked to call the kitchen. Giles had never been in a kitchen that contained a grand piano. Had the floor slid open to reveal a swimming pool and dancing girls he wouldn't have been surprised.

'I'm worried,' said Mrs Rivetti.

Nothing new here. Every parent of every kid he'd ever tutored was worried. That's why they hired him.

'I'm worried he won't get in. Since the beginning of term he hasn't really settled. I know you're doing your best and we appreciate that.'

Giles knew the code. 'Doing your best' meant 'we think you could be doing more.' 'We appreciate that' meant 'we don't appreciate it at all.' Everything Mrs Rivetti was saying suggested a new level of concern – even that subtle shift from 'I' to 'we'. Luigi Rivetti was in on the case as well – or if he wasn't, Lucia would get him on it soon. Vesuvius was rumbling.

'Paolo always finds it difficult at the beginning of the school year,' said Mrs Rivetti. 'Summer is fine. He loves his holidays.'

A life of luxury in villas, on private planes and in yachts. Who wouldn't love his holidays?

'But back here in London . . .'

Paolo may not have liked being back in London, but

Giles was relieved. He was enjoying seeing the nights draw in and feeling the temperature drop.

He was glad to have a chance to recover. A chance to forget. A chance to wipe the slate clean and make a new start.

'We think you should see him more,' said Mrs Rivetti.

More? He was already seeing Paolo for two sessions in the week and one at weekends. There was no point seeing him more than that. One of the things he'd learned since he had taken up tutoring was that reluctant pupils didn't lose their reluctance through increased exposure to what they didn't want to do.

'You're the only one he'll respond to, Giles. We saw that right from the start and we certainly saw it in the summer. I know it wasn't easy for anyone what with . . . but you were good to have around. Good for all of us, but especially for Paolo. He gets on so well with you and that is so valuable.'

Giles knew how valuable it was. He still couldn't believe how much he had been paid.

'The thing is, Giles, that Sam's decided she can't carry on tutoring Anna.'

'Really?'

This was news to him. He hadn't seen Sam since they'd got back. They'd messaged a few times, but not about anything important. Not about what had happened.

He was surprised she hadn't told him she was stopping.

'Did she say why?'

Mrs Rivetti shrugged. 'Personal reasons.'

Personal reasons? What did that mean?

'And we were wondering if you could take over.'

'Take over from Sam? I, er . . .'

Taking over from Sam would mean teaching both the Rivetti children. It would double the time he spent at the Rivettis' and double the pressure.

'We'd pay you well. Extremely well.'

Giles tried to imagine what, in the Rivettis' world, paying extremely well might mean.

'The thing is, Paolo will only have this one go at getting into that school and we really can't leave anything to chance. We need to get him the best. And you, Giles, are the best.'

'I'm very flattered, Mrs Rivetti, but—'

'Think about it, Giles.'

'The thing is I do have other clients—'

'Whatever you earn from your other clients, we will double it, triple it, if you take over Sam's side of the teaching. Think about it.'

Giles thought about it. It had been a busy Saturday, cycling from house to house to tutor teenage kids. How much easier would it be if he only had two students? And if he earned more from them than he did from the others?

'The coming weeks are crucial for Paolo,' said Lucia. 'The more he can get of you, the better his chances. We know that. He responds to you, Giles, in a way he doesn't respond to his teachers at school and sometimes he responds to you in a way he doesn't even respond to us, his parents . . .'

Giles didn't need telling. He had seen the parental shortcomings of the super-rich in close-up.

'And if you agree to take on Anna as well, we were thinking that you could even move in here for a while.'

Move in? He hadn't seen that one coming.

Mrs Rivetti's eyes fixed tightly on his. 'We have a lot of room here. And there is a self-contained apartment at the back that you could have. When you're not tutoring Paolo and Anna you would have complete independence. Come and go as you please.'

A self-contained apartment? Giles tried to imagine it. If they called this room a kitchen what would their apartment look like?

'I'm very flattered, Mrs Rivetti, but can I think about it?'

'Of course. But Luigi wanted me to mention something else for you to consider. If you come to us, live with us, and work exclusively as our tutor we would cut the ties with the agency. You would be our employee.'

'So I wouldn't be working for Forum at all?'

'No,' said Mrs Rivetti. 'Just for us. Ideally as a live-in. Maybe you would like to see the apartment before you go?'.

'OK,' he said, 'that would be great.'

When Giles left the Rivettis' and set off on his bike down Castelnau towards his parents' house in Ranelagh Avenue, his mind was spinning. The prospect of working exclusively for the Rivettis held many attractions, the greatest of which were undoubtedly more money and the chance to move out of his parents' home. The annexed apartment had been the size of a small house and he couldn't stop thinking of what it might be like to live there. Nor could he stop thinking of how many noughts might be on the end of the Rivetti live-in tutor pay cheque – more, he sensed, than the number of apostrophes Paolo had placed correctly.

On the other hand, the idea of being owned by the rich Italians, of working only for them and, despite the apartment's apparent independence, in effect living with them and being constantly at their beck and call, was not something he could seriously consider. His experience in the summer had confirmed his sense that this kind of tutoring was not for him, and his instincts were telling him that, far from moving in with the Rivettis to be a live-in tutor for Paolo and Anna, now might be the time for him to do what Sam had done and stop working for them completely.

As he cycled past the Sun Inn, Giles reached a couple of decisions.

The first was to say no to the Rivettis.

The second was much bigger and would have more far-reaching implications. He should have done it years ago but now, at last, he would do the right thing.

And he would do it tonight, after the Forum party.

4

'So tell us all about it,' said Simon.

Giles took a sip of his beer and looked round the early Saturday evening crowd in the Coach and Horses.

'About what?'

'The summer.'

'It was good.'

What else could he say? Three weeks in a Tuscan villa and a cruise round the Med. Four hours a day tutoring Paolo, and the rest of the time to himself.

'How come you land all the good jobs? Whenever I apply for these exotic placements I never come close. And now here we go again. Another September.'

September. The beginning of another academic year. The return of schools and, with their return, the demands and requests of parents anxious for extra help. Extra help that would bring their kids up to scratch and get them the grades. Extra help that would get them into the right school or university. Extra help that would give their kids the edge and keep them ahead. Extra help that would ensure they weren't missing out on the extra help that other kids were getting

It was a busy time for tutoring.

And it was time for the annual Forum drinks party.

'I don't know why they do it,' said Emily. 'I mean, what's the point?'

'It's because Forum's a *family*,' said Simon. 'Haven't you seen their website?'

'Silly me,' said Emily. 'I forgot.'

'Yeah,' said Simon. 'One big happy family, and one with . . .' He turned to Giles. 'One with favoured sons.'

'You've got it wrong,' said Giles.

'I don't think so, 'said Emily. 'If you don't watch it, you'll become a . . .' She looked over her shoulder at the early evening drinkers in the Coach and Horses and leaned into the table as if about to deliver a confidence. 'You'll become a *supertutor*.' She italicised the word with a whisper.

'A super tutor?' said Giles.

'Yeah.' Emily leaned back and smiled. 'One of those tutors who works for the super-rich and earns an absolute fortune.'

'I really don't think so,' said Giles.

Emily took a swig of beer from her bottle and licked froth from her lips. 'You're almost there.'

'One family,' said Giles, holding up his index finger. 'One.'

'Yeah,' said Simon, 'a super-rich one.'

'Exactly,' said Emily. 'Perfect for a . . . supertutor.'

'I do have some principles, you know.'

'Of course,' said Emily. 'We've all got principles. I mean, I'm only tutoring because—'

'Because it's something that pays while you pursue your dream?' said Giles. He'd heard the line many times before. He knew all about Emily's and Simon's dreams.

'This time next year,' said Emily, 'I won't be doing this.'

'Yeah, right,' Giles laughed. 'You said exactly that this time last year.' He turned to Simon. 'Both of you said it.'

'Yeah well it takes time, doesn't it?' said Simon. 'It's all right for you, landing jobs like that. Must be the Hugh Grant looks. The floppy hair. The posh voice.'

'Radley and Cambridge,' said Emily. 'That's what gets you these jobs. Comprehensive and Cardiff like me you've got no chance.'

'Or Radley and Newcastle like me,' said Simon. 'Not quite the same, is it? The thing is, Giles, the reason you'd make a good supertutor is there's nothing else you're desperate to do.'

'How do you know?'

'Because you've never said there is.'

'That doesn't mean I don't want to do something else. I just haven't worked out what it is yet.'

'Exactly,' said Emily. 'So why not go for it? Spend your time jetting round the world and getting paid a fortune.'

'You're forgetting that while I might spend some of my time on yachts in the Med, I also spend some of my time in inner city state schools.'

'Ah yes,' said Simon. 'Pro bono!'

He smiled at Emily. 'Pro bono!' she repeated.

'You may laugh, but I'd like to point out that of all those sitting round the table right now there's only one person who offers his tutoring services for free in an area that might need it more than the Rivettis.'

'It's not that we don't want to,' said Simon, 'it's that we can't afford to.'

'Yeah,' said Emily. 'Principles are really expensive.'

'Whereas you're raking it in,' said Simon, 'so principles are a bit easier.'

'I don't *have* to do it, you know. No-one's forcing me to.'

'And Forum don't have to do it either,' said Emily. 'But it makes them feel better and it looks good. Maybe it does the same for you.'

'Look,' said Giles, his tone suggesting he wanted to bring this conversation to a close. 'I'm not claiming to be a saint or anything. The fact is I do the pro bono stuff because I want to and so what if it makes me feel better? What's the harm in that? Maybe I do it to keep my feet on the ground, to remind myself that all the flashy stuff is OK but it's not real. The thing about these glamorous jobs . . .'

He paused. For a moment, a very brief moment, he was tempted to tell them about the summer.

'The thing is, at the end of the day, you're left in no doubt about where you stand. You're their employee, their servant. You're part of their domestic staff. A maid with a degree.'

'But you're like a fashion accessory,' said Emily, 'their bit of British class they like to show off. They don't show off their maids.'

'Look,' said Giles, 'I only go abroad with them in the school holidays. If you wanted to make serious money out of it you'd have to live with them the whole time.'

He thought again of the Rivettis' offer. Ditching Forum and moving into the self-contained apartment in their Lonsdale Road mansion. The more he thought about it the more appalled he was.

'You still haven't told us about the summer,' said Simon.

Giles tensed. 'What's to tell?'

'Was she there again?' said Emily.

'Was who there?'

'You know who I mean.'

'Do I?'

'Yeah,' said Simon. 'The other tutor.'

'The other tutor? Yeah, she was there.'

'And . . . ?' Emily leaned forward.

'And what?'

'What happened?' said Simon.

'Nothing happened.'

Simon stroked his chin. 'Yeah, right.'

'You can believe what you like, but it's the truth.'

'What's her name again?' said Emily.

'Sam.'

'Oh, yeah. Sam. And is Sam going to be there tonight?'

'I don't think so.'

'You don't think so? You mean you don't know?'

'When I last spoke to her, she said she couldn't make it.'

Emily gave a knowing smile. Was Giles imagining it, or was that a jealous glint in her eye?

'I still don't understand why they needed two tutors.'

'I was there for the son and Sam was there for the daughter.'

'And what are they like, this Italian family?' asked Emily. 'You must have got to know them pretty well.'

'The parents? Not really.'

'What about the kids?'

'Yeah, I got to know them quite well.'

'No, I mean what about the kids telling you stuff about the parents? Kids always tell you stuff.'

'Yeah,' said Simon. 'The kids always tell you things. Those little breaks you take for a chat – that's when they let things slip about mummy and daddy. I mean, the things you find out!'

Simon started to tell them the things he'd found out. The cross-dressers in Chiswick. The father in Kew who put hidden cameras in all the rooms. The couple who made loud love in the bedroom while he was tutoring.

'Are we listening to your next Edinburgh show?' said Giles.

'Could be,' said Simon. 'What do you think?'?

'Is any of it true?' said Emily.

'Every word of it.'

'And what about you?' said Emily, turning to Giles. There was something about the way she was looking at him. Was she flirting?

'What about me?'

'Found out anything interesting about your parents? I mean the parents of the kids you teach.'

'Nothing special.'

'I sometimes worry about you, Giles . . .' Emily leaned forward and he saw the glint again. 'All those mothers.'

'What about them?'

Emily gave a suggestive wink.

Giles shook his head. 'Sorry to disappoint you.'

'What about the fathers?' said Simon.

'Afraid not.'

'I don't believe you,' said Emily.

'About the dads?'

'About any of them.'

Simon downed his drink and stood up. 'OK. Let's get this over with. A big smile for Felicia and Roddy so they know we've turned up and then back to the pub as early as we can.'

'Good idea,' said Emily. 'What about you, Giles? Fancy slipping out early to the Red Lion?'

'Or does the blue-eyed boy want to hang out with Felicia and Roddy?' said Simon.

'You've got the wrong idea,' said Giles. 'Really.'

'No we haven't,' said Simon. He poked Giles in the ribs. 'Teacher's pet.'

Teacher's pet. That's what Simon had called him at Radley and he'd carried the habit, together with so many others, beyond the school walls. The two of them went back such a long way and shared so many things that whenever they were with others they were sometimes accused of lapsing into a code that people didn't understand, making references from which others felt excluded.

Tonight Giles had been more than usually conscious of this, and he knew exactly why. It was because of what he had decided to do. He had lived with it for too long and now was the time to sort it out. Now was the time to come clean.

'Yeah,' said Emily. 'Teacher's pet!'

'You've both got the wrong idea.'

'I don't think so,' said Emily, placing her hand on his shoulder and giving it a squeeze. 'Mr Supertutor!'

Giles laughed with them but his mind was elsewhere, thinking of when he should turn down the Rivettis' offer and when would be a good time to have a quiet word with Simon.

5

DCI Deighton's office, like Deighton herself, revealed nothing about her private life. No family photos. No personal touches. A business-like, no-nonsense affair.

'No ID?' said Garibaldi.

Deighton shook her head.

'No phone?'

Another shake.

'And why there?'

'Strange place, isn't it?'

'Yeah,' said Garibaldi. 'Did you know it's where Ebenezer Morley's buried?'

Deighton raised her eyebrows. She tolerated many things about Garibaldi – his inability to drive and his QPR season ticket, for example, but she found other things more difficult to take. Like his tendency to show off.

'Ebenezer Morley?'

'OK,' said Garibaldi, sensing that her face was turning into a no-tolerance zone, 'I didn't know who he was either. Had to look him up. Amazing what you can find on Wikipedia. Turns out he's the man who formulated the rules of modern football. Pretty big news in football terms. And he lived in Barnes. Funny that. Coming from Barnes you'd think he'd be more of a rugby man, but good old Ebenezer, eh? And it seems he's not the only famous person buried in the Old Cemetery.'

Deighton raised her eyebrows again.

'F.T. Palgrave.'

'And who did he play for?'

Garibaldi smiled. '*Palgrave's Golden Treasury*. A famous poetry anthology.'

'Of course,' said Deighton. 'And what did your Wikipedia research tell you about the times you couldn't move in the Old Cemetery for used needles and condoms?'

'Maybe that's what brought him there. Sex and drugs.'

'Maybe.'

'Unlikely to be rock and roll.'

The blank look again.

'It's a song. Ian Dury. "Sex and Drugs and Rock and Roll".'

'I see.'

'Had it been a bit closer to the Marc Bolan shrine we might consider it.'

Deighton nodded. She got this one – a reference to the memorial at the sycamore tree on Queen's Ride into which the T. Rex singer's car had fatally crashed in 1977.

'It's surprising,' said Deighton, 'how few people know about Barnes Old Cemetery.'

Garibaldi nodded. Those who knew about the cemetery at the edge of the Common often referred to it as a well-kept secret, the term 'well-kept' applying to the secret rather than the cemetery. Long ago abandoned, neglected and overgrown, the place had in the past attracted cruisers, drug addicts and gloom-seeking goths, but in recent years a local environmental group had kept it in better shape, clearing rubbish and tending the paths, while allowing nature to take its course and the place to become a sanctuary for birds and other wildlife.

'Anything on the man who found him?' said Garibaldi.

'A banker called Simon Mulholland. We've got a statement. Seems more embarrassed about needing a crap before he got home and throwing up than worried about what he found. DNA check will confirm whether the bodily expulsions are his.'

Deighton paused and gave Garibaldi a look he had come to recognise. The pastoral concern look. The unspoken but implied recognition of what he had been through.

'So, Jim, how are you?'

He gave a non-committal shrug. Deighton's face still wore the pastoral care look, her eyes inviting Garibaldi to speak.

'I'm, you know, getting by,' he said.

'Like the rest of us, then,' said Deighton. She let out a slow sigh. 'You know, I sometimes wonder if we shouldn't expect more.'

'More than what?'

'More than getting by.'

'Getting by seems good enough to me. Beats expecting too much and always being disappointed.'

'Look, Jim, if you ever want to talk about things—'

'Talk about things?'

'If you're, you know, finding it tough.'

Garibaldi felt accused, as if he looked like a man who needed to talk about things, as if he'd done something wrong and everyone had noticed.

'Talk about things?'

'We all know how difficult it was for you a few years back.'

They all knew, but it was only in the car with Milly and

here, in Deighton's office, that the divorce and depression were ever mentioned. Or at least mentioned to his face.

'And,' said Deighton, 'it's difficult to find the right time when we're here.' She waved her hands to suggest she was referring to the whole station. 'So I was wondering if you might fancy a drink one night after work.'

'OK,' said Garibaldi, trying hard to hide his surprise.

'Let me know. It's sometimes easier to say things away from this place.'

Garibaldi had to pinch himself. The closed book that was DCI Deighton was threatening to open.

'Right,' said Deighton in a back-to business tone, looking down at her notes. 'Another young life gone.'

Another young life. He thought of Alfie. He'd always assumed that the older he got, the less he would worry about him, but his first year at university had shown him otherwise.

Deighton's phone rang. 'DCI Deighton.'

She nodded and scribbled on her pad.

'We've got a name,' she said when she hung up.

'How did they get that?'

'His clothes. Apparently his jumper had one of those name tags your mum used to sew in. Maybe he had it when he was at school.'

From nowhere a memory rushed back and, in the corner of Deighton's office, Garibaldi saw his mother stitching labels in his grammar school uniform. There she was in their Fulham council flat, her eyes flitting between the needle and thread and the TV. And there was his father in the chair beside her, his head in a paper, ready for his evening trip to the pub. How many years ago was it? Thirty? Forty? And how many years before the fateful accident that took them both away from him?

Even now there were nights when Garibaldi heard again the knock on the door and the policeman's words. Even now there were times when he saw all of his life after that point as some kind of crazed grief – joining the police rather than going to university, marrying Kay, becoming a father, and then the shit of a couple of years ago when everything unravelled, as if it had taken all those years to comprehend the enormity of what had happened to him just before he was about to take his A Levels.

'Jim?'

Garibaldi turned away from his mother and father and saw Deighton looking at him across her desk, eyebrows raised.

'Are you OK, Jim?'

'Sure. I'm fine.'

'You seemed miles away.'

'Did I? Sorry, I was just thinking.'

'About the victim's jumper?'

'Yeah. I was thinking that it might not be his.'

Deighton nodded in the way she always did when Garibaldi surprised her with an unexpected line of thought.

Garibaldi shook his head, trying to shake the memory away.

Penny Gallen, still in her dressing gown, wore the waxwork face of a woman frozen by shock. Her movements were slow, her speech uncertain and her manner that of someone recovering from a dizzying blow to the head.

Jeremy Gallen sat beside his wife, clutching her hand, his white fingers tightly wrapped round hers. He was dressed in a suit, looking as if, despite the news they had just received, he would go off to work after this interview and carry on with his life as normal. Garibaldi sat opposite the couple.

DS Gardner sat beside him and the Family Liaison Officers stood outside in the hall, ready to offer support when their visit ended.

The room was heavy with pain, numb with shock.

'I can't begin to imagine how you must feel,' said Garibaldi, 'and I'm sorry to have to ask you questions so soon after hearing such terrible news.'

Jeremy Gallen nodded. His wife gazed into space.

'But given what seem to be the circumstances of his death, it's important that our investigation starts as soon as possible.'

'Who would do such a thing?' said Mr Gallen, looking imploringly from Garibaldi to DS Gardner and then back to Garibaldi. 'Who could possibly want to kill . . . to kill Giles?'

Mrs Gallen flinched at the mention of her son's name.

'I don't understand,' said Mr Gallen. 'Who could have done this?'

'Everything in front of him,' said Mrs Gallen, still staring into space. 'Why?'

Garibaldi leaned forward. 'When did you last see Giles?'

Mrs Gallen turned to him, but her look was blank, as if she had no idea what he'd said.

'We saw Giles yesterday lunchtime,' said Mr Gallen. 'Before he went out.'

'Where did he go?' asked DS Gardner.

'He said he was going to work.'

'Where did he work?'

'All over the place,' said Mr Gallen. 'He was a tutor. A private tutor.'

'I see,' said Garibaldi, 'so do you know where he went?'

Mr Gallen shook his head. 'He was tutoring several students, but he never told us who they were or where he was going . . .'

'Twenty-six!' said Mrs Gallen.

Twenty-six. The words echoed in the silence like a doomed bingo call.

'We never asked him where he was going,' said Mr Gallen. 'As long as he told us if he wouldn't be coming back.'

Wouldn't be coming back. Another silent echo.

'That's all we asked,' said Mrs Gallen 'Let us know if he wouldn't . . . He said he'd be back early evening and then he'd be going out again to a drinks party.'

'Where was this party?'

'I think he said it was at the agency.'

'The agency?'

'The tutoring agency he works for. Worked for.'

The wrong tense of the recently bereaved. One of the few grammatical errors Garibaldi never felt the urge to correct.

Mrs Gallen shook her head again, her eyes blank and wide.

'The drinks were at the tutoring agency he works for,' said Mr Gallen.

'Do you know the name of this agency?'

'Forum. It's called Forum Tutors.' The barely audible words came from Mrs Gallen. 'They're based here in Barnes.'

'And Giles had been working for them as a tutor?'

Mr Gallen nodded. 'He's been doing it for several years. Ever since he left Cambridge. At first it was just something to tide him over. I kept going on at him to get a proper job—' He broke off as if remembering, and regretting, the discussions. '—and he kept telling me he would, but then over the last year or so he started to get different kinds of placements. More money. Travel abroad. So he decided to carry on. I still wish . . .'

'Where did he go?' said Garibaldi.

'All over the place.' Mr Gallen sounded disapproving. 'Italy. The Greek islands. Mainly Easter and Summer holidays. The rest of the time the family were here.'

'The family?'

'An Italian family. Massively wealthy.'

'And do you have any idea who Giles was tutoring on Saturday? Was it this family?'

'I don't know,' said Mrs Gallen. 'He's always busy on Saturdays. And terms have just started, I suppose, so . . .'

Mr Gallen gave a heavy sigh. 'Do we really have to answer questions now? This is unbearable.'

'I'm sorry, Mr and Mrs Gallen, but we need to—'

'They need to know!' Mrs Gallen almost shrieked the words. 'They need to know!'

Mr Gallen rested another hand on his wife's.

Mrs Gallen looked at her husband's hands and then up at his face, as if unable to make a connection between them.

She turned to Garibaldi. 'Will I be able to see him?'

'His body will need to be identified,' said Garibaldi, 'but you don't have to . . .'

'Are you sure it's him?' said Mrs Gallen, her eyes brightening at the possibility of a mistake. 'What if it's not him?'

Garibaldi looked round the room. The elegant dark furniture. The book-lined walls. The tasteful prints. The framed photographs. His eyes rested on the two graduation photos, a girl and a boy.

'How did you identify him?' said Mr Gallen.

'There was a name tag in his jumper.'

'A blue jumper?' said Mrs Gallen, her eyes suddenly alive and warm.

Garibaldi nodded.

'He had it from Radley,' said Mrs Gallen. 'I sewed it on for him!'

'I'm sorry,' said Garibaldi.

Mrs Gallen smiled at a memory. 'He adored his time at Radley. Loved every minute. Cambridge was fantastic, of course, but I still think the school meant more to him. There's something about your schooldays, isn't there? And he made such good friends.'

'Did you know his friends?'

'Oh, yes.' Mrs Gallen turned to her husband. 'Such good friends, weren't they, dear? A big group of them, but it was really Simon and Hugo, wasn't it? From day one. And Simon lives here in Barnes, so they were close in every sense.' She turned to Garibaldi. 'He'll have to know! They'll all have to know. All his friends. Simon, Hugo, Alex, James, Henry . . .' She trailed off, as if she were a teacher distracted in the middle of reading a register. 'But especially Simon and Hugo.'

'And did Giles have a . . . did he have a partner?'

'You mean a girlfriend?' said Mr Gallen.

Garibaldi gave a non-committal nod. 'Anyone.'

'He did have a girlfriend,' said Mrs Gallen. 'A lovely girl, but they broke up earlier this year.' Her face flashed with concern. 'We'll have to tell her. We'll have to tell everyone . . . Beth, that was her name.' She turned to her husband. 'Can you remember where she lived?'

'We don't need to worry about that now, dear.'

'But she'll have to know. Everyone will have to know!'

Mrs Gallen's face froze. She bowed her head.

Garibaldi turned to Gardner and nodded. They both got up. 'Thank you, Mr and Mrs Gallen, and our deepest condolences again. If there's anything you remember about where he was last night, or anything that you think might be significant, please do get in touch.'

'His jumper,' said Mrs Gallen, her head still bowed. 'Can I have his jumper?'

Garibaldi said nothing, knowing that not much of the jumper would remain after extensive forensic testing. He held out a card to Mr Gallen. 'We will do our very best to find out who did this.'

Mr Gallen looked at the card. 'What on earth was he doing there? Of all places. And . . . why?' He looked up at them. 'Please . . .'

'We'll do all we can,' said Garibaldi. He moved to the door with Gardner, beckoning the Family Liaisons back in.

Mr Gallen looked at them with puzzled, pleading eyes. 'Thank you.'

'Poor bastards,' said Garibaldi as they headed for the car.

6

Garibaldi looked at the board behind DCI Deighton. The crime scene photo of Giles Gallen, face down in the cemetery, blood pooled beneath his body, sat in the middle. Beside it was a photo from Gallen's Instagram profile. Underneath was a map of the area, rings round the Old Cemetery, the Gallens' house in Ranelagh Avenue and the Glebe Road house of Felicia and Roddy Ireland, the owners of Forum Tutors.

'Gallen's parents,' said DCI Deighton, pointing at the Ranelagh Avenue ring, 'last saw their son yesterday evening before he went out to meet friends before going to the Forum Tutors drinks party. We don't know where Gallen met his friends or, as yet, who those friends were, but we do know that Gallen was at that party. We have no idea of his precise time of departure and we don't know where he went after the party. All we know is that his body was found here.' She pointed at the ring round Barnes Old Cemetery. 'It was found this morning by a jogger, a Simon Mulholland, who was taken short towards the end of his run and went into this area . . .' She pointed at the ring round the Old Cemetery. '. . . to relieve himself. As he was doing his business . . .'

Garibaldi smirked. There were things about Deighton he didn't quite get. Capable, yes. Tough, yes. She must have been to have risen as she had. But she was still an enigma, her private life a mystery, and her prim, schoolmistressy turns of phrase at odds with the brutal realities of her job. Doing his business? She might as well have said big jobbies. Or even, echoing his own crime scene gag, number twos.

'As he was doing it, he saw the body. This made him throw up. That explains the vomit and faeces found at the scene.' She pointed at the photos at one side of the board. 'We've taken a DNA swab from Mulholland and wait to have the match confirmed. Doc Stevenson can't be precise about the time of death, so all we can say with certainty is that it happened between the time he left the party on Saturday night and the time the body was discovered on Sunday morning. So it all comes down to working out what happened to Gallen after he left the Ireland's house. We're expecting the post-mortem later today, and we do, of course, assume nothing, but the picture seems to tell a pretty clear story. A fatal stabbing. The search for a weapon continues.'

DCI Deighton scanned the room. Garibaldi looked at Gardner, waiting for her arm to go up. There it was. Always the first to ask a question.

'That cemetery's a pretty odd place. Do we have any idea why he might have gone there?'

Gardner's questions tended to be either a statement of the obvious or unhelpful, often both at the same time. This one was an improvement.

'You're right,' said Deighton. 'The cemetery's an odd place. And in years gone by it was a place for drugs and sex. It pulled in some odd birds.'

Odd birds. There she went again. If she'd come out with

ne'er-do-wells or scallywags it wouldn't have surprised him. Deighton was teacher-like, but St Trinian's rather than Grange Hill. Or maybe, fuelled by some strange fantasy of his own, Garibaldi was imagining the St Trinian's thing.

'Tidied up now by the Friends of Barnes Common, but still pretty wild.'

'Any CCTV?' asked DC McLean from the back.

'Nothing near. There could be some security cameras at Rocks Lane Sports Centre and there may be some residential cameras on the houses between Glebe Road and the Cemetery. At the moment, the problem is we know nothing about Gallen, and we need to. In particular we need to know about his movements on Saturday night. No phone on the body but we've asked for records of his calls and cell site analysis. We need to look at his computer, at his bank transactions. He had friends. He worked as a tutor. There's plenty to find out about him if we're going to get some kind of narrative.'

Narrative. A Deighton favourite. Just like ABC. Assume nothing. Believe nobody. Check everything. Incredible how far you could rise from one read of the Ladybird Book of Detection.

'We need everything we can get on Giles Gallen. Find out how the . . .'

. . . victim lived and you'll find out how the victim died. Garibaldi finished the line in his head.

'Right,' said DCI Deighton. 'Let's get on it.'

Let's get on it. Another Deighton gem.

DS Gardner drove out of the station car park up onto the Shepherds Bush Road and turned right towards Hammersmith Broadway. 'I'm beginning to forget what it was like to drive over the bridge.'

'It's OK for you,' said Garibaldi, 'you live north of the river.'

'OK for the station but not much use when you need to get to Barnes.'

Garibaldi laughed. Barnes had always felt cut off – a historical result of the loop in the river that enclosed it – but its sense of isolation had been accentuated by the closure of Hammersmith Bridge to traffic. Being a non-driving cyclist, it made little difference to him as you could still get across the bridge by bike or on foot, but for the majority of Barnes residents it was a major inconvenience. Drivers had to cross the river via Chiswick or Putney, while those using public transport had to get off on one side and walk across to the other.

Nothing – war, famine, terrorism, injustice – had angered the good people of Barnes as much as the bridge's closure. Nothing had come as close in uniting them in communal protest or in bringing them to the brink of insurrection.

'You know what?' said Garibaldi. 'You're right.'

Gardner gave her head a small turn, as if she was surprised to hear such words come out of her boss's mouth.

'About the bridge?'

'About Barnes Old Cemetery.'

'Yeah?'

'Yeah. It's a strange place, and we need to know what Giles Gallen was doing there. We also need to know what he was doing before and after that drinks party. All we've got is that he was tutoring in the afternoon.'

'Funny thing, tutoring, isn't it?' said Gardner.

'Can't say I've given it much thought. All I know is it's big business.'

'So you never got Alfie a tutor?'

Garibaldi laughed. The idea had never crossed his mind, though he knew it had crossed Kay's.

'I mean,' said Gardner, 'I can understand it if your kid's fallen behind badly or needs some special help or you think they need a leg-up because they're not getting what they need at school, but from what I gather, everyone does it. I've got a friend who gets a tutor in for her kids and she said something like a quarter of school kids in the country get private tuition of some sort, and when it comes to London, it's more than that – it's nearly half! That's crazy. And a lot of these kids are already at private schools. People fork out millions in fees and then fork out more for a private tutor. I don't get it.'

'Money and ambition,' said Garibaldi. 'It's a heady cocktail. The world's full of parents wanting the best for their kid and being prepared to pay for it. And when I say wanting the best for your kid, read wanting your kid to do better than everyone else's.'

He thought of Alfie moving schools for A Levels. Had that been the best thing for him? Was that why he had ended up at Oxford? And was that why he had changed so much in his first year there?

'What's more,' said Gardner, 'my friend says loads of these tutors aren't even properly qualified. Young. Just out of university. They could be completely useless. She says the whole thing's a jungle and you have to be careful. A load of firms are out to rip you off.'

Garibaldi nodded his agreement. 'Everyone's out to rip you off.'

They drove in silence towards Chiswick.

As they crossed the bridge Garibaldi asked, 'So how's it going with Tim?'

Something about sitting beside DS Milly 'Uber' Gardner,

their eyes on the road ahead rather than on each other, made it easier to ask such questions.

'Three months now,' said Gardner.

'So you're counting, then?'

'Yeah. Is that good or bad?'

'Depends what the three months have been like.'

'They've been good.'

'Count away, then.'

Garibaldi glanced sideways and was pleased to catch the end of a smile. Ever since he'd accepted that nothing would, or should, happen between them, he'd developed an almost paternal protectiveness towards his sergeant.

'Yeah, it's all going well. Except that I sometimes worry . . .'

She broke off, as if thinking better of what she'd been about to say.

'Worry about what?'

'It's nothing.'

'Really?

'OK,' sighed Gardner. 'This is going to sound silly, but sometimes I worry that I might not be good enough for him.'

'Good enough for him? Don't be ridiculous! Surely the question is whether he's good enough for you?'

'The thing is he's . . . he's a bit like you.'

'A bit like me?'

'Yeah. Clever.'

Garibaldi knew his reputation. A bit of a smart-arse, fond of showing off his learning, not averse to making the occasional literary reference, a novel always tucked away in the inside pocket of his jacket (currently a Muriel Spark). And a recently developed habit of pointing out grammatical errors. He tried to rein himself in but sometimes he couldn't stop himself. And all, according to his ex-wife, because he never went to university and needed to overcompensate.

'You shouldn't think like that.'

'I try not to,' said Gardner, 'but when we're talking about things I sometimes think what I say's a bit, you know, obvious.'

'What kind of things?'

'Oh, I don't know. Maybe we'll be watching a film or some TV programme or talking about something and he'll come up with these comments and I'm like . . .'

Was it Garibaldi's fault? Had he in some way contributed to her feelings of inadequacy? He'd resolved many times to encourage Milly rather than criticise her, but he knew he'd often fallen short.

'I mean,' said Gardner, 'I know lawyers are clever, and I know I've read less books than him . . .'

The word 'fewer' knocked on the doors of Garibaldi's lips. He had the good sense to keep them shut.

'. . . but we get on really well, even if we're from different backgrounds.'

'It's a myth,' said Garibaldi.

'What is?'

'That you need to have similar interests and be from similar backgrounds to work as a couple. Often it's better to be different.'

He knew his own experience proved otherwise. He never had much in common with Kay and look how that turned out. And in Rachel he'd found a woman who loved Townes Van Zandt.

'Maybe I should get myself a tutor.'

Garibaldi laughed. 'No, Milly, whatever you do, do not get yourself a tutor. You don't need to do an Eliza Doolittle!'

Gardner looked baffled and Garibaldi kicked himself.

'Eliza Doolittle as in Pyg . . . as in *My Fair Lady.* You know, the musical.'

'I don't think I've seen it.'

'You haven't seen *My Fair Lady*?' He kicked himself again.

'I'm sure Tim has though.'

'What you've got to remember, Milly, is people are never as clever as they think they are or as you fear they might be.'

'Really?'

'Yeah, really.'

'Does the same go for you?'

'The same goes for everyone. The thing to do,' said Garibaldi, 'is trust your instincts and do what you want. Don't be swayed by what you think your opinion should be about things. Just say what you think.'

'Yeah, but whenever I do that . . .'

'Milly, believe me, if there's one thing you don't need it's a tutor.'

'You're right. I mean, I could always ask you for a few lessons, couldn't I?'

'That's a joke, right?'

There were limits to how much he wanted to encourage her advancement.

'The thing is,' said Gardner, 'it's all very well to say you should say what you think, but what if what you think's a load of bollocks?'

'You've been in team briefings, haven't you? Just think how much of what's said in them is a load of bollocks. The thing is if everyone waited until they knew what they were about to say was going to be one hundred percent on the money, no-one would say anything.'

'But in meetings we're coming up with ideas, testing them out, asking questions.'

'Exactly, and how's that any different from anything else? So, when smartypants Tim—'

'He's not a smartypants.'

Smartypants? Where had that come from? He sounded like Deighton.

'You know what I mean. Whenever he talks about books and things just say what you think. Don't hold back.'

'But what if you haven't read the books he's talking about? What if you haven't heard of whatever he's referring to?'

'Just be honest. It's the only way.'

'But then he'll think I'm . . .'

'The worst thing to do is pretend.'

Gardner fell silent, as if weighing up the advice. She didn't seem convinced.

'But if you really do want private lessons,' said Garibaldi, 'I'm sure I can arrange reasonable rates.'

He winked. It was as difficult to stop himself flirting as it was to stop himself pointing out grammatical errors.

7

Felicia Ireland knew her way round schools. A product of Westminster and Trinity College, Cambridge, she had, since the establishment of Forum Tutors, devoted herself to securing a comprehensive knowledge of the system she herself had sailed through so successfully. She had an agile brain and could absorb information quickly, so it didn't take her long to master the details. Prospectuses. Websites. Inspection Reports. League Tables. The Good Schools Guide. Mumsnet. She set about her research with enthusiasm, coming to the conclusion so many others had reached – that when it came to educating your kids, the world was full of parents who only wanted the best and were prepared to go to extraordinary lengths (and fork out huge sums of money) to secure it.

She spoke to as many people as she could. Headteachers. Admissions Officers. Journalists. Parents. Pupils. Agencies. Tutors. She spread her net far and wide as she gathered insight into the world of tutoring. Soon she had what she felt was a sharp sense of the market's possibilities and, with her husband, Roddy, launched Forum Tutors confident that, provided she recruited the right sort of people, there was an almost insatiable demand for what they would offer.

Roddy applied the skills he had gained from working as a graduate trainee in the marketing department of a large consumer goods company to examine the tutoring market with a different approach. His wife may have been adept at research, but he knew that her real understanding of the world was more intuitive than scientific. She liked to talk and pick up on gossip, listening to the rumour and speculation and working out what was being said round the dinner tables of the tutor-employing classes. Schools that were in and schools that were out. How to play the entrance exam game. How to get your kids into the best universities. How important extra-curricular activities were in any application. Felicia was a people person, not a numbers person, and Roddy liked to think he brought a much-needed business brain to the operation. He covered the stats and the percentages – most importantly, he came up with a sense of how much money they could make from the enterprise. Between them they covered the bases. Forum Tutors thrived and life was good.

Felicia liked to think her life was as comfortable as she could have reasonably expected it to be by the time she hit forty. An eight-year-old daughter (her name already pencilled in for a string of prestigious schools). A huge house in Barnes inherited from Roddy's parents and the place from which they ran their business. A golden Labrador they walked each day on Barnes Common. And a wide circle of interesting friends, all of whom she was sure looked on her success with a degree of envy.

In the early years she had often felt the need to justify her involvement in the tutoring business, but now she felt on much safer ground. When they had started out, tutoring was something to be ashamed of. Private tutors were almost smuggled in through the back door with a sack over their head. Now they were picked up by drivers and taken in private jets to exotic locations. Not all of them, admittedly, but those whose face and CV fitted, those who could offer what her clients wanted or, more significantly, what they thought they wanted, could make very good money, a sizable percentage of which ended up in the Forum coffers. The very best tutors had become almost status symbols, and tutoring had moved from the back door to the shop window.

Ever since its foundation, Felicia liked to think that Forum Tutors did things differently from other agencies. They always went for the personal touch, with both clients and employees, and liked to look on themselves as an extended family. She knew the family analogy may have been some way from the truth, but the image appealed to her and she frequently used it – in interviews and in profiles and in the Forum publicity material. Felicia always had a good eye for the PR opportunity.

Now she was experiencing a family bereavement. A Forum tutor was dead – not just dead, murdered – and she was facing questions from two detectives.

'I know this must be a very difficult time for you, Mrs Ireland,' said the one who had introduced himself as Garibaldi. 'We understand that Giles was one of your employees and we understand that he was here, in your house, on Saturday evening. Is that correct?'

'Yes,' said Felicia. 'We had a party here for our tutors. We do it every year.'

'And did you speak to Giles during the evening?'

'Yes I did. We both did – Roddy and I.'

'Roddy's your husband?'

'That's right.'

'And how did Giles seem to you?'

'Absolutely fine. His usual charming self.'

'I see. And what time do you think Giles left?'

'I have no idea.' Felicia paused and took a breath. She couldn't take it in. She was being bombarded with these questions as if she might somehow be involved. 'Look, Inspector, I'm really struggling to come to terms with this. When you say murdered, where—?'

'He was found dead this morning in Barnes Old Cemetery.'

'Where?'

'Near Rocks Lane Tennis Courts.'

'And how—?'

'He was stabbed.'

Felicia covered her mouth with her hands. 'I don't believe it. I can't . . .'

'I hope you understand that we need to find out as much as we can about him and about his movements on Saturday evening.'

'Of course. What can I tell you?'

Felicia looked at the detective. He took out his notebook. It seemed strangely old-fashioned, like something from a previous age.

'Do you have a list of those who were at the party?'

'I can get you one.'

'With contact details as well, if possible.'

'I can email it to you later.'

'A printout now would be useful if you could manage that.'

There was something about his manner that Felicia didn't like.

'How long had Giles been working for you?'

'Three or four years.'

'Can you be more precise?'

'I can look it up if you like. We have careful records.'

'I'm sure you do. And what was Giles like as a tutor?'

'Excellent. One of our best. He was exactly what a lot of our clients are looking for. The right sort of background. Personable. Charming. Played by the rules.'

'What rules are those?'

'We expect high standards of our tutors. I don't know how much you know about the tutoring business—'

'I know it's booming,' said Garibaldi.

Felicia nodded. 'It certainly is. Hundreds of agencies, but we like to think we're different.'

'In what way?'

'We – Roddy and I – take great care over recruitment and keep a careful eye over what's going on. Unlike many others, we take a real interest in our tutors. That's why,' she said, blowing her nose, 'this is such a shock.'

'How many students did Giles have on his books?'

'I can't remember offhand, but I can check.'

'If you could. A list would be great.'

'You don't surely think that any of them—'

'I don't think anything, Mrs Ireland. I'm just trying to get a picture of Giles Gallen and what he did.'

'You can't for one second think that any of his students are involved. The parents will be so shocked when they hear and then to have the police—'

'I'm not saying any of them are involved but we need to know who they are. We may need to speak to them.'

'They'll be devastated. Absolutely devastated. Especially the Rivettis.'

'The Rivettis? The Italian family he went abroad with?'

'Yes. How do you know that?'

'His parents told us.'

'But not all his pupils were like that. I'd hate you to get the wrong impression. You see, although we do have the very wealthy on our books, we don't like to see ourselves as exclusive in any way. Not all of our tutors spend their time swanning round the Mediterranean on a yacht or in villas on Caribbean islands. And we do run a pro bono scheme . . .'

Felicia always enjoyed delivering the line. There was something about the very words 'pro bono'. They lifted her onto the moral high ground, disarming those ready to criticise.

'Pro bono?' said the detective, as if there was something odd about the idea.

'Yes. We do free work in several inner-city state schools.' It was only one, but several always sounded better. 'And Giles was one of the first to get involved. He still— he was working there only last week.'

'What was Giles's subject?'

'He was an English graduate, so that was his speciality when it came to entrance exams, GCSEs, A Levels, university entrance. But we do expect our tutors to broaden their range and he would have covered other subjects, particularly with the younger students.'

The door opened. Felicia was relieved to see Roddy walk in. She had been beginning to feel very much on the defensive.

'So sorry,' said Roddy. 'I was talking to a client. I do apologise.' He sat down next to Felicia. 'This is such a terrible thing. I mean, who would murder Giles Gallen? It's unbelievable. Unthinkable. His students will be devastated. And their parents.'

'To say nothing of his own parents.'

'Of course. I mean—'

'We need to find out as much as we can about what Giles had been up to, Mr Ireland. In particular, we need to know what he was up to on the night he was killed and given that he spent a large part of the evening here . . .'

'I understand. And we'll do everything we can to help.'

'Well, that list would certainly be a great help.'

'List?' said Roddy.

Felicia turned to him. 'Of who was at the party last night. I said we could provide one.'

'OK,' said Roddy. 'Yes, we can certainly get that to you.'

'Now would be most helpful.'

'Now?'

The detective said nothing, but his look made the 'now' very clear.

'And if we could also have a list of who Giles was tutoring.'

'Why do you need that?'

'If Giles was tutoring during the day, we need to know where he was and who he saw. We might need to speak to them.'

Felicia sensed Roddy bristle.

'You don't think that his murder could be in any way connected to his work as a tutor, do you?'

'At the moment, Mr Ireland, we are pursuing all lines of enquiry. We're assuming nothing – all we're looking for is as full a picture as possible of Giles Gallen and what he was doing yesterday.'

'OK,' said Roddy. 'I'll print them off for you.'

He left the room and Felicia felt uncomfortable again. Something about the way the detectives were looking at her, especially the man, was unnerving.

'I suppose this will be in the news,' she said, looking from one to the other.

'I should think so,' said the man. 'A press release went out this morning.'

'What will it say about Giles?'

'What do you mean?'

'Will it say he worked as a tutor?'

'It may do.'

Felicia weighed up the PR implications.

'And if it doesn't,' said the detective, 'I'm sure people will find out, and I'm sure they'll also find out that he worked for you.'

It was as if he had read her thoughts.

'But there's no connection between his murder and . . . and us. There can't be!'

'We can't rule anything out.'

A sound of a whirring printer from the next room punctuated the brief silence that followed.

Felicia looked towards the door, desperate for Roddy to return with the printouts and for the detectives to leave.

There was something about the way they were looking at her, especially the one with greying hair and the Italian name. Every time she caught his eye she sensed he already knew, or would soon find out, things she'd rather he didn't. Like her suspicions over the last year or so about Roddy – the way he acted as if he was hiding something, the way he so often showed the excessive charm of the guilty, the way uncharacteristic emotional outbursts had ruffled his customary calm. Sometimes she thought Roddy's behaviour was a sign that he was having an affair, but sometimes she thought he was harbouring a different kind of secret, something to do with the business. The way he had reacted to the news of Giles Gallen's murder, his uncharacteristic nervousness in the presence of the detectives – it all pointed to the possibility that he might have more to hide than an extra-marital fling.

Felicia was ruling nothing out and, as she looked at the

Inspector's dark probing eyes, she got the sense that he too was considering all kinds of possibilities.

Garibaldi paused outside Gail's Bakery and turned to Gardner. 'Fancy a coffee?'

'Why not?'

'And a pastry?'

Gardner patted her stomach. 'Just a coffee.'

'Yeah, I shouldn't either. Tell you what, why don't we share?'

'Go on then, you've persuaded me. Didn't take much, did it?'

It was warm enough to be outside, so Gardner pulled up a couple of chairs to a table, while Garibaldi went inside to order.

He came back with two lattes, an almond croissant and a Danish.

'I thought we were going to share.'

'We are.' Garibaldi took the drinks and pastries off the tray 'We're having half of each. I'm going for a run later. What's your excuse?'

'Fitness DVD in the living room. No-one sees you, you can pause if you need a breather and you can fast forward if you want it to end quickly. In fact, if you feel like it you can just stop it completely, give up and have a cup of tea. Perfect.'

Garibaldi reached for the almond croissant and cut it in half. 'So what do you make of them?'

'I think I prefer the Danish.'

'I meant Forum Tutors.'

Gardner smiled. 'I can see their appeal.'

'And what's that?'

'Pretty smooth, aren't they? Posh. Charming. Clear idea

of their market and how to appeal to them. Certainly give the impression they know what they're doing.'

'Oh they know what they're doing, all right.'

'And it seems that Giles Gallen was a bit of a star.'

'Yeah. They rated him, didn't they?

'Nice work if you can get it. Summer holidays in luxury locations.'

'There must be drawbacks,' said Garibaldi, taking a bite of his croissant.

'Such as?'

'I don't know, but name me a job that doesn't have bits that are shit. Maybe the kids are brats. Maybe the parents treat him badly. Maybe he gets sunburn.'

'Even so.'

'A couple of things I noticed about them. First was that they made a big thing of saying they're not exclusive when they clearly are. And the second was that, although they were clearly upset about Giles, they seemed just as concerned about something else.'

'What's that?'

'Have a guess.'

Garibaldi kicked himself. He'd promised to stop himself asking his sergeant to have a guess and also to stop giving her the look he was now giving her in the silences that tended to follow.

This time the silence was surprisingly short. 'They were worried about damage to their firm's reputation, weren't they?'

He stopped himself adding 'well done', but took careful note. Maybe he shouldn't quit the 'have a guess' thing after all.

'My thoughts exactly. Their eyes were on the PR implications pretty quickly. Just like that pro bono stuff. Had to slip that one in, didn't they? Makes them sound good when everyone knows it's half conscience salve, half PR gimmick.'

Gardner's look suggested that 'everyone' might be an overstatement and Garibaldi kicked himself again – this time for wondering whether Gardner thought pro bono might be something to do with U2.

'Or maybe I'm just being cynical. I have been known to be.'

His phone rang. He reached into his pocket, pulled it out and looked at the screen.

Alfie.

He got up from the table and raised an apologetic hand.

'I'm going to have to take this,' he said, walking away.

'Hi, Dad.'

'Hi. How's things?'

'Good.'

Garibaldi crossed the road to Barnes Green and walked down the path towards the pond, trying to work out what kind of a call it was.

'It's about the Fulham game.'

A QPR call. His favourite.

'Can't wait,' said Garibaldi. 'Fulham. And midweek under the lights. Always tasty.'

'Yeah, look, the thing is I . . . I won't be able to make it.'

'Really?' Garibaldi couldn't hide his disappointment. Home games were a bond established long ago, important fixtures in more than one sense.

'Why's that?'

'There's stuff going on up here.'

'Stuff?'

'Yeah. A party.'

A party? What kind of party was more important than a West London local derby?

‘I see. And you can’t . . . ?’

Alfie wasn’t far away. Hop on the Oxford Tube and he’d be in West London in no time – comparative proximity was one of the few positives Garibaldi had been able to find in his son going to Oxford in the first place.

He’d missed only one or two home games in the last few years and always for good reasons – holidays, exams, illness. Even when Garibaldi had been unable to make it himself when he was on a case and working weekend shifts, Alfie had gone to the game by himself or taken along a mate.

And here he was, missing two games in succession.

‘But you missed the last one,’ said Garibaldi, trying to be adult about it but sensing he sounded like a whingeing kid.

‘I know, but—’

‘Couldn’t you come down and get back up in time? Parties go on till all hours, don’t they?’

‘It’s not that kind of party. It’s a dinner party.’

‘I see.’

‘And it’s in the country.’

Dinner Party. In the Country. The fears that had been brewing through Alfie’s first year seemed confirmed.

‘OK, Alfie. That’s no problem. But how about I come up and see you soon?’

‘Yeah, that’d be great. Mum wants to come up as well, so . . .’

‘Let’s fix up a date. Maybe Rachel can come as well?’

He hated it when anyone’s voice went up at the end of a sentence, but here he was, doing it himself, turning a statement into a question. Anyone would think he was insecure.

‘That would be good.’

He tried to gauge Alfie’s level of enthusiasm. He was desperate for him to like his partner in the way that he was desperate for him not to like Kay’s.

'OK. Speak soon.'

He hung up and, instead of turning back to Gail's, walked to the pond. He wanted time to sort himself out, to go through yet again what he felt about Alfie. Was it anger, or was it a sense of betrayal? Or was it a feeling of helplessness, a sense that he had no control over the decisions his son was making and there was nothing he could do about it?

He remembered a recent case which had brought him into contact with a group of smug, entitled, self-regarding Oxford graduates.

The thought that his son might end up like them was too terrifying to contemplate.

8

bbc.co.uk/news

BARNES CEMETERY VICTIM NAMED

The man found murdered in Barnes on Sunday morning has been named as twenty-six-year-old Giles Gallen. His body was discovered by a jogger in the Old Cemetery, an abandoned graveyard next to the Rocks Lane Tennis Centre.

Scenes of Crime Officers have been examining the scene since the discovery at 9.00 BST. Reports suggest the victim died as a result of stab wounds. A post-mortem is being carried out and the police have launched a murder investigation.

DCI Karen Deighton said detectives are trying to trace Gallen's movements on Saturday night. She appealed for anyone with CCTV or dashcam footage in the Rocks Lane area to come forward and for anyone who may have seen Gallen or been with him that evening to contact the police.

Gallen, a Cambridge graduate, had been living at home with his parents while working as a private

> tutor. His father said, 'We cannot believe this has happened. Giles was a wonderful son with the world at his feet. Our lives have been ripped apart by this senseless act of brutality. We cannot understand why anyone would want to do this to him.'
>
> Barnes Old Cemetery was abandoned many years ago. Its graves and monuments were subjected to considerable damage and vandalism but it has in recent years been tended by a local environmental group intent on preserving its 'Gothic charm'.

Garibaldi turned away from the screen, scrolled through his iPod, reached for the remote and pressed play. The plaintive guitar of First Aid Kit's 'Emmylou' came out of the Bose speakers on the floor.

He loved the Swedish sisters' song, their promise to be Emmylou Harris to his Gram Parsons, June Carter to his Johnny Cash. And he loved it even more when Rachel sang along to it, which is what she was doing now, sitting at the table, head down over her work.

'Won't be long,' she said, breaking off from her singing. 'Last few.'

A lot of things had improved since Rachel had moved in three months ago. They no longer had to plan nights together in advance, deciding on who would go to whose (Rachel had stopped him referring to 'home' and 'away' fixtures), there were no more decisions about at which flat you needed to leave things (more of an issue for Rachel) and there was no longer the assumption (mainly one that Garibaldi had indulged in) that each overnight stay would involve sex. Now they were together the whole time there was less pressure in that area – something that Garibaldi felt might have led to less frequency (a thought he had the good sense to keep very much to himself). Above all, though, and as Garibaldi reminded himself to keep telling Rachel regularly, it was great to be together so much more. Knowing Rachel was there filled out the contours of emptiness that had mapped two years of living by himself.

But, in honest moments, he recognised there were also drawbacks to cohabiting. Some of the irritations he had felt in all those years of marriage had returned. Not always being able to watch what you want on TV. Someone else choosing the music. Not being able to eat what and when you'd like to. Sharing a bathroom. And above all, despite not having enjoyed his previous state of loneliness, finding it more difficult to be by yourself, to find the private space everyone needed. Sometimes all Garibaldi wanted was to sit in the flat by himself reading, watching Italian films on Netflix and listening to music.

But he was generous enough to concede that some of what he regarded as problems could easily be seen as positives. Rachel's viewing preferences had introduced him to *The Bureau* and *Call My Agent* and she had opened some cultural windows that he had assumed would always, for him, remain closed. Jazz, for example. He'd never got beyond a bit of Miles Davis and John Coltrane but he now found himself enjoying what Rachel was playing on her laptop and asking about it. And food. Garibaldi had become practised at polite tactful praise when faced with the meals she cooked, but, though still thankful that his unpredictable hours meant they couldn't always eat together, there had been several occasions when his praise had been genuine.

While he waited for Rachel to finish her marking, Garibaldi googled Felicia Ireland and clicked on the first of the large number of results.

Daily Telegraph

ELITE FIRMS RIDE CREST OF TUTORING BOOM

Private tutoring is booming. It seems nowadays everyone wants a tutor and the very wealthy are prepared to pay the very highest money to secure the best. Long gone are the days when hiring a tutor was seen as an admission of inadequacy or failure. Now they're status symbols. Just like you might show off a new car, now you might show off your tutor, the one you've brought with you on holiday this summer to keep the kids up to the mark, making sure they're not falling behind in the academic rat race, and, when the tutoring's over, maybe keeping the kids entertained as well. It's a win-win. You feel you're doing your best to give your kids a great education (topping up what's on offer at the already-pricy private schools they go to) but you're also getting a bit of high-class babysitting on the side.

It's not a view shared by the woman who set up one of London's leading tutoring agencies. I visited Felicia Ireland at her Southwest London home to talk about the tutoring boom.

'Tutoring often gets a bad press. It's seen as the preserve of the wealthy, but we here at Forum know it is so much more than that. The media like to latch on to stories about the super-rich. They ignore the rest because it's not such a good story. They don't want to know about the parents who want the best for their child and make sacrifices to get the extra help the school cannot provide. The child with learning difficulties who desperately needs the one-to-one attention that isn't always available in schools. The media isn't interested in so much of the everyday, run-of-the-mill, down-to-earth work we do. And nor are they quick to recognise our pro bono initiatives. They're more interested in the tiny percentage at the very top – the agencies who deal with them, the tutors who they employ. They don't realise that it's much more than that. But here at Forum we do.'

It may be that some of Forum's clients are of modest income but there is no doubt that the agency's big money comes from the rich. It's the Dubai clients who have tutors working on private jets as they ferry their children back and forth from Nice to London who pay the big money. It's the parents who put up a tutor in a hotel five minutes' walk from their son's boarding school to give him easy access who pay the bills. It's the Russian oligarchs and hedge fund billionaires who allow their business to prosper.

Garibaldi looked at the photos – Felicia Ireland at the desk, Roddy standing behind her – and skimmed through the article. Felicia's justification was smooth and polished. Laws of supply and demand. Bespoke service. Advantages of one-to-one tuition. The need for committed professional tutors and the high standards expected from Forum.

When the article picked up on Forum's hope that by using money from the wealthy to fund pro bono initiatives, not only the rich would benefit from what they had to offer, Garibaldi felt Felicia seemed less convincing. And when it asked whether such a Robin Hood idea would ever work and whether it was anything other than crumbs from the rich man's table, he even found himself nodding in agreement – something he seldom did when reading the *Telegraph*.

'Right,' said Rachel, tidying up her papers and getting up from her desk. 'Emmylou at your service.'

Garibaldi shrugged. 'I think I'm more Johnny than Gram tonight. The old Johnny, that is, the grumpy one with the gravelly voice nearing his end.'

'Bad case?'

'If it was a black kid stabbed on an estate we'd shrug our shoulders and look for the usual. Posh white man in Barnes and everyone's puzzled. We've got nothing.'

The song ended. Garibaldi fiddled with the iPod and found another. Gillian Welch. 'And there's more bad news.'

'What's happened?'

'Alfie can't make the game.'

'Why not?'

'A party. No, hang on, not a party. A dinner party. In the country.'

'Oh, well. It's what happens when you go to uni.'

'I wouldn't know.'

'Yeah,' said Rachel. 'All part of trying to find out who you are.'

'How about trying to realise who you're not?'

'Comes to the same thing, doesn't it?'

Garibaldi was lining the culprits up in his mind. Kay. Dom. The school they sent him to.

'So that's why you're pissed off,' said Rachel. 'It's not the case, is it? It's Alfie.'

She was right. Garibaldi could endure the other

stuff – Alfie's decision to apply to Oxford (despite his reservations, he had been very proud when he got in), his choice of friends and changed behaviour in his first year. But giving up on QPR? Was this what his parents would have felt if they'd lived to see him ditch their Catholicism?

'Maybe I need to grow out of it. I mean, it's not *that* important, is it?'

He knew, as he said the words, that he didn't believe them, and tried to cheer himself up with the thought that Alfie's lapses might be only temporary. Maybe, after these moments of wobbly faith and wavering commitment, he would see the error of his ways and return to the fold.

But what if he didn't? What if it was like him and the church? What if this was Alfie's dark night of the soul?

He shook the thought away, reached for his glass and changed the subject. 'Tell me, do your kids at Hillside go for much private tutoring?'

Rachel laughed. 'Private tutoring? You're joking. Our kids can't afford it. No, what happens in schools like Hillside is that the private tutoring comes to us.'

'What do you mean?'

'Some of these posh tutoring firms offer us their services for free. You know – wanting to do a bit of good for the needy.'

'And do you use them?'

'We do now. One of Kevin Johnson's great initiatives. We've been using one firm for the last year. Sixth form stuff. University entrance, that kind of thing. So as Head of Sixth Form I've been pretty involved.'

'Yeah? What firm's that then?'

'Forum Tutors.'

9

DCI Deighton looked over the glasses perched on the end of her nose.

'The post-mortem shows that Giles Gallen died from a single stab wound to the heart. The depth and shape of the wound suggests a single-bladed knife with a serrated edge. Maybe a bread knife or a kitchen knife. Forensics are still on the scene at the Old Cemetery and the search for the weapon continues there and in surrounding areas.'

Deighton hooked the glasses off her nose and looked at the room. 'Any questions?'

Garibaldi glanced at Gardner. She started to raise her arm but stopped herself.

'The alcohol levels in Gallen's blood are yet to be determined, but the stomach content odours suggest heavy consumption, maybe linked to his attendance at the Forum drinks party on Saturday evening, which is the last confirmed sighting. No confirmation of the time he left and nothing as yet on his movements between then and the discovery of his body.'

Deighton looked down at her file. 'There's one other thing. Evidence of recent ejaculation. It's not clear whether he had sexual intercourse – penile swabs are still being examined – but there was semen on Gallen and on his underwear. We await DNA confirmation but, given the semen's location it seems reasonable to assume it is likely to be Gallen's.'

'So that's why Gallen was in that cemetery, then – for sex?' said Gardner.

'He could have been there for all kinds of reasons,' said Deighton. 'Assume nothing.'

'But if the ejaculation was recent,' said Gardner, 'doesn't that suggest . . . ?'

'There could be other explanations,' said Deighton.

'Such as?'

Deighton gave Gardner a headmistress stare.

'We need to ask ourselves why Gallen was in Barnes Old Cemetery. Sex is a possibility, but we need to keep an open mind.'

'Maybe he was caught short,' said DC Hodson from the back of the room. 'Just like the bloke who found him.'

'Yeah right,' said Gardner. 'He lives in Ranelagh Avenue. Just round the corner. If he wanted a crap, he could have gone home for one.'

'Maybe,' said DC McLean from his seat next to Hodson, 'it was a pick-up gone wrong. The Old Cemetery was notorious for it a few years back. A big cruising spot.'

'But why pick someone up there?' said Gardner. 'Why not use Grindr or whatever and go somewhere comfortable?'

'Some like it outside,' said Garibaldi. 'Apparently.'

'But *there*?'

Garibaldi nodded. 'And some like it weird. Apparently.'

'Well that place is weird all right,' said Gardner. 'Totally freaked me out.'

'So the question is what *was* he doing there?' said Deighton. 'Did he go to meet someone? Or did he go there by himself for some other reason? Why would he go there by himself that late at night?'

'Maybe he was walking home and something took his attention,' said Gardner. 'A noise. A disturbance.'

'So he heard a noise coming from an abandoned cemetery,' said Deighton, 'and he wandered towards it out of interest? Really?'

'Alcohol,' said Gardner. 'It clouds your judgement.'

'Maybe he had a habit of going there,' said Garibaldi.

'For what?' said Deighton.

'It's just round the corner from where he lived,' said Garibaldi. 'Maybe he just liked going there? Maybe he went there when he was younger. Perfect place for a moody teenager.'

'What? At that time of night?' said Gardner.

'Perfect time for a moody teenager. And let's face it, it's not that long ago since he was one. He was only twenty-six.'

'He was at boarding school, right?' asked DC Hodson.

'Radley,' said Garibaldi. 'The jumper he was wearing was from his schooldays. Name sewed into it.'

'Bit odd, isn't it?' said Deighton, 'to be wearing a jumper he wore when he was at school?'

'Yeah,' said Gardner. 'Nothing I wore at school would have still fitted me when I was twenty-six.'

'I've said it before,' said Garibaldi, 'but it's what those places do to you. They're the Larkin's mum and dad of the educational world.'

The room fell silent and Garibaldi had the familiar sense of puzzled eyes turning in his direction.

'They fuck you up,' he said, by way of explanation.

A glance at some of the faces suggested not everyone felt illuminated.

'The papers are onto it,' said Deighton. 'Lots of

speculation about the Old Cemetery. They're digging up all kinds of things.'

'Good place for it,' said Garibaldi.

Deighton looked at him blankly.

'A cemetery. For digging things up.'

'Right,' said Deighton, giving Garibaldi one of her just-about-tolerate-you looks. 'We need to work out all we can about Gallen's last movements, in particular what he did on Saturday. Who did he tutor on Saturday afternoon and where was he doing it? Who was at the party in Glebe Road? Was he with anyone before and after the party? Any CCTV cameras pick him up? And we need to find out more about what Gallen was up to in his life.' Deighton stood up. 'OK,' she said. 'Let's—

'Let's get on it.' Garibaldi muttered the words in time with his boss but very much under his breath.

10

Hilary Ainsworth was not surprised when the man and woman standing on the doorstep of her Cleveland Road house showed their cards and announced themselves as detectives from the Metropolitan Police. She'd been expecting the visit ever since she heard the news and she greeted it with a sense of relief – at least she no longer had to debate whether she should get in touch with them or wait for them to come to her, no longer had to wonder whether giving them a call might make them more likely to think she had nothing to hide.

'We'd like to ask you a few questions, Mrs Ainsworth.' said the short, dark man who had introduced himself as Detective Inspector Garibaldi, 'and take a statement.'

'Of course. I'm really sorry, but I'm still struggling to take it in. And I can't think of how I might be able to help. I mean . . . *murder*?'

'Tell me, Mrs Ainsworth, did Giles Gallen come here last Saturday to have a lesson with your daughter?'

'Not that I know of,' said Hilary. 'I can check with Briony of course but I would have known if he was coming.'

'How often did Giles tutor your daughter?'

'Once a week during term time. Usually on a Saturday afternoon.'

'But not last Saturday?'

'No.'

'How did Giles seem when you last saw him?'

'Absolutely fine. He came in and did his lesson. Perfectly polite. Charming as ever. He was very charming, Giles. And he's . . . was he really stabbed?'

The detective nodded.

'Nothing that struck you as odd or unusual in any way?'

Hilary shook her head. 'He was a good tutor. Briony really enjoyed his lessons. She's totally devastated. Still in a state of shock.'

'Is Briony in?' said the woman. Hilary nodded. 'We'd like to speak to her.'

'Of course.'

Hilary walked into the corridor and called upstairs. 'Briony!'

There was no response, so she called again. This time there was a muffled 'what' from behind her closed bedroom door.

'Can you come down, please?'

The bedroom door opened and Briony thumped downstairs, her mouth dropping open when she saw the two detectives standing in the hallway.

'I know this is very upsetting for you, Briony,' said the woman, 'but we need to ask you a few questions. Did Giles come to give you a lesson last Saturday?'

Briony shook her head. 'No. Definitely not.'

Hilary hoped her daughter was telling the truth. Bitter experience had taught her that this wasn't always the case and part of her wondered whether Giles *had* come round on Saturday and Briony was keeping it quiet, though she couldn't imagine why she might feel the need to. Unless ... Surely not. Giles Gallen may have been charming and handsome and not much older than Briony, but it was ridiculous to think that something might have been going on between them.

She shook the thought away. Just because Briony's parents had, on that very weekend, been involved in their own acts of betrayal, she shouldn't suspect her daughter had been doing the same. And she shouldn't be so quick to wonder what Vince might do if he found out she had.

Briony may have had only a vague idea of where their wealth came from, the money that had bought their Barnes house and paid for the private education, but Hilary had a more informed knowledge of how Vince had made a fortune from the string of clubs he owned. She also knew more about the kind of contacts Vince had and what he was capable of when things didn't go his way or when he came upon something he didn't like. That's why it was important not to do anything that would anger him, or if you couldn't do that, make sure you never got caught – a lesson she had learned many years ago and one that Briony was beginning to understand.

'And tell me, Briony,' said the sergeant,' What was Giles like?'

'He was like ...' Briony gasped for breath. 'He was like a friend. A real friend.'

It was all so sad, thought Hilary, all such a tragedy, a senseless waste of a young life. And murdered. She knew people got murdered in London, but it happened to other people and in other places. Not to people like Giles. PLU. People Like Us.

What could he possibly have done to deserve that? Maybe nothing. Maybe it was some sicko, some random attack and Giles was simply in the wrong place at the wrong time. That kind of thing happened all too easily.

Or maybe Giles wasn't what he seemed. When it came to appearances, you never could tell. Giles could have all kinds of secrets.

She thought back to last Saturday. She knew only too well where her husband had been. Away on a golfing weekend with business associates. That's what he'd said, but Hilary knew the truth. She knew that Vince had been with her old friend Ginny and she knew exactly what they had been up to.

The question was whether Vince knew that on Saturday afternoon she had been up to the same thing – that, far from visiting her aunt in Surrey, she had been somewhere else entirely, and that her affair had been going on for just as long as his.

The thought of what he might do if he found out she'd been pulling the wool over his eyes frightened her. Never mind that he'd been doing the same to her for years – his mind didn't work like that.

And yet she continued to do it. Why?

Maybe she was simply a bad person.

And maybe it was because she was a bad person that her thoughts turned to Briony's future. She needed good grades, and for those, she had no doubt, she would need another tutor.

Much as she was shocked and saddened by the murder of Giles Gallen and while she recognised that it was a terrible thing, the world had to go on, and that world was a tough place, one where you needed to look after your own.

She would get in touch with the agency as soon as she could.

Briony couldn't believe it. This was someone she knew, someone who came to their house and gave her lessons. She'd got to know him really well. All those one-to-one sessions. It wasn't as though you spent the whole of the hour working. There was plenty of chat. And it helped that he was so easy to talk to. A real charmer. Good-looking too. She could tell her parents thought so as well because they kept making these comments about how they needed to leave the door open in the living room and how she shouldn't have lessons with Giles when neither of them were in the house. Especially her dad. He'd even made suggestions that Briony might be better off with a woman tutor.

Briony was churning inside and her hands were shaking. She hoped the detectives hadn't noticed. They'd think she was hiding something. That one with the Italian name had been looking at her in a very odd way throughout the whole interview, as if he already knew things about her she'd want to stay hidden.

The woman's eyes weren't quite so sharp. She seemed kinder somehow.

'When Giles came to give you a lesson,' she said, 'did he talk to you about things?'

'What kind of things?'

'Things other than work.'

Briony shrugged. The truth was he did. Sometimes they spoke more about other things than they did about Emily Dickinson or Sylvia Plath. Those were the good weeks.

'We'd have a break sometimes,' she said, 'and talk about films and music and stuff . . .'

The man leaned forward. 'And there was nothing Giles said that suggested he might be in some kind of trouble?'

Briony shook her head.

Should she tell them?

It wasn't anything huge, but ever since she heard of his murder, she'd been thinking a lot about some of the things Giles had said in their last lesson together.

What should she do? What should she put in her statement?

She took a deep sigh and decided there was only one thing to do. She had learned its power a few years ago and since then she had turned it on and off to good effect. It had even got her a main part in the school play.

'I still can't believe it! I can't believe someone's killed him!'

Her voice wobbled and her lower lip trembled. She braced herself and, reminding herself of how well she had done it in that audition, she started to cry.

11

When Laura Barker heard it on the news, she thought it was a mistake. There had to be two Giles Gallens. That was the only way it could make sense.

But when the man and woman on the doorstep held out cards and introduced themselves as detectives she realised there was, when it came to the news she had heard, only one Giles Gallen – the charming, mild-mannered young man who had been coming to the house for over a year to give Freddie some extra help.

The detectives followed her into the living room where they chose to stand rather than accept the offered armchairs.

'When did you last see Giles?' said the man.

'Last Saturday,' said Laura. 'He had a lesson with Freddie.'

'Can you remember what time?'

'It was in the afternoon. Two o'clock I think.'

'And how did he seem to you?'

'Much as he always did. I still don't believe this. Murdered?'

'Does Freddie know?' said the woman.

Laura nodded. 'He's devastated. He liked Giles. They got on well.'

'What was Giles tutoring Freddie in?' said the man.

'GCSE English.'

The thought struck Laura that she would have to find a replacement. She knew there were more important things to be thinking of at this particular moment – the sad and senseless loss of life, the tragedy of a young man with so much ahead of him cut down in his prime, the unbelievable pain and anguish his poor parents must be feeling, the sense that London's streets, even those in leafy affluent areas like Barnes , were no longer safe from the violence usually associated with other places– but she couldn't shift the thought that Freddie would need someone else for the extra help he so clearly needed.

'Is Freddie in?' said the woman.

'He's upstairs, doing his homework.'

She knew this was unlikely. The chances were Freddie was on his laptop, on social media or in the middle of some dreadful video game, or even up to something worse. That was why they had got Giles in the first place. Yes, King's was a good school. Yes, the teaching was up to scratch. But, even so, it was worth the extra money to maximise Freddie's chances. No matter how good a school and no matter how good the teaching, you couldn't do too much to ensure that your son got the best results possible. And English was essential. Not only that, it was also Freddie's weakness. That's why they'd taken Giles on, and if they could find tutors as good as him in other subjects, they'd seriously consider hiring them as well.

'Could we have a word with him?' said the man.

'I'll go and get him,' said Laura.

She went upstairs and knocked on Freddie's door, giving him time to shut down whatever inappropriate site he might be on before coming down to face the detectives.

What was it about the police? Why did she feel so

awkward whenever she was in their presence? Clearly some kind of guilt. It was like being a kid in primary school when the teacher tells the class that one of them has perpetrated some terrible misdeed and she (all her primary school teachers had been women) intended to find out who it was. Whatever the crime – bullying, teasing, playing in forbidden areas, saying rude words, jumping the lunch queue, not doing what you'd been told, doing something unmentionable to your own or someone else's body in the privacy of the toilets – Laura would always think she had committed it. She never *had* committed it (apart from one memorable occasion when she made a rude sign out of the coach window on a school trip to the Cutty Sark) but she always thought she could have done, and that was why, when confronted with an angry teacher in search of a culprit, she would always blush. And the more she blushed, the more she would think everyone thought it was her, and the more she thought that, the more she would blush.

This childhood habit had stayed with her into adulthood. And that was why, as she followed Freddie downstairs, she was trying not to think about Giles Gallen. Whenever she did, she started to blush and sensed the detectives registering her tell-tale crimson cheeks.

She may have had nothing to do with the murder, but that didn't mean there weren't things about her she'd rather the police didn't know.

Freddie couldn't believe he was being interviewed by two detectives in his own house. It was like something out of a film or a TV show. The difference was this was real. His tutor had been murdered. Stabbed. And the police wanted to talk to him.

'How did you get on with Giles?'

Freddie wasn't sure about the man who asked the question. The woman seemed nice – lots of smiles and nods, as if she realised he was finding this difficult and needed some help. But the man kept looking at him in a strange way.

'I liked him,' said Freddie. 'He really helped me.'

'It must have been quite a shock for you,' said the woman, 'to find out he'd been murdered.'

Freddie nodded. They had no idea how much of a shock it had been.

The man leaned forward. 'Did Giles ever say anything to you when he gave you lessons that made you think he might be in trouble?'

Freddie shook his head.

'Did you talk about things with him?' asked the woman. 'You know, have a break from work and chat?'

'Sometimes.'

In other words, as often as Freddie could manage it. Football was always a good side-track. As well as the other stuff, the stuff he couldn't tell them about.

'The thing is,' said the man, 'we're talking to everyone he was tutoring and especially the ones he saw on Saturday afternoon, just to get some sense of how he was and what he was up to.'

What he was up to? It was as if they already knew and were waiting for Freddie to come out with something to confirm it. These detectives were just like teachers. They had this creepy way of asking you questions, making it seem as if they knew things already and were just waiting for you to confess what they already knew. Like their Head of Year when he'd been accused of smoking. Was it something that teachers learned from watching cop shows on telly? Or did the cops learn it from teachers, remembering how they'd been grilled at school?

'So nothing seemed unusual on Saturday afternoon?' asked the man.

'No. It was like it always is, usual stuff.'

'And what was that?'

'What was what?'

'Usual stuff. We went through a couple of past papers. One English Language and one English Literature. I don't find it easy. Hemingway. *The Old Man and the Sea*. I don't get it.'

The man nodded. It was the first time he had seemed in complete agreement.

'And was Giles a good tutor?' asked the woman.

'Yeah, he was. I'd, you know, be finding things a bit difficult and then after Giles had been I'd feel different about things.'

Should he tell them? He couldn't believe it was relevant and he couldn't see how it might connect to the murder, but it might be the kind of thing they needed to know. In all the cop shows he watched it was always those tiny details that at first seemed unimportant that turned out to be crucial. And should he also tell him what Giles had said in their last lesson that had upset him so much?

He looked from one detective to the other and was on the point of telling them when the man got up from his chair and the woman did likewise.

He breathed a sigh of relief.

And he breathed an even bigger sigh when they left the house.

Freddie went up to his room, sat at his desk and flipped open his laptop. His world had been difficult enough when it had only involved the challenges of GCSEs, finding a girlfriend and getting his parents off his back.

The arrival of Giles as his tutor had, in so many ways,

made life easier to bear, but his murder, and the arrival of the detectives, had thrown everything into a state more disturbing than any he had encountered in his sixteen years.

12

Since his wife walked out on him to live with a woman in Brighton, Clive Marsh had found things tough in ways he had never imagined possible. The day-to-day responsibilities of clothing and feeding two kids, the mechanics of keeping a house clean and functioning – had he attended to these things during the years they were a couple like the liberal new man he had claimed to be, they wouldn't have been a problem. But the truth was he had only paid lip service to the idea. Only now was he realising that things would be easier had he not, underneath the veneer, been as much of a gender stereotype as the next unreconstructed caveman. And when it came to gender issues he now had enough to keep any therapist in business for years.

Not that he was in a position to afford a therapist. Financially, things were tight. His job as a copywriter, precarious at the best of times, now seemed, in times that were clearly a long way from best, even less secure.

Things might have been easier if one of his reactions to Helen's walk-out hadn't been to reacquaint himself with a habit he had discarded many years ago, but the stress of keeping on top of his job while coming to terms with his wife's walk-out and adjusting to his new responsibilities had made him more dependent on cocaine than he had been in his twenties. And it was now much more expensive.

That was why, when it came to plans for Amy's secondary schooling, he was putting all his eggs in one particular educational basket – the girls' grammar school in Kingston that Chloe, the older daughter, already attended. It was as good as any of the fee-paying options and, like the primary school, it was free. It may have been a long journey from East Sheen but, in the scale of things, that wasn't a huge problem.

The real problem was the eleven-plus exam.

Clive had approached it thinking that it was what it claimed to be: a test that recognised those of the necessary level of intelligence to benefit from a grammar-school education, a test for which no special preparation was needed. He soon discovered that this was as far from the truth as it was possible to be. The harsh reality was that if you didn't start tutoring your daughter at least two years before the test and, most significantly, if you didn't get her to the right tutor, one who knew the specifics of the eleven-plus ropes and had years of experience dancing through them, you had no chance.

The stats told the tale, and so did anyone you spoke to on the subject who had been down the same route.

Helen had been in charge of arranging tuition when Chloe had been preparing for the exam, and it had all happened, like so many things in their family life, without Clive knowing too much about it. With Helen no longer on the scene (though happy to provide email and telephone advice – she still cared about their daughters' wellbeing) Clive was at the helm, but by the time he got involved he was already very late to the eleven-plus tutoring party. All the slots at the best tutors, the ones with proven track records, had already been taken.

His frantic search for a tutor ended with the arrival on their doorstep of Giles Gallen from Forum. When Clive first saw him he didn't hold out much hope but as the weeks passed he couldn't believe his luck. Giles may not have had the years of experience of the ageing experts (all of them women) who had cornered the market and had punters queuing round the block, but he had worked wonders with Amy, not only effecting a remarkable improvement in her performance, but also making her actually want to do well and get into the place. His fingers were still very much crossed but at least Giles had given Amy's hopes of a good free secondary education some kind of fighting chance.

In fact, Clive was so impressed by what Giles had done for one of his daughters that he wondered whether he could possibly work the same magic on the other.

If the school's assessment were to be believed, Chloe was heading for disaster in next summer's A Levels and there was little chance of her pulling off the trick she had performed at GCSE. It pained Clive to see her show so little interest in anything academic and in particular to see her lose her appetite for English, the subject she had always enjoyed the most, and when it emerged in conversation that Giles was an English graduate he asked him, in some desperate last effort, whether he could give Chloe a few extra lessons in the remote hope that they might spark some renewed enthusiasm.

He knew it may have been a risk, putting Chloe in the charge of a handsome twentysomething, but he considered it a risk worth taking, and felt entirely vindicated when Chloe told him how great her first lesson had been. Soon she was having regular weekly sessions with Giles, who had joined the small, select and shrinking list of those people in the world who understood her.

Having so much to thank Giles for made the news of his murder even more painful to process. Hearing about it had been unbearable but telling Amy and Chloe about it had been worse.

And now detectives had called at the house.

'What we would like to know,' said the man standing next to his female colleague in the hallway, 'is whether Giles came here to tutor Chloe last Saturday afternoon.'

'Yes, he did,' said Clive. 'Look, I can't tell you how upset we all are. We're completely devastated.'

'I'm sure you are,' said the detective, whose name he hadn't quite caught. It had sounded Italian.

Clive didn't like his tone. It was almost as if he doubted his devastation.

'How did he seem to you that afternoon?'

'Absolutely fine.'

'And how was he as a tutor?' asked the woman.

'He was brilliant,' said Clive. 'Really brilliant.'

He shook his head, shocked at the speed with which his thoughts had turned from sadness at the loss of such a young life to worries about how he might find a replacement.

He felt awkward in the presence of these detectives. There was something about them, in particular the way they were looking at him, that made him uneasy.

Or was it simply paranoia?

Ever since Helen had walked out and he'd resumed his coke habit, Clive had become increasingly erratic and unpredictable. He'd done his best to keep his aberrations hidden from Chloe and Amy but he'd be surprised if they hadn't picked up on it, especially Chloe, who had been going through shit of her own ever since her mother moved out. The arrival of Giles as her tutor may have got her back on track academically, but from what Clive could see (and he had been seeing more than he wanted to) she was still sleeping with every available boy who came her way. He wanted to protect her and give the fatherly advice she so badly needed, but he had no idea how to set about it. So far, his clumsy attempts at intervention had been greeted with either sullen hostility or accusations of hypocrisy.

And Helen hadn't been much help. The first thing she said was that it wasn't at all unusual for girls of Chloe's age to behave like that and he was probably making a fuss about nothing, but she did promise to have a word. Whatever that word had been, it seemed to have had little effect, and Clive still found Chloe's behaviour impossible to deal with.

Maybe that was why he had the row with Giles. It came from nowhere, starting with a fair and polite query from the tutor about a change of times, but it soon became something bigger. And it was completely irrational. Why on earth would he turn on the person who had helped Chloe so much? It was frightening the way something in him had snapped, as if a switch had been suddenly flicked, and he had started ranting and raving, accusing Giles of all kinds of things, including taking advantage of his troubled, vulnerable daughter. Even more frightening was the way he had felt an uncontrollable urge to hurt him, to do something violent.

And with it all came the fear that Chloe, who he thought had gone out at the end of her lesson, may well have been upstairs, listening to every word.

Chloe couldn't believe Giles was dead. And not just dead – murdered. She also couldn't believe that she was being interviewed by two detectives about it, as if she might know something about who killed him or (and she was increasingly feeling that's what they were thinking) that she might in some way be involved, even *responsible* for it. Her life had been pretty fucked up ever since her mum had moved in with Caroline in Brighton, but this had taken fucked-upness to an entirely new level.

'I realise how distressing this must be for you Chloe,' said the short dark man, 'but we're trying to find out as much as we can about what Giles was up to and we understand that he was here on Saturday afternoon giving you a lesson.'

'That's right, he was.'

'And how did he seem to you?'

'He seemed fine.'

He had seemed more than fine. Chloe could still hear him taking her through John Donne's *The Flea.* She knew it was a seduction poem but there was something about the way Giles spoke about it that made it sexy beyond words. When he told her that in John Donne's day the printed 's' would be elongated and would look like an 'f' on the page and then read aloud that line 'it suck'd me first and now sucks thee' Chloe knew exactly what she wanted to do with Giles Gallen and was pretty sure that he wanted to do the same thing with her.

Ever since her mum's lesbian bombshell, Chloe's love life had been a disaster area, a string of short-term relationships, more like flings, and often no more than one-night stands. She knew it was wrong, and she knew she was earning herself a reputation, but she didn't seem able to stop herself. And when her dad shouted at her about it she felt the urge to do it even more. Who was he to talk about how to behave? She knew all about what he'd been up to recently, and not just his Tinder dates and his attempts to find someone new. She knew what he was doing.

She simply couldn't cope with what had happened to

Giles. There had definitely been something between them. She'd felt it, and she was pretty sure he'd felt it too. And it was more than flirtation, more than physical attraction, more than the need to scratch the itch of sexual desire. It was different from anything she had felt for any other boy.

'How long had Giles been tutoring you for?' asked the woman.

'A few months.'

'For English A Level?' said the man.

'Yeah. I haven't been doing too well at school and Dad thought it might be a good idea.'

'And what texts are you studying?'

It was the man again.

'Is that relevant?'

The man shrugged. 'I have no idea. But I definitely won't know if you don't tell me.'

'OK. Well, we've been doing John Donne and Shakespeare's Sonnets. Does that give you any clues?'

The man smiled. 'Maybe it does. Both about sex and death, aren't they?'

Chloe looked closely at his face. It was difficult to tell whether he was being serious.

'What do you mean?' she said. 'Are you saying that his death was . . . ?'

The man shrugged. 'That his death was linked to sex? I have no idea.'

He was making her feel uncomfortable, as if he already knew something but didn't want to reveal it.

'Do you have *any* idea who did it?' she said, trying to get the conversation away from sex and death.

'We have a few leads.'

'Such as?'

'Too early to reveal.'

'It just seems so difficult to believe. I mean *stabbed.* Knife crime! And to be found in that place . . .'

'Do you know Barnes Old Cemetery?'

'No. Never heard of it before all this.'

'So you've never been there?'

'Been there? No, I . . . you don't think I – no, I've never been there.'

'It's a very strange place and I'm trying to work out what Giles was doing there on Saturday night.'

'I've no idea. I was at a party in Sheen.'

'I'm not asking you for an alibi, Chloe.'

'I know, but—'

Chloe bit her lip. Had she said the wrong thing? Was she giving too much away?

'It's just that . . .' She paused and took a breath. 'It's just that I can't tell you how much it's shaken me up. I've been going through some difficult times and . . .'

'Difficult times?' said the man.

'Yeah, family stuff, school stuff.'

'I see.'

'Yeah, and Giles's lessons, well they sort of made me think differently about things . . .'

'Sounds like he was a good tutor.'

'He was. Yeah he was . . . great, you know? That's why . . .'

Chloe hadn't meant to cry. She thought she had everything under control but it welled up suddenly and overwhelmed her.

The woman took a pack of tissues from her pocket and offered them to her. Chloe took one, blew her nose and wiped her eyes.

'Take your time,' said the man. He held out a card. 'We'll be off, but here's my number and if anything occurs to you, absolutely anything, just get in touch. OK?'

Chloe looked at the card as the two detectives got up. *DI Garibaldi*. An odd name. Italian. Just like the biscuit.

She looked up at him, wondering whether she should have mentioned her Dad's behaviour and his row with Giles. Surely not. Her Dad may have been up to all kinds of strange things since her mum walked out but no-one in their right mind could possibly think him capable of murder.

13

Ginny Murray, like everyone else in the world, wanted the best for her kids. And when it came to Jade, the best meant the kind of education she herself had been deprived of. It had looked for a long time as though Jade would fulfil her mother's wishes. She had always been a good student and had sailed through her GCSEs with top grades. This gave Ginny every reason to be proud of her, especially as her daughter had done this at a local comprehensive, something she liked to remind all her friends of, the vast majority of whom had paid, and were still paying, through the nose for private education.

Had Jade listened to Ginny and stayed at the all-girls comprehensive, where the Sixth Form was successful and well-established, Ginny was convinced that her daughter's academic success would have continued. But Jade, strong-willed and independent-minded, had decided that the freedoms of a Sixth Form college were what she needed. For freedoms read fewer rules, a relaxed attitude to discipline, and boys.

Ginny felt so strongly about the prospect that she had even considered asking Phil to have a word with their daughter, but she quickly dismissed the idea, remembering the awful scenes, the threats of violence, the stomach-churning tension that had characterised the final stages of their relationship. Jade going to Sixth Form College was a very small problem when placed beside the prospect of increased contact with her father.

So, despite Ginny's urging, despite her subtle and often very unsubtle attempts to persuade her to stay where she was, Jade started at Sixth Form College. After the discipline and structure of the all-girls comprehensive, she found the freedom intoxicating. It wasn't the more relaxed discipline, and it wasn't boys (she had gone out with a perfectly acceptable boy called Robin for six months) – it was more her newly acquired desire to do anything but work. It wasn't that Jade became idle. Far from it. If anything, she became too active. In that first year of the Sixth Form she threw herself into a bewildering range of activities. Acting. Singing in a band. Writing for the college newspaper. Volunteering. She committed herself to all of these with admirable enthusiasm and energy. The problem was she did it all at the expense of her academic work.

Ginny had never considered herself a tiger mum – and she was quick to criticise those who put excessive pressure on their children to achieve the highest grades and to outperform their peers in everything they did. But as Jade went through her first year of sixth form she became increasingly worried about her university prospects. She had no doubt that Jade would have an impressive range of extra-curricular activities to support her application but feared that, having taken her eye off the academic ball, she had lost the edge she would need for a place at a top university.

Ginny's approach had always been hands-off and had become even more so when her marriage to Phil had ended. She had her own life to rebuild and was pleased that Jade needed so little parental intervention. But it was now clear to her that hands needed to be applied and she was unsure how to go about it.

That's why when her old friend Hilary spoke of the fantastic English tutor they had found for their own daughter Briony, she was quick to grasp the opportunity.

It was ironic that old schoolfriends who had very much gone their separate ways should end up living so close to each other, or given that they were both Barnes residents, should end up being able to afford to live so close to each other. But that's where they had ended up, Hilary at one end in Cleveland Road and Ginny at the other in Baronsmead Road.

Over recent years Ginny had been wary in her dealings with Hilary. They spoke now and then on the phone and met up for lunch every couple of months and, given that they both lived in Barnes, they often bumped into each other, especially on Saturday mornings when if you went to the Farmers' Market or sat down for a coffee outside The Olympic or simply walked up and down the High Street and Church Road it was difficult to avoid bumping into people you knew. But whenever Ginny was in contact with her old school friend she was overwhelmed by a guilt and an anxiety that she hoped didn't show. Guilt that ever since she had started working for Vince she had been sleeping with him. And anxiety about whether or not Hilary knew or was likely to find out.

Giles's details, though, had proved a godsend and Ginny was more than glad that she had followed them up, as the beginning of Jade's lessons with him marked a change in her daughter's attitude. Jade seemed a little slower, more reflective, more prepared to spend time in her bedroom at her desk with her books than gallivanting round in a whirl of activities. OK, it may have been only English she was beginning to take more seriously but that was the subject she wanted to read at uni and so a good place to start. Maybe she would move from there to her other subjects. Maybe, if she could find other tutors as good as Giles, she would get them in as well.

Things had been looking much better and that's why the news of Giles Gallen's murder had hit Ginny so hard. She couldn't believe he was gone, and as she looked at the two detectives facing her in the living room, she felt guilty that her thoughts were turning so quickly to wondering how she could find someone to take over from him.

'So tell me, Mrs Murray, why did you employ Giles Gallen?'

'Why? He's a tutor. He'd been tutoring my friend's daughter and she recommended him.'

'Who is your friend?'

'Hilary. Hilary Ainsworth. An old school friend.'

The man took out his notebook and flicked through some pages. 'Her daughter would be Briony Ainsworth?'

'That's right.'

'Have you spoken to Hilary since Giles was murdered?'

Since Giles was murdered. The words seemed unreal.

'Yes,' said Ginny, 'of course I have. I was so shocked and so was Hilary. We couldn't believe it.'

'Do you have any idea *why* it might have happened?'

'Why should I have any idea? He was Jade's tutor. He came to give her lessons. How could that be connected to what happened to him?'

There was something unnerving about the man. The way he had asked the question made her feel uncomfortable.

'Did Jade talk about Giles at all?'

'All she said was that the lessons were great and that she

wanted to carry on. Which, as far as I was concerned, was a result. Now . . .'

Ginny clasped her hands together and shook her head.

'Is Jade at home?' said the woman.

'She's in her room.'

'Could we speak to her?'

'Of course.'

Ginny went into the hall and called upstairs.

When Jade came down, Ginny left the room. She closed the door behind her, wondering whether she should stay where she was, lean close to the door and try to hear what her daughter had to say.

Jade had never been interviewed by the police before and was finding it a strange experience, less exciting perhaps than her memories of TV cop shows had led her to expect. There was something downbeat, homely even, about the detectives sitting opposite her, the short dark man who she thought kept looking at her in a strange way and his kinder-looking colleague.

'I'm sure that what happened to Giles Gallen,' said the man, 'has nothing at all to do with his work with you, but we're talking to everyone he had been tutoring and all those he saw on that Saturday afternoon just to get an idea of what he'd been up to.'

'What he'd been up to? I don't know. I mean – he was my tutor and . . . what can I say?'

'I understand,' said the man, 'but it's strange how, in cases like this, what might seem an irrelevant detail can turn out to be revealing. So tell me, how did Giles seem last Saturday when he came to give you a lesson?'

'OK. Much as he always was. We did some Larkin poems.'

'Larkin, eh?'

The man leaned forward in his chair, as if excited by mention of the poet's name. 'Which poems?'

Jade looked at the detective. Was he being serious? Did he really think what Larkin poems they had been through could be in any way significant?

'Which poems?' she said. 'I don't see how—'

'It's not important. I'm just interested.'

'We looked at *An Arundel Tomb . . .'* The man nodded in recognition. 'And *High Windows*.' Another nod.

'What will survive of us is love,' said the man, looking to one side. 'And when I see a couple of kids . . .'

Jade's jaw dropped. He had quoted the last line of one and the first line of the other.

'I'm a big Larkin fan,' said the man. 'It's the misery I like. Though I always say if you look closely . . .' He left his thought unfinished. 'Did you talk about things other than Larkin?'

'Any other writers, you mean?'

'Anything.'

'We took a break in the middle and had a chat.'

'What did you talk about?'

'I can't remember. Just things.'

'And he didn't say anything that, in the light of what happened to him that night, strikes you as significant?'

'I'd have told you if he did.'

Jade was feeling increasingly uncomfortable, mainly because of the man – his questions had made her uneasy from the start. She knew she hadn't answered them truthfully. Not so much in what she had said, but in what she had chosen to keep quiet about. And she sensed that he knew it as well.

Should she tell him? She knew what she was doing was

illegal, but thousands were doing the same and she couldn't believe this kind of thing would be high on the detectives' list of priorities, not when they had a murder on their hands. But she'd still rather they didn't know, especially as she couldn't see how it could be directly connected to Giles. All he did was say something in one of their early sessions. It wasn't a direct suggestion and certainly not a recommendation – he'd said it pretty much in passing – but Jade had picked up on it and done the rest herself. She knew there were risks, but it had worked so far, and she was hoping it might see her through.

No. It was best to say nothing, best to protect herself from closer examination – especially from that detective with the Italian name.

The way he had quoted Larkin had really freaked her out.

14

Gardner turned right into Rocks Lane and headed north, passing the Old Cemetery where the cordon and tent still surrounded the murder scene.

'You know what I find funny about this tutoring thing?' said Garibaldi. 'It's the way it's so, I don't know, so *private*. Normally your kid leaves home and goes to a school where they sit in classes with other kids and get taught stuff. It's a public thing. It's communal. But with tutoring your kid doesn't leave home. They stay put, and someone comes to the house, the home. One to one lessons in the home. It's as far from public as you can get. Private lessons. Private tutors. There's something secretive about the whole idea.'

'They all seemed pretty upfront about it all.'

'Did they? I'm not so sure. I think there's still this sense that you don't want anyone to see or know about it. And the other thing I don't get is the way this stranger – or at least it's a stranger at first – comes into the family home and sits I don't know where – in the living room, at a kitchen table – and gives a lesson. I mean how does it work? Presumably doors are left open all the time. I'm not trying to be sensational here, but there's a safeguarding issue isn't there. Are all these tutors checked? What's it called? CRB?'

'That's the old one,' said Gardner. 'It's called DBS now. Disclosure and Barring Service.'

Garibaldi nodded, impressed by his sergeant's knowledge. 'Of course. DBS. When we get back could you check whether Giles Gallen had DBS clearance? And could you check whether Forum demands it of all their tutors?'

'Do you think Giles Gallen . . . ?'

'I don't know what I think.' Garibaldi turned to look at Gardner. 'What did you make of them?'

'All clearly devastated.'

'Yeah. Notice anything else about them?'

Gardner bit her lip. He could tell she thought he was testing her.

'Can't say I did. I'm assuming you did, though.'

'I thought they all looked a bit sheepish, as though they were uncomfortable about the whole thing.'

'Well you would be, wouldn't you, if your kid's tutor's been murdered?'

'As I said, I don't think they've been upfront about everything. They all looked like they were hiding something.'

'You think everyone's hiding something.'

'That's because everyone is. The kids gave it away more than the parents. They're not so good at hiding things. Maybe they haven't had as much practice.'

'So what do you think they weren't telling us?'

'There was something in the air. Yeah, they were all shocked, but they also seemed if not exactly guilty, then embarrassed about something. Maybe it's the whole private tutor thing. Maybe there's still a sense you shouldn't be doing it, or shouldn't need to.'

'But everyone's at it. Look at the numbers. And these parents, when it comes to their kids' education they don't give a toss about what's fair, do they?'

Garibaldi thought of Alfie and gave a quiet laugh of recognition.

'And those kids,' he said, 'looked like they'd been hauled up in front of the head. Even if they were completely innocent they couldn't stop themselves looking guilty. I remember feeling it myself, but then I was at a Catholic school so guilt was part of the curriculum. I almost did it for A Level.'

'But what could those kids possibly know?'

'Remember the way when you were at school you used to speculate about all the teachers?'

Gardner didn't look as if she did.

'We did it the whole time,' said Garibaldi. 'We'd be there in lessons looking at them but most of the time we weren't listening to them. We were thinking about their lives outside the classroom. That's where all the rumours came from, all the speculation. Most of it sexual as I recall. And the funny thing is so many of them turned out to be true. Like there was this story that one of the priests, the *priests*, was knocking off the woman who taught French. Seemed ridiculous but you heard the story everywhere. When the priest taught you that's all you could think of and it was the same when you had a French lesson with the woman. Then, a couple of years after I left I heard that the priest had left the priesthood and left the school and was getting married. Guess who to? The woman who taught French!'

'I don't get it. Do you mean—?'

'Kids pick up on things. They're more intuitive than we sometimes give them credit for. They tune into things.'

'OK, but that lot haven't left us any clearer about what was going on in Gallen's life, have they?'

'The thing is most of us can seem to be living our lives

normally while all kinds of shit's going on beneath the surface. A bit like swans and their legs.'

Gardner looked blank. Garibaldi decided not to explain.

'I mean, look at me. Look at you.'

'Speak for yourself,' said Gardner. 'I'm fine.'

'No you're not. You're worried about not being good enough for smartarse Tim.'

'Not likely to lead to murder, though, is it?'

'You tell me.'

'OK,' laughed Gardner. 'And what about your shit?'

'Which bit do you want? Kay? Dom? Alfie?'

'And are you going to kill anyone?'

'Not at the moment, but I'm thinking about it. The thing is you never know what's going to push someone over the edge.'

'But we've got no idea about Giles Gallen's shit, do we?'

'Not yet. But tell me, why are most murders committed?'

Gardner turned down the edges of her mouth in a thoughtful frown. Garibaldi caught himself enjoying the silence, and, true to his new resolution, broke it early. 'I mean what are the most common motives?'

'I know what you mean, I was just thinking.'

'I'll give you a clue. They're on the "L" page of Deighton's A–Z of Detection.'

Another short silence.

'"L"? You'll have to tell me,' said Gardner.

'OK. Love, Lust, Loathing and Loot. The big four. But I always like to add Lunacy and Luck, or rather Lack of Luck, you know: wrong place wrong time. With Gallen we have no idea. It could be any, it could be none. The question is whether we need to add another L to the list.'

'What's that?'

'Learning.'

Garibaldi turned to see Gardner smiling and nodding her approval.

'Been working on that one, have you?'

'"A little learning is a dangerous thing." Know who said that?' Garibaldi kept the silence very short. 'Pope.'

'Yeah? Which one?'

'One of them,' he said, deciding not to tell her it was the eighteenth-century poet, 'can't remember which.'

He didn't want to dent his sergeant's confidence with smartarse Tim. Especially as, at that very moment, he himself was experiencing his own feelings of doubt and insecurity. Why had he thought that every single one of those they had just visited had been either lying or keeping something very much to themselves? Could he possibly be right? Or was he losing his ability to sift truth from lies, to read people accurately?

His phone rang.

'DI Garibaldi.'

'Archie McLean here, boss. We've had a call from one of Gallen's tutoring friends. Says they were with him on Saturday night.'

Garibaldi took out his notebook and jotted down the address.

15

Garibaldi and Gardner sat facing Emily Francis in the living room of her parents' Putney home.

'Thank you for getting in touch, Emily.'

'I had to. I knew I had to talk to you. You see, I think I may have been one of the last people to see Giles, to see him . . .'

The word 'alive' hovered in the short silence.

'I hope you don't mind answering a few questions.'

'Of course not. Anything to help find out who did this. It's so . . .' Emily shook her head in disbelief.

'So you were with Giles on Saturday night?'

'Yes. We were both at the party but I was with him before and after as well. We were in the Coach and Horses before and we went to the Red Lion afterwards.'

'So you were with him all evening?'

'I wasn't *with* him. I mean we weren't . . . I wasn't by his side the whole time.'

'You mean you're not his girlfriend.'

'Girlfriend! No, nothing like that.'

'How did you know Giles?'

'I met him at the Forum drinks party about three or four years ago. We'd both just started tutoring. I don't know him that well. We've had the occasional drink with mutual friends, messaged every now and then. That kind of thing.'

'But you spoke to Giles on Saturday evening?'

'Oh, yeah, we spoke all right. Mostly in the pub before the party. I mean there were only three of us there.'

'So that's you, Giles, and . . . ?'

'Simon.'

'Simon . . . ?' Garibaldi flicked through his notebook to find the list of tutors at the Forum drinks party.

'Simon Prest.'

'I see. And on Saturday night was there anything Giles said or anything about his behaviour that struck you as unusual?'

'Not at all.'

'Nothing that made you think he might be in trouble?'

Emily shrugged and spread her hands, palms-up. 'He certainly didn't say anything to suggest that someone was going to kill him!'

'Did Giles have a partner?' said DS Gardner.

'He had a girlfriend, but I think they'd broken up.'

'And did he have a current girlfriend, anyone he was seeing?'

'No, I don't think so. Simon thinks he might have been seeing this girl he was tutoring with abroad, but when he asked him about it on Saturday Giles was very coy about it.'

'Do you know the name of Giles's girlfriend, the one he broke up with?'

'I think she was called Beth, but I can't swear on it.'

'Surname?'

'No idea.'

'And the girl he tutored with?'

'Sam, I think.'

'Surname?'

'Again, I don't know. Look, do you have any idea at all who did this?'

'We're pursuing several lines of enquiry,' said Garibaldi. 'Tell me, what did you speak about with Giles on Saturday evening?'

'I can't remember. I . . . does it really matter what I said to him?'

'I won't know that until you tell me, will I?'

'Well, I can't remember exactly. It was just the usual stuff. Catching up on our summers, that kind of thing.'

'And Giles had been abroad in the summer, is that right?'

'Yeah. With this Italian family.'

Garibaldi looked at his notebook. 'That would be the Rivettis.'

Emily nodded. 'The Italians. He started working for them about a year ago.'

Garibaldi scribbled in his notebook. 'I see. Tell me about this drinks party. You were with Giles in the pub before and after the party. Were you with him *at* the party?'

'No. I mean, I may have had the occasional word with him, but I didn't see much of him. He seemed to be with the Irelands most of the time, Felicia and Roddy. They had a lot of time for Giles. I think he was their blue-eyed boy and he played up to it.'

'What do you mean?'

'He milked it. He knew they rated him, knew that they put him forward for glam jobs like the Rivettis, so Giles made sure he was always onside with them. You know, said the right thing. Told them what they wanted to hear.'

'And what did they want to hear?'

'That he was committed to being a tutor. Most of us really want to do something else. I mean, I really want to be a . . .' Emily stared wistfully out of the living room window as if her ambition had just floated by. 'I really want to be a journalist and I'm doing it to make ends meet. It's not what I *want* to do. Just like I don't want to be still living at home with mum and dad. But the Irelands, they have this thing about career tutors and they think that's what they have . . . had in Giles.'

'And *is* that what they had in Giles?'

'Giles said no, but we didn't believe him. It wasn't like he kept banging on about what he really wanted to do – unlike the rest of us. And he's got the perfect background for Forum.'

'What's that?'

'Public school. Cambridge. That kind of thing helps when it comes to tutoring.'

Garibaldi looked round the living room of Emily's Putney family home. It didn't scream lack of privilege, and Emily herself, in jumper, jeans and Converse with the clean, fresh-faced confidence of youthful affluence, came across as someone from a background not a million miles from Giles's.

'I take it you didn't go to private school then.' Private. Garibaldi always opted for the more accurate adjective.

'Lady Margaret's.'

Garibaldi knew it. A far from shabby all-girls comprehensive and a favourite choice of the middle classes.

'And Cardiff,' added Emily. 'I'm not saying it's counted against me or anything – it's more that what Giles had definitely counted for him.'

'I see. So let's get this straight, you didn't speak to Giles at the party, but you went to the pub with him afterwards.'

'The Red Lion was on the way home for us and close to where Giles lived so we headed there. We went early and Giles joined us later when he'd managed to pull himself away from the Irelands.'

'Who's we?'

'Giles, me and Simon.'

'And can you remember what time Giles left the pub?'

'Not exactly, but I think it was round about ten thirty.'

'And what time did you leave the pub?'

'Shortly after him. I fancied one last drink but Simon was in some kind of hurry and I didn't want to stay by myself so, yeah, we left very soon after Giles.'

'And how did you get home?'

'I got an Uber.'

'And Simon?'

'He lives in Barnes, so he walked home.'

'I see. So there was nothing at all unusual in Giles's behaviour on Saturday night?'

Emily shook her head. 'Nothing I noticed. It's completely unbelievable. That kind of thing happening to Giles. It doesn't make any sense.'

Garibaldi got up and reached for his card. 'If you think of anything, absolutely anything, do get in touch.'

Emily looked at the card and shook her head. 'I mean, what the fuck was Giles doing in a cemetery at that time of night? Maybe it was some weirdo. Or maybe they, I don't know – maybe they thought he was someone else.'

'We're not ruling anything out,' said Garibaldi.

He headed for the door, adding mistaken identity to his list of possibilities. Luck. Or Lack of Luck. Not such a silly idea. Maybe he'd bring it up at the next meeting.

Simon Prest sat in the living room of his parents' Barnes home, leaning back in his chair, one foot resting on a jiggling knee. He ran a hand through his mop of curly blond hair and sighed.

'This kind of thing,' he said, 'it just doesn't happen to ... people you know. Do you know what I mean?

Garibaldi knew what he meant. People you know. White. Middle-class. Educated. Privileged.

'It's freaked me out completely. I really don't know what to say.'

'Maybe you could start by telling us where you were with Giles on Saturday night?'

'Saturday night? Yeah, sure. I met Giles and Emily in the Coach and Horses before the party and we went to the Red Lion after it.'

'So you spent a lot of time talking to him, then?'

'Not much at the party, but before and after, yeah.'

'And did Giles say anything to suggest he was in trouble of any sort?'

'Trouble?' he said. 'Giles? Trouble wasn't Giles's thing.'

'What do you mean?'

'He was Mr Clean. Mr Squeaky Clean. Always was.'

'Was there anything about his behaviour that evening that struck you as odd?'

Giles gave a slow shake of his head. 'Nothing. He was just . . . just Giles. I can't believe he's gone. It doesn't make sense.'

'I understand that he'd been tutoring abroad in the summer.'

Prest chuckled. 'Yeah. Lucky sod. A holiday in the sun, luxury lifestyle, all expenses paid. I never get gigs like that. Mainly because I'm in Edinburgh in the summer performing to half-empty rooms.'

'So you're a comedian?' said Garibaldi.

'The jury's out but, yeah, that's what I'd like to do. So when it comes to August I have to leave the swanky jobs in the sun to the likes of Giles and head off to rainy Edinburgh. Not that I ever get offered swanky jobs in the sun.'

'How did you know Giles?'

'We were at school together.'

'I see. That would be Radley. And you both live in Barnes.'

'Yeah. My family moved here after my first year at Radley.'

Garibaldi looked round the living room of the Nassau Road house, close to the pond and the heart of the village. Public School. Huge houses in Barnes. Where did these people get the money?

'So schoolmates and neighbours? You must know – have known – each other pretty well, then.'

'Yeah, we did. At school obviously but we hung out down here as well. As close to best friends as you can get. Which makes it all the more . . .' Prest bowed his head, screwed up his eyes and rubbed them with his hands. 'It's difficult. I can still remember meeting him on our first day at Radley. We were in the same Social.'

'Social?'

'Sorry, house. You're so used to the lingo you forget. But, yeah, Giles was a real success at school. More than me. He was Head of So – House. Clever. Good at games. Good at everything. Whereas I was good at games but not so hot at the rest. He went off to Cambridge and I went off to Newcastle. I was always the joker. He was, you know, the real deal.'

Garibaldi looked at his notebook. 'Giles's mother mentioned another old school friend. Hugo. She said the three of you were particularly close.'

Prest smiled and gave a wistful sigh. 'Yeah, we were. Hugo's devastated. I mean, we all are, everyone is.'

'And you saw each other often?'

Prest nodded. 'We kept in touch. And we'd meet up for a drink every now and then.'

'And tell me,' said Garibaldi, flipping over a page in his notebook. 'How did both you and Giles end up tutoring?'

'Funny, isn't it?' laughed Prest. 'You'd have thought Giles would be destined for something better, wouldn't you? Not that there's anything wrong with tutoring, but you know what I mean. I'm doing it because it fits in with my comedy. But Giles? I'd always expected him to go into the City or the Law or even head off to teach in some public school like Radley but no, he moves back to Barnes with nothing planned and drifts into tutoring. I'd already got myself on Forum's books, told him about it and he came on board. Said he never thought he'd do it for more than a couple of months but it seems he liked it.'

Garibaldi consulted his notebook. 'Emily says you were talking to Giles about the woman he tutored with in the summer.' He consulted his notes. 'Sam.'

'Yeah. Sam.'

'Were they an item?'

'I don't know, but Giles was a real charmer. Always was. And spending weeks together in a Mediterranean villa or on some yacht. All that sun and sand . . .'

'But he didn't mention it?'

'Giles didn't give much away.'

'I see. It seems that you were one of the last people to see him alive. You were in the Red Lion together after the drinks party. How did he seem to you then?'

'He'd clearly had a drink. I mean, we all had.'

'What time did he leave?'

'I can't remember exactly. Maybe round half ten.'

'Did you leave with Giles?'

'No. He left before us.'

'And you and Emily left shortly afterwards.'

'Yeah, about half an hour afterwards.'

'And where did you go when you left?'

'Where did I go? I walked back here.'

Garibaldi glanced at his notebook. 'So there was nothing in his behaviour, nothing about him that made you think he might be in any kind of trouble?'

Simon Prest shook his head. 'He seemed perfectly OK. Nothing to suggest he was about to be . . .'

'Well, thanks for your time, Simon.' Garibaldi got up from his chair and nodded to Gardner. 'If you think of anything at all that might be of interest and I mean anything, however small, however much you think it might be irrelevant, do let us know.' He handed him a card. 'You'd be surprised how helpful small details can be.'

'I will,' said Simon. 'It's difficult to think of Giles not being . . .'

He trailed off, leaving Garibaldi to wonder whether it was a sentence he couldn't finish or whether his old schoolmate's not being was a state Simon Prest found difficult to contemplate.

16

As Gardner drove along the Lower Richmond Road towards Barnes, Garibaldi turned to look at the Half Moon, his mind going back to his first date there with Rachel – the evening listening to country covers that had marked the real beginning of their relationship.

Did either of them think then that they would end up where they were now? And did either of them imagine that in the time since they wouldn't go back to the Half Moon once? Maybe he should look up what was on, find a good band or singer, and take Rachel back to where it had all started.

At the top of Castelnau, Gardner took a left into Lonsdale Road, drove past St Paul's School, and pulled up on the gravel drive outside a huge house set back from the road. They got out and Garibaldi paused, taking in the double-fronted building and its adjoining coach house.

The doorbell rang deep within the house. Garibaldi showed his card to the man who came to the door.

'Mr Rivetti?'

'No. I work for the Rivettis.'

'Is Mr Rivetti at home?'

'He's at work.'

'Mrs Rivetti?'

'I'll see if she's free.'

'It's not a matter of seeing if she's free,' said Garibaldi. 'We're Metropolitan Police detectives investigating a murder and we would like to talk to her.'

The man reluctantly pulled back the door and ushered them in.

Garibaldi and Gardner followed him through a marble-floored hall into a spacious, light-filled reception room. It was strangely furnished, a combination of the classical and the modern – wooden dressers and tables, Queen Anne chairs, Chesterfield sofas, Greek pottery and abstract paintings which looked like Picassos and Chagalls. It looked as though it shouldn't work, but it did. Just about.

'I'm Mrs Rivetti.'

Garibaldi turned to the woman who stood in the doorway. She was dark and petite, elegantly dressed in linen trousers, blue cardigan and pearls.

'Is this about poor Giles?' she said.

Garibaldi nodded.

'Maybe you'd like to come this way.'

Mrs Rivetti led them through to another huge room. Kitchen/dining room was the closest Garibaldi could get to describing it, but that gave no sense of its scale and variety. On one side of the room a grand piano sat under two tapestries. In the middle was a long table with twelve chairs opposite three ground-to-ceiling glass windows giving onto a manicured lawn and landscaped garden. On the other side, beyond an island, were shining state-of-the art kitchen appliances.

Mrs Rivetti stood by the table and held out her hands, inviting Garibaldi and Gardner to sit down.

'We can't believe it,' said Mrs Rivetti taking a seat

opposite them. 'All of us, but Paolo especially. He's devastated.'

'Is Paolo at home? We'd like to have a word with him if possible.'

'I'm afraid he's having a tennis lesson at the Riverside.'

'I see. Maybe tomorrow then.'

'Of course, but I have to warn you he is very distressed about it all.'

'We'll tread very carefully, I can assure you.' Garibaldi leaned forward, resting clasped hands on the table. 'Tell me, Mrs Rivetti, how long had Giles been tutoring Paolo?'

'Just over a year, I think. Yes, he started at the beginning of the last school year.'

'When did you last see him?'

'He was here on Saturday afternoon. When was he . . . ?'

'When was he murdered? Some time late Saturday night, early Sunday morning. How did he seem when he was here in the afternoon?'

'Absolutely fine. He had a session with Paolo and then . . .'

The hesitation was brief but Garibaldi caught it. Together with the darting of the eyes to one side it gave her away. She was either about to lie or change what she was about to say.

'And then we had a chat about how Paolo's getting on, whether he'll get in.'

'Get in?'

'To his school. Entrance exam.'

'I see,' nodded Garibaldi. 'And am I right in thinking that Giles spent the summer abroad with your family?'

'He did. He came away with us at Easter to help Paolo and he was with us over the summer as well.'

'You must have got to know him well.'

'We did, Paolo especially. He spent more time with

Paolo. We did things together but he was with Paolo mostly.'

'I understand there was another tutor working with you in the summer. Sam?'

Mrs Rivetti nodded. 'Yes, Sam was with us.'

'Did you get her through Forum as well?'

'We did.'

'Do you have her contact details, Mrs Rivetti?'

'Of course. Do you need them now?'

'That would be very helpful.'

Mrs Rivetti reached for her phone and scrolled through it. 'Here we are. Sam Bannister.'

Gardner jotted down the number.

'I see. Tell me, Mrs Rivetti, when did you find out about Giles's murder?'

'When did I find out?' Mrs Rivetti looked puzzled. 'I don't know. The news. I heard it on the news.'

Garibaldi took out his notebook and scribbled something down. Or rather, made a squiggle. He wanted Mrs Rivetti to think she'd said something significant.

'And when you heard the news what did you do?'

'What did I do? I don't know. I was so shocked – I think I called my husband to tell him.'

'And did your husband know?'

'He had no idea. He was as shocked as me. He said to wait until he was home before telling Paolo.'

'Why did he say that?'

'He wanted us both to be there. He was worried about how Paolo might react.'

Garibaldi flicked through this notebook. 'Wasn't there a chance that Paolo would find out himself? Online. Social media. Things like that tend to spread pretty quickly.'

'Luigi said to wait, so I did.'

'And what about your daughter? Did she know?'

'Anna?' Mrs Rivetti shook her head. 'Neither of them knew before we told them that evening. It was terrible. They were so shocked. Paolo cried all night.'

'And tell me, Mrs Rivetti, when you and your husband heard the news did you think of getting in touch with the police at all?'

Mrs Rivetti shrugged and held out her hands. 'Why would we do that?'

'To say you knew him. To say that he was here on that Saturday afternoon, to say that he tutored your son and had spent the whole summer with you. Sometimes people come forward with information in case it might prove to be of some help.'

'I'm sorry, it didn't occur to us. We were in such a state.'

'What time did Giles come to you on Saturday afternoon?'

'I can't remember. I think it was about four o'clock, maybe five. He spent an hour with Paolo going through some entrance papers.'

'I see. So he spent an hour with Paolo and then left.'

'That's right. I had a chat with him and he went off.'

'You had a chat with him?'

Mrs Rivetti's eyes flashed as she gave an extravagant shrug. 'Inspector . . .'

'Garibaldi.'

'Garibaldi?'

'My grandfather was Italian.'

'Where from?'

'A little village in the south. Between Rome and Naples.'

Mrs Rivetti's smile left Garibaldi in no doubt that she was from the north.

'I see. Do you go back?'

Did Garibaldi go back? Only in his mind. Only when he was thinking of his father and the Italian grandparents he never knew. Only when he was working his way through Duolingo and watching classic Italian films on Netflix. Only when he took out the embryonic family tree that still had most branches missing and visited Garibaldi genealogy websites. Only when he looked up photos of his ancestors' hilltop mountain village.

'I hope to go back soon,' he said.

Mrs Rivetti smiled. The Italy of the Rivettis and the Italy of his farmer grandfather may have been poles apart but the brief sense of shared heritage seemed to have taken some of the sting out of her.

'Inspector Garibaldi.' She pronounced it the Italian way, with a short 'a'. 'I don't see how any of these questions are at all relevant to what happened to Giles.'

'We're just trying to get some sense of what he was up to.'

'Up to? You make it sound like he was doing something wrong.'

'Not at all. We'd like to talk to your husband, Mrs Rivetti. Will he be in this evening?'

'He's at work. He's back late most nights.'

'Do you have his number? We'll give him a call and see what's a good time.'

'He's a busy man, Inspector.'

'And so am I, Mrs Rivetti. And I'm investigating a murder, so I'd appreciate everyone's cooperation.'

'Of course.' Mrs Rivetti reached for a notepad, scribbled down a number and handed it to Gardner.

As they walked to the car Garibaldi turned back to look again at the house's imposing frontage.

'It's one thing,' he said, 'going into people's houses to tutor, but it must be another thing entirely going on holiday with them for months, actually *living* with them. Takes the intimacy thing to new levels, don't you think?'

'It must do,' said Gardner as she opened the car door and climbed in.

Garibaldi got into the passenger seat and clipped on his belt. 'Would *you* feel comfortable having a live-in tutor as part of the family for the whole summer?'

'I don't think we'd have room in a caravan.'

'Hypothetically.'

'I can't imagine it. I mean, I just can't see Tim thinking he'd need one.'

Garibaldi smiled his approval as they headed towards Chiswick Bridge. DS Gardner was coming on.

17

'So where does she live?' said Garibaldi.

'Hoxton.'

Garibaldi sighed. Hoxton was a long way from home, a long way from the river. Unlike the hills of North London, it didn't give him the sense he was about to have a nosebleed, but it did always give him a headache. At first it was the excesses of hipster colonisation that caused the pain, but now the discomfort came from his sense that the area was populated by people who had turned up late for a party, not realising that the cool guests had long ago left for somewhere more interesting. The place was like a tribute act – never as good as the original and coming close to parody.

'I've Googled her,' said Gardner, 'and guess what?'

Garibaldi paused the way his sergeant did when asked to guess anything.

'She's got a famous dad.'

'Bannister? Not . . .'

'Yeah. Harry Bannister. Fancy that.'

Harry Bannister. Famous multimillionaire tycoon. High media profile. Star of TV shows. Quick to embrace any opportunity for self-promotion. First port of call for a right-wing, reactionary soundbite on any issue.

Garibaldi sighed. 'Probably best not to mention it.'

'OK.'

'And let's hope she's dodged the gene.'

Gardner pulled up in Hoxton Square and they walked through several blocks to Harrow Cloisters.

Sam Bannister's flat was large and light, its long window looking out onto the Cloisters' courtyard. It had the kind of minimal style achieved only through colossal effort and huge amounts of money. Lots of bare floor, glass and exposed brick.

Garibaldi wriggled in his chair. It may have been fashionable, but it was far from comfortable. He took out his notebook and gave Gardner a let's-get-going smile.

'We're here to ask some questions about Giles Gallen.'

In leather jacket, jeans and trainers, Sam Bannister had the kind of beauty that meant she didn't have to try too hard when it came to clothes – she would look good in anything. There was something about her – an air of confidence that Garibaldi suspected had its roots in more than money.

She reached for a packet of cigarettes, took one out and offered the packet to Garibaldi and then Gardner. Both shook their heads. Garibaldi was surprised that she smoked (he knew few people who did and most of those were in the older generation) and that, even though this was her flat, she was going to do it in their presence. He thought of telling her he'd rather she abstained but decided against it.

'Fuck, yeah, I just don't believe it. I mean—' She took a deep drag on her cigarette.

'Do you mind if we open a window?' said Garibaldi.

Sam Bannister looked at the cigarette in her hand as if she'd forgotten it was there. 'Sure. Sorry. Do you mind? It's just that I'm pretty stressed . . .'

She got up and opened two windows.

'What can I tell you?' she said as she sat down.

'We understand you knew Giles. You worked together for the Rivettis this summer.'

'That's right. We were in Italy and around the Med.'

Around the Med. She made it sound like popping round the corner to the shops.

'As we understand it,' said DS Gardner, 'Giles was tutoring the boy and you were tutoring the girl.'

'That's pretty much it. But there was a lot of free time. It sounds glamorous and everything, the villa, the yacht, but it wasn't always.'

Garibaldi raised his eyebrows. 'Really? You didn't enjoy your time cruising . . . around the Med?'

'Don't get me wrong. It was pretty luxurious. Accommodation. Food. Drink. No expense spared, but tutoring those kids wasn't always easy.'

'And why was that?'

'They weren't interested in studying anything. Who could blame them? It was their summer holidays and here they were expected to work every morning. We could tell they weren't interested. It wouldn't have been a problem but the Rivettis . . .' She let out a big sigh. 'Mr and Mrs Rivetti would let you get on with it. They'd almost ignore you and get on with their socialising and partying and having fun and you'd get the sense that they were really relaxed about it all and then suddenly they'd sort of panic and get really stressed about how the kids were doing, about whether Paolo would get into his school and how Anna was shaping up. And Mrs Rivetti, she had a real temper. She'd be OK one moment and then explode.'

'Explode at who?'

'Anyone in range. The kids mostly, but not always.'

'And when you say explode, what exactly do you mean?'

'I don't mean it literally, like, pow! I mean it as a metaphor.'

'I didn't for one moment think you could have meant anything else,' said Garibaldi. 'When we spoke to Mrs Rivetti earlier she seemed very much intact.'

'OK.' Sam Bannister looked taken aback, as if regretting her reference to metaphor. 'She shouted a lot and there were a few times when she threw things. To be honest Giles and me were sometimes a bit frightened of her. I sometimes thought Mr Rivetti was as well.'

'Did she ever get physically violent?'

Sam Bannister's hesitation was brief, but Garibaldi noticed it.

'No.' Her voice was firm, perhaps too firm. 'Or if she did, we never saw it.'

'So she never, for example, smacked the kids?'

'Look, all I said was that she had a temper. I wasn't saying anything else.'

'I'm well aware of that, Sam , but we're investigating the murder of her tutor and we have to pursue all possible lines of enquiry.'

'Are you suggesting she—?'

'I'm suggesting nothing.'

'This is ridiculous. Just because you've got a temper doesn't mean—'

Garibaldi held up his hand. 'Let's get back to Giles, shall we? You must have spent a lot of time with him?'

'A fair bit, yeah.'

'So you got to know each other pretty well.'

Sam Bannister looked taken aback. 'Look, nothing happened between us, OK? No relationship, no holiday fling. OK, so there was one night . . .'

She trailed off. Garibaldi sensed she was weighing up whether or not to finish the sentence.

'One night?' he prompted.

Sam Bannister shook her head. 'No, it was nothing. We had a thing one night after too much wine.'

'A thing?'

'It was nothing. We didn't have sex.'

Garibaldi smiled at her frankness. He never could have spoken about sex like that when he was her age. He wasn't sure he could now.

'Some of Giles's tutoring friends think he might have split with his girlfriend because of you.'

''Fraid not. It really was nothing and it was very silly. It's what happens when you're on holiday and you've had too much wine.'

'So how long have you been working for the Rivettis?'

'I started the same time as Giles. About this time last year. We both went away with the Rivettis at Easter. That's when I got to know him.'

'And how often do you see Anna?'

'I used to see her once a week after school.'

'Used to?'

Sam Bannister's face tightened. 'Yeah. I don't tutor her anymore. I've stopped.'

'Really? Mrs Rivetti didn't mention it.'

'Yeah, I gave my notice in last week. I've stopped tutoring altogether.'

'So you no longer work for the Rivettis or for Forum?'

'That's right.'

'Why have you stopped?'

Sam Bannister looked at Gardner and then turned back to Garibaldi. She again seemed to be deciding whether or not to say more.

'I got a job. A proper job.'

'Where's that?' said Garibaldi.

A slight pause. 'It's digital publishing.'

'Digital publishing?' There was something about the very word 'digital' that made Garibaldi uneasy. 'But you're not at work today?'

'Not in the office, no.'

'What is it? A digital day off?'

'I'm working from home.'

'I see. And this digital publishing firm, what are they called?'

'It's a very small outfit. Compass Publishing. As I said, very small, but I'm lucky to get a foot in.'

'Absolutely,' said Garibaldi. 'Must be good to be able to stop tutoring.'

'Don't get me wrong, I didn't dislike it. It's just that I know it's not what I want to do long-term. Like most tutors, I suppose.'

'Tell me, Sam,' said Garibaldi. 'Did you ever notice anything about Giles, his behaviour, what he said, that made you think he might be in trouble of any sort?'

'You mean anything that might suggest someone would want to kill him?' Sam Bannister shook her head. 'But there is one thing—'

That look again. That sense of consideration, of whether or not to tell.

'I've no idea whether it's at all relevant but I got a text from Giles on Saturday evening.'

'What time?'

Sam reached for her phone and scrolled through. 'It was at 5.32 in the afternoon.'

She handed the phone to Garibaldi. He held it between himself and Gardner as they both read the screen.

just been to Rivettis'. They tell me you've resigned. What's happened? They've also made me an offer. Give me a call.

'I never got the chance to call him. I rang him next day but no answer. His phone was dead and so, it turns out, was he.'

'Do you have any idea what they offered Giles?'

Sam shook her head. 'I never got to talk to him, did I? Could be anything.'

'Could be anything?' said Garibaldi. 'What do you mean?'

'I mean, it's obviously about his tutoring. That's why he's there in the first place, but I don't know what it was.' Sam gave a thoughtful look, as if searching for a possibility. 'It could have been to do with getting a replacement for me, I suppose. Yeah, maybe that's what it was.'

'Well, look, Sam, thanks for your time.' Garibaldi wriggled in the uncomfortable chair and reached out to her. 'Here's my card. If you think of anything else that might be significant, please do get in touch. And we've got your number so if we've got any more questions . . .'

Garibaldi looked at Sam as she left. Underneath the poise he sensed that all was not well with her. He was convinced she had been lying, or if not lying then not revealing the full truth. But he'd thought the same about everyone he'd spoken to so far about Giles Gallen.

Was he right, or was he simply losing his touch?

18

Rachel's baths were an important part of her day – a restorative ritual involving candles, books and music that lasted for up to an hour and, much to Garibaldi's as-yet-unarticulated displeasure, one that used up most of the hot water. He had learned, to his cost, that it was a good idea not to interrupt them so when he came into the flat to find a shut bathroom door and the sound of music beyond it he poured himself a whisky, put on Gillian Welch and lay on the sofa.

His phone rang.

Kay. His heart sank.

'Jim, it's me.'

'Hi.'

'We need to talk about Alfie.'

So what was new? Had there ever been a time in recent years when they hadn't needed to talk about Alfie?

'How was he?' said Garibaldi, remembering that she'd seen him at the weekend.

'I'm worried.'

That made two of them, but he knew their worries were different. Alfie's attendance at QPR games had never been of great concern to his ex-wife.

'When did you last speak to him?' asked Kay.

'Yesterday.'

'How did he seem?'

'Look, Kay, no need to play games. Why don't you just tell me what you're worried about?'

'I'm not playing games. I just want to know how you found him.'

'I'll tell you when you've told me what you're worried about.'

It was like being back in the playground.

'I don't think he's working hard enough. In fact, I don't think he's working at all.'

So that was it. No work. Nothing about the company he was keeping, the social reinvention that had caused Garibaldi many a sleepless night.

'What makes you say that?'

'He's partying all the time. Dominic says . . .'

Garibaldi winced. It was bad enough every time Kay uttered her partner's name, but when she uttered his name and followed it with 'says', he felt his face twitch. It was twitching now as he shut his eyes and listened to Dominic's analysis of Alfie's university experience.

'Alfie should be aiming for a First. Nowadays that's what employers are really looking for.'

So that was it. The demands of the market. The need for a good job. The assumption that his son would end up in the City. An assumption he had, until recently, dismissed as ridiculous.

'What he should be doing at Oxford is aiming for a First and making contacts.'

'Well, he's making contacts all right,' said Garibaldi. 'Dinner parties in the country.'

'I don't have any problem with that. It's the good degree I'm worried about.'

What had happened to the woman he married all those years ago? Could anyone change so much?

'Well I do have a problem with that,' said Garibaldi. 'Wouldn't surprise me if he ends up joining one of those drinking clubs, the sort of thing those wankers like Johnson and Cameron and Osborne were in. What was it? The Bullingdon.'

The woman he married would have agreed with him. No son of theirs should be hanging out with that sort of crowd, or even be close to that sort of crowd.

'Don't be ridiculous. He's not thinking of joining the Bullingdon.'

'Not yet he isn't.'

'Look, Jim, I don't have a problem with him making interesting friends.'

'Interesting?'

'That's his choice. It's what you do when you're young.'

'It's not what I did when I was young.'

'Yes, well—'

'Yes well what?'

'Look, Jim, I don't want a row. I just want to talk about Alfie.'

Garibaldi tightened his lips. It was impossible to talk to Kay about Alfie and not have a row. And it was difficult not to apportion blame when what to blame was so clear. That move to the private school sixth form. Alfie's girlfriend and the school's air of expectation and entitlement. And now that he was at Oxford, hanging out with a load of kids from schools posher than the one his father thought he should never have gone to in the first place.

Of course, he'd been proud when Alfie had got in. And of course, he enjoyed going up to see him. But when he thought of the changes his son was going through he couldn't help but wonder whether he'd have been better off somewhere else.

'I was ringing,' said Kay, 'to ask whether when you see him—'

'He'll be OK,' said Garibaldi, cutting across her, not wanting her to have the chance to tell him what to say. 'Whatever it is, he'll get through it.'

He spoke the words with a conviction he knew he lacked.

The bathroom door opened and Rachel, one towel wrapped round her body, another cocooning her hair, emerged.

'Look, Kay, I've got a work call coming in. I've got to go.'

'Maybe we should meet.'

The last thing he wanted.

'You and me,' said Kay, adding after a pause. 'And maybe Dominic and Rachel.'

Correction. That was the last thing he wanted.

'Let's think about it,' he said before saying goodbye as nicely as he could bring himself to.

Rachel sat on an armchair and started to dry her hair. 'Who was that?'

'Have a guess. She's worried that Alfie's not doing any work. Not at all worried that he's hanging out with a load of toffs.'

'And not at all worried that he's not coming to QPR?'

Garibaldi smiled. She knew him well.

'Look,' said Rachel, sounding like she was about to deliver a teacher explanation. 'These things are always worse when you're thinking about them at a distance. Maybe you should go up and see him.'

As was so often the case, Rachel was speaking sense.

'Yeah, maybe I should. Fancy coming with me?'

'Sure.'

'OK, let's try and find a time. Might be difficult with this case.'

Rachel stopped patting her hair and sat up. 'By the way, I've got something for you.'

Garibaldi perked up, thinking that Rachel was about to let her towel slip and call him over.

'About the case. I went through the records of who came from Forum Tutors to Hillside and guess whose name was in the list? One Giles Gallen.'

'Gallen? At your school?'

Rachel nodded. 'Yeah. I only found it today. I was going to ring you—'

'Why the hell didn't you?'

He hadn't meant to sound so aggressive and immediately regretted it. This always happened after conversations with Kay.

'Sorry, I didn't have any time.' She sounded wounded. 'And I thought it would be OK to tell you this evening.'

'It's pretty important, isn't it?'

'I know it's important and I'm sorry I didn't ring. I thought if I told you as soon as I saw you it would be OK. And I've been in the bath and . . .'

Garibaldi held up his hand. 'I'm sorry. I shouldn't have snapped. And it's fine. Absolutely fine.'

'I mean I *could* have called you, I suppose, but it's not that easy at school . . .'

Garibaldi moved towards Rachel and took her hands in his. The last thing he wanted was a row. 'It's OK. It really is.'

Rachel nodded and smiled. All was forgiven. Garibaldi reminded himself to look up what was on at the Half Moon.

'So tell me,' said Garibaldi, 'what was Gallen doing at Hillside?'

'University stuff with Sixth Formers,' said Rachel. 'The Head's desperate for some of our kids to get into Oxbridge. It may not have happened yet but he's already written the Press Release for when it does. And he's always banging on about access schemes and the like. That's why he jumped at Forum's pro bono offer. And Giles Gallen apparently came in a couple of times in the summer term to talk to some Year 12 kids who were thinking of applying. Gave them some advice and interview practice. Came in again at the beginning of this term as well.'

Why had Forum not mentioned it? When Garibaldi had asked Felicia and Roddy Ireland for a list of who Gallen had been tutoring why had no mention been made of his work at Hillside? Especially given their eagerness to flag up the pro bono work they offered.

'I think I might need to come in.'

'Come into school? Will I have to pretend I don't know you?'

'Depends whether you're into that kind of role play.'

Rachel reached for the towel wrapped round her body. Garibaldi wondered whether his luck was in but was disappointed when he saw Rachel pull it tighter and go back into the bathroom.

He lay down on the sofa again, picked his laptop off the floor, turned up Gillian Welch, looked up 'What's on at the Half Moon' and Googled Barnes Old Cemetery again.

19

'There's something I need to tell you, boss.'

DCI Deighton looked up at Garibaldi from her desk. 'What is it?'

'Can I shut the door?'

Deighton nodded and Garibaldi closed the door behind him.

'Have a seat,' said Deighton.

Garibaldi sat down. 'It's like this. The thing is, I'm in a relationship . . .'

The pastoral care look spread across Deighton's face.

'OK,' she said, in a tone that suggested any relationship was fine by her.

'I've been living with a teacher for several months – we'd been going out for a couple of years – and the thing is she works at a school that Giles Gallen did some work at.'

Deighton listened as Garibaldi explained the nature of Forum's pro bono initiative at Hillside Academy.

'I see,' she said, 'and you're telling me this because Hillside will be part of our investigations.'

'Exactly. I'm declaring an interest. Rachel, my partner, organised the programme so it could be that I have to go to the school where she works. I hope you understand why I felt the need to come clean.'

'I'm glad you did, Jim. Very glad.'

'If you'd rather someone else did it—'

'Did your . . . did Rachel meet Giles Gallen at all?'

'From what I can make out, she just greeted him and showed him to a classroom. I'm going up to Hillside after the meeting to speak to the Head, but the chances are I'll have to speak to Rachel. I just wanted you to know where I got the information and make you aware of the connection.'

Deighton hooked the glasses off her nose and leaned back in her chair.

'Thanks, Jim. And do you know what? I think it's fine for you to go to Hillside with Milly. Keep me posted and if there are any developments which make it impossible for you to carry on we'll deal with them as and when.'

'What kind of developments would those be?'

Deighton shrugged. 'I don't know. Maybe if you think your partner stabbed Gallen last Saturday in Barnes Old Cemetery we might have to rethink things.'

Garibaldi laughed and got up from his chair. 'OK. Thanks.'

'But before you go,' said Deighton. 'How about that drink? I think we might find we have a few things in common.'

A few things in common with DCI Deighton? Garibaldi was intrigued.

'Do I have to wait to find out what they are?'

'Well, for a start, I'm also living with a teacher.'

This was it. Deighton was letting him in. Soon he'd be calling her Karen.

'Yeah, well that's a bit of a coincidence, I guess,' said Garibaldi.

'She's not called Rachel, though.'

Garibaldi found himself nodding but he couldn't work out

why. Was it to show this was much as he had thought (and much as everyone else in the station thought but had never known for sure)? Or was it to show this was all fine by him?

Either way he felt awkward and embarrassed and was relieved when Deighton got up from her desk and said, 'Let's get this meeting done, shall we, and then we can get out our diaries.'

DCI Deighton peered at the team over her glasses.

'Forensics confirm that the vomit and faeces found at the crime scene are from Simon Mulholland, the man who found Giles Gallen's body. So that's his story confirmed from both ends. Blood spatter on the gravestone and the ground matches Gallen's but it also gives DNA from someone else. This DNA matches the traces found on Gallen's clothes and in the traces of flesh under Gallen's fingernails. There's no match for this DNA on the national database. The blood and flesh under the nails suggests there was a struggle – so it seems Gallen resisted whoever stabbed him. Several footprints were found in the cemetery's soil. Leaf cover of the crime scene and the dry weather meant forensics were able to get good prints. Some have been matched to the trainers Gallen was wearing. We'll have to get whatever Mulholland was wearing to forensics as soon as possible. Any questions?'

Garibaldi saw DS Gardner's arm twitching. Up it went. 'If Gallen had been drinking to excess, how much resistance could he put up?'

'You'd be surprised how much you can do when you're drunk.' Deighton allowed space for the sniggers that followed. 'And the evidence clearly suggests a struggle.'

'What about the headstones near the body?' said Gardner, clearly on a roll. 'Any prints on them?'

Deighton scanned the report. 'No fingerprints apparently. The stones are too old and porous.'

'And what about the rubbish?' said Garibaldi. 'Seemed to be quite a bit on the ground. Anything there?'

Deighton flicked over the pages. 'Crisp packets, cigarette packets, a few cigarette butts and a tennis ball from the Rocks Lane courts. Clearly an ambitious first serve.' A few laughs. 'But nothing significant. It would seem, though, there's a good chance we've got the killer's DNA.' She looked up at the room. 'Right. Where are we on the Forum drinks party?'

'We've tracked down all of the guests, 'said DC McLean. 'Not all of them knew Gallen which is obviously quite likely given the nature of the job and that they don't work in the same place, but those who did know him confirmed his presence—'

'We know he was present, Archie. That's not in dispute.'

Deighton was in a strange mood. First her invitation and revelation. And now this spikiness.

'OK,' stumbled DC McLean. 'A few said a brief hello how are you to him but none of them spoke to him at length. Many said that he seemed to be speaking to the Forum owners quite a bit. Felicia and Roddy Ireland.'

DC Hodson spoke up. 'We've run a check on the tutors who were there, but nothing on the PNC. One had a speeding caution from some time ago, but that was it.'

'What about the ones he was in the pub with?' asked Deighton.

'Emily Francis and Simon Prest,' said Gardner. 'In the Coach and Horses before the party and the Red Lion after. Said Gallen left by himself at about ten thirty. They left after him.'

'Where did they go?'

'Francis says she got an Uber to Putney and Prest says he walked home.'

'Have we checked?'

'Francis's Uber's confirmed,' said Gardner. 'And we can see Prest leaving on the pub's CCTV and a camera in Church Street shows him walking to his parents' house in Nassau Road.'

'OK,' said Deighton. 'And where are we on these?'

She stood aside and pointed at the names on the board behind her.

BRIONY AINSWORTH
FREDDIE BARKER
CHLOE MARSH
JADE MURRAY
PAOLO RIVETTI

'These are the kids Gallen was tutoring.'

'OK,' said Garibaldi. 'Gallen saw all of them apart from Briony on the Saturday afternoon. We've seen all of them apart from Paolo and we've spoken to the parents. Nothing leaps out.'

'Have we run a check on the parents?'

'Not yet.'

'We need to do that,' said Deighton, looking to DCs Hodson and McLean. 'ASAP.'

'There's something else,' said Garibaldi.

He got up from his seat, picked up a marker pen from the desk and walked to the board. He gave Deighton a smile as she made way for him.

'We can add to this list.' He wrote on the board, then stood back, pointing at his words:

HILLSIDE ACADEMY

'Apparently Gallen was working for free—' he glanced at Gardner. 'Pro bono, that is, at Hillside Academy, a school in Shepherds Bush. Helping Sixth Form kids with their university applications.'

He stepped back from the board, imagining Rachel doing the same in front of her Hillside classes.

'We don't know who he saw but I'm going up there today.' Garibaldi pointed at the list. 'In terms of all these kids, nothing leaps out about any of them. Gallen was seeing most of them once a week but he's recently spent much more time than that with these guys.' He pointed at Paolo Rivetti's name. 'The Rivettis. Wealthy Italian family. Massive mansion on Lonsdale Road. Gallen went away with them to tutor Paolo in the Easter and summer holidays at their villa in Tuscany and around the Med . . .' He paused. '—iterranean. There was another tutor there with him. Sam Bannister. It turns out she's stopped tutoring for the Rivettis. In fact, she's stopped tutoring altogether. She hadn't been in touch with Gallen since they got back from Italy but he did send her a text on Saturday afternoon after he'd seen the Rivettis saying they'd made him an offer. We don't yet know what that offer was, but we're seeing the Rivettis again later. One other thing about Sam Bannister. She's got a famous dad. Harry Bannister.' A few groans from the room. 'Might be of no significance but we need to be aware.'

'Right,' said Deighton. 'Any questions?'

'Yes' said Gardner, 'this tutor thing. We're spending a lot of time looking at Gallen's tutoring, but how do we know his murder's connected to it?'

'We don't,' said Deighton. She stretched her arm towards the board. 'He'd been tutoring that afternoon and spent the evening with other tutors and at the agency drinks. His murder could have nothing at all to do with any of this, but we need to look at it. We need to check everything.'

'What I mean,' said Gardner, 'is so what if he was seeing these kids? I mean, if a teacher got murdered we wouldn't interview all the kids they taught, would we? Or if it was a doctor would we look at all the patients they saw the day they were killed? Shouldn't we be looking elsewhere?'

'We are,' said Deighton, unable to hide her irritation. 'And we will.'

'I hear what you're saying,' said Garibaldi, turning to Gardner, wanting to support her, 'but the thing is that being a tutor's different from being a teacher. When you see kids it's one to one. It's not a whole class. And it's different from being a doctor. You see the kids for longer. And the biggest difference is you see the kids in their homes. Or if you're lucky, their villa or yacht. The thing is we have to start somewhere and until we know more about what was going on in Gallen's life we have to start with what we've got.'

'Exactly,' said Deighton, giving a quick glance at Gardner.

'So what if he was at the agency drinks party?' said Garibaldi. 'So what if he was in the pub before and after it? It may all be nothing. But we need to know for sure it's nothing. The same with tutoring. It may have nothing to do with it. It could be a sex assignation. It could be a mugging that got out of hand. It could be the random act of a psycho. It could even—' Garibaldi smiled as he recalled Emily Francis's words, '—be a case of mistaken identity. We don't know.'

'Where are we on Gallen's phone records?' said Deighton.

'Right,' said DC Hodson. 'No phone was found on the victim and the search for it continues. Cell site analysis shows it was last used in Barnes, somewhere near the Red

Lion, which is much as we'd expect. We have a call detail record from the service provider. A lot of numbers and we're trawling through them. Nothing significant yet.'

'What about his card transactions, bank details?'

'No strange spending pattern,' said DC McLean, 'but a few big amounts paid into his account recently from the Rivettis, which may well be for his work in the summer.'

'OK,' said Deighton. 'A search of Gallen's room revealed very little. Bundles of cash in his drawer but not a huge amount. Digital forensics have his laptop. Search history pretty much what you'd expect. Nothing illegal. A few symptoms checkers which might be of interest. Must have been a few weeks when he was worried he had an STD.'

'Can we have the dates for those?' asked Garibaldi.

'Sure,' said Deighton. 'And as far as social media goes, looks like he stopped bothering with Facebook some time ago, wasn't a big one for Twitter but used Instagram a bit. A few posts from exotic locations in the summer. It's all on file so you can have a look yourself. Right. Anything else?'

Deighton looked round the room, and hooked her glasses off her nose.

'Right,' she said. 'Let's—'

'Get on it,' said Garibaldi under his breath.

20

Emily Francis said goodbye to Flora's mother at the door and headed towards the Lower Richmond Road. It had been a difficult hour – hours with Flora always were – and she needed a drink. Still, at least Fran was free. A couple of spritzers with her in The Spencer were just what she needed before heading back to her parents' house in Putney.

Going through a past GCSE paper with Flora had, as ever, been challenging. A familiar blend of stupidity and teenage truculence, Flora found concentration difficult and took every possible opportunity to side-track Emily into red herrings. Such red herrings were usually welcomed – chatting with her student was much easier than trying to teach her – but tonight Emily was more conscious than usual of Flora's mother hovering within earshot by the open door and felt under pressure to keep on task.

At the end of the lesson Flora's mother took Emily aside. This was usually her opportunity to voice her concerns about Flora's doubtful prospects and the inadequacies of her teachers (one a direct consequence of the other) but tonight all she wanted to talk about was Giles Gallen. Having discovered that Emily had been with him on the night of his murder, she assumed Emily must be privy to information unknown to, or as yet unrevealed to, the media and pressed her for details.

There was nothing Emily could tell her. She had no idea who could have murdered Giles and was still struggling to take it in. The idea that a young graduate working as a tutor and living at home with his parents, in other words a person in exactly her position, could meet such an end, brought home to her the slenderness of life's thread, especially her own.

Emily shivered, turned up her collar against the evening chill and picked up her pace as she walked towards the pub, unable to stop herself reflecting on where she was in relation to what she liked to call her life plan. Was she kidding herself that she would ever become a journalist? Was she wasting her time flooding commissioning editors with ideas for articles, sending off speculative reviews and features, trawling her world for connections and opportunities? Loads of people out there were doing exactly the same, cherishing the same dreams and ambitions. Was she kidding herself that she had something they didn't? Was there anything about her ideas and her prose that marked them off from the rest?

It was the old insecurity, that competition-fuelled fear of failure that had been with her since her schooldays. Its shadow had accompanied her to university and had now followed her into the world. It wasn't the world she'd hoped to join – living in her parents' Putney home and working as a tutor wasn't what she had imagined on graduation. She'd always seen herself living in a flat in some youthful edgy postcode far from Putney's tepid gentility, working as a journalist and with a long-term boyfriend, and that's still how she liked to see herself, especially when her mind wandered, as it so often did, in tutoring sessions with the likes of Flora.

The boyfriend thing shouldn't be a big deal, but she knew it was. There had been boyfriends at school but nothing serious and there had been Phil at Cardiff – something that had seemed serious but had proved itself flimsy in post-uni life – but there had been nothing for the last few years apart from some ill-judged one-night stands and dating app disasters. She was always on the lookout, and maybe that was the problem. Maybe she came across as too keen, too anxious. That evening of the Forum party, for example. She hadn't meant to flirt with Giles, but she hadn't been able to stop herself, and as the evening passed her flirtation had become more and more outrageous. But it wasn't as though it was all down to her – Giles had been doing exactly the same. If anything he'd been worse.

Of course she regretted it, but given that she could see no possible connection to Giles's murder, she'd seen no need to tell the police. Giles certainly wasn't going to say anything, so why should she? They need never know.

Lost in reflection, Emily was unaware of anything around her. It was only when she shook her head to clear her thoughts that she heard the footsteps behind. At first she thought nothing of them. Plenty of people walked along the Lower Richmond Road at this time of night. But something about these steps unnerved her. Sometimes they came so close that she thought whoever was behind her (and the weight of the steps suggested it was a man) was about to overtake, but then they receded as if they had deliberately retreated.

Emily kept telling herself that it was all her imagination. Thinking about Giles had made her see, and in this case hear, danger where there wasn't any. All she needed to do was turn round to see who it was. She'd then see there was no threat and could give whoever it was a friendly smile and step back to let them pass.

But something stopped her turning. She picked up her pace again and sensed the steps behind following her pattern. Here they came again, getting closer. She tensed, and the steps receded. It was as if they were playing some game, taunting her, tempting her to turn. Maybe that was why she wouldn't – she refused to play their game.

The pub was within sight. She would be safe there.

'Emily!'

The voice came from the other side of the road. She turned towards it.

'Fran!'

Never had she been more pleased to see her friend. She stopped and waited for Fran to cross the road. As she did, she watched her follower walk past. It was, as she had thought, a man. He looked harmless enough – puffa jacket, jeans, trainers and a peaked cap. She had imagined it all.

It was good to catch up with Fran. Whenever they met they regressed to their days at Lady Margaret's, almost as if the years that had followed had never happened. And the good thing was that Fran was in a similar position to hers. No boyfriend, living with her parents, and still looking for the job she really wanted. Being with her didn't make Emily feel like some kind of failure, and she was in a much better mood when she left the pub and walked towards Putney Bridge.

It was when Emily turned into her road that she heard them again.

The steps.

The same pattern, the same approach and retreat.

This time, maybe emboldened or maybe befuddled by the couple of drinks she'd had in the Spencer, she decided to turn.

It happened in a flash. She saw the peaked cap under a hood but nothing of the face as a hand covered her mouth and an arm tightened round her neck. She was almost lifted off her feet as she was pulled into a side road. Suddenly she was up against a wall, the man's body pressing against her back. The arm pulled itself tighter and she gasped for breath.

Was this it? Was this how it happened?

The hand stifled her attempted scream, muffling her desperate grunts. She wriggled against the gripping arm and kicked back with her heels. One caught a shin.

'Listen!' came a voice. Half-snarl. Half-whisper.

The arm released its grip as the body pinned her closer to the wall.

He pulled her away from the wall, the hand pushing harder against her mouth and she heard a zip.

'Feel this?' he said.

What was happening? Had he unzipped his flies?

The arm came back into the gap between her face and the wall and she felt something sharp against her neck.

'Feel this?' he repeated, his mouth close to her ear.

Emily felt it. A sharp steel edge.

'It's a knife,' said the man. 'Remember Giles?'

Emily grunted.

'If you don't keep your mouth shut the same thing will happen to you.'

The knife pressed harder against the neck. Had it cut her?

'So keep your mouth shut. Understand?'

Another grunt.

'When I let you go, keep facing this wall and you'll be OK. If you turn you get this.'

Another press of the knife.

'Understand?'

The weight of the body lifted. Emily thought of turning but she was frozen, unable to move.

She heard him running away. By the time she turned he was out of sight.

21

'How can I help you, Inspector?'

Kevin Johnson looked every inch the 'charismatic' head Rachel had described. Sitting behind a desk, the surface of which was absolutely clear and a source of great uneasiness to Garibaldi, whose own desk was notoriously untidy, he looked more like a CEO than a headmaster. His smartly-cut suit hung comfortably on his muscular physique, his shirt was a crisp white and his tie a bright yellow. His voice, deep and resonant, full of resolution and purpose, carried authority.

'As you know,' said Garibaldi, 'a young tutor who had done some work for you here at Hillside was found murdered last Saturday. And we'd like to ask a few questions.'

'I hope you're not suggesting that his murder might be connected to Hillside Academy, Inspector.'

'Not at all. We're just trying to get a picture of what Giles Gallen was up to and we're speaking to everyone he was tutoring. He worked for a firm called Forum and I understand they came in to do some pro bono work here.'

'A grand gesture,' said Johnson. 'But, alas, probably not enough. Do you know how many black students there are at Oxford, Inspector?'

Garibaldi paused, unsure whether the question was rhetorical.

'Not enough is the answer,' said Johnson. 'More than it was four or five years ago but still not enough. Compared to the percentage of the UK population that's black the percentage of Oxford undergraduates is alarmingly small. There may be many reasons for this and I've heard most of the explanations, but as the first black head of Hillside Academy—' Kevin Johnson paused, as if giving time for the significance of what he had said to sink in. '—As the first black head, I am determined to do something about it. And that's why I jumped at Forum's offer of pro bono tutoring. Not just for the black kids here, you understand, but for all of them. They need to have their expectations about what's possible raised. Their horizons need to be broadened.'

The lines sounded practised. Garibaldi sensed that Johnson had delivered them many times before.

'So I spoke to my Head of Sixth Form . . .'

Garibaldi imagined Rachel and Johnson together. Maybe they were in this very office. Maybe Rachel was sitting in the same chair.

'And we decided to get Forum in to speak to some of our brightest Year 12s last year, to talk about the process, to demystify it and to give them advice. And if any of our Hillside students were thinking of Oxbridge then Forum would come back this term to give them some more help. And that's what they did. Giles Gallen as I understand it was one of the three Forum tutors who came in. Our Head of Sixth Form will be able to give you more details. Do you have any questions, Inspector?'

'How long have you been head here, Mr Johnson?'

'My third year.' Kevin Johnson made it sound like a stage

on a well-mapped journey. His was the voice of a man going places, a man with a five-year plan.

'How have they been, those three years?'

'Not without their challenges, but then what's life without a challenge? That's what I've been trying to do here, Inspector. Get everyone to recognise challenges, and to rise to meet them. And if a firm comes offering tuition to our brightest pupils I have no choice but to take it, to help them raise their sights and rise to the challenge. Not that I'm only concerned with the brightest. Of course I'm not, but I'm also not worried about fostering excellence, about nurturing achievement. And when we get our first pupil accepted by Oxford or Cambridge that will be a great moment—'

Garibaldi remembered Rachel's reference to the already drafted Press Release.

'—other kids will look at him or her and think, it could be me. Just like I hope they might sometimes look at their headteacher and think the same.'

Garibaldi nodded. It was exhausting listening to him. Kevin Johnson may have had the good sense to promote Rachel but he couldn't have been easy to work with. Charisma was bad enough, but combined with a colossal ego it was lethal.

'I like to think I've made some progress,' said Johnson, 'but it's not for me to say.'

It may not have been for him to say but Garibaldi sensed he was not in the habit of stopping himself.

'We're a genuinely mixed school, Inspector. A high proportion of free school meals. A high proportion of ESL. And ethnically very mixed. And, as Hillside's first black head that last point is very important. When I came here discipline was poor. That's why I came in tough. Zero tolerance. Strict uniform policy. It was messy at first. No-one likes suspensions, exclusions and expulsions, least of all me. But I did what had to be done and after a while I realised it's what everyone wanted. Everyone needed to know where they stood. Not just the kids but the parents too. They like to be clear about things. And gradually things are turning. A school is a bit like a big ship, Inspector. It takes a while to turn and sometimes you don't realise it's turning at all until you look up and see you're facing in a different direction.'

Kevin Johnson smiled and nodded as if to say he had finished.

Garibaldi sensed he had just heard an extract from a longer, frequently delivered speech.

'But you don't want to hear about that, do you, Inspector? You want to hear about what this poor tutor had been doing with us. If you follow me,' he got up from his chair and walked to the door, 'I'll bring you to our Head of Sixth Form, Rachel Monroe. She's excellent, one of my best appointments, and I'm sure she'll tell you all you need to know. She says that the tutor had helped one of our very brightest students, Devon Furlong, and I'm sure she'll be able to get him to talk to you and answer any questions.'

'So you didn't tell him? '

Garibaldi shook his head.

'Shouldn't you have declared your involvement with me?'

'I've told Deighton,' said Garibaldi. 'That's enough.'

Rachel sat behind her desk, looking at him over her glasses in a way that reminded him of his boss. She seemed unconvinced. 'Even so. It still seems a bit, I don't know, deceptive.'

Rachel may have been right, but Garibaldi was prepared

to take the risk. When it came to playing by the book he had, over the years, chosen to ignore many of its pages. Sometimes he'd ignored whole chapters.

'Nice office,' he said looking round the room.

'No it's not. It's cramped and it's noisy.'

'Yeah, but it's yours, isn't it? You should try open plan. Probably only a matter of time before we're hot-desking.'

'So what did you make of Mr Johnson?'

'It's all about him, isn't it?' said Garibaldi. Rachel laughed. 'But he spoke very highly of you.'

'OK, and what am I supposed to do for you?'

'Find me the student he came in to help.'

Rachel peered at her computer. 'Just see where Devon is.' She pressed some keys. 'OK, he's in a Politics lesson. I'll go and get him for you.'

When Rachel left the room Garibaldi got up and walked to the window. It was quiet. Most of the kids were in class but a few were coming and going – late arrivals, perhaps, or those who needed to leave early.

Was it so long ago that he was one of them? Was it so long ago that his own schooldays were marred by tragedy? He thought of the Larkin poem (why did he always come back to the most gloomy of writers?) about long perspectives open at each instant of our lives and the way they link us to our losses. That phrase had always stuck. Not a day went by when he didn't think of his loss, when he didn't think of the long perspective, the possibility that things might have turned out differently.

'This is Devon.'

Garibaldi turned to see Rachel holding her arm out, introducing the young black student standing beside her. 'I'll leave you to it.' She closed the door behind her.

'Have a seat,' said Garibaldi, resisting the temptation

to go behind the desk and sit in Rachel's chair. 'I'm Detective Inspector Garibaldi and I want to ask you a few questions.'

Devon sat down with a nervous smile. 'This is about Mr Gallen, isn't it?'

'It is.'

'Miss Monroe told us about it.' Devon shook his head slowly. 'I can't believe it. Terrible.'

'I understand Giles Gallen came in to talk to you about university applications.'

Devon nodded. 'Yeah. He helped me a lot.'

'What's your subject, Devon?'

'I want to do English.'

'And how did Giles help you?'

'He got me to write essays over the summer and he went through them with me and then he came in to give some interview practice. And then . . .' Devon looked up at Garibaldi with pleading eyes. 'It's terrible what's happened. I mean . . . who would . . . ?'

'What was he like?'

'He was, like, really encouraging. I mean the school's really good, especially Miss Monroe – she's done so much to help but there was something about this guy who was at Cambridge only a couple of years ago telling me it wasn't just a dream and that I had a chance. It made me feel different about it. He was saying things that other people don't.'

'What do other people say?'

Devon looked to one side and winced. 'Not everyone's so encouraging. Not a place for me. Ideas above my station. You know the kind of thing.'

'I see. So not everyone approves of your ambitions?'

Devon shrugged. 'There've been a few comments, yeah, but nothing I can't handle. I'm used to it. I've always been a bit different from the crowd, I guess. When everyone else was out doing their thing I'd be at home with a book.'

Garibaldi nodded his approval. 'So Giles helped?'

'He was great. Didn't think he would be. Thought, you know, given his background and everything he'd be . . . but it was like he understood. And he was happy to answer any questions. Gave me his email and his number, said call any time.'

'And did you?'

'Did I what?'

'Call him.'

'No. I emailed a couple of times asking questions about the essays I was doing, but no I didn't call him.'

'I see. Well thanks for your help, Devon. I'll let you get back to your lesson.' Garibaldi stood up but Devon stayed where he was. Garibaldi walked to the door and looked back as he turned the handle. Devon was still in his chair.

'Is everything OK?'

Devon's face suggested it wasn't. 'Look, when I said I didn't call him that's not quite true. I did call him. I was having doubts about the whole thing so I gave him a call.'

'So why didn't you tell me?' said Garibaldi.

'Because I didn't just talk to him, I met him. Giles – Mr Gallen – he said why don't we meet up to talk things through. So we met for a coffee. And ever since I heard about the murder I don't know . . . I've felt a bit uneasy about it.'

'What are you uneasy about?'

'I feel guilty.'

'Guilty? Why?'

'It's like I shouldn't have done it.'

Garibaldi nodded as if he understood. He had no idea whether this kind of thing was allowed, whether any boundaries had been crossed.

'Did you tell the school about it?'

Devon shook his head.

'So you feel guilty because you didn't tell anyone?'

'Yeah, maybe.'

'Was it just the once?'

'No, that's the thing. We met two, three times. He said he was happy to see me any time and go through stuff. And I'd been finding things tough . . .' Devon trailed off and held his head in his hands. 'I still can't believe it's happened.'

'Take it easy, Devon,' said Garibaldi. 'Take your time. Are you ready to go back to your lessons?'

Devon lifted his head and shook himself down. 'I'm OK.' He got up from his chair and walked to the door.

Garibaldi opened it for him and reached into his pocket for a card. 'Give me a call if you think of anything.'

'Will you have to tell anyone?'

'I may have to,' said Garibaldi, 'but I'll make sure you don't get into trouble.'

'Feels like I already am,' said Devon as he walked away.

Garibaldi watched him walk down the corridor, wondering why he felt so uneasy about his encounter with the bright seventeen-year-old.

'Tell me more about Devon Furlong,' he said when Rachel returned.

'What do you want to know?'

'Obviously a bright kid who's aiming high.'

'Yes,' said Rachel, 'one of our best. Really talented.'

'English at Cambridge?'

'He's got a chance. They're desperate to broaden access and then you get all this support from places like Forum. Everyone seems to want to help kids like him. And the Head, as I'm sure you picked up, would love him to make it. So, yeah, he's got a chance.'

'How many sessions were Forum lined up for?'

'Two last term and three this term.'

'And what contact would you expect there to be between your students and the Forum tutors outside those times?'

'They email to send essays through and some email with questions or to ask for advice.'

'And would your students ever meet up with their tutors?'

'Meet up? What do you mean?'

'Outside school.'

'Outside school?' Rachel looked as though she had never considered the possibility. 'If they have, I haven't heard about it. It's not something we'd encourage. Could be a safeguarding issue. I mean, Forum are pretty good. All their tutors are DBS checked and everything but, even so, I don't know how happy we'd be about it. On the other hand, I don't know if we could stop them. Are you asking because that's what Devon's done?'

Garibaldi nodded. 'He met Giles Gallen to talk about his work. Two or three times.'

'Really?' Rachel screwed up her eyes as if to work out how much of a problem this was and its likely implications.

'As Head of Sixth Form, you probably need to know about it.'

'Right. Well, thanks for that.'

'No problem.' Garibaldi gave her a wink and opened the door. 'See you later, miss.'

22

The girl who opened the door looked very different from the one who had done the same only a few days ago. She was tense and drawn. Her colour had drained.

Emily invited Garibaldi into the living room, offered him a chair and sat down opposite. Mrs Francis put a head round the door to express shock at what had happened and concerns about the safety of her daughter. Garibaldi turned down her offer of tea and did his best to reassure her.

'Why didn't you report this last night?' he said to Emily when her mother had closed the door behind her.

Emily took a breath, and puffed out her cheeks as she exhaled. 'I was in shock. I didn't know what to do.'

'Did you suffer any injuries?'

'A couple of bruises but nothing serious. The knife—' She shuddered at the memory. 'It touched my neck but it didn't draw blood.'

'You'll have to come into the station to give a statement, but take me through what happened.'

Garibaldi listened, giving encouraging sympathetic nods as Emily took him through the assault.

'And those were his words?' he said when she had finished. '"Remember Giles." "If you don't keep your mouth shut the same thing will happen to you," and, "Keep your mouth shut"?'

Emily nodded.

'Have you any idea why he said that?'

'That's the thing. I haven't got a clue what I'm supposed to be quiet about. I don't know any . . . secrets. Keep your mouth shut? I've no idea what I'm keeping it shut for. And if this is the man who murdered Giles . . . I mean I could have been killed! I was yards from my home! I could have been killed!'

'Can you remember anything else about the man?'

'As I said. Peaked cap, hood, puffer jacket, jeans and trainers.'

'His voice?'

Emily shrugged. 'No accent or anything. I mean he had an accent, but London.'

'Roughly spoken?'

'I thought I was about to be raped. I didn't pay much attention to his voice. Am I safe? What should I do?'

'Do you have the clothes you were wearing last night?'

'They're upstairs.'

'You haven't washed them?'

'No.'

'We'll need those clothes. There may be DNA traces.'

'OK. But I don't get it. What did he mean "keep your mouth shut"? I don't know anything!'

'Nothing that Giles told you about that might be important to someone?'

Emily shook her head. 'The thing is it makes it sound as though Giles was murdered because he *didn't* keep his mouth shut, as if he was killed because he said something, revealed some secret. But how could that be?'

'You can't think of anything from that evening, perhaps,

in the pub before or after the party that Giles said or hinted at? Anything he did?'

Emily shook her head again, but this time it was bowed as well, as if she didn't want her face to be seen. It was a tiny gesture, but Garibaldi noticed it. Was it shame? Was it guilt? Or was it simply shock?

'Who have you told about this, Emily?'

'My parents obviously and I told Fran. And I messaged Simon because he was with us on that night and he knew Giles. He couldn't believe it.'

'Right,' said Garibaldi. 'Let's get you to the station then. If you could get those clothes.'

He took his phone out and called DS Gardner.

Garibaldi had expected to find Gardner waiting for him in the car outside the Mulholland's house, but as was so often the case when it came to travelling in London, and even more so since the closure of Hammersmith Bridge, it had been quicker by bike. His inability to drive, together with his refusal to do anything to remedy the problem, may have made things difficult for him at times and may have been a source of bafflement to his colleagues, but Garibaldi enjoyed the way it marked him out as different, pointing out whenever the issue was raised or whenever anyone cracked the Milly 'Uber' Gardner gag that he couldn't see what the fuss was about.

Five minutes later, Gardner pulled up.

Simon Mulholland came to the door, glass of wine in hand. Garibaldi showed his warrant card, introduced himself and followed him through into the living room, sitting down in the armchair he was offered.

'Hope you don't mind our coming to ask a few questions.'

'I can't think I've got anything to add to what I've already said in the statement.'

'I'm just curious to know more about the moment you found the body.'

'Well, as you know, it's all rather embarrassing. I was out for my usual Sunday morning run and I was, er, taken short and needed to relieve myself. And then I saw it.'

'So having relieved yourself, you saw the body and then you threw up. Is that right?'

Mulholland gave a nervous laugh. 'Hugely embarrassing, but we'd been out the night before and they'd served Indian food, and I'd also had a fair bit to drink . . .'

'So what did you do after you saw the body? Apart from throw up, that is?'

'I rang the police.'

'You didn't touch the body at all?'

'Touch it? I wanted to get away from it. I was totally freaked out.'

'Funny place, Barnes Cemetery, isn't it?' said Garibaldi.

Mulholland gave a dismissive shrug. 'To be honest that was the first time I'd been in there. I've run past it so many times and I've glanced in occasionally and seen a couple of headstones, but I didn't know much about it.'

'Well, you're not alone there.'

'The whole thing,' said Mulholland. 'It's dreadful. Who would do such a thing and in Barnes. I mean—'

'We're not entirely cut off from the real world, you know. It might seem that way sometimes.'

'I know. Such a young man. Public school. Cambridge.'

He spoke the words as if they provided some kind of immunity.

'And,' he added, 'working as a tutor. I should think he was raking it in round here. Everyone does it. Funnily enough we were talking about that very thing the night before. We got onto schools, which always happens at these things, and it didn't take long to get from there to tutors. I guess we're going to have to look into it ourselves pretty soon.'

Garibaldi raised his eyebrows.

'Two daughters,' said Mulholland. 'Three and five. If you want to get them into anywhere decent you have to start pretty early.' He looked at his watch. 'Look, Inspector, I really don't have much to add to what I've already said. And—'

'We won't keep you long, Mr Mulholland. Can I confirm that you didn't know Giles Gallen at all, that you have never had contact with him?'

'None at all.'

'So none of your friends, no-one at this dinner party, knew Giles. None of them had used his services?'

'Not as far as I know. You're surely not suggesting—?'

'I'm not suggesting anything. I'm just curious. And in the dinner party discussion did anyone mention Forum Tutors?'

'Forum?'

'The agency Giles worked for. They're based here in Barnes.'

'No. I don't remember.'

The door opened and a woman walked in, giving a double take when she saw Garibaldi and Gardner. Fresh complexion, hair tied back, navy cardigan, white shirt with collar turned up, jeans and expensive trainers. She had hundreds of lookalikes in Southwest London.

'Darling,' said Mulholland, extending his arm by way of introduction. 'The police have come to ask a few more questions.' He turned to Garibaldi and Gardner. 'My wife, Fiona.'

Fiona Mulholland gave a polite smile and nod. She turned to her husband. 'I thought you'd given a statement.'

'He had,' said Garibaldi, 'we're just following up on a few things.'

'Darling,' said Mulholland, 'have you heard of Forum Tutor agency?'

'Forum? Yes, I have. Some of the girls were talking about them. Pretty good apparently. Is that the one this poor chap worked for?'

'It is,' said Garibaldi. 'Did any of the g—' he stopped himself just in time. 'Did any of your friends know Giles Gallen at all?'

'Know him? No. I mean . . . you don't think we or any of our friends could possibly be involved in any way?'

'We don't think anything at the moment, Mrs Mulholland. We're merely making inquiries. And as your husband was the one to find the body . . .'

'Look, Inspector,' said Mulholland. He had sat up in his chair as if bracing himself for a fight. 'I may have been the one who found the body but I can't possibly be under any suspicion, can I?'

'Of course you're not, darling,' said Mrs Mulholland as if she had become a police spokesperson. 'How could you be?'

'OK,' said Garibaldi. 'Well thanks for your time. There is one other thing, though, before we go.' He shot Gardner a glance.

'Mr Mulholland,' said Gardner, picking up the cue. 'Can you remember what shoes you were wearing on Sunday morning? I'm assuming they were some kind of trainers.'

'I was on a run. Of course they were trainers.'

'And can you remember which ones?'

'Yes. I only have two pairs. One for running and one for tennis.'

'Several sets of footprints were found on the soil where Giles Gallen was found and we need—'

'Sorry?' said Mulholland. 'Am I some kind of suspect here? This is ridiculous! I found the body and I phoned the police. What—'

Garibaldi leaned forward, his hand raised. 'It's for the purposes of elimination, Mr Mulholland. We know you were there, so we need to know which are your prints. If you could go and get the trainers you were wearing then DS Gardner can put them in her evidence bags and we can get them to the forensics lab.'

Mulholland looked to his wife and then got up to get his trainers.

'I still can't believe it,' said Fiona. 'Such a shock. And for it to happen there.'

'Are you familiar with Barnes Cemetery?' said Garibaldi.

'Only from dog walks,' said Fiona. 'I often take Bertie down to Barnes Common and he has a habit of heading off into the cemetery when we go past it. That's how I discovered it. And when some of us were walking our dogs together one day we followed them in and looked around. Very Gothic.'

Garibaldi nodded his approval. A woman who used the same description of the place as Martin Stevenson. A woman who, despite her haughtiness and SW13 air of entitlement, clearly had brains.

Simon Mulholland came in carrying a pair of trainers. 'They're not very clean, I'm afraid.'

'That's no problem,' said Gardner reaching for them and putting each of them in a separate evidence bag.

'How long will you need them for?'

Mulholland sounded concerned, as if being deprived of his running shoes for a few days, even in the service of a murder investigation, constituted a huge personal inconvenience.

'We'll get them back to you as soon as we can,' said Gardner, following Garibaldi to the front door.

'Just a matter of elimination, you understand,' said Garibaldi.

'Of course,' said Mulholland. 'Happy to help.'

Outside the house Garibaldi unlocked his bike.

'Tell me,' he said, looking up at Gardner. 'Does everyone in Barnes have a dog?'

'It seems so, boss.'

'And does everyone have different trainers for tennis and running?'

'All part of the kit.'

'Right. Like having a private tutor.' Garibaldi patted his bike. 'OK if I leave this at home and come up in the car with you?'

'Sure. I'll even give you a lift back.'

Garibaldi hopped on his bike, rode the short distance to Rutland Court, locked his bike in the covered rack outside the entrance to his flat and went back to join Gardner.

A few minutes later, they were at the top end of Lonsdale Road outside the Rivettis' mansion.

23

Luigi Rivetti regarded the English education system as the best in the world, and it was the one he wanted his children to pass through. A prestigious public school followed by Oxford or Cambridge. The perfect path. An educational key that would open all kinds of doors.

This was one of the main reasons why, when an opportunity arose at the London branch of his Italian investment bank ten years ago, he was quick to take it. They kept their home in Italy, where his wife and children returned most holidays, but during school terms the Rivetti family lived in Barnes.

Luigi Rivetti loved England and he loved London. But most of all he loved Barnes – the tree-lined roads, the independent shops, the village feel, the very Englishness of the place. Whenever he sent friends back in Italy photos of the duck pond and the Sun Inn they thought he'd sent them pictures of somewhere else. They couldn't believe it was London.

Luigi knew that getting his children through the top levels of the English system would not be easy, but he had bought the best advice and hired the best help and it had all, until very recently, looked so promising. But now the outlook was far from bright. They currently had no tutors for Paolo and Anna and he was facing questions from two detectives.

He leaned back in the antique Chesterfield chair and steepled his hands in front of him. 'How can we help, Inspector?'

'We were here yesterday to talk to your wife.' Garibaldi turned his head to Mrs Rivetti. 'And we'd like to ask you a few questions as well.'

'With or without my wife?' said Luigi.

'No need for your wife to leave,' said Garibaldi. 'I'm sure you have no secrets.'

Luigi laughed loudly. 'Of course, Inspector. No secrets! Why would there be secrets?'

As he said the words into his mind rushed all the secrets he'd rather these detectives didn't know.

Like how he had acquired most of his massive wealth.

Like what had happened in the summer.

'Tell me, Mr Rivetti, when did you last see Giles?'

'I haven't seen him since we've been back in London. But before we go any further, Inspector, can you tell me why you need to talk to us?'

'We're talking to everyone Giles was recently involved with. And as he'd been working for you in the summer and had seen Paolo on Saturday afternoon that includes you.'

'I see,' said Luigi, 'but I can't think I have anything to add to what Maria's already told you. We valued Giles very highly. He was the perfect tutor. Well mannered, and with the kind of breeding you only get from a top-class English education. I can't imagine anyone wanting to kill him.'

'So neither of you noticed anything odd about his behaviour, nothing about him that made you think he could be in some kind of trouble?'

Luigi turned to his wife. They both shook their heads.

'As I said, Inspector,' said Luigi. 'I haven't seen him since the end of the summer but from what I saw there seemed nothing unusual.'

'And how much of him did you see?' said the woman.

Luigi turned to her. 'What do you mean?'

'I mean, how much was he actually with you? There must have been times when he was free.'

'Of course,' said Luigi, 'It's not a twenty-four/seven kind of thing. He and the other tutor had time to themselves. We're not slave drivers.'

'This other tutor,' said Garibaldi. 'Sam Bannister.'

'Ah yes,' said Luigi. 'Sam. She was very good too.'

'I understand that Sam stopped working for you recently. Handed in her notice.'

'Yes,' said Luigi. 'We were sorry to lose her. But these things happen.'

'Did Sam say why she was stopping?'

'She said she'd found a job in publishing.'

'I see.' Garibaldi looked at his notebook. 'Apparently Giles sent Sam a text on Saturday afternoon saying that you had made him an offer.'

Garibaldi paused and looked from Luigi to his wife and then back to Luigi, his eyebrows raised.

Luigi turned to Maria, as if unsure who should answer. Maria kept her eyes on Garibaldi. Neither spoke.

'Had you made him an offer?' said Garibaldi.

Maria turned to her husband. Luigi nodded his approval.

'Yes,' said Maria. 'We had made him an offer. We had just found out that Sam was stopping and we were worried about getting a replacement, a good replacement that is. Tutors are easy enough to come by but good tutors, ones you know are going to deliver and ones you can be confident your child will like – those are a different matter entirely. And so we asked Giles if he would be prepared to take over Sam's work and tutor both our children.'

'Your son and your daughter?'

'That's right.'

'So your daughter liked Giles as well?'

'They both liked him.'

'That would have been a lot of work for Giles, wouldn't it?'

'We would have paid him well,' said Luigi.

'I'm sure you would have.'

'We'd have made it work,' said Maria.

The inspector looked at both of them. 'What do you mean?'

'What Maria means,' said Luigi, 'is that we would have worked out a schedule, made it as easy as possible for Giles.'

'And what did Giles say to your offer?' asked the woman.

'He said he'd think about it.'

'I see,' said the inspector. 'And, Mr Rivetti, what did you think of this idea?'

'What did I think? I thought it was a good idea. In all these matters I yield to Maria's better judgement. I'm a busy man, Inspector. Don't get me wrong. I take a great interest in my children's education. To be honest that's why we are here in London, because your education system is the best in the world. But in most of the day-to-day matters it's Maria who's in charge so when it comes to our offer – the offer Maria made, I trusted her.'

Garibaldi got up from his chair. 'Is Paolo in or does he have another tennis lesson?'

'Not tennis,' said Maria, 'but he's not here again. He's at a friend's.'

'I see,' said Garibaldi, 'Maybe when his diary's less crowded . . .'

'Of course,' said Luigi. 'I'm sure there's nothing he can tell you but—' he turned to his wife, '—will he be in tomorrow after school, Maria?'

'Yes, he will. Nothing tomorrow.'

'Well, thank you for your time, both of you,' said Garibaldi. 'If anything else occurs to you, do get in touch.'

Luigi waited until he heard the car drive off before turning to his wife. She smiled at him nervously and he sensed she was, like him, thinking of all that had been left unsaid.

'Where are we on new tutors?' he said, breaking the uneasy silence.

'I've been on to Forum again.'

'Good. We need to sort something out quickly.'

'And Paolo knows not to say anything?'

'You've told him and I've told him. I've made it absolutely clear to him that he should say nothing about it.'

'You think we can trust him?'

'Oh, yes,' said Maria. 'I made it very clear. He knows there would be consequences.'

'Good.' Luigi smiled at his wife. He knew that if Maria had threatened his son with consequences then he wouldn't step out of line.

Finding replacement tutors was a big concern but it was nothing compared to what might emerge in the police investigation into Giles Gallen's murder.

24

'Last night Emily Francis was assaulted at knifepoint.' Garibaldi stood by the board, addressing the team. 'She wasn't injured but she was told to keep her mouth shut. She was also told to remember what happened to Giles Gallen. Emily works for Forum Tutors, the firm that Gallen worked for and she was with him on Saturday night. She's given us a statement and the clothes she was wearing last night are at the lab. This is a significant development and one which might affect where we look for Gallen's killer.'

'What's she being told to be quiet about?' said Gardner, quickly out of her blocks.

'We don't know. More to the point Emily doesn't know either, or at least she says she doesn't. The obvious link between her and Gallen is Forum. To have one of your tutors murdered may be regarded as misfortune but to have one murdered and another one attacked with a knife looks like carelessness.'

He paused and looked at the room, wishing he'd been able to stop himself. The room looked back at him blankly. 'Oscar Wilde,' he said.

Some looked at him expectantly, as if he had just named a likely suspect.

'So we need to talk to Forum. I should think they're already shitting themselves at the likely press coverage.'

DCI Deighton stepped forward. 'Thank you.' She pointed at the board where Emily's name had been placed next to Gallen's and a picture attached. 'Emily Francis says she has no idea why she was told to keep her mouth shut, can't think of any big secret she and Giles shared that they might need to be quiet about. As always, we need to keep an open mind, but this looks very significant.' Deighton looked round the room. 'Right, an update on Gallen's tutoring.'

She stepped away from the board and nodded to Garibaldi. He picked up a marker pen and added the name *Devon Furlong* to the list of students Giles Gallen had been tutoring.

'Devon Furlong, seventeen, a high-achieving student at Hillside Academy and one of the pupils on the receiving end of Forum's pro bono work. Gallen was helping him with his Cambridge application. Devon liked him a lot and asked him for advice. Emails at first, but then they started to meet. They met several times. We're not sure if that was breaking any rules but it's not what you would expect. Safeguarding. Child protection. It's a bit of a grey area and we need to find out what the Forum line on that kind of thing is.'

Garibaldi paused. He didn't want what he was about to say to come out wrong.

'Devon Furlong is a different kind of student from the ones Gallen was seeing in Barnes and Chiswick and Sheen. He's a black kid living on the White City Estate.'

He looked round the room, hearing the unvoiced assumptions. Estate. Black kid. Gangs. Knives.

'Devon is simply another kid Gallen was tutoring. As

with all the other kids there is nothing at all to suggest he's connected in any way to the murder, but, like the others, he needs checking out.'

Garibaldi squirmed, kicking himself for not having said it more directly. After all that had happened – in the world and in the Met – he shouldn't have needed to say it at all.

'Right,' said Deighton, breaking an awkward silence, 'so where are we on the others? The Rivettis?'

'Sam Bannister resigned from tutoring the Rivetti kid last week,' said Gardner, 'and stopped working for Forum. Got a job in digital publishing. And it appears that the offer made to Giles Gallen by the Rivettis was to take over Sam's tutoring of their daughter, Anna.'

'OK,' said Deighton, 'and the other families?'

'Only thing on the PNC about any of them,' said DC McLean, 'is to do with Clive Marsh. Gallen was tutoring one of his daughters for her eleven plus and the other for A Level. It appears that Marsh was arrested for possession of cocaine in 2016. Works in advertising so no surprise there. Nothing on the others, though one of the dads looks a bit dodgy. Vince Ainsworth owns a string of clubs. When I say clubs we're not talking Pall Mall. Looks a bit shady but there's nothing on him. And it seems that one of the other parents, the mother of Jade Murray, works for him.'

'Yeah,' said Garibaldi. 'The Ainsworths and the Murrays are old friends. The Ainsworth mum and Ginny Murray were at school together. Hilary Ainsworth recommended Gallen to her.'

'OK,' said Deighton. 'CCTV on the Emily Francis attack?'

'There's a camera on the Lower Richmond Road,' said Gardner, 'at the junction with the road her home's in. And we've got him.'

Gardner fiddled with her computer and an image appeared on a screen at the front of the room.

It showed Emily Francis turning for home and, seconds after, a man following. Puffa jacket, jeans, trainers, peaked cap, hoodie. His face was well hidden.

'I can't see anything beyond what we've been given in her description,' said Gardner.

Garibaldi screwed up his eyes and looked closer. He couldn't see anything either.

'But I've got something else,' said Gardner. 'Footage from the Red Lion. She pressed a few keys. 'It's at 22.00, so about thirty minutes before Gallen left.'

The camera showed the outside of the Red Lion. A few people were coming in and out of the side door, all turning to the right when they exited and coming back from the same direction. 'It's now,' said Gardner. The door opened and a man came out. Gardner paused. 'That's Gallen.' She pressed a key and Gallen moved not to the right where the Ladies and Gents were located, but to the left into the garden.

The CCTV camera stayed focused on the door. One minute later it opened. Gardner paused and Emily Francis stood freeze-framed in the doorway. Gardner pressed play again and Emily Francis also took a left into the garden.

'There's one camera covering the whole garden. It doesn't show Gallen and Francis, but we do have them coming back in.'

Another key press and the screen showed Gallen walking towards the door by himself.

'Look at this,' said Gardner. She froze the picture and moved into close-up. Gallen was tucking in his shirt and smoothing his hair. His hand reached for his groin, scratched it and checked his flies.

A minute later Emily Francis came to the door from the same direction as Gallen. She also ran fingers through her hair.

Gardner froze the picture again and moved in on the untucked shirt hanging below the back of Emily Francis's jacket.

'That shirt,' said Gardner, 'was tucked in when she went into the garden.'

Garibaldi looked at his sergeant, impressed.

'So the question is,' said Gardner, 'what Gallen and Francis were doing in the pub garden shortly before they left and shortly before Gallen was murdered. They may have just been talking. If so, about what, and why the need to do it in the privacy of a dark garden? And if the state of their dress and their gestures suggest they were up to something else in the garden, is it significant?'

'This could, of course,' said Deighton, 'account for the semen on Gallen's body. Something that happened *before* he got to the Old Cemetery. Thank you, Milly. Great work.'

'Yeah,' said Garibaldi. 'Great stuff.'

'We need to have a word with Emily Francis,' said Deighton.

25

Evening Standard

TUTOR IN KNIFE ATTACK

Last week tutor Giles Gallen was murdered in Barnes. Last night a friend of his was threatened at knife point in Putney. **Emily Francis** *gives an account of her experience.*

Whenever I see statistics about knife crime in London or about sexual assaults on women I always think they are about other people. These things never happen to me. They never even happen to people I know.

But in the last few days that's all changed. First, last Saturday, a friend of mine, who I was with that evening, was stabbed to death. Then, last night, I myself was attacked at knifepoint.

A friend of mine murdered. A horrific attack on me by a knife-wielding assailant. But these things didn't happen in an inner-city estate, a crime-ridden area of social deprivation. No. We're talking Barnes and Putney.

When I heard Giles had been murdered I reacted with sadness and shock, but also with the realisation that it could easily have been me.

And last night it very nearly was.

London is more dangerous now than it ever was, and young middle-class graduates in areas of affluence aren't immune.

I'm frightened for myself. And I'm frightened for my generation. I'm frightened for us all.

Turn to page 4 for Emily Francis's lowdown on working as a private tutor.

TURNING TO TUTORING

I got to know Giles Gallen through our work as private tutors. There are thousands like us – twentysomething graduates who have come back to live in their parental home while they contemplate their future. They turn to tutoring for many reasons. For some it may well be what they want to do and they're happy to do it. Some are whisked off to exotic locations to tutor the children of the super-rich (my friend Giles was one of these) and are very highly paid. Some (and that includes me) work in less glamorous places but can see the advantages. The hours are flexible, you can take on as much or as little as you choose and sometimes you can actually enjoy it.

And for those, like me, who want to work in a

> highly competitive field (journalism in my case) it is the perfect way to explore avenues and possibilities while earning money and, who knows, maybe doing some good somewhere along the line . . .

Emily put down the paper. She'd read the piece many times and knew its every word, but she couldn't stop herself looking at it, especially her name. There it was. In print in the *Standard*. Not only in print but in bold.

How smart had she been to turn the horrific experience to her advantage? The speed of the editor's response had told her she was on to something good, and here it was in front of her – a feature on private tutoring on the back of the news story.

She was pleased with the way she'd edited the original. What had been intended as an anonymous exposé of the world of private tutoring, flagging up its questionable ethics and dubious practices had become something much more general with enough unattributed stories, all given a suitable Metropolitan spin, to hook the *Standard* readership. She was already thinking about how she could develop the piece for the nationals.

There was nothing in the piece that might get in the way of the police investigation – nothing about her attacker's threats, nothing about 'remember Giles' or 'keep your mouth shut'. And she'd taken anything out that might connect the events to Forum.

But that didn't mean Felicia and Roddy wouldn't go ballistic. The chances were they'd probably fire her but she thought it was a risk worth taking. Getting her feature in the *Standard* might be just the kick in the arse her so far unsuccessful attempts to become a journalist needed. It might even mean that her tutoring years would soon be behind her. How clever to say she wanted to be a journalist – the whole thing was like a calling card, a CV in a prestigious newspaper. And if Forum did fire her she could really let rip with her original piece, making it even more scandalous and damning, dishing the dirt secure in the knowledge that she would never have to tutor again.

Her phone rang. She looked at the screen. As expected.

'Emily, are you all right?' said Felicia.

'I'm fine. I—'

'I've just read the paper. What a terrible thing. How awful for you!'

'I'm OK. It was a shock but I think I've recovered.'

'You may think you have but be careful. That must have been a huge trauma. But, Emily, why on earth didn't you tell us?'

'I was going to, but—'

'To read about it in the paper like that. It was distressing.'

'I'm sorry. Haven't had time. I . . .'

'Do the police know?'

'Yes. I've given a statement.'

'Emily, I'm so glad you're OK and that you haven't been . . . that nothing worse has happened to you.'

'You mean glad that I haven't been murdered? Yeah, so am I.'

'But Roddy and I are very concerned.' Felicia paused and cleared her throat. 'That article . . . I really don't know what to say.'

'The *Standard* are very pleased with it.'

'I'm sure they are, I just hope it doesn't cause problems.'

'What kind of problems? I didn't mention Forum, I just said Giles and I worked for the same agency. And I didn't say anything defamatory. I didn't say anything that anyone who knows anything about tutoring wouldn't know already.'

'We're still worried, Emily. We're worried about you, of course, but this article . . . there may be implications.'

Emily imagined a list of possible implications. Being fired sat at the top of it.

It was time to go on the offensive. 'Look, Felicia. There's something I haven't told you but I think maybe you should know. I've told the police and it's in my statement. The thing is my attacker said some things to me. He made some threats.' She sensed Felicia holding her breath. 'He told me to remember what happened to Giles and said that if I didn't keep my mouth shut the same thing would happen to me.'

'What?' Felicia couldn't hide her surprise. 'So was whoever attacked you the man who murdered Giles?'

'Who knows? He could be.'

'And does that mean that Giles was killed because of something he knew, or because he said something?'

'It's a reasonable assumption, isn't it?'

'So you know something as well, then?'

'That's the thing. I have no idea what they were talking about. There's no big secret that Giles shared with me or anything. We didn't know each other that well.'

'Hang on.' Felicia paused, as if sorting out her train of thought. 'If you don't know anything why would they threaten you?'

'Exactly. I have no idea. But the reason I mention it is that even though we might not share a secret so big that Giles could be killed to make sure it stays a secret we do share something else . . .'

'What's that?'

'We both work for you. We both work for Forum.'

Emily paused, giving Felicia time to take it in.

'I'm well aware of that, but how is it relevant?'

'I have no idea.'

'I think we need to talk, Emily. Can you come in? Roddy and I would very much like to see you.'

Emily sensed from the tone of Felicia's voice that they were now unlikely to fire her.

'What the hell is this?'

A hand thwacked the paper onto Garibaldi's table. He turned to see DCI Deighton standing over him.

'Have you read it?'

Garibaldi nodded. Not only had he read it, he had tried to find out whether Emily Francis had in any way impeded the progress of the investigation. Even if she hadn't he was half-minded to tell her that she had and threaten to charge her.

'So much for keeping it out of the papers,' said Deighton. 'It won't take them long to be running "tutor-killer-on-the-loose" stories. Why the hell has she done it?'

Garibaldi picked up the paper, open at the page of the tutoring feature and pointed at a sentence – *And for those, like me, who want to work in a highly competitive field (journalism in my case).*

'Like so many things in life,' he said, 'you need to look at what's inside the brackets to see what's really important.' Deighton put on her glasses as he held the paper up. 'She wants to be a journalist.'

'She might need to become one quick. I can't imagine Forum are going to be pleased.'

'It doesn't mention them, does it?'

'No, but they'll hate it.'

'Boss.' DS Gardner was walking towards them brandishing a piece of paper. 'I've got something.'

'What is it?' said Garibaldi.

'I've run a check on Devon Furlong. Not him so much as his family. Devon lives with his mum, and one younger brother on the White City Estate. His other brother also lives on the estate but in a flat of his own. And this brother . . .' Gardner consulted the sheet in her hand. 'Terrell Furlong, twenty-six, has a record. Arrested on suspicion of theft, possession of weapon, and a range of gang-related offences. Nothing big has stuck and it seems remarkable that he hasn't done time. What I'm thinking though is . . .'

Garibaldi held up his hand to stop her. 'Hang on a minute.'

'I'm not saying—'

'No, but it's tempting, isn't it? Gangs. Knives. It's too easy a . . . narrative.'

He cast a sideways glance at Deighton before delivering the last word. She nodded her approval.

'Knife crime doesn't exist in Barnes,' said Garibaldi, 'but it does up there, so let's say that's where it came from.'

'I'm not saying that, boss. I'm just—'

'What percentage of stabbings are perpetrated by black kids?'

'I know, but—'

'Haven't got the exact number but it's very high, isn't it?'

'That's not what I'm saying.'

'What are you saying?'

Gardner sighed with frustration. 'I'm saying that I've got something, that's all. We can't ignore it.'

'OK,' said Garibaldi, 'we can't ignore it, but nor should we start constructing narr . . . we shouldn't assume.'

'I'm not assuming anything, I'm just saying—'

'You're saying maybe Terrell Furlong tracked down Gallen and stabbed him to death?'

'No, I—'

'Maybe he didn't like him giving his kid brother a few extra English lessons? Maybe he thought he was getting ideas above his station? Maybe—'

'You're right,' said Deighton. 'We assume nothing but, yes—' she turned to Gardner and nodded, '—we investigate.'

Garibaldi's phone rang. He took the call.

'Inspector Garibaldi? It's Felicia from Forum Tutors. I expect you've seen the article in today's *Standard*?'

Garibaldi mouthed 'Forum' at Deighton and Gardner.

'You mean Emily Francis's article?'

'Yes. We're shocked. Everyone will find out that she and Giles worked for us.'

'And you're worried about your reputation?'

'Actually, Inspector, we're more worried about the safety of our tutors. First Giles Gallen stabbed to death and then Emily Francis threatened at knifepoint. You don't have to be Sherlock Holmes to think someone might be after us.'

'After you? You mean Giles Gallen was killed because he worked for you, and that's also why Emily Francis was assaulted?'

'I'm not saying that but in our position it's something we have to seriously consider. We'd like to talk to you, Inspector.'

'That's good, because we'd like to talk to you too.'

Garibaldi hung up and looked at Deighton and Gardner. 'They're scared shitless.'

'OK,' said Deighton. 'I'll let you and Uber get off.'

Uber. Garibaldi forced a smile. So what if he didn't drive? Not only was it often faster on his bike, it was also greener. What's more, if he could drive he would never have come up with the first verse of his yet-to-be-completed and as-yet-unperformed country song: 'If I'd passed my test I'd get away tomorrow/If I could drive I know where I would go/Far away from the city's heartbreak/To a place where things are nice and slow.'

Sometimes he dreamed he was on stage singing it with Guy Clark. Sometimes with Steve Earle. Never, as yet, with John Prine.

It had hit written all over it.

26

Felicia Ireland tried to look cool but she was clearly rattled.

'Obviously we're upset about what happened to Emily,' she said, 'and her welfare is our primary concern, but we're also concerned about the article she wrote. The story of her attack is one thing, but the feature on being a tutor is another thing entirely.'

'I see,' said Garibaldi. 'And what is it, precisely, that concerns you about the article?'

Felicia's shrug suggested she thought explanation unnecessary. 'It doesn't do much for the reputation of private tutoring.'

'Really?' said Garibaldi. 'It seemed innocent enough to me. Just saying what everyone probably already knows – that a lot of young people do it as a way of getting money while they look around for jobs.'

'Exactly,' said Roddy, 'which is not the impression we like to give at Forum. We don't want our clients to think our tutors are only doing it because they can't think of a better way to earn some money. We like to think we employ tutors who aren't so obviously fly-by-night.'

'Correct me if I'm wrong,' said Garibaldi, 'but I don't

think Emily Francis actually said that she worked for Forum, did she?'

Felicia threw her head back and laughed. 'People will know. People *already* know and believe me word will spread. She used her own name, for goodness' sake. What about the people she's tutoring for? They'll know she works for us.'

Roddy Ireland leaned forward and rested his elbows on his knees. 'As Felicia says, we're worried about Emily's wellbeing and very distressed by what she experienced. I hope you realise, Inspector, that our concern is not with any damage to our reputation. Not at all. As you say, Emily Francis said nothing surprising and didn't mention us by name. I think what we have here is a misjudged attempt by an aspiring journalist to get her name noticed. We'll talk to her and we'll carry on using her services. You can't fire someone because they have different views.'

Garibaldi thought of all those fired over the years for that very reason.

'More importantly,' said Roddy, 'are we any closer to finding out who killed Giles?'

'We're pursuing several lines of enquiry and we're getting very close.'

It was his stock response – far from the truth but a good way of fending off the implication that not finding the perpetrator within a few days amounted to failure.

'I have to be honest with you, Inspector. Giles Gallen was murdered only a matter of days ago and now Emily Francis is threatened at knifepoint, and we're worried that in some way these things might constitute a real threat to us, to Forum. It's not our reputation we're worried about so much as our safety.'

'There's no evidence to—'

'But what if someone's out to get us?'

'Do you think that's the case?'

'I'm stating the possibility. Giles worked for us and so does Emily.'

'There might be no connection at all,' said Garibaldi.

He knew it was a lie. Or at least he knew what Emily Francis had told them. Remember what happened to Giles. Keep your mouth shut.

But he wasn't going to tell the Irelands. Not yet.

'But what if there is?' said Felicia. 'Should we be doing anything? Should we be warning our tutors?'

'I don't think there's any need to panic.'

'No need to panic? One of our tutors murdered and another one attacked. Why wouldn't we panic?'

'I don't think there's any special advice you need to give your tutors, Mrs Ireland. Giles Gallen wasn't murdered while he was giving a lesson and Emily Francis was attacked as she was walking home. There's no evidence at all that these events are anything to do with their tutoring work.'

'Even so . . .' said Roddy.

Garibaldi gave them both a stern look, the kind he imagined Rachel giving recalcitrant Hillside students. 'Perhaps you could help us with a few questions.'

'Of course,' said Felicia, 'but I hope you understand we're only trying to do the best by our tutors, our clients, everyone.'

'And we're trying to find out who murdered Giles Gallen, so your cooperation would be appreciated.'

Felicia turned to Roddy as if she needed his approval. He nodded and she turned back to Garibaldi.

'We'd like to know a little more about your pro bono

work at Hillside Academy,' said Garibaldi, 'and Giles Gallen's involvement in it.'

'The pro bono work is very important to Forum,' said Felicia. 'We—'

Garibaldi cut in. 'Forget the PR. We know all about that.'

'What do you want to know, then?' said Roddy.

'How many tutors. What the deal was. What Giles did.'

'OK, Inspector,' said Felicia. 'We put feelers out to several schools a couple of years ago. Not all responded positively, but the new Head at Hillside, Kevin someone . . .'

'Johnson,' said Garibaldi. 'Kevin Johnson.'

'He was very keen, so we advertised the opportunity amongst our tutors. We hadn't expected a big take-up and to be fair we didn't get one.'

'Why did you think you wouldn't get a big take up?' asked Gardner.

'Because the majority of our tutors, while they may have a social conscience and altruistic impulses, are doing it because they need the money, so to take on an unpaid commitment was asking a lot.'

'So how many went to Hillside?' said Garibaldi.

'Three of them,' said Felicia. 'We were particularly pleased that Giles was one of them. Having worked for such high-profile wealthy clients like the Rivettis, it was good to see him getting involved.'

'And how often did you expect your tutors to see the Hillside students?' asked Gardner.

'We offered five sessions.'

'I see,' said Garibaldi, 'and would your tutors have any contact with the students outside those sessions?'

'We encouraged email support, so yes there was contact beyond the sessions.'

'But you wouldn't expect your tutors to meet up with any of the students?'

Felicia and Roddy both shook their heads.

'The reason I mention it is because Giles Gallen was helping a boy at Hillside called Devon Furlong and it seems that Devon and Giles met up several times away from the school.'

'That's most unusual,' said Roddy. 'We don't encourage that at all.'

'So you have rules about that kind of thing.'

'Nothing written down,' said Felicia. 'Nothing formal.'

'You surprise me,' said Garibaldi. 'I'd have thought you'd want to make it clear there were boundaries that shouldn't be crossed. I'm thinking of young teenage girls meeting male tutors. Or of course meeting female tutors. Or of course young teenage boys doing the same.'

He winced, embarrassed by his clumsiness.

'Are you suggesting,' said Roddy, 'that Giles seeing this boy for a coffee has anything to do with his murder?'

'Not at all. I'm just asking about usual practice.'

'I think all this shows,' said Felicia, 'is Giles's extraordinary level of commitment. He really cared about his Hillside work. He told us. I really don't see how this could be at all relevant.'

'You never know what's relevant,' said Garibaldi, 'until the connection reveals itself.'

Garibaldi thought briefly of revealing one possible connection but decided that for the moment the Irelands would be better off not knowing about Terrell Furlong.

He decided to go for something else.

'One thing I must tell you is that Emily Francis's attacker said things to her that may be significant and may link her attack to Giles's murder. Apparently . . .' He liked the apparently and paused to give the word some space. 'Apparently he said, "remember what happened to Giles". He also said, "keep your mouth shut". It would seem they both knew something, some secret.'

'We already know this, Inspector,' said Felicia.

'Really?'

'Yes. Emily told us.'

'In which case,' said Garibaldi, 'you've had some time to think about it.'

'And I still don't know what to make of it. I mean, what kind of secret?'

'If I knew that it wouldn't be much of a secret, would it?'

'Well, it can't be a secret about us,' said Roddy.

'I never for one moment thought it could be. The secret could be anything. There's also a chance that there's no secret at all, just as there's a chance that whoever killed Giles Gallen is not the person who attacked Emily Francis.'

'But surely—?' Roddy looked baffled. 'There has to be a connection. If he said those things—'

'We have to keep an open mind,' said Garibaldi. 'What might help is to know who Emily was tutoring. Do you have a list of her clients?'

'You can't possibly think . . . ?'

'I'm capable of all kinds of thoughts, Mr Ireland. So if we could have that list?'

'Of course,' said Roddy. 'I'll send it through tomorrow.'

'Now would be better,' said Garibaldi. He held Roddy's gaze until he got up and went to the office.

'It's very difficult to take all this in,' said Felicia. 'Murder, and now this!'

'That's troubles for you,' said Garibaldi. 'Never single spies are they? Always come in battalions.'

Felicia Ireland looked at him, shocked.

Garibaldi couldn't tell whether it was because of what had happened to two of her tutors or because the visiting detective had just quoted from *Hamlet*.

27

Whenever Garibaldi reflected on how and why he had ended up living with Rachel, he always came back to the same two defining moments. One was, inevitably, the night they met and slept together. The other was the evening they spent at the Half Moon. What was so memorable about the first was not so much the night itself (though the speed and ease with which things happened had taken him by surprise) as the morning after. On the few occasions since his split with Kay when he had found himself in similar situations, the morning after had been awkward and embarrassing. But with Rachel this was far from the case. At first Garibaldi had wondered whether this was because Rachel, unlike him, was used to such scenarios, but when she admitted that what she had done was quite out of character, he felt the first glimmer that this could be the beginning of something significant. When she had picked up the Townes van Zandt CD and said how much of a fan she was he felt the second.

And then there had been the date at the Half Moon listening to Patty Nelson's evening of country covers. By then they had already spent a few more nights together, but that evening was when they opened up to each other, and in many senses it marked the real beginning of their relationship. Garibaldi could still remember how pleased he had been when Rachel had said he was too educated and intelligent to seem like a typical policeman and he had loved the way she responded when he told her about the loss of his parents and his decision to join the police rather than go to university. It wasn't that she understood, it was that she was prepared to admit that she didn't, that she couldn't begin to comprehend the pain he had been through.

When Garibaldi saw that Kimmie Rhodes was playing the Half Moon and that tickets were still available he was quick to buy a couple. He did so in the knowledge that he might not be able to make it but he enjoyed telling Rachel what he'd done. Not that it marked a particular anniversary or anything. And not that it would give him a chance to go down on one knee and produce a ring (though he'd be kidding himself if he hadn't imagined doing this at some later date). It was just good to let her know that, even when he was in the middle of a case, he thought about these things.

As it happened, the cards fell Garibaldi's way and he got away from work in good time.

He had just got home when his phone rang. He checked the screen. Alfie.

'Hi Dad, how's things?'

'OK. And you?'

'Good. I'm on a coach.'

'A coach? Where are you off to?'

'I'm coming down to London.'

'Yeah?'

'For a party.'

'Another dinner party?'

'No, but was wondering if I could come round and get changed.'

'Get changed? Sure. What time will you be here?'

'About an hour, I reckon.'

'OK. The thing is we're going out later, so—'

'I tried mum but they're not at home. I won't be long. It's just that I didn't want to come down in my gear.'

'Gear? What is it? A fancy dress party?'

Alfie laughed. 'Will it be OK? You'll still be able to go out?'

Garibaldi checked his watch. Alfie had a key and could let himself in to change. That wouldn't be a problem, but it felt wrong not to see him.

'Yeah, no problem.'

Rachel came out of the bedroom as he ended the call.

'That was Alfie. He's on his way down.'

'To see you? I thought—'

'We can still go out. He's just popping in to get changed before he heads off to a party. He would have gone to Kay and Fuckwit's but they're not in, so he wants to come here.'

'Well, that's good.'

'What? To be second choice?'

'No. To see him. You know your trouble?'

'I get the sense you're about to tell me.'

'It's always a glass half-empty, isn't it?'

'At the moment it's no glass at all.' He went to pour himself a drink.

Rachel sat down on the sofa and switched on the TV to check that she'd recorded *Richard Osman's House of Games*. They liked to watch it together, in the same way that they liked to watch *University Challenge*, keeping careful scores in both. Given recent performances, Garibaldi suspected that Rachel might have been indulging in some sneaky advance viewing.

'Devon Furlong,' said Garibaldi, sitting down next to

Rachel with a small whisky. 'How much do you know about him?'

'Not much beyond what I've told you. Clever kid. Lives on the White City Estate with his mum and kid brother.'

'Did his older brother go to Hillside as well?'

'I don't remember him. If he did it was before my time. Why do you ask?'

'Just curious.'

'Just curious? You're a detective. Detectives aren't just curious.'

Garibaldi leaned forward and picked up his iPod from the coffee table. He scrolled through, put it in the speaker dock and pressed play. Lucinda Williams filled the room. *Car Wheels on a Gravel Road.*

'Here's the thing,' he said, leaning back and sipping his drink. 'Devon's got two brothers, right? Turns out his older one, Terrell, has a bit of a record.'

'What for?'

'Drugs, knives, assault.'

Rachel turned towards him. 'So what are you suggesting?'

'I'm not suggesting anything. I'm just trying to understand Devon Furlong's background.'

Rachel straightened herself and sat upright. 'Wait a minute. Are you saying Devon Furlong's brother's linked to the murder?'

'Not at all.'

'Not at all? Why else would you ask about him? White City Estate. Black kid. Criminal record. He obviously stabbed Giles Gallen to death, didn't he? Tracked him down to Barnes and killed him because . . .' She held her hands out in exasperation. 'Well, why exactly?'

Garibaldi regretted starting the conversation. Now was not a good time. Not with Alfie on his way round.

'The thing is Devon Furlong saw Giles Gallen outside the allotted tutor sessions at Hillside. They struck up some kind of relationship that isn't the normal tutor-pupil one. And, yes, of course it may be nothing at all, but I'm afraid it's what we need to do. We have to look at all possibilities, however unlikely and far-fetched they seem.'

'But . . . listen to yourself!'

'I just wanted to know if you knew more.'

Rachel shook her head. 'Sorry to disappoint you. Look, a lot of black kids . . . You know what? I don't believe I'm having to say this.'

Garibaldi held up his hand. 'OK. I'm sorry . . .'

Rachel's face softened as she nodded. 'No. I'm sorry. I didn't mean to snap, it's just that whenever people, especially you lot —'

'You lot?'

'You know what I mean.'

'Now who's being prejudiced?'

'It's not as though there isn't a track record, is it?'

'I'm not part of it. When it comes to this, and when it comes to a whole load of things, they're a long way from being "my lot".'

'You think that lets you off the hook?'

Garibaldi held up apologetic hands. 'OK. What can I say? You'd have thought by now they might have learned some lessons.'

'You would, wouldn't you?'

Garibaldi nodded his agreement. 'Your head thinks very highly of you, doesn't he?'

'Are you trying to change the subject?'

'Of course I am. He does, though, doesn't he?'

Rachel gave a modest shrug. Garibaldi reached for her hand and squeezed it. She squeezed it back and they sat there listening to Lucinda Williams, waiting for Alfie, and looking forward to returning to the Half Moon.

He was still his son. Nothing – illness, divorce, stopping coming to QPR – could ever change that. And it was always good to see him.

Garibaldi gave Alfie a hug and Rachel kissed him on the cheek, a gesture which seemed less strange and more comforting each time he saw it.

Alfie put down his bag and glanced round the flat – it may have been an innocent enough look, but Garibaldi saw it as judgemental. His place may have been smaller than Dominic's Putney house and no doubt less grand than the houses of his new Oxford friends but it didn't seem that long ago that Alfie was telling him, after a home game, a few pints and a Saturday night takeaway curry, how much he enjoyed being there with them both, how relaxed the place was, how cosy.

'Time for a drink?'

Alfie checked his watch. 'Have to get moving but, yeah, a quick one would be nice.'

'Beer OK?'

Garibaldi motioned for Alfie to sit down next to Rachel on the sofa and went to get a beer.

'I hear mum came up to see you,' he shouted from the kitchen.

'Yeah. She did.'

No mention of Dominic. Once, just once, he would love to hear Alfie say that he thought he was a prick.

'Did she tell you about it?' said Alfie.

'A bit.' Garibaldi came back in with a bottle of Budweiser and handed it to Alfie. 'Cheers!' he said reaching for his glass of whisky and raising it.

'What did she say?'

'She was worried you weren't doing enough work.'

Alfie laughed and swigged from the bottle. 'Yeah, well she could be right there.'

'And she was worried that if you didn't do enough work you wouldn't get a good degree and if you didn't get a good degree you wouldn't . . .'

'I wouldn't get a good job,' said Alfie, finishing the sentence for him. 'Yeah I picked up on that.'

'Whereas I'm worried,' said Garibaldi, 'that if you don't do enough work you're going to get kicked out.'

'Seriously?'

'Seriously. They do that kind of thing, don't they? Probably got a funny name for it as well.'

'Yeah, but you have to be, like, really bad. I know what I'm doing.'

Garibaldi wanted to debate it but now wasn't the time or place – for that, or for all the other things he wanted to ask his son but couldn't. Why he was still hanging out with his newly acquired rich friends. Whether he had a girlfriend. Whether his missing QPR home games was a temporary blip or a sign of things to come. Whether Alfie would ever forgive him for the mistakes he had made. What he felt about the shit he had put him through.

'Seriously, Dad, don't worry about the work. It's all under control.'

Maybe it was. Alfie was clever enough to get by doing very little. He'd always been like that.

'Still enjoying it?'

'I'm fine, Dad. And about the Fulham game . . .'

Garibaldi waved his hands. He didn't want to hear.

His son was drifting away from him. That's what

happens. Everyone changes as they grow up – it would be odd if they didn't. Alfie at twenty should not be the same as Alfie at fifteen.

So why did he find it all so difficult to accept?

'Still,' said Alfie taking another swig from the bottle, 'I won't miss much, will I? We never beat Fulham.' He got up from the sofa, picked up his bags and headed into Garibaldi's bedroom.

He emerged five minutes later in a dinner jacket and black tie. It shouldn't have surprised Garibaldi but it did.

'Look at you!' said Rachel.

Alfie did his best to look embarrassed but Garibaldi could tell he was enjoying the impression he had made.

'So this party,' said Garibaldi. 'Somewhere posh is it?'

'North London.'

Garibaldi shuddered.

'How are you getting up there? It's miles away.'

'They're laying on Ubers.'

Laying on Ubers? An inappropriate image of DS Gardner flashed in his mind.

'If you want to stay the night . . .'

'It's OK. I'm staying at a friend's.'

'An Oxford friend?'

As if it could be anything else.

'Yeah,' said Alfie, 'someone my girlfriend knows.'

Girlfriend. He'd let it out.

'Girlfriend?'

'Yeah.'

'Is that recent?'

'A few months now. Look, Dad, this really isn't a good time for the third degree. I've got to get off. Maybe when you come up to see me—' he turned to Rachel to include her in the invitation, '—you can meet her.'

'Look forward to it,' said Garibaldi. 'Did Mum meet her when she came up?'

'Yeah, she did.'

But she hadn't told him. He felt a phone call coming on.

'Anyway,' said Alfie, picking up his bags. 'Let's fix up a date for a visit.'

'OK, let's do that.'

Alfie gave Rachel a kiss on the cheek and turned to Garibaldi, who gave him a hug, making it a light one just in case he creased the dinner suit.

What did the scene remind him of?

Was it *Great Expectations* – Pip leaving his home at the forge to become a gentleman in London? Or could it be *Frankenstein* – the scientist shocked by what he had created?

He couldn't place the memory, the scene or the lines he was grasping for.

Then they came to him. Larkin. The ending of *The Whitsun Weddings* – the sense of falling and the arrow shower sent out of sight somewhere becoming rain.

An ambiguous image. He'd never been able to work out whether it was optimistic or pessimistic – exactly what he felt now as he looked at his son head out of the door to find his North London-bound Uber.

28

Daily Mail

ARE LONDON'S PRIVATE TUTORS SAFE?

A murder and a knife attack. Such crimes are not unusual in London but a couple of things about these two set them apart from the usual knife crime scenarios.

First, their location. These weren't committed in the inner city or in areas associated with high rates of such crimes. These happened in Barnes and Putney, leafy areas of Southwest London.

Secondly, the occupations of the victims– both were private tutors. Emily Francis, the victim of the knife attack, wrote about this in yesterday's *Evening Standard*, but she omitted to say what sources confirm – that they were both working for the elite agency, Forum Tutors. A spokesperson for Forum said, 'We are deeply saddened by the murder of Giles Gallen. He was an exceptional tutor, highly regarded by all he worked for. Our sympathies go to his family and friends at this sad time. We are also distressed to hear of the attack on Emily Francis, and we are glad she is safe. Both worked for Forum but we can see no reason at all to connect these terrible incidents to our agency.'

DCI Deighton of the Metropolitan Police, in charge of the investigation into Gallen's murder, denied any connection. 'We are pursuing several lines of enquiry but have no reason to believe that there is any connection between the murder, attack and Gallen and Francis's line of work.'

Although Forum deny any connection between the attackers and their firm, others have wondered whether working as a private tutor can potentially expose you to dangers.

A tutor, wanting to remain anonymous told the *Mail* 'I recognised all that Emily Francis described in her piece about tutoring. Tutors are invited into the houses of those they teach and become very close to the families. In many cases the tutor almost becomes another member of the family. But that doesn't mean it's always cosy. You're dealing with kids' and parents' hopes and ambitions and that can bring out extreme emotions.'

Felicia Ireland threw the newspaper onto the table. It didn't look good, but it could have looked one hell of a lot worse. When the *Mail* had phoned she had been briefly tempted to offer 'no comment', but that would have made it look like Forum had something to hide. So instead she had expressed her sadness and played down the idea that there was any possible connection between the incidents and Forum. And it seemed to have worked. It wasn't a great position to be in but they didn't come across too badly and, if they were lucky, it might do them less harm than they feared. They would have to wait and see.

Roddy had seemed more worried than her. Since the attack on Emily Francis and since the appearance of the article, he had been jumpy and nervous, the veneer of public school charm and unflappability unable to disguise his anxiety. He was particularly concerned that the Rivettis had not been in touch to find a replacement. The prospect of losing such a profitable connection worried him.

'Do you know how much money the Rivettis have been bringing in?' he had asked.

Felicia didn't, but she knew it was a lot.

'And we still haven't given them replacements, have we?'

'I've made a couple of suggestions but they haven't been impressed. That was the trouble with Giles. He was so damned good.'

'And what about for Sam? Don't they need to replace her too?'

'It's the same with her. But I'll keep trying. They can't afford to be too fussy, can they?'

'That's the problem. They probably can. Any sentence about the Rivettis containing the words "can't afford" is probably untrue.'

Felicia had reassured him by promising to contact more tutors and make more offers. It may not have entirely satisfied Roddy but it did seem to make him less agitated.

As for Emily Francis, Felicia was naturally concerned about the attack and about Emily's wellbeing, but her publicly expressed concern was nothing compared to the level of private distress she felt about Emily's knee-jerk journalistic response. It didn't bode well. She knew that Emily's article was far blander than it could have been, and that there was plenty she could have said that she had chosen to omit, but she also knew there was no guarantee that she wouldn't say such things at some later date.

The truth was Emily Francis was a danger, and she didn't trust her any more than she trusted her husband.

Garibaldi was on his phone in the station car park, the place he went to when he wanted to have a private conversation or when he thought he might need to raise his voice.

This was where he went when he needed to call Kay.

'You could have told me.'

'I didn't think it was relevant.'

Kay's tone was cold, distant, defensive. It was difficult to remember that it hadn't always been like that.

'You didn't think it was relevant? I'd have thought Alfie having a new girlfriend is pretty damn relevant, wouldn't you?'

'She seems very nice.'

'That's not the point!' He was shouting. 'Alfie's my son as much as he is yours and there are things I ought to know about him, things you should share with me.'

'I can tell you're annoyed. Maybe we should wait until—'

'Of course I'm annoyed. I know things aren't always easy, but—'

'No they're not always easy and whose fault is that?'

Garibaldi bit his lip. Not metaphorically, but literally, top teeth pinching his lower lip to stop him from saying what he really thought.

'Whose fault?' he said. 'How long have you got?'

It would take them forever. How many hours had they spent going through it, raking through the ashes of their marriage, teasing out the chronology of pain, looking for any comforting sense of cause and effect? Kay's affair with Dominic had been going on for some time, from long before Garibaldi's depression, and his discovery of it shortly after the onset of his illness did irreparable damage to their relationship, ending their marriage at a time when he could not have been more vulnerable.

But it did even greater damage to himself. That he should have recovered as he did was nothing short of miraculous. That he could not forgive her – not just for what it had done to him but also for what it had done to Alfie – was understandable.

'All I'm saying is that you could have told me he had a new girlfriend.'

'Maybe I assumed he'd tell you himself. You do talk to him, don't you? It's not as though I'm the only one he speaks to.'

The thought that Kay might be right pained him. OK, Alfie had told him, or at least let it slip, when he had popped in to change before his party, but why hadn't he told him before? First, missing QPR games, now telling his mother things he wasn't telling him.

'He did tell me actually,' said Garibaldi, 'when he popped in last night.'

'Popped in?'

'Yeah. He was on his way to a party.'

'A party?'

'Yeah.' He couldn't resist adding, 'Didn't you know?'

Squabbling and fighting over Alfie was undignified. They both knew it but they couldn't stop themselves. Whenever they spoke about Alfie each of them picked up an end of the tug o' love rope.

'Look, I've got to go.' Garibaldi ended the call and

walked back to the building, trying to imagine what the new girlfriend was like and how much she had to do with the changes that had come over his son.

At his desk he went through the case notes again trying to get some handle, an angle or a possibility that no-one else had seen.

He couldn't find one.

29

Sam Bannister often wished her dad wasn't who he was. Throughout her childhood she may have enjoyed the things his massive wealth provided and felt a shiver of pride when others connected her name to her father's, but when she left her prep school and went off to Wellington she started to feel differently. There were other kids of famous parents there – it was that kind of school – but there was something about hers, or more specifically her dad, that made her an object of real curiosity. Every time he was on the front pages or on TV, shooting his mouth off in some knee-jerk far right rant, Sam sensed the eyes of all upon her.

At first she had longed for the anonymity of the other kids, those whose parents conducted their lives out of the media's glaring spotlights. Then, realising that she could do nothing about her dad's fame, she had longed for a sudden turnabout in his views, so that, rather than feeling an object of ridicule amongst the school's left-leaning hip intellectuals, she might be admired or revered. If he stopped going on about immigration, tax cuts and the need for less state interference and started to espouse human rights, gender equality and redistribution of wealth, she might be pleased rather than embarrassed to see his name in the papers or watch him on TV. She often fantasised about having a different kind of father, trading him in for another famous Dad – Barack Obama or Bob Geldof or even Gary Lineker. She knew it was crazy, but she couldn't stop herself wanting as a father someone who would stand up for decent things rather than shoot his mouth off about being a self-made man who made his millions through hard work and who had no time for shifters, idlers and socialists and especially not for the woke younger generation.

Getting away from her father was one of the reasons Sam chose to leave her sister's twenty-first birthday party early. It was one way to avoid the discussion she usually ended up having with him whenever she returned to the Hampstead family home – the one in which she expressed her disapproval of his political views and he reminded her of how much he'd given her.

But there was another reason for her early departure shortly before eleven.

She had thought no one would disturb her when she'd sought refuge in her old bedroom and burst into tears, and was surprised when her sister, looking for somewhere private to make a quick adjustment to her dress, came in and found her. Sam tried to pass off her tears as nothing, but before she could reflect on the wisdom of what she was doing, she'd told her sister everything about what had happened in Italy.

She had no idea why she'd done it. Maybe it was because the two of them had always been close and found it difficult to keep things from each other. Or maybe it was simply because she was caught with her guard down and couldn't resist the urge to share, and perhaps lighten, her burden. Whatever the reason, she had immediately regretted it, worrying not only that being found in tears and blurting out her secret might somehow have ruined her sister's big night, but also that her revelation might have serious consequences. That's why she had sneaked out a few hours later, hoping no-one would notice, intending to give her sister a call tomorrow to tell her that she'd made up the Italy story because she didn't want to reveal the real reason for her distress.

As Sam walked towards Hampstead High Street, trying to come up with another plausible reason for why she had been crying in her bedroom, she hoped the last thing her sister would do on her big party night would be tell anyone what she had heard.

She was so wrapped up in these thoughts as she walked to the tube that she didn't at first notice the footsteps behind her. It was only when they came close and then receded, only to come close again moments later, that she thought there was something odd about them, and turned.

Directly behind her was a man in a hoodie. He looked to one side when he saw Sam turn.

Sam picked up her pace. She thought the man had dropped back, but then she heard the steps again, falling in time with her own.

The man closed, and then backed off.

Closed and backed off.

Closed . . .

A hand grabbed her arm.

So this is what it felt like to be mugged. In all her years of living in London it had never happened to her. Until now.

Instinctively, Sam gripped her bag tightly, holding it close to her chest.

The man fell in step beside her, his hand tightening its grip on her arm.

'Listen to what I say.'

Sam turned to look at him, but she could see nothing of his face – just two eyes looking straight ahead from above a black scarf. She tried to wriggle away but his grip tightened even more.

'Don't struggle,' said the man, his eyes still fixed straight ahead.

A sharp point dug into her side.

'Feel that? It's a knife.'

Sam shivered. She looked at the people walking past. Could they see what was happening? Would they help her if she screamed?

'Just do what I say,' said the man, 'and you'll be fine. Don't struggle. Don't call out. If you do—' Sam felt the point against her ribs '— you get this. There's a little alley next on the left. We're going to turn in there. OK?'

Sam nodded. She tried to speak but her mouth was dry, her tongue stuck to the roof of her mouth.

A couple walked towards them as they neared the alley. The man allowed them to pass, then pulled her to the left.

'In here,' he said.

A few yards down the alley he pulled her to the right into a small courtyard. His hand, still on Sam's right arm, pinched it tightly. His other hand grabbed Sam's left arm as he put his leg in front of her shin and pushed.

Sam spread out her arms to break the fall. Her hands and knees smarted as they hit the concrete.

The knife hit the ground.

Sam tried to scream but his weight fell on her from behind, pinning her down, and a hand muffled her mouth. She grunted against his fingers and wriggled under his body.

'Just listen to what I have to say, OK?'

Sam grunted again.

She felt a sharp sting on the side of her neck.

'Feel that? It's a knife'

Another grunt.

'The kind of knife that killed your friend. It could kill you too and it will if you don't keep your mouth shut. Understand? We know who you are. We know where you live. And if you say anything . . .' The knife point pressed in. '. . . you'll go the way of Giles. Understand?'

Sam grunted.

'Understand?'

Sam grunted again.

'OK,' said the man. 'Nothing. OK?'

The weight lifted and Sam heard running steps receding.

Was that why Giles had been murdered?

Was it all because of what had happened in the summer?

She lay on the ground, unable to move, her mind racing.

30

Garibaldi looked across the table in Interview Room 2. 'Thank you for coming in.'

Emily Francis looked uncomfortable. It was probably the first time she had ever been in a station.

'I'm not being charged or anything am I?'

'Not at all,' said Garibaldi, 'it's just that we've got a few further questions and thought it would be better to go through them here.'

'So I don't need a solicitor or anything?'

Garibaldi shook his head. 'You're welcome to get one if you want but all you're doing is helping us with our enquiries.'

Garibaldi picked up a copy of the *Standard* open at the page of Emily's article. 'How's this gone down?' he said.

'The *Standard* loved it.'

'And what about Forum?'

'They weren't so keen. Worried about bad publicity I suppose, though I did point out that I didn't mention them.'

Garibaldi picked up another paper from the table – the *Mail* this time. 'Didn't take this lot long to get on to it, did it? Maybe Forum were right to be a bit concerned.'

'I don't see that I did anything wrong—'

'We're not saying you did.'

'The fact is that I was attacked. The fact is that Giles Gallen was murdered. And we both work for the same tutoring firm. Look—' Emily broke off, as if she were losing patience with her self-justification, 'OK, I really want to be a journalist, that's no secret, and so I saw the opportunity and took it. I had this feature on tutoring that I wrote some time ago and so I offered it to the *Standard* and they took it. All I had to do was make a few changes . . .'

'And what kind of changes would they be?' said DS Gardner.

'Well, the original was a kind of exposé, you know *Secret Diary of a Private Tutor* kind of thing, giving the lowdown, telling the truths. It didn't seem appropriate to offer that, so I took out all the juicy bits.'

'Do you have a copy of that original article?' said Garibaldi.

Emily looked flustered. 'Well, yes, but . . .'

'I'd love to see it, just out of interest you understand. Nothing more.'

Emily's eyes darted from side to side. 'I'd love to give it to you but the thing is I've actually pitched it to some editors and I'm waiting for them to get back so maybe . . .'

'Not to worry, Emily,' said Garibaldi holding up his hand. 'Not to worry. It's just that the more I find out about this whole private tutoring thing the more I'm fascinated. Anyway . . .' He put down the papers and picked up his notes. 'I'm interested in what you say about changing that article, about taking out the juicy bits because, you see Emily, and this is why we've called you in today, we think you might have been taking out some other juicy bits.'

'I'm sorry?'

'The account you gave us of the Saturday evening you spent with Giles at the pub and at the Forum party . . .'

Garibaldi paused. He loved creating silences like this, the chance they gave to look closely at a face and evaluate the reaction.

'I don't understand.' Emily seemed unruffled but Garibaldi could tell her mind was whirring, busily rebooting and refreshing, trying to work out what was coming.

'I thought you said I wasn't in trouble.'

'I'm not saying you are.' Garibaldi scanned his notes. He didn't need to but he knew it had an unnerving effect, as if referring to something already written gave more weight to the spoken words. 'All I'm saying is that in what you've told us about that evening you've done what you did to that article – you've left out the juicy bits. And just as I would very much like to see that original article so would I like to hear the full version of that Saturday night. In the case of the article, you have every right not to show us it – or at least you do at the moment, who knows what might happen in the future? – but in the case of the Saturday night, as this is part of a murder investigation you have a duty to give us what is often referred to as the whole truth.'

Emily shifted in her seat. Her inner computations had finished. She knew the game was up.

'Which bit of the evening are you talking about?'

'You know which bit, Emily.'

'I'm not sure I do.' She wasn't giving in too easily.

'We've got CCTV footage.'

'Of what?'

'Of the side door to the Red Lion. The one you use to go to the loos. If you turn that way, that is.'

Emily's defiance shrivelled. Her nod of acknowledgement was slow and resigned.

'We could show you the footage,' said Gardner, 'but if you tell us the truth we won't need to.'

'Take your time,' said Garibaldi.

Emily gathered herself. 'Look, it was really silly. I mean nothing like that had ever happened between us before. Ever. And I hadn't expected it to. But Giles was in a strange mood at the pub and I'd had quite a bit to drink and I suppose we'd been flirting in a way all evening. I'd been teasing him about being a supertutor and about what he got up to in Italy with the other tutor . . .'

'What did he get up to?'

'Nothing. Or at least that's what he claimed. So I was teasing, flirting. I wasn't with him much at the party but then at the pub it was different and just before we were all thinking of going he made this suggestion . . .' Emily broke off and looked across the table at Garibaldi and Gardner. 'Do I really have to spell it out? How much detail do you need?'

Garibaldi leaned forward. 'Did you, Miss Francis, have sexual intercourse with Giles Gallen in the garden of the Red Lion on that Saturday night?'

'Well . . .' Emily shook her head, a mixture of disappointment and embarrassment. 'How relevant are these details?'

'We won't know until we hear them.'

'OK. Sexual intercourse? No.'

'But you got up to something in that garden?'

'We couldn't do it standing up. He was too . . .'

'So you didn't have sexual intercourse but you did something else?'

'Do I really have to answer this?'

'I'm afraid you do.'

'Yeah. We did something else. He . . . I . . .'

She paused, her eyes darting from one to the other, pleading not to have to spell it out.

Garibaldi said nothing, his eyes fixed on her in a steady gaze. Now was not a time to look at Milly Gardner.

'I gave him . . . look I really don't see how—'

'Thank you, Miss Francis,' cut in Garibaldi. 'You wonder why we're asking you about this and I quite understand your concern, but the thing is if you've chosen to exclude this very important element of the events of that Saturday night we are concerned that you may not have been entirely truthful about other things.'

'Such as?'

Garibaldi looked at Gardner. She took up the baton.

'Such as,' said Gardner, 'whether you were privy to some secret that Giles Gallen shared with you, whether you were threatened at knife point and told to keep quiet because there were in fact things that you knew.'

'I've told you already. There's nothing I know.'

'Why should we believe that?' said Garibaldi. 'You lied to us about what happened between you and Gallen that night —'

'I didn't lie! I didn't say anything that wasn't true. I just . . .'

'You just didn't tell us.'

'It didn't seem relevant.'

'Didn't seem relevant?' said Garibaldi. 'Sex – or something close to it – some kind of job, let's say, with a man who hours later was stabbed to death a mile or so away.'

'So you're saying I lied by omission?'

Omission. Emission. Now wasn't the time for a pun.

'We're not playing lawyers here, Miss Francis, even if that may have been what you studied at university.'

'I studied Psychology.'

'I see.'

He had no idea what he saw, apart from further evidence

that he found Emily Francis's generation irritating beyond words.

He leaned forward, rested his elbows on the table and clasped his hands. 'The thing that puzzles me is that you spent a large part of Saturday evening with Giles Gallen. Pub before the party. Pub after the party. Pub garden after the party. In all that time did he say nothing that might suggest some secret?'

Emily Francis shook her head. 'That's the thing about secrets. They're not secrets if you tell anyone.'

'It's psychology you studied, right? Not philosophy.'

No smile. Total seriousness.

'The question that I'm really asking myself here,' said Garibaldi, 'is why you were threatened at knife point and told to keep quiet, why you were told to remember what happened to Giles Gallen if you had no idea what you needed to be quiet about. Strange, isn't it?'

'Very strange. I don't understand it at all.'

'There is one possibility, though, which is also nagging away at me. I don't want to think it's true but the thought won't go . . .'

Emily looked at him expectantly.

'And that's the possibility that your account of the attack isn't completely truthful.'

'You think I've left out the juicy bits?'

'I'm not talking omission here, Miss Francis.'

'You think I made it up? Why the fuck would I make it up?'

'Exactly,' said Garibaldi, 'why would you?'

Emily sat back in her chair and folded her arms. Her gaze swivelled back and forth between Garibaldi and Gardner, her eyes bright and defiant.

'So the question I'm asking here,' said Garibaldi, 'is why

would your attacker say those things to you if you have no idea what he could be talking about? You see my problem. Maybe he didn't say those things—'

Emily banged her fist on the table. 'He *did* say those things!'

'Or maybe you *do* know whatever Giles Gallen knew.'

Another fist bang. 'I *don't* know!'

'So if neither of those things is true why did the attack happen at all?'

Emily raised her fist for a third time but thought better of it. 'Exactly. And do you know what? Sometimes I think it was a mistake. Sometimes I think they maybe got the wrong person.'

The wrong person. It was the second time Emily had said it. When he first spoke to her she'd suggested that Giles Gallen may have been murdered in a case of mistaken identity. And here she was saying the same about her assault.

To suggest one case of mistaken identity looked like misfortune, to suggest two . . .

Garibaldi looked across the table at Emily Francis, thinking of her and Giles Gallen in the Red Lion pub garden. Lines from Larkin came to him – the ones in *High Windows* about seeing a couple of kids and guessing he's fucking her . . .

Giles Gallen may not have been doing that (or able to do that) with Emily Francis on that particular Saturday night but he found it difficult to believe that he hadn't done it with her before.

Was that why he found it difficult to see Giles Gallen as the squeaky-clean character his old schoolmate had described?

Was that why he also found it difficult to believe anything that Emily Francis said?

31

Terrell Furlong's flat was on the fifth floor of a block on the north side of the estate between Commonwealth Avenue and the Westway.

Garibaldi knocked and waited with Gardner. There was no answer.

A woman came along the walkway, stopped outside a door, reached for her key and turned to them.

'You looking for Terrell?' she said.

'Yeah,' said Garibaldi. 'This is his flat, right?'

'Yeah. It's his flat.'

The woman looked them up and down as if she knew who they were and was working out whether she should say any more.

'He's working.'

'Working?'

'At the Day Centre.'

'Where's that?'

The woman pointed over the walkway wall towards the noise of the Westway traffic. 'Over there,' she said.

Garibaldi and Gardner thanked her and set off. When they reached the Day Centre, a council-run enterprise which offered, according to the board outside its entrance, classes, groups and support for estate residents, they asked the man behind the food counter where they might find Terrell Furlong.

The man passed the tea he had just poured to an old lady.

'Why do you want to know?' he said.

'We want to speak to him,' said Garibaldi.

'Who are you?'

'Do you know where he is?'

'Yeah, I do.'

The man reached for a cloth, mopped up the slops round the tea urn and wiped his hands on the back of his apron.

'If you could tell us where he is,' said Garibaldi.

'You're talking to him.'

'Right. Could we have a quick word?'

'About what?'

Garibaldi looked round the room and discreetly took out his warrant card so that no-one apart from Furlong could see it. Gardner, following his lead, did the same.

'We're here to talk about Giles Gallen,' said Garibaldi. 'He was found murdered last Saturday.'

Terrell turned to a woman behind him. 'Marje, can you take over for a few minutes? I need to talk to these—' He turned to Garibaldi and Gardner. 'These people.'

He put down his cloth, came out from behind the counter and led them to a plastic table in the corner. Garibaldi took a seat and glanced round the room at the other tables where people sat with cups of tea and sandwiches. Some were talking, some reading a newspaper and some simply staring vacantly into space. The place had the feel of a care home.

'Tell me again,' said Terrell, 'who's been murdered?'

'Giles Gallen.'

'Never heard of him. Where did this happen?'

'Barnes.'

Terrell looked puzzled. 'Where?'

'Barnes. The other side of Hammersmith Bridge.'

Terrell still looked puzzled.

'The thing is,' said Garibaldi, 'your brother Devon knew him, and that's why we want to talk to you.'

'Devon knew him but you want to talk to me. Wouldn't it make more sense to talk to Devon?'

'We have,' said Gardner, 'but he said a few things that made us think it might be worth talking to you too.'

'How did Devon know him?'

'Giles Gallen was a tutor and he came into Hillside to give Devon some help in his university application.'

Terrell nodded, as if he now understood a little more. 'So. Devon and his brains, yeah?'

'Tell me,' said Garibaldi, 'did Devon ever mention Giles Gallen to you?'

'Devon doesn't tell me about school. That's Devon. He don't shout about it. He just does it.'

'We're told that not everyone approved of Devon's ambitions.'

'Yeah? Who told you that?'

'Devon did. Didn't he tell you we saw him?'

'No. I was over there only yesterday and he didn't say anything.'

'So what do you think of Devon applying to Cambridge?' said Gardner.

'What do you mean? Isn't he allowed to?'

'Of course he is,' said Garibaldi. 'It's just—'

'Devon's got brains, right? He should use them. Get out and get on, that's what he should do. Look, I still don't get what it is you want to know.'

The truth was Garibaldi wasn't sure either. The link was

so tenuous, the possibility that there could be a connection between Gallen's murder and Devon's brother so slight that he almost felt embarrassed.

'The thing is,' said Garibaldi, 'it seems Giles Gallen didn't only come into the school, he also saw Devon outside school. They met up a few times to talk about his essays.'

'Is that a problem?'

'We don't know. We're just looking into Gallen's dealings with Devon.'

'His dealings? You said he was giving Devon some lessons. What's there to say?'

Garibaldi looked round the room. 'How long have you been working here?'

Terrell smacked his hand on his forehead in an exaggerated gesture of sudden dawning. 'Oh, hang on, now I get it! That's why you've come to see me! Terrell Furlong the bad brother. Devon's a good guy but let's talk to the bad guy.'

'That's not why we're here.'

'Look, let me explain how it is. OK, so a few years ago I got into trouble. You know that. I know that. But that's behind me, right? Nothing now for a long while. Ever since I started at the gym and ever since I started coming here—' He spread his arms wide to take in the whole room. 'It's been different.' He paused, giving Garibaldi a firm confident stare. 'The church has helped as well.'

'The church?'

Garibaldi braced himself for a tale of born-again saw-the-light conversion.

'Not like you think,' said Terrell. 'Not singing, not clapping, not shouting about it. I just started going – about three years ago – and it's made a big difference. And I help out there as well.'

'You help at the church?'

'Yeah. The youth group. So that's me. Day Centre. Youth Group. Gym. I'm sorry to disappoint you guys, but if you've come looking for Devon's big bad brother you've got the wrong man.'

'We're just trying to find out more about Giles Gallen and what he was doing.'

'And you're worried about him giving Devon some extra lessons.'

'Not so much the lessons in school. More the meeting up outside it.'

'Yeah? Where did they meet?'

'They met for a coffee somewhere. Devon didn't say where.'

'And you didn't ask?'

Garibaldi was beginning to feel morally inadequate in the presence of this do-gooding help-the-community former gang member.

'Does it matter where they met?' said Gardner.

'I won't know that,' said Terrell, 'until I know where it was.'

'Look,' said Garibaldi, 'we don't really think there can be any link between Giles Gallen tutoring Devon and meeting up with him and his murder, but we need to explore the possibility . . .'

'And the White City Estate seems a good place.'

'It's where Devon lives.'

'Of course it is.'

'I don't want you to get the wrong impression.'

'I haven't. I think I've got the right one.'

Garibaldi felt uncomfortable.

'Tell you what,' said Terrell. 'I'll do you a favour, I'll have a word with Devon myself and see if there's anything about him seeing this bloke that might be important. And I'll ask around. If I pick anything up, I'll let you know. '

'As I said . . .' Garibaldi was still feeling uncomfortable. 'It's probably nothing. We just have to check. We're speaking to everyone Gallen tutored to get the whole picture.'

'Of course you are.'

'I hope you understand.'

'Yeah. I understand all right.'

Terrell Furlong stood up, as if to indicate that the interview was over and he needed to get back to serving tea to the White City old folks.

Garibaldi nodded to Gardner and they got up to leave.

'I don't know about you,' he said to Gardner as they walked to the car. 'But that's made me feel like shit.'

'Yeah,' said Gardner. 'Me too.'

32

Felicia Ireland knew things were bad, but she also knew they could have been one hell of a lot worse.

The articles could have caused huge damage, provoking a flood of emails and phone calls from concerned clients, but the signs were they were getting away relatively lightly – enquiries from potential clients, far from falling off, might even have increased. Maybe there was, after all, no such thing as bad publicity.

But Roddy wasn't quite so relaxed. All he could see was the worst-case scenario – unusual for someone who had always liked to look on the bright side.

'Look,' he said to Felicia over the kitchen table, 'we have no idea who killed Giles Gallen. It could have been anyone, and it could have been for any reason. And it could have nothing to do with us at all. But this attack on Emily Francis and the things the attacker said to her connect her to Giles and connect both of them to us.'

'How do they connect them to us? They were friends. They knew each other. That's the obvious connection. The fact that they both worked for Forum's irrelevant.'

'The *Daily* Fucking *Mail* doesn't think so. They've made the whole fucking country aware of the connection!'

'There's no need to swear.'

'There's every fucking need!'

'I think you need to calm down a bit.'

'I am calm!' He paused and, seeming to realise that he had been shouting, lowered his voice. 'I'm just worried. Aren't *you* worried?'

'If I could think of any possible reason why anyone would want to target us then I might be. But the whole thing seems so preposterous . . .'

Roddy threw his arms in the air. 'Everyone's talking about it. When I was walking Hector on the common this morning all the other dogwalkers said the same – "Hope you're safe. Be careful, won't you?" You can say there's no link, but the *Daily* Fucking *Mail* has done its best to suggest otherwise, haven't they? And that's without knowing what the attacker said to her! Imagine what they'd do if they knew. They'd have a fucking field day! And you know what? Given our dear Emily's track record, the chances are they might find out. I wouldn't put it past her to ring them up and tell them or, better still, write another fucking article about it. Anything to advance her career. You know what we should do?'

Felicia looked at her husband, waiting for him to calm down. This was the worst she'd seen him for some time.

'I'll tell you what we should do,' said Roddy. 'We should fire her.'

'We can't do that. Think how bad that would look. Think of the headlines. "Victim of attack fired by tutoring agency". "Assaulted tutor fired for writing article." "Murdered man agency sacks—"'

'OK,' said Roddy, getting up from the table. 'I get the picture.'

He grabbed the dog lead and shouted, 'Hector! Walkies!'

Roddy's reaction to stress had always been to walk away from it. More specifically to walk away from it with his dog.

He had always found it difficult to express his emotions – a result, Felicia had no doubt, of his education: the separation from his parents at the age of eight when he was sent away to board, first at a prep school in Berkshire and then to public school. How that could not have caused psychological damage, and how the practice should still be considered acceptable, she could never understand. OK, she may have been to Westminster, but at least she went home each day to her family.

Felicia still loved Roddy, or at least she thought she did, but his recent emotional outbursts had made her more aware of the damage his stiff-upper-lip repression might have done to him and of the flaws in their relationship. She had started to wonder whether she'd ever really understood him, ever really known what he was thinking and, most unsettling of all, whether she'd ever really satisfied him. And she had also started to wonder why Roddy found it easier to be demonstrably affectionate with Hector than he did with her and why, in times of stress, he reached for the lead.

He used to walk Hector morning and afternoon, popping out with him briefly last thing at night. Since the Giles Gallen murder and the newspaper articles Roddy had added a midday walk to Hector's schedule and had also, fuelling Felicia's suspicions, taken to going out for a walk by himself after Hector's late-night excursion. The dog had never been so exercised and when he scampered into the room in response to Roddy's magic words Felicia thought he looked half-hearted about it all, as if, much as he loved romping on Barnes Common, he wouldn't mind a rest every now and then.

'I tell you,' said Roddy, 'someone's after us. There's someone out there who wants to get us.'

'Who would want to? That's what I don't get. Why–?'

Roddy put Hector on the lead. 'Let's assume Giles Gallen knew something. He knew something so serious that someone killed him to keep him quiet for good.'

'What did he know? Must have been pretty serious.'

'I have no idea. But look at what they said to Emily – "keep your mouth shut", "remember what happened to Gallen".'

'Well, it can't be anything about us, can it?'

Roddy walked to the door and turned. 'Nothing about us, no. Not about us directly. But our clients . . .'

'You think one of our clients murdered him? A parent?'

'It's unlikely, I know, but . . . I just want it to be something other than what I fear – that someone's targeting Forum Tutors.'

Roddy shut the door behind him and headed out with Hector.

Felicia went to the window and looked at her husband walking down the road towards Barnes Common. She knew all about the dog-walking community.

Most of them were women.

It was only a suspicion, but it wouldn't go away.

Nor would the suspicion that Roddy was keeping something else from her, something about Forum.

As she turned from the window her phone rang. She didn't recognise the number.

'Hello?'

'Is that Felicia?'

'Speaking.'

'It's Mrs Rivetti here.'

'Mrs Rivetti! How are you?'

Felicia went into the kitchen, sat at the table and reached for a pen and pad of paper. Experience had taught her that when clients phoned instead of emailed it was a good idea to take notes.

'Felicia, we still have not got a tutor for Paolo.'

'I'm sorry. This is a difficult time for everyone . . .'

'Of course it is, but I hope you understand this is also a difficult time for us.'

'I'm sorry you didn't like the candidates we sent to you, Mrs Rivetti. We thought they would be a very good match for you and for Paolo.'

'I liked them, Felicia, I liked both of them. Nice boys. But Paolo did not like them. His exams are in a few weeks and he needs someone to get him through them. He needs someone like Giles.'

'They were both highly qualified and with a lot of experience.'

'I know. But even Luigi is getting worried about it now. Usually he leaves it all to me but he wanted to look at the profiles of the tutors you suggested and he also said they weren't right.'

'Did he say why?'

'He just said they weren't up to Giles.'

Felicia sighed. Giles had lost his life but this somehow seemed less important than the Rivettis having lost their tutor.

'Tutors like Giles are very hard to come by.'

'We've managed to find a replacement for Sam. That was not as difficult. She came for an interview and we all liked her.'

'Was that through another agency?'

Felicia nervously waited for the answer, imagining Roddy's response if he discovered they were in danger of losing the Rivettis' custom.

'Yes it was,' said Mrs Rivetti. 'And we can look at the same agency for Paolo . . .'

As she feared.

'But we would like to use you if we could, Felicia. So what I'm ringing to ask is whether there are any other tutors on your books who might be good for Paolo? Because if not . . .'

Felicia thought quickly. 'I do have one other suggestion for you, Mrs Rivetti, and the only reason I haven't told you about it before is because I wasn't sure of his availability . . .'

She had no idea whether this would work, but she had started now and saw no way of turning back.

'You say you want someone like Giles, well this man is a friend of his. More than a friend, he's an old school friend. They were at Radley together. And this guy, Simon, is very much like Giles. I've already told him about the possibility. He's devastated by what happened to his friend and obviously feels a little uneasy stepping into his shoes like this, but I did explain that it's an emergency and he said he's interested.'

'This sounds good.'

'So maybe I could send through his details and we could fix up an interview.'

'Thank you, that would be very helpful.'

Felicia hung up, let out a huge sigh of relief and scrolled through her laptop to find Simon Prest's contact details.

She had no idea how he would respond but knew she had to try.

33

Garibaldi wriggled in the uncomfortable Hoxton chair.

'This must be very distressing for you, Sam, but it would be good if you could tell us what happened.'

Sam Bannister lit a cigarette and dragged deeply.

'Take your time,' said Garibaldi, getting up to open a window.

He sat down and listened as Sam took them through the sequence of events – from leaving the party at her parents' Hampstead home to the attack.

'Tell me about the knife,' said Garibaldi.

'I felt it against me, I heard it fall to the ground and then I felt it again when he was lying on top of me.'

'And the words he said to you. Are you absolutely clear about them?'

'As clear as I can be. "If you say anything you'll go the way of Giles". I remember it because I thought at the time it was a strange way to say it. Go the way of Giles. Funny, isn't it? You're lying on the ground with someone on top of you holding a knife to your throat and you have thoughts like that. But, yeah, go the way of Giles, that's what he said.'

'And when he said, "if you say anything" do you have any idea what he meant?'

'Not a clue.'

'Did they mean some kind of secret that Giles knew and that you knew as well?'

Sam held her hands out wide and laughed in disbelief. 'I have no fucking idea. None at all.'

'Or did they mean that you know who killed Giles and they were telling you, warning you, to keep your mouth shut?'

The thought had come to Garibaldi from nowhere and he was pleased with it. He should have asked Emily Francis the same question.

'Look, Inspector, I have no idea at all who killed Giles and I have no idea what they were telling me to keep quiet about. At the moment I'm more worried about my safety.'

'You're aware of the attack on Emily Francis?' said Gardner.

'Of course. I've read the newspapers. I've been online. Everyone's talking about it, speculating.'

'Speculating about what?'

'About whether there's a link to Giles, about the tutoring thing . . .'

'The thing is, Sam, the attack on you and the attack on Emily Francis are remarkably similar. Both of you were followed, both of you were threatened with a knife and both of you were told to keep your mouths shut. And both you and Emily Francis say you have no idea what your attackers were telling you to keep quiet about. Strange, isn't it?'

'Are we assuming it's the same man?'

'We don't know. We have CCTV of Miss Francis's attacker and we're looking into the Hampstead CCTV coverage to see if we can get yours. The descriptions suggest the same clothes and similar height and build. So it could very easily be the same man.'

'And is it the man who killed Giles?'

'We can't say.'

'Because if it is, I'm in danger aren't I? I mean he could do it again . . . any time.'

'Your link with Giles is that you worked with him for the Rivettis. Until recently, that is. You also, until recently, worked for Forum. Can you think of any way all these incidents could be connected to them?'

'No. I mean I have no idea. And even if I did—'

'And even if you did you wouldn't tell us?'

'No. I mean he told me to keep my mouth shut. He threatened me with a knife.'

'That shouldn't stop you telling us anything you know.'

'Giles was murdered! I've been attacked and threatened! I'm not safe! I could have been killed. Whoever did it is still out there and they could do it again. What am I supposed to do? Lock myself up? Get twenty-four-hour protection?'

Garibaldi thought of pointing out that her father could probably arrange it.

'What do you suggest I do?'

'I advise you to be careful, Sam.'

'Be careful? What does that mean?'

'It means look after yourself. Maybe avoid walking by yourself alone late at night. I'm sure that's something you'd do anyway, but, given what's happened . . .' Garibaldi got up and nodded to Gardner. 'We'll be off.'

He thought of walking to the door and doing a Columbo as he reached for the handle, but decided to do it where he was.

'One more thing, Sam. We asked the Rivettis about

making an offer to Giles and they said they had no idea what he meant.'

'But the text . . .'

'Exactly. Giles sends a text saying they had made him an offer and the Rivettis say they didn't make one.'

'That doesn't make sense.'

'It doesn't, does it? You suggested that it might have been about finding a replacement for you and it would make perfect sense if they'd asked Giles to take over, but apparently not.'

'I don't understand. Why would Giles send me that text if it wasn't true?'

'I know. There is, of course, one other possibility.'

'What's that?'

'That Giles was telling the truth and the Rivettis weren't. That they did make him an offer but they didn't want us to know what it was.'

Sam's mouth opened, but no words came out. She looked stunned.

'You know them well, Sam, don't you? After all, you've been on holiday with them, you've lived with them. Can you think of any offer that the Rivettis might make to Giles that they wouldn't want us to know about?'

Still no words, but a slow shake of the head.

'Well, if you do have any thoughts about that, do let us know, won't you?'

'Of course.'

Garibaldi and Gardner walked out of Harrow Cloisters towards their car.

'What did you do that for?' said Gardner. 'You know exactly what offer the Rivettis made to Giles.'

'Of course I do,' said Garibaldi, 'but I wanted to see how Sam Bannister would react.'

'So you lied to her?'

'Only for the purposes of the investigation. Perfectly legitimate.'

'And how *did* she react?'

'In a way that justified the lie. You could tell that she was unsettled. Confirms what I've thought all along. That there was something going on with the Rivettis that's not quite right. There's something that's hidden, something no-one's saying.'

Gardner stopped in her tracks. 'Hang on, you're reaching that conclusion just from looking at Sam Bannister respond to your lie?'

'Not just that. Remember when we were speaking to the Rivettis and I mentioned the text about the offer?'

'Yeah, what about it?'

'Did you see the way they reacted? There was a hesitation. Luigi Rivetti looked surprised. You could see it in his face and then he turned to his wife and you could sense confusion. It didn't last long and then you could see his relief when she answered. It was only a moment but it was the same kind of moment we saw in Sam.'

'So you think the Rivettis might have made some other kind of offer?'

'I'm sure they didn't. Not on this occasion. But I reckon there could be other offers that might have been made in the past.'

'Such as?'

'I don't know. I just have this feeling that something might have been going on beyond tutoring.'

'Sex?'

'With Maria Rivetti? Who knows? Giles was a handsome chap. And we know Maria Rivetti has a temper. She's pretty volatile.'

'So what are you thinking?' said Gardner. 'Something going on between Maria Rivetti and Gallen. He puts a stop to it and she kills him. Bit unlikely, don't you think?'

'Each man kills the thing he loves.'

'Yeah but she's a—' Gardner broke off, realising her boss was quoting again.

'Oscar Wilde. But you're right. It's unlikely.'

'What if Luigi Rivetti found out what was going on and he killed him?'

'Again, a bit unlikely, but we can't rule anything out.'

'Or maybe something was going on between Gallen and Luigi?'

'Even more unlikely, but you never know.'

Gardner nodded. 'OK. But there's one thing I don't get about this offer thing. If Sam thought it might have been something ... secret, something that needed to be kept quiet, why would she show us Giles's text like that?'

'Maybe she wanted us to look into it.'

'And we have looked into it. And we've found that it was all about tutoring, about Giles taking over from Sam.'

'That's assuming that there was only one offer.'

'What do you mean?'

'The way the Rivettis reacted, it was as if Luigi was thinking of a different offer. It was as if maybe they had *both* made him offers, but they were very different.'

'So Maria Rivetti's was about tutoring. What would Luigi's have been about?'

'I have no idea. That's why I said what I did to Sam.'

Gardner gave a big sigh. 'Why didn't you tell me that was what you were going to do?'

'Because I didn't know I was going to do it. It just came to me.'

'And has it left you feeling any clearer about things?'

'I'm clear about one thing, and that's that Sam Bannister knows something she's not telling us.'

'And what's that?'

'That's the problem. I have no idea.'

34

bbc.co.uk/news

HARRY BANNISTER'S DAUGHTER IN LATEST TUTOR KNIFE-ATTACK

Yesterday, the daughter of businessman and TV star Harry Bannister became the latest victim in a series of attacks on the capital's private tutors. Sam Bannister, 26, was attacked as she walked to the tube from her parents' 20-million-pound Hampstead mansion where she had attended her sister's 21st birthday party.

Her assailant approached her in the street, took her into an alley, pinned her to the ground and threatened her with a knife. The police are investigating the attack and are linking it to the recent murder of Giles Gallen in a Barnes cemetery and the assault on Emily Francis in Putney.

The victims in all three cases had been working as private tutors. Bannister had recently resigned from Forum Tutors, the agency that had employed both Gallen and Francis, who wrote an article in last week's *Standard* describing the tutoring experience common to so many recent graduates.

Harry Bannister told the *Standard*, 'I am appalled by what has happened to my daughter. She was simply walking along the road not far from our house on her way home and was subjected to the most distressing attack. Our streets are no longer safe. Knife crime is rife and it is no longer happening in the places it used to. It is spreading to different parts of our city, threatening different people. What I want to know is what our police are doing about it. Where are they? Where is their presence? And what are they doing about the murder of a young private tutor? What are they doing about the other attacks? What's going on?'

Forum Tutors were unavailable for comment. DCI Karen Deighton, in charge of the investigation, said 'We are pursuing several lines of inquiry and making progress. We have no evidence to suggest that private tutors or the Forum agency are being targeted. There could be other, unrelated reasons for these attacks.'

Garibaldi looked up from his screen at Deighton. '"Different people"? We know what Harry Bannister means by that, don't we? White people in Hampstead.'

'And we also know what it means by other unrelated reasons for the attacks.'

'And what's that?'

'It means we haven't got a clue. None of us have.'

Garibaldi let the 'has' remain unuttered.

'One thing that puzzles me,' he said, 'is why Giles Gallen

was murdered and Emily Francis and Sam Bannister weren't. Why were they only attacked and threatened?'

'Exactly,' said Deighton. 'If Gallen was killed because he needed to be silenced and if Francis and Bannister also needed to be silenced, why didn't he kill them as well?'

'Not that we want to be dealing with a tutor serial killer.'

'Of course. But why the different MO?'

'There's no evidence that it's the same man behind the murder and the attacks.'

'Sure, but they have to be connected, don't they?'

'Looks like it. But if Francis and Bannister need to be silenced why do they say they don't know anything? Both claim to have no idea why Gallen was murdered, no idea of what they're being told to be quiet about.'

'But we know Francis has already lied to us about one thing. What's to say she hasn't lied to us about others? And what's to say that Bannister's not keeping things from us as well?'

Garibaldi nodded. 'We need to keep at them.'

'We need more, Jim.' Deighton pointed at the screen. 'And now that bigmouth Harry Bannister's on the case we need it quickly.'

Garibaldi leaned back in his chair. 'It all comes back to the same thing, doesn't it?'

'And what's that?'

'Tutoring.'

'Yeah. We need to look more closely at Forum.'

'And we also need to look again at the kids he was tutoring. And their parents. I get the sense they might have more to tell us.'

'Right,' said Deighton turning away and heading back to her office.

'Let's get on it,' said Garibaldi under his breath.

*

'I've told them you're an old friend of Giles. Same pedigree. Very similar.'

When Simon Prest had heard Felicia Ireland's words he should have thought twice about it.

He'd always been aware, since his time at Radley, that he wasn't Giles Gallen and he was convinced the Rivettis had, in the last hour, made that same discovery for themselves. He'd been distracted throughout the whole interview, if not thinking about what it would be like to spend the summer on a yacht or in a flash villa then thinking that the only reason he was sitting opposite the Rivettis was because of what had happened to Giles. He was hesitant to step into a dead man's shoes, especially when that man had been murdered, and murdered in a way that kept haunting him. The cemetery. The knife. The blood.

When the interview ended he knew he hadn't made a good impression.

Mrs Rivetti had been the easier of the two. A bit over-anxious about her son's prospects (what parent wasn't?) but straightforward enough in her questions. Mr Rivetti, on the other hand, had unnerved him. When Simon was answering the mother's questions he had sensed her husband's scrutinising eyes. And when Mr Rivetti himself was speaking he felt even more under the microscope.

Mr Rivetti stressed the need for any tutor to be flexible and cooperative, willing to help in things beyond the merely academic, happy to involve himself fully in the life of the family, whether here in London or abroad. He then started to ask about Giles. How well had he known him? Had he spoken to him about his work for the family? Had he said anything about his summer abroad? Had he mentioned the other tutor who had worked for them?

That was when Simon had felt most uncomfortable.

It brought home to him something he had been aware of for many years – that when it came to him and Giles, people were always more interested in Giles. Even when he was dead.

But as he walked away from the Rivettis' house along Lonsdale Road towards Barnes, cutting through the path by the Swedish School towards the river and joining the towpath, he reminded himself that he hadn't ever really wanted the job, that there were other reasons why he had turned up to the interview.

He checked his watch. He had to hurry.

35

Milly Gardner was glad to have the car to herself. Driving Garibaldi around was all well and good but they said too much to each other sitting side by side. She knew too much about Alfie, Kay and Dom (or Fuckwit, as Garibaldi liked to call him). And Garibaldi knew too much about what went wrong with Kevin and her new boyfriend, Tim (or Smartarse, as Garibaldi liked to call him).

She couldn't stop herself seeing similarities between her boyfriend and her boss. They were both clever, and they both liked to show it. With Garibaldi it was often a case of coming up with a quote or a reference, something off-beat or unexpected that others wouldn't get, or at least not get immediately. It was different with Tim. He didn't go out of his way to show how much he knew but whenever she said something wrong or revealed her own ignorance he would make her aware of it.

That conversation in the car with Garibaldi about tutors and *My Fair Lady* had really got to her. She'd even looked it up on Wikipedia when she got home that evening to see what he was getting at. She'd also tried to put into practice his advice about saying what she really felt rather than what she felt she ought to, but so far the results hadn't been good. On each occasion Tim had looked at her as if she'd lost her senses. He'd not even bothered to correct her – just gave her a what-the-fuck look.

Maybe she should take Garibaldi up on his offer of lessons? On the other hand, maybe not. The more she found out about private tuition the less she liked it.

'And did you enjoy having him with you in the summer?'

Paolo nodded. 'It was good.'

'It must have been a terrible shock to you to find out he'd been murdered.'

Paolo nodded again. 'He was so nice. I don't understand it.'

'Tell me, Paolo, what was Giles helping you with in particular?'

'Everything I needed for my exam.'

'What exam is that?'

'The one I need to take to get into the school.'

'Which one's that?'

'St Mark's. It's difficult. A lot of people take it and not everyone gets in.'

Milly looked at the young boy in front of her. Poor kid. You could see the strain on his face, sense the pressure he was under.

'I see,' she said. 'And do you really want to go there?'

Paolo shrugged and gave a little smile. 'I'd like to. It would make my parents very happy.'

'But what about you?' said Milly.

Paolo tilted his head to one side with a thoughtful look, as if he wasn't in the habit of considering what he himself wanted.

'It would be good. My dad says it opens all kinds of doors

and sets you up for life. A good school and a good university. He says it's important.'

'And your mum. What does she say?'

Paolo laughed. 'She goes on about it even more.'

'So you've had to work very hard for this exam?'

'Yeah. I have.'

Gardner nodded, as if she knew all about working hard for exams. Paolo Rivetti wasn't to know that when it came to exams she'd never pushed herself. Maybe if she'd had a Maria Rivetti on her case it would have been different.

'And you had to work so hard that you even brought Giles with you on holiday in the summer. That must have been strange, having to study when you're on holiday.'

'Yeah, but it wasn't that much. Just a couple of hours a day and Giles made it fun. We hung out a lot as well doing, you know, fun things. It wasn't really like having a tutor out there.'

'So it didn't stop you having fun?'

Paolo smiled. 'Yeah we all had fun. Lots of fun. And there were parties.'

'Parties?'

Paolo paused. His face flushed. 'Nothing big,' he said. 'Just, you know, some evenings people came round.'

'I see.'

'Do you . . . ?' Paolo broke off and looked at Milly with large pleading eyes. 'Do you have any idea who did it?'

'That's what we're trying to find out, Paolo. That's why I'm asking you these questions. You never know what might be important, even the tiniest detail.'

The door opened and Maria Rivetti put her head round.

'Everything OK?' she said.

'Fine,' said Milly. 'I've just been asking Paolo a bit more about being tutored by Giles.'

Maria looked at her son. 'You liked him so much, didn't you?' She shook her head in disbelief. 'It's still so difficult to take in.'

'And I was asking Paolo about the summer.'

'The summer?' said Maria, as if she couldn't see the relevance.

'His time with you on holiday.'

'We didn't want Paolo to go off the boil in the holidays. It's so easy to do.'

'But Paolo tells me it wasn't all work and no play.'

Maria threw back her head and laughed. 'All work and no play? If only! Sometimes it's difficult to get any work out of him at all!'

Milly got up to leave. 'Still, it's nice to know you still had time to party.'

'Party?'

Maria Rivetti looked surprised, as if party was a word she didn't understand. She glanced at Paolo and then turned back. 'Of course,' she said. 'Just because we expected the kids to do some work each morning didn't mean we weren't going to have a good time. It was our holiday after all. You can't let this tutoring stuff get too much, can you?'

'Couldn't agree more,' said Milly, heading for the door. 'And, please, if anything occurs to you that you think might be relevant to Giles's murder, however small it is, please give us a call.'

'Of course,' said Maria Rivetti.

'And if I don't see you, Paolo, before you take your exam, good luck!'

'Thanks,' said Paolo.

'Thank you,' said Maria Rivetti, closing the door behind Gardner.

Milly walked to her car, wondering why she had such a

strong sense that there was more to the summer than they were revealing.

Maybe Garibaldi was right – everyone did have something to hide.

Chloe looked at DS Gardner. She seemed different without the other one, the one with the Italian name. More confident, perhaps. More probing. She was certainly managing to make her feel uncomfortable, but that was probably more to do with her own guilt than the detective's questioning.

'I'm sorry to have to ask you these questions again, Chloe,' said the detective, 'but we need to double-check a few things and we also need to know if anything else might have occurred to you.'

'No problem,' said Chloe, trying to give a confident smile. 'I quite understand.'

'And *has* anything occurred to you since we last spoke?'

Chloe furrowed her brow as if she was trying hard to think of something. The truth was nothing new had come to her in the interim. What she knew had been there all the time. The question was whether or not she should tell anyone.

'Look,' she said. 'when you came to see me I was in a real state of shock. I still am, but I've, you know, had a bit more time to reflect . . .'

She paused for a breath.

'Take your time,' said the woman.

'I think I referred to tough times. My mum walking out. Stuff like that. What I didn't say was . . .'

Should she do this? There was no point telling them about the problems she'd had ever since her mum walked out, about her trouble with boys or about the way she had fancied Giles something rotten and still swooned when she remembered some of the sessions with him and the things he said about poems. But surely there was some point telling them about her father and the row she overheard? Not that she thought he could have anything to do with the murder, but because she should, because in some strange kind of way she felt she owed it to Giles.

The woman was leaning forward, waiting for her to speak.

'Look,' said Chloe, 'I don't think this is really relevant, but I just feel I should tell you. Ever since my mum left, my dad, well he's behaved a bit strangely. Maybe it's just a reaction to mum, but he's been really over-protective when it comes to me and . . . and boys. It's like he's trying to, I don't know, control me. And the thing is, I think he thought there might be something going on between Giles and me.'

'And was there?'

'No. Nothing.'

'Did your dad say anything to you?

'Not to me, but he did to Giles. He thought I was out and he had this big row with him. It was terrible. He was accusing Giles of doing all sorts of things. I couldn't believe how angry he was.'

'Did Giles say anything to you about it?'

'No. I thought the next time I saw him he might have been a bit cooler towards me, but he didn't say anything.'

'And did you say anything to your Dad?'

Chloe shook her head. Did she really have to explain? Couldn't she see how bad her relationship with her father was?

'Look,' said Chloe. 'I'm sure he's got nothing at all to do with it and I didn't even think it was worth mentioning because it all seems so unlikely . . .'

'You've done the right thing,' said the woman, leaning forward. 'You really have.'

'Are you going to have to talk to my Dad about it?'

'We'll have to follow it up.'

'It's just . . . well things are pretty shit between us already and I don't want them to get worse.'

'Don't worry. We'll tread lightly.'

Milly flicked through her notebook as she sat opposite Freddie Barker. She'd already filled up a couple of pages with notes on Paolo Rivetti and Chloe Marsh.

'I won't keep you long, Freddie. I just want to go over a few things again to do with Giles Gallen.'

'Have you found out who killed him?'

'Not yet.' Remembering an old trick of Garibaldi's, Milly added, 'but we're very close.'

'I keep thinking about it,' said Freddie. 'It's horrible.'

'It is horrible, Freddie, but you must try not to think about it.'

'It's a bit difficult when you keep coming round asking questions, isn't it?'

Milly tried to ignore Freddie's tone, feeling waves of sympathy for anyone who had ever tried to teach him.

'This will be the last time. I promise.'

'OK,' sighed Freddie.

'I just want to know if there's anything you haven't told us. Anything at all you remember of Giles. Anything he did. Anything he said.'

Freddie scratched his head. 'I can't think of anything. He was great. I mean he . . .' He broke off and looked to one side. 'What was so good about him wasn't what he taught me. I mean, that was good and it really helped, but it was the other stuff that was the best.'

'The other stuff?'

'The chats we had. Football. Music. Films. And he used to give me things.'

'What kind of things?'

'He tried to give me books at first, you know, things he thought I might really like as opposed to the crap I have to do for GCSE. But he could see I wasn't really interested so he started to give me other stuff. CDs. DVDs. I mean, when I say "give" I mean lend. I gave them back. And he told me not to tell my mum because she'd think he was trying to distract me from school work. That's why I didn't tell you. I didn't want my mum to know about it.'

'Any particular CDs you remember him giving you? Any DVDs?'

Freddie thought for a moment and then came up with a few titles.

Gardner jotted them down, but not many of them rang a bell.

'There's one other thing I probably should have told you.'

'What's that?'

'It was the last time I saw him, that Saturday. When we'd finished and he was about to leave he said something. I probably should have told you . . .'

'What did he say, Freddie?'

'He said he would probably have to stop tutoring me.'

'Did he say why?'

Freddie shook his head. 'That's all he said. He said he hadn't said anything to my mum yet, but he was probably going to stop a lot of his tutoring.'

'Did he say when he was going to stop?'

'No, that's all he said. Like I said, I didn't really think anything of it at the time but it's funny, isn't it? I mean, he was right, wasn't he? He's not going to be coming round here again, is he?' Freddie sighed. 'And I never got the chance to return the CDs and stuff.'

He sniffed a couple of times and his lips tightened. He looked like he was fighting back tears. Under the teenage truculence Milly suddenly saw a vulnerable, frightened boy.

Jade Murray looked at the detective sitting opposite her and wondered what it would be like to do her job. How would it feel to go from house to house asking questions, to be constantly on the hunt for some truth that you felt people were keeping from you? Pretty frustrating, she reckoned, and maybe even close to boring. It seemed a long way from the exciting things she saw detectives do on telly, and she certainly wasn't tempted to add it to her list of possible careers.

This detective seemed a bit different without the other one, the one who freaked her out by quoting Larkin. She seemed more relaxed, more friendly, and it was maybe this friendliness that caught her out. Jade had been in two minds about whether or not to tell the police the whole truth. She knew Giles hadn't done anything wrong, certainly nothing illegal, but she also knew that the same couldn't be said about herself. When the detective started asking her questions, smiling and laughing at some of her answers, Jade felt like she was talking, if not to a friend, then at least to someone who was a sympathetic listener, and she let her defences down.

Before she knew it, she had told the detective what it was that Giles had mentioned and what she had done in response.

She didn't tell her the whole truth. She said she'd stopped some time ago, and wouldn't dream of doing it again, and she hoped this meant they wouldn't be interested in doing anything about it.

But she still felt uneasy when the detective left, and kept asking herself why she had told them.

Briony Ainsworth was having a bad day. School was shit. Home was shit. Life was shit. She'd spent the whole day wondering what it would be like to be at another school, to live in a home where your parents weren't cheating on each other and where the family wealth wasn't derived from, at best questionable, and at worst illegal, activities. She knew all about her parents' affairs and she was beginning to discover things about her father's clubs.

And to round off a brilliant day, she was now facing more questions from the police. At least it was only the woman this time, and she was being nice enough, but, even so, she was still finding the whole thing distressing.

Maybe that was why she decided to tell her what Giles Gallen had said the last time she had seen him, the Saturday before his murder.

'Look,' she said to the detective, who sat opposite her, pencil in hand, notebook open on her lap. 'I should probably have told you this when you first came to see me but I was all over the place, I mean really upset by the whole thing.'

The detective straightened in her seat, eyebrows raised.

'He said he had to stop seeing me.'

'You mean stop giving you lessons?'

'Yeah, don't worry. He wasn't seeing me in any other sense. There was nothing like that going on.'

'Did he say why?'

'No. All he said was that he was going to have to stop.'

'Did he tell your parents?'

'He said he was telling me first so that I knew.'

'And this was a week before he was murdered?'

'Exactly. I don't know if it's of any significance but I thought you should know.'

The detective scribbled in her notebook. 'Well, thanks for your time,' she said, getting up to leave.

'I'm sorry I didn't tell you. It's just that everything's been shit. I hope you understand.'

'Of course I do. You take it easy, OK? It must have all been a terrible shock.'

Briony looked at the detective leave. Life was still shit but she felt a little better for having told the truth.

36

Milly stood in reception at Hillside Academy, facing the woman who had just come through the door.

'I'm Miss Monroe, detective sergeant. I understand you need to see Devon Furlong.'

'That's right.'

'He's in lessons at the moment, but I'll go and get him out for you. Is this to do with the Giles Gallen murder?'

Milly looked at Miss Monroe. Was this Rachel? She knew Garibaldi's partner worked here and that she was Head of Sixth Form – he'd made quite a big thing about her promotion. Was this her?

Miss Monroe had gone before she had a chance to say anything. When she came back she took Milly into a room adjoining the reception area, where Devon was waiting, and shut the door behind her.

'I have a few more questions about Giles Gallen,' said Milly. 'When you met him outside school—'

'I didn't know that was wrong.'

'I'm not saying it was, Devon. I just want to know more about it.'

'What more do you want to know? We were talking about my essays and my application. You have to send work up before your interview and I was struggling. So that's what we spoke about.'

'Where did you meet?'

Devon shook his head in frustration. 'You say I didn't do anything wrong but you're making me feel pretty guilty about it. Feels a bit like a stop and search. I've had enough of them.'

'I'm sorry, Devon, but all we're trying to do is find out as much as we can about what Giles Gallen was up to.'

'Up to? There you go again. It's like he's guilty as well.'

'I've spoken to the other students Giles was teaching and a couple of them said that he told them he was going to stop. Did he say anything about that to you?'

'Stop? No. If anything it was the opposite. He offered to see me more often, said he'd see me any time. That's the thing. He really wanted to help me, like *really*. That's why it's so bad. He was making a big difference and I . . .' Devon paused for breath, gathering himself. 'I miss him, you know.'

'OK, Devon. I know how difficult it must be for you.'

Devon looked at her, wide-eyed. 'I'm not sure you do.'

'How many times did you see Giles outside school?'

'Three, maybe four. I can't remember.'

'Where did you meet him?'

Devon threw his arms wide, a footballer pleading his innocence after a foul. 'Does it matter?'

'You never know what might be important.'

'It was the *Big Toe*.'

'I see.'

Milly paused, looking over her notes. She sensed Devon shifting in his seat, as if something was troubling him. She looked at him and said nothing, allowing the silence to grow. It was a trick Garibaldi had taught her.

They looked at each other. Devon looked like he was about to speak but stopped himself several times.

Eventually he broke the silence. 'What's so sad is how nice he was, how kind. He was, you know, generous. Generous with everything.'

'When you say generous, do you mean he gave you things?'

'Yeah. He gave me books. They weren't his own, I could tell. They were brand new. He'd bought them and he gave them to me.'

'Books to help with your essays?'

'Yeah. And they did.'

'When did he give you these books?'

'In the café.'

'Did Giles ever give you anything else?'

'Like what?'

Gardner shrugged. 'Anything.'

Devon laughed. 'He lent me twenty quid once but I paid it back. It was just books. I can tell you what they are if you need to know.'

Gardner held up her hand. 'That's fine, Devon.' She got up from her chair. 'I'll let you get back to your lessons.'

'You any closer to getting who killed him?'

'Pretty close.'

Give the impression that you're nearer than you are. Another trick she'd picked up from Garibaldi.

Garibaldi looked at Simon Prest's hand as he held it out towards him.

'It's nothing, really nothing.'

Garibaldi nodded his agreement. The red mark on the palm was short and thin. It was only a graze.

'Did you get it seen to?'

Prest shook his head. 'No need. It was the shock more than this.'

'I know you've already given a statement, Simon, about the details of the assault, but there are a few questions I'd like to ask. Maybe you could take me through what happened.'

'Again? I've already—'

'Even so, Simon, I'd like to hear it.'

'OK.' He took a breath. 'I'd just been interviewed by the Rivettis.'

Garibaldi held up his hand. 'Sorry. Interviewed? What for?'

'As a replacement for Giles. As you can imagine, it was a pretty difficult position to be in, but anyway I thought I'd go back home the long way via the river to give me some time to think things over. I often walk by the river to think, I always have done. So I went along Lonsdale Road and then cut down to the river beside the Swedish School and I was walking along the towpath towards Barnes Bridge when it happened. It all happened so quickly, and I still can't believe it . . .'

Prest broke off and took another breath to steady himself.

'I was beside the nature reserve. I was lost in thought, going over what had happened to Giles. I didn't hear anything at all. And then an arm was round my neck, a leg in front of my shin, a shove in the back and I was on the ground with the weight of a body on top of me. I remember feeling my cheek against the gravel path. Then the point of a knife against my neck and a man's words.'

'What did he say?' said Garibaldi.

'"Remember Giles. Keep your mouth shut or you'll get the same".'

'And then what happened?'

'I figured that if I could wriggle enough to get him off me . . .'

'While he was holding a knife against your neck? Bit risky, wasn't it?'

'Yeah, but you don't think, do you? The adrenaline. He was heavy, but I managed to roll and roll him with me. I tried to hit the hand with the knife in.'

'Did you catch a glimpse of him? Did you see his face?'

'No. He had a hoodie pulled low. He may even have had a cap and a mask. It happened so quickly I didn't really get a look at him. Before I knew it he'd run off.'

'Did you run after him?'

Prest looked puzzled. 'No. I . . .'

'A fit lad like you?'

'He had a knife. I saw the blood on my hand. I was shocked. Look, Inspector, what the fuck's going on? Giles killed and then Emily and Sam. And now this. What do Forum say about it all?'

'They're worried, obviously, but they see no reason why they would be targeted like this.'

'But that's the link! That's what connects it all!'

'Tell me again, Simon, where you had been before you were attacked.'

'At the Rivettis' . . . but, surely not. That can't be . . .'

'I have no idea, but we need to consider all possibilities.'

'I never thought . . . I mean it never occurred to me.'

'Tell me, Simon, why do you think you were told to keep your mouth shut?'

'I have no idea! If I knew anything relevant to Giles's murder I'd have already told you. I think the question, and the thing I'm worried about, is whether I'm safe. If this is the bloke who killed Giles . . .'

'I'll ask you again, do you know of anything Giles Gallen was doing that might have got him into trouble?'

'I've told you. Nothing. Giles? He's not that sort.'

'And what sort would that be?'

'The sort to get in trouble. I mean he's . . .' Prest gave his head a series of short shakes. 'No way. Not Giles. He's clean. Squeaky clean.'

Garibaldi got up to leave. 'In my experience, they can often be the worst. If there's anything more you can think of . . .'

'Of course.'

Simon Prest opened his palm and looked at the thin red graze running down its centre. He turned to Garibaldi, a young boy again, fear in his eyes.

'How's this all going to end?' he said.

'We're getting there,' said Garibaldi, knowing as he stepped out into the rain that this was far from the truth.

As he unlocked his bike from the Nassau Road railings, his phone rang.

He didn't recognise the number.

'DI Garibaldi.'

'Terrell Furlong here. I've found out something you might find interesting.'

'What is it?'

'Look, if it's OK with you I'd rather not talk on the phone. Can you come to me?'

'Sure.'

'I'm in the centre.'

37

DCI Deighton looked at the team over the reading glasses perched on her nose. Her hair, touched with grey, was cut short. Her clothes were business-like: black trousers, cream blouse, linen jacket. Very much the headmistress. Very much the woman of secrets. Everyone speculated about her private life, especially after a few pints in the Duke's Head, but no-one had come close to discovering the truth. The assumption was that she went home to a woman when she finished her shifts, but no-one had yet furnished the evidence.

It was only Garibaldi who knew.

'Thanks to some sterling work from DS Gardner,' said Deighton, 'we have some updates on the kids Giles Gallen was tutoring. Gallen told two of his students – Freddie Barker and Briony Ainsworth – that he'd be stopping giving them lessons. No reason given and he told the kids but not the parents. It also appears he was in the habit of giving things to some of his students. CDs and DVDs to Freddie Barker – these were loans. And books to Devon Furlong. These weren't loans – he bought them for him. And, oddly, while he told some of the kids he was stopping, he told Devon he'd be prepared to see him more often. A couple of other things. It seems that Chloe Marsh's dad had a huge row with Gallen, accusing him of taking advantage of his daughter. And it also seems that when Gallen first tutored Jade Murray and they spoke about her difficulties focusing and concentrating, Gallen mentioned that some of his friends at uni took Ritalin. And that's what Jade Murray did. No evidence at all that Gallen provided it. According to Jade, he just mentioned it in passing. She did the rest and claims to have stopped after trying it for a couple of weeks. So there's plenty to follow up there. Any questions?'

Garibaldi looked at Gardner. She kept her hand down.

'OK. And we've had another attack on a Forum tutor – Simon Prest. The same MO, the same threat. Just as with Emily and Sam, a suggestion that they might know something which could be connected to Gallen's murder and telling them to keep their mouths shut. What connects these attacks and what connects the attacks to the murder seems to be Forum.'

'You're right,' said Garibaldi. 'Forum's an obvious link. But there's another one. The Rivettis. Gallen worked for the Rivettis. He was murdered. Sam Bannister worked for the Rivettis. She was attacked and threatened.'

'But Emily Francis didn't work for them,' said Gardner, 'and she was attacked.'

'And what about the latest attack?' said Deighton. 'Simon Prest worked for Forum but he didn't work for the Rivettis.'

'OK,' said Garibaldi, 'but where had he been before he was attacked? In the Rivettis' house being interviewed as a possible replacement for Gallen.'

Garibaldi listened to the silence. He wasn't sure where his logic was taking him but he was enjoying the bafflement.

'I don't get where you're going,' said Deighton.

'The point is they all had Rivetti connections. And the thing about Emily Francis is that she might not have worked for the Rivettis, but we do know that she had sex with Giles Gallen shortly before he was murdered. Well, when I say sex . . . Anyway, it could be that Gallen told her something, something that someone else didn't want her to reveal.'

'What?' said Gardner. 'He told her when they were having sex, or rather . . . ?'

'That's not what I'm saying. Someone could have found out that they were close and—'

'But Emily says it was a one-off. Spur of the moment.'

'All I'm saying is there's a Rivetti connection as well as a Forum connection, and we need to look at it. But I've got something else.' He cleared his throat. 'I've just been to see Terrell Furlong, Devon's brother. He got in touch because he heard something. Nothing definite, but enough for him to let us know. It appears that when Gallen met Devon for coffee it didn't go unnoticed. It was in a café close to the estate and apparently a kid works there and saw them each time. Apparently, this kid saw Gallen hand over a package to Furlong. Furlong didn't open it, he just took it. This kid also saw Gallen give Furlong money. And this kid's brother is a big figure up there. Terrell knows him and knows what he's into.'

'What are you suggesting?' said Deighton.

'I'm not suggesting anything,' said Garibaldi. 'No assumption. I'm not feeding any . . . narrative.'

'So what do we make of the fact that they were seen together?' said Deighton.

'I don't know,' said Garibaldi, 'but Terrell Furlong knows his way around that place and he thought it was significant enough to tell us. Look, Terrell isn't going to grass. He may be a reformed church-goer. He may be bad-boy-turned-do-gooder, but he knows the rules and he's not going to take any risks like that.'

'Why's it such a big thing,' said Gardner, 'for a kid like Devon to have a coffee with someone like Giles Gallen?'

'I'm not saying it necessarily is,' said Garibaldi. 'All I'm saying is that if Terrell Furlong thinks it's worth mentioning then we need to take it seriously.'

'OK,' said Deighton. 'Thanks.' She looked at the sheet of paper in her hand. 'We now have the forensics report on the clothing of Emily Francis and Sam Bannister. The DNA traces found on both are the same. We don't yet know whose they are, but we know they're from a man. We can assume it was the same man who attacked Francis and Bannister, but those traces don't match the DNA found on Gallen's body – so it looks like whoever attacked them didn't kill Gallen. And there's no match for them on the national database.'

'And Simon Prest's clothing?' said Garibaldi.

'We're waiting.'

'Also,' said DC McLean, 'Simon Mulholland's footprints have been confirmed as some of those at the murder scene.'

'One other thing,' said DC Hodson, 'We've tried to get more on one of the parents of a kid Gallen was tutoring. Vince Ainsworth, Briony's dad. Runs a string of clubs and they were investigated a few years ago as a possible front for drugs and prostitution. Nothing stuck, but that doesn't mean nothing was going on.'

'And' said DC McLean, 'it seems that Jade Murray's mum, Ginny Murray, works for Vince. No idea whether that's significant but Jade and Hilary Ainsworth are old friends.'

Garibaldi looked at McLean and Hodson. As soon as one of the DCs spoke, the other spoke as well. He couldn't work out whether it was competition or mutual dependency.

'We've been through Gallen's phone calls. Nothing leaps out. But we did pick up on one thing. The last call Gallen received on the night he was murdered was at 10.35, shortly after he left the Red Lion. And it was from Simon Prest. It may be nothing, but it seems a bit odd, given that Prest had just been with him in the pub. We need to ask him.'

'OK, 'said Deighton. 'Let's get on it. The thing is—'

She turned to the board and pointed at the picture of Giles Gallen.

'We're still no closer to his killer, are we?'

She pointed at the list of names beneath it – Gallen's Forum students, their parents, the Forum tutors who had been attacked.

'The question is where, amongst this lot, do we find him?'

'The Rivettis are hiding something,' said Garibaldi. 'I know it.'

'What is it?' said Deighton.

'I don't know. It's hidden.'

Deighton gave Garibaldi a stare. 'Well, maybe you should get over there and find out what it is. Do Forum know about the Prest attack yet?'

Garibaldi shook his head.

'They need to know, preferably before they read it in the press. OK?'

'Am I missing something?' DS Gardner took a right at the end of Putney Bridge and headed up the Lower Richmond Road towards Barnes. 'We don't know why Gallen was murdered, but we do know that three tutors have been attacked and threatened, told to remember what happened to him and to keep their mouths shut. What links them all? You say the Rivettis but that doesn't cover them all. Emily Francis didn't work for them and she denies that

Giles told her anything. And Simon Prest had only just been interviewed by the Rivettis for a job. That's moving pretty quickly isn't it? How would the attacker know that and what could Simon possibly know about the Rivettis? He'd only just met them.'

Gardner stopped, waiting for Garibaldi to respond.

'Go on,' said Garibaldi, interested to see where she was heading.

'So we're back to the obvious link which is Forum Tutors. All four worked for Forum. So, yeah, Felicia and Roddy are right. They *are* being targeted. Someone's out to get them.'

'OK,' said Garibaldi. 'But what are they being told to keep quiet about? They all say they don't know anything that anyone would threaten them about.'

'Exactly,' said Gardner. 'There's one possibility, though, which we need to consider.'

'What's that?'

'They could all be lying. Every one of them.'

Garibaldi nodded his approval. Assume nothing.

'You're right,' he said. 'They could all be lying.'

'Maybe we need to talk to them again. Bring them in. Raise the stakes.'

'We could,' said Garibaldi, 'but it'll bring the same result unless we've got something new to present them with.'

'We could always make something up.'

'Completely unethical,' he said, 'But out of interest what kind of thing did you have in mind?'

'You could always say one of the others had coughed up, confessed to what he knew.'

'We can't do that. Or if we did we'd have to be pretty careful how we worded it. Something like "what if we told you someone's already told us who the killer is? Would that help you tell us the truth?"'

'How's that different?'

'It's hypothetical. It's a what if.'

Gardner nodded, taking it in.

'But there's another question we haven't answered,' said Garibaldi.

'What's that?'

'Why was Gallen killed and why were the others only threatened?'

'I don't know, 'said Gardner, 'maybe it's a case of to kill one Forum Tutor may be regarded as misfortune. To kill two looks like . . .'

Garibaldi laughed.

'And remember,' said Gardner, 'it looks like it wasn't the killer behind the attacks.'

They drove on in silence for a minute or two.

Garibaldi broke the silence. 'Milly,' he said, 'I've got a confession to make.'

'Yeah?' Gardner sounded cautious, worried about what was about to be revealed.

'Yeah. I keep thinking of Devon Furlong.'

'What's wrong with that?'

'I keep thinking of him in a way I shouldn't be. It's too easy. Easier than it is to look at a load of middle-class white kids tutoring other middle-class white kids.'

'You're not alone.'

'That doesn't make me feel any better.'

'Everyone's thinking it. Gallen goes up there to help Devon Furlong, makes the mistake of seeing him outside school because he's a nice guy and wants to help and he's seen by someone giving Furlong a package, giving him money. What's he seen as? An intruder? A threat?'

'Exactly. And then you think what they might do if . . .'

'They?'

Garibaldi kicked himself. Gardner was right. Who were *they?* He was as bad as the rest of them.

'OK,' he said, 'but it's a big leap from that to thinking someone came down to Barnes to kill him.'

'I don't know. Maybe someone warned him and he ignored the warning.'

'What would they warn him about?'

'Maybe someone thought Gallen was doing more than giving Devon extra English lessons, thought something else was going on.'

'Yeah, but what?'

Gardner pulled up opposite Peas in a Pod in Church Road. They climbed out and walked down Glebe Road to the Forum offices.

As they did Garibaldi's phone rang.

Alfie.

'I'm going to have to take this, Milly.'

'OK. I'll wait in the car.'

Garibaldi turned into the Crescent and walked towards the pond.

'Alfie. Hi.'

'Hi, Dad. How's things?'

He sounded different. Garibaldi sensed something had happened. 'I'm fine. Look, sorry I haven't fixed a date to come up yet. I've been busy.'

'A case?'

'Yeah, a case. Anyway, haven't spoken since that party. How was it?'

'The party? It was OK.'

Garibaldi's mind was already working hard, trying to find the reason for the call.

'How's the work going?'

A short silence. Something was definitely up.

'Look, the reason I'm ringing is . . .'

Garibaldi braced himself for the next chapter in his son's book of social reinvention, the latest step in his journey away from what he used to be. Or maybe for something worse. Something about Fuckwit Dom, perhaps. Something about plans for internships in banks or consultancies. Or maybe Alfie's lack of work had caught up with him and he was being threatened with expulsion or whatever fancy-pants name they had for such a thing at Oxford.

All these thoughts in that brief silence.

'Things have changed,' said Alfie.

Garibaldi steadied himself.

'And you know I said I couldn't make the Fulham game tonight—'

The game. He'd completely forgotten about it.

'Look, don't worry about it, it's OK.'

'The thing is I can come now after all.'

Garibaldi's heart fluttered.

'I thought you had a party to go to.'

'I did, but I'm not going anymore.'

Something had happened. Alfie was a little boy again, working up the courage to tell.

'I see,' said Garibaldi. 'Has something . . . ?'

His first thought was the girlfriend. Last year's break-up with the one from school had been bad enough. Had it happened again?

'We can talk tonight, Dad. The thing is I'm all right, but I'd really like to come down for the Fulham game. Maybe stay the night and come back early tomorrow. Just wanted to check it was OK by you.'

OK by him? Garibaldi couldn't express how OK by him it was.

'That's great, Alfie. See you later. Where shall we meet? The Bush?'

Garibaldi was already juggling shifts and commitments, desperate to clear the space to be at Loftus Road.

'Yeah. Sounds good.'

'Seven?'

'Yeah, I should make seven.'

'Great. See you later.'

Garibaldi hung up and did a little jig. The swans on Barnes Pond looked at him, unmoved.

38

Evening Standard

TUTOR ATTACKS CONTINUE

Police yesterday warned the capital's private tutors to be extra vigilant after another tutor was attacked and threatened with a knife. The assault took place on the towpath in Barnes and police are connecting it to a recent series of similar attacks on tutors and to the murder of Giles Gallen, found stabbed in Barnes Old Cemetery last Saturday.

Sources suggest that the recent victim worked for Forum Tutors, the agency that employed both Gallen and the other assault victims. Felicia and Roddy Ireland, the owners of Forum, were unavailable for comment but today issued a statement. 'We were absolutely devastated to hear of the murder of Giles Gallen and are horrified by the assaults on our tutors. Their safety is our priority and we are issuing guidelines to them all about the need for care and watchfulness.'

DCI Karen Deighton of the Metropolitan Police, in charge of the murder investigation, said, 'We are shocked by the series of attacks and believe they may be linked to the murder of Giles Gallen. We are pursuing several lines of enquiry but urge anyone who has any information which they think may be of relevance to get in touch on 02088789472.

When asked whether the murder and attacks are specifically linked to Forum Tutors DCI Deighton said, 'We are in regular contact with the agency but are keeping an open mind.'

Emily Francis is one of those assaulted. She recently wrote of her experience in the *Standard* and yesterday said that 'my fears have been confirmed. There is something very sinister going on and I would urge anyone working as a tutor, in particular those working for Forum, to be extra vigilant and avoid being by themselves, especially at night.'

Roddy Ireland threw the paper onto the desk with a violent flick of the wrist and glared at Garibaldi and Gardner.

'My question is what the *fuck* are you doing about it?'

'We're pursuing several—'

'Don't give me your several lines of enquiry bullshit! One of our tutors was murdered and three have been attacked. If ever there was any doubt that someone is after Forum Tutors then that doubt has gone. Have you got *nowhere* in your investigation?'

Felicia Ireland placed a restraining hand on her husband's arm.

'The thing is,' she said, keeping her voice low and calm to

offset her husband's, 'we're very worried. Our first concern is our tutors but you have to realise that in a business such as ours there are a lot of people who are being affected by what's going on. There are the kids we teach of course but there are also the parents. And parents talk. My God do they talk. And this—' she reached for the *Standard* '—doesn't help.'

'And as for that bitch Emily Francis,' said Roddy. 'She can't stop herself talking to the press, can she? Writes a couple of articles and then gives them a quote warning all Forum tutors! I don't believe it!'

'We're suffering,' said Felicia. 'At first clients were supportive when they heard the news about poor Giles. But now they're worried. They don't want their kids' tutors attacked. They don't want their kids' tutors murdered.'

'There's no evidence to suggest that they will be murdered,' said Garibaldi. 'These were threats.'

'Serious fucking threats, though,' said Roddy. 'And there's already been one murder. What more evidence do you need?' He looked aggressively at Garibaldi and Gardner. 'And tell me, what exactly *are* your lines of enquiry? How close are you to finding Gallen's killer and the man behind these attacks?'

'I'm afraid we can't answer that,' said Garibaldi, 'the details of an ongoing murder investigation have to remain confidential.'

'Very convenient.'

'But,' added Garibaldi, 'we are of course looking closely at Giles's activities and that means we have been looking closely at those he tutored. And their families.'

Roddy pointed at the paper on the desk. 'And what have you found out?'

Felicia waved a restraining hand in front of her husband. 'Maybe you should calm down, dear.'

'What do you mean? All I'm asking is a perfectly reasonable question—'

'Look,' said Garibaldi, 'Given the way the press works and especially given the way people talk and gossip it's extremely unlikely that you'll be out of the spotlight for some time. I think you should prepare yourself for that.'

'Maybe we should prepare another statement,' said Felicia.

Roddy looked at his wife. His face was red and puffed. 'Someone's out to ruin us, aren't they? And whoever it is, they're doing a fucking good job!'

'As I was saying, Mr Ireland, we've been speaking to the kids Gallen was tutoring. We've been talking to all his Forum pupils here in West London and also in the White City.'

'White City? We don't have any clients in the White City.'

'He did some pro bono work, remember? Hillside Academy and one of the kids he was helping lives in White City.'

'White City?' said Roddy, as if the words had triggered something significant. 'A boy, was it? And this boy . . . what was he like?'

'I think what Roddy means,' said Felicia, 'Is that—'

'I know what I mean,' said Roddy. 'I'm asking what the boy was like.'

Garibaldi knew exactly what Roddy Ireland wanted to know, but he wasn't prepared to tell him. 'If you think we should be looking in the direction of Hillside Academy and the White City more than in the direction of Barnes because this sort of thing simply doesn't happen here, may I point out that—'

'I'm not saying that. I'm asking a simple question.'

'OK,' said Garibaldi, 'if you're suggesting that a high-achieving student aiming for Cambridge is likely, simply because of where he lives, his background, to be involved in those activities, then I'm afraid I have to put you right.'

'Go on then, put me right! So much for pro fucking bono, eh? Look where it gets you!'

'You don't mean that, Roddy,' said Felicia. She turned to Garibaldi and Gardner. 'He doesn't mean it. We're proud of it. Tutors like Giles were making a difference up there. A real difference. All we want is something that will help us understand what's going on, something to give us the hope that all this will stop.'

'And all I want to say to you,' said Roddy, 'is that you don't have to be Inspector Fucking Morse to work out that someone is after Forum. We're under threat. What are we expected to do? Our tutors need to get out and tutor. They need to move about, travel across London. We can't just stop everything, shut down our business. Maybe that's what they want us to do. Well, if it is they're going to be disappointed.'

'I understand, Mr Ireland,' said Garibaldi.

'Do you? I'm not sure you do. Well let's not keep you. I'm sure you've got plenty of lines of enquiry you need to explore.'

'Before we go,' said Garibaldi, 'are you absolutely sure you have no idea of anything Giles may have been up to that would make someone want to murder him?'

'We've already told you, Inspector. What's more we have no idea why, since his murder, three of our tutors have been attacked.'

'And if your theory is right and whoever's behind all this is after you, after Forum, can you think of any reason why they might be?'

'Of course not! That's the whole point. That's why we're so distressed. I can't think of any reason in the world!'

Roddy Ireland's face had turned purple. His wife looked at him and as she did Garibaldi caught a fleeting expression in her face. It showed fear and worry but he thought it showed something else as well – a suspicion that there might, despite her husband's claims, be some kind of motive for targeting Forum.

Garibaldi had no idea whether his instincts were right, but he left the Glebe Road house unconvinced by Roddy Ireland's protestations of innocence.

39

The Bush Theatre bar was busy. Most of the customers were there for that evening's production of *Taking the Knee* but Garibaldi's mind was on a different kind of drama. A few hundred yards further down the Uxbridge Road and under a different kind of lights, QPR and Fulham were about to face each other in a midweek clash.

He sat at a corner table, tuning out the pretentious pre-show chat of the committed theatregoers and picking up on the banter of the pre-game fans, colours and scarves hidden to avoid being denied entry or ejected from the premises for being the wrong sort. Garibaldi was no enemy of the theatre but its smugness got to him – not so much the smugness of theatre itself, but the smugness of those who went.

Smug was not a word ever applied to QPR fans.

Garibaldi nursed his pint and tried to read his book but it was difficult to concentrate. It was nothing to do with the book. And nothing to do with where he was or with pre-match excitement.

It was all to do with Alfie.

All afternoon he'd been unable to focus on the Gallen case. Sitting at his desk, scrolling through statements and reports all he could think about was seeing Alfie, wondering what had led to his change of mind.

Their greeting hug was closer and tighter than usual. Garibaldi could sense something was up.

'Seen the team?' he said.

'Yeah,' said Alfie. 'Three at the back again.'

'Yeah, they never learn, do they? Time for a drink?'

'Sure.'

When Garibaldi brought the drinks back to the table Alfie took his glass and raised it. 'Cheers!'

'Cheers.'

Alfie took a couple of gulps, licked his lips and looked around the bar.

'I expect you want to know why I can make the game after all,' he said, turning back.

'Don't feel you have to tell me. If you—'

'I'm not sure where to start, but the thing is there's this girl . . .'

Garibaldi nodded. *Cherchez la femme*. As he suspected.

'Lily. She's in this big social group and there's been a lot of partying and, yeah, a lot of money. I guess. I didn't realise at first how much I was getting through.'

The bank of Fuckwit Dom, no doubt.

'At first we were just friends. You know, part of the whirl, having a good time with everyone else. And, yeah, I was probably doing too much of it. Not enough work etcetera. Then it started to get a bit more serious and we started going out together.'

Garibaldi gave another I'm-listening-and-I-understand nod.

Alfie reached for his beer and looked towards the bar before taking a couple of gulps. It was as if he was bracing himself.

'Look, Dad, I'm OK. You don't need to worry about me or anything. It's just that I think I . . . I think I might have lost my way a bit.'

He'd lost his way. What Garibaldi had wanted to hear him say for months. Any minute now Alfie would say that he thought Dom was a prick and he could die a happy man.

'The truth is the Lily thing's over. We had a big row, a horrible row. So I obviously wasn't going to go to this dinner party. It was her friends. The crowd. And I thought, fuck it, why was I thinking of doing it anyway, even when I was going out with her? Whatever made me think I should do that kind of thing rather than come down to see the R's.'

Garibaldi swallowed. Christmas had come early.

'I had no idea,' he said.

'No idea about what?'

'Any of it. I mean I knew you were doing a fair bit of . . . socialising, but I didn't know about your girlfriend and, obviously, I didn't know you'd split. When you came down for that party everything seemed great . . .'

Though it hadn't. He could still remember what he felt as he saw Alfie head off to the party in his DJ. *Frankenstein*. *Great Expectations*.

'That party was the start of it,' said Alfie. 'I mean, it was huge. Lily's friend Rosie's twenty-first at this massive place in Hampstead. And when I say massive I mean . . . it was like something out of *The Great Gatsby*. And I was standing there thinking what the fuck am I doing. All these people and there were a *lot* of people. Monied. Entitled. Privileged. I just sort of had this moment and that's when we had our first row. It seemed nothing at the time. I was in a group of people from Oxford, people Lily knew from school and stuff and people I'd hung out with quite a bit. Then Lily went off because her friend was upset about something to do with her sister and when she came back she seemed in a strange mood and I asked her what was up and she told me. And I can't remember what happened or what I said but she snapped. "You don't understand," she said. "People like you just don't understand." I could see she was upset and I didn't want to push it but "people like you"? I couldn't let it go. So I asked her what she meant and she wouldn't say. But it stayed with me and when we were back in Oxford I asked her again. And all she said was "can't you see how different we are?" And, yeah, in that moment I could. And I could see how different I was from everyone I'd been hanging out with, how I'd sort of lost myself. I don't know how I hadn't realised it before and I know what you think, Dad. You think it all started when I changed school. Maybe it did. Who knows what would have happened, where I would have ended up if I'd stayed put? But the thing is I can't change where I am. All I can do is kind of start again, make the most of what's left. Realise I've made some mistakes recently. And get back to Loftus Road.'

Garibaldi felt for Alfie but he also felt for himself. This was what he had wanted for some time – to get his son back, to reclaim him.

Yet throughout Alfie's confession his mind had been mulling over something else, a possibility that was gnawing away at him and wouldn't stop.

Garibaldi looked at his watch. 'Right,' he said standing up and draining his pint, 'we'd better get going. Look, I'm so pleased you've told me this. I hadn't wanted to say anything, but I was concerned, mainly because I didn't want to see you get hurt.'

'I can't say I'm not hurt,' said Alfie. 'But it's good to have told you. The thing is you start doing something and you get sucked in and because you're with a load of people who all think what they're doing is perfectly normal you start to think it's normal yourself. You just can't see it. I should never have fallen in with that . . . that lot. And, as I say, it was when I was at this ridiculous party that I realised it. Maybe if Lily's friend hadn't been upset . . .'

Something suddenly clicked. A girl attacked while walking back from her sister's twenty-first in Hampstead. The dates tallied.

'Alfie.' Garibaldi couldn't stop himself. 'This is a complete longshot but I have to ask. Is Lily's friend's sister called Sam?'

'Sam? Yeah. How do you know that?'

'And is Sam's surname Bannister?'

'Yeah. I was going to tell you. That's why it was such a massive thing. It was at Harry Bannister's house. I had no idea Lily's friend was his daughter and I got a big shock when I found out. I mean, what a prat!'

'And did Lily say what was upsetting her friend's sister?'

Alfie nodded. 'Yeah, she did. She swore me to secrecy, but you know what? "People like me"? Fuck it. I might as well tell you. She said it was all to do with the summer when she was working as a tutor in Italy. Something had happened.'

'Did she say what?'

'No, but she said she was worried that all kinds of shit had been going on because of it. She was worried something might happen to her.'

As they walked down the Uxbridge Road joining the hooped blue and white shirts of QPR and the white ones of Fulham, Garibaldi's mind whirred with narratives.

40

Garibaldi stood onstage in the centre circle at Loftus Road. Beside him was Emmylou Harris and in his hands was a guitar. He looked down at it, baffled. Emmylou smiled, leaned towards him and mouthed something Garibaldi couldn't decipher. He raised his eyebrows.

Emmylou leaned in further and put her mouth to his ear. 'People Like Us,' she said. 'You know it?'

People Like Us? Garibaldi had never heard of it. He shook his head. Emmylou gave him the chords but they were just letters to him – he had no idea how to play them.

He looked down at his hands on the guitar. They were frozen, unable to move.

Emmylou nodded and counted him in. 'One, two, three . . .'

The Loftus Road tannoy system blasted out a loud ring. Emmylou looked at him in a panic.

'It's all right,' said Garibaldi. 'We're OK. People like us are OK.'

The ringing continued, loud in Garibaldi's ears.

He opened his eyes, turned his head and picked up the phone.

'Garibaldi.'

'DI Garibaldi? It's Roddy Ireland. Something's happened.'

'What is it?'

'I've been assaulted.'

Garibaldi wiped his eyes and looked at the clock. He'd slept in. A 2–0 win over Fulham and more beers with Alfie in the pub afterwards . . .

'Are you OK?'

'No, I'm not OK. I've been assaulted. At knifepoint.'

'Are you injured?'

'A cut, but it's nothing. Could have been worse, so much worse.'

'When did this happen?'

'Last night when I was out for a walk. I would have rung you then but I thought it was too late.'

'OK. I'm on my way round.'

Felicia Ireland sat beside her husband on the sofa, her hand clasping his. Roddy looked tense, his brow furrowed, the corners of his tight-lipped mouth turned down in a grim frown. His hand touched the white bandage on the side of his neck.

'I don't believe it,' said Roddy. 'I really don't believe it.'

Garibaldi took out his notebook. 'You'll need to come in and give a statement, Mr Ireland, but maybe you could take me through what happened.'

'It was last night at about eleven, I think. I'd just taken Hector out.'

'Hector?'

'Our dog. I take him out last thing at night so he can relieve himself. Last night I got back in and I was still feeling a bit restless, going over everything that had happened, so thought I'd go out for another walk by myself to clear my head. So I set out as I said at about eleven.'

'Where did you go?'

'I headed to the pond. There were a few people about, but not many. A few youngsters on the benches, some other late-night dog-walkers. And it was when I was heading back via the common and I came to the bridge over Beverley Brook that I got the sense I was being followed. I could hear steps behind me. Some way off at first but they grew closer. I thought someone wanted to overtake me so when we got close to this little bridge – which as you know is only wide enough for one person – I turned round to see if he wanted to pass.'

'He? You knew it was a man at this stage?'

'Not at this stage, no. But I did pretty soon after.'

'So you saw what this man looked like?'

Roddy shook his head. 'No. He had a hoodie pulled over his head and when he saw me turn he turned his head away. In the brief flash I got of him it looked like he might have had a mask or a scarf over his face. It was all very quick, I didn't see much.'

'So you turned round. Then what happened?'

'I walked over the bridge and I heard the steps breaking into a run and the next thing I know I've got an arm round my neck and I'm being dragged down through the bushes and I've been shoved on my front right by the brook and there's a body pinning me down. There's a weight on my back and I can't move and there's a hand round my mouth and . . .'

Roddy stopped and took a breath to calm himself.

'I'm sorry, just telling it to you brings it back and . . .'

Felicia gave his hand a squeeze.

'Take your time, Mr Ireland,' said Garibaldi. 'I know this must be painful for you, but it's important we get every detail.'

Roddy sighed. 'OK, so one hand was round my mouth, then I felt something against my neck. Something sharp. And the bloke said, "Feel this? It's a knife and I'm happy to use it. Understand? So listen. Remember what happened to Giles? Keep your mouth shut. One step out of line and you'll get this." And then I don't know where I got the strength from but I wriggled and pushed up against him and I managed to get him off – I don't know how – and I tried to hit him with my hand and that's when he did this—'

Roddy pointed to the bandage on his neck.

'Looks pretty bad.'

'It's nothing. Just a scratch.'

'Can I see?'

'Sure.' Roddy undid the bandage.

Garibaldi leaned close. It was a small cut, one or two inches long. It didn't look too deep.

'Did you get anyone to look at it?'

'Felicia cleaned it and dressed it last night. Good to have a wife who's done a first aid course.'

'You should get it checked out.'

'I'll see if I can see a nurse at the GP today,' said Roddy. 'It's certainly not a case of A and E.'

'Can we go back over what this man said,' said Garibaldi. '"One step out of line". Were those his exact words?'

'Absolutely.'

'And tell me, Mr Ireland, how long did the struggle last, would you say?'

'I can't be exact. Seemed to go on forever.'

'What clothes were you wearing?'

'I'm wearing them, I'm afraid. I'm still shocked, couldn't be bothered to find anything else this morning. And a jacket, I had a jacket on.'

'I'd like to take those clothes away now, Mr Ireland. DNA.'

Roddy looked momentarily baffled. 'It has to be the same man.'

'It may very well be, but we need all the evidence we can get.'

Felicia let go of Roddy's hand. 'Detective Inspector, this is extremely serious. If there was any doubt that Forum Tutors is being targeted, it's gone. And my question is, what should we do to protect ourselves and more importantly what are you going to do to protect us?'

'I advise caution,' said Garibaldi. 'That applies to both of you and to all your tutors.'

'Is that it?' said Felicia. 'Is that all we get?'

'We're doing all we can, Mrs Ireland. Believe me.' Garibaldi looked at Roddy. 'Your clothes?'

Roddy had the look of a reluctant schoolboy being told to change for swimming.

He left the room leaving Garibaldi to his wife's glare and frosty silence.

41

Garibaldi sat at his desk reading through the case notes – statements, reports, interviews, forensics. It was a matter of wood and trees. The more he looked at the details the less he saw of the overall picture.

One Forum tutor murdered. Three Forum tutors attacked. The Forum owner attacked. All told to keep their mouths shut and remember what happened to Giles Gallen.

Garibaldi leaned back, stretched and yawned.

'Boss?'

He straightened up. Gardner was standing in front of his desk, holding a sheet of paper.

'I've found something strange. Or rather I haven't found something and I'm not sure what it means.'

'What is it?'

'It's Sam Bannister. She stopped working for the Rivettis, right? And she also stopped working for Forum.'

'That's right. Got a job in publishing. Sorry, *digital* publishing.'

'Exactly. Well, when you asked her who it was for she said Compass Publishing. I wrote it down, put it in my notes. It's on file. The thing is I've been trying to find them but I can't. Compass Publishing. There's no trace. You'd have thought that a digital publishing firm would have some kind of digital presence but no, there's nothing.'

'But why would she lie? Why would she say she had a job with a firm that doesn't exist?'

'Maybe she doesn't have a job at all.'

'Then why would she pretend she has?'

Gardner nodded. She'd clearly thought this through. 'The only reason I can think of is that she left the Rivettis for some other reason but didn't want anyone to know. The Rivettis were told the same – she'd got a job in digital publishing. But if that's not the case, why did she stop? She stopped for the Rivettis and she stopped tutoring altogether. The question is if there's no job at Compass Publishing because there's no Compass Publishing, then why did she leave?'

'She could have made a mistake,' he said. 'Could have got the name wrong.'

'You don't forget the name of the firm you've just started working for, do you?'

'Maybe it's something close to Compass and it came out wrong.'

'Close to Compass? Give me an example.'

Gardner was right. They needed to talk to Sam Bannister.

But first Garibaldi needed to do some Googling.

Garibaldi wriggled in the uncomfortable armchair.

'We have a few more questions to ask you, Sam.'

Sam Bannister gave an if-you-must shrug. 'I can't believe there's anything more for me to tell you.'

'Let's see, shall we?'

Garibaldi took out his notebook and flicked through some pages, making a show of close consultation.

'Can we go back to the night of your assault, Sam. You were on your way from your sister's twenty-first at your parents' house in Hampstead. Is that correct?'

'That's right.'

'That would be your sister Rosie?'

Garibaldi flicked over a couple of pages of his notebook, paused, then flicked over a couple more. He looked up at Sam and held her gaze for a few seconds before speaking. Sam turned away.

'Sam, you told us that you stopped working for the Rivettis because you'd found a job in publishing. Is that right?'

'Yes, as I said, a job in digital publishing.'

'Sorry. *Digital* publishing. I see. When you told us I asked you what the firm was you were working for and you said . . .' Another glance at the notebook. 'You said Compass Publishing.'

Sam Bannister's face said it all. A rabbit in the headlights. A cornered animal. Wide-eyed, caught-in-the-act guilt.

Garibaldi looked across to Gardner and nodded. She allowed herself a little smile.

Sam Bannister said nothing, turning to look out of the window at the East London sky.

'The thing is, Sam,' said Garibaldi, 'We've looked for Compass Publishing but can't find it. And as my colleague DS Gardner points out, it's very odd for a digital publishing firm not to leave what I believe is referred to as a digital footprint. There is, of course, the possibility that you got the name wrong and if that's the case we would love to know the real name so that DS Gardner can do another Google search, but if that's not the case—'

Sam Bannister said nothing and kept her head turned away to the window.

Garibaldi allowed the silence to stretch for a few more seconds. 'Tell me, Sam. What happened in the summer?'

'What do you mean?'

'What happened in Italy at the villa? When you were tutoring the Rivetti daughter. When you were working with Giles Gallen.'

Sam turned back. Her face was flushed. 'What do you mean what happened?'

Her eyes were looking at Garibaldi steadily. Too steadily.

'I mean, I don't think you've been telling us the truth about things, or rather you haven't been telling us everything. I did a bit of research last night. My Italian wasn't up to it but Google Translate is a wonderful tool. Found the most fascinating story about something that happened at a Tuscany villa. Not in the English newspapers of course but a fair bit of coverage in the Italian press. You know what I'm talking about?'

No response.

'I had no idea the Rivettis were into parties. You didn't mention them, did you? But then you wouldn't, I suppose. Especially not the one where a young woman was found dead in the swimming pool.'

'I don't know what you're talking about.'

Garibaldi paused for a few seconds. 'Really? I think you do.'

'It was nothing to do with me!'

'So you do remember it, then?'

'Of course I do.'

'So why didn't you mention it?'

'I didn't think it was relevant.'

'Giles Gallen, who was with you when it happened, was found murdered and you didn't think it was relevant?'

'That's ridiculous! What are you saying?'

Garibaldi snapped his notebook shut and leaned forward. 'I'm saying that you know more than you have told us and I want you to tell us everything now. You can do it here or if you continue to be a little reluctant I can formalise it and bring you in for questioning.'

'Am I in trouble?'

'That depends on what you choose to do, on whether you tell us all you know.'

'But he's a powerful man.'

'Who is?'

'Mr Rivetti.'

'Don't worry about Mr Rivetti. We'll make sure you're OK.'

'Like the way you made sure I was OK when I was walking to the tube that night? Like the way you made sure those other tutors were OK when they were attacked and threatened?'

'This is different.'

'Is it? How do you know it wasn't Rivetti attacking us? Or, given that Rivetti pays people to do things for him, one of Rivetti's men? The man who attacked me said "keep your mouth shut, remember what happened to Giles." Are you surprised I haven't said anything? I'm frightened.'

'When we first spoke to you, Sam, you hadn't been attacked or threatened. Why didn't you tell us when we first interviewed you?'

'Just because I hadn't been threatened didn't mean I wasn't frightened. I've been frightened ever since ... Remember the text Giles sent me on Saturday?'

'About the Rivettis' offer?'

'I was convinced it was nothing to do with taking over my tutoring. I know that's what I said, but I thought it was something else.'

'Like what?'

'A threat. Maybe even money to buy him off. And then when I heard that Giles was murdered that night . . .'

Garibaldi softened his voice and spoke calmly. 'I think you should tell us what happened in Italy, Sam, and what you think might have happened to Giles Gallen.'

He opened his notebook again and reached for a pencil as Sam Bannister started to talk.

42

'OK,' said Deighton at the front of the incident room. 'We've a couple of updates on some of the parents of the kids Gallen was tutoring. First the father of Briony Ainsworth. It's pretty clear that not all the activities in the string of clubs he owns are above board.'

Above board. A very Deighton term. Garibaldi looked at his boss and smiled, trying to imagine what his drink with her would be like.

'Nothing anyone's been able to pin on him and nothing that seems to connect him to Gallen's murder. Seems the two of them had very little contact and he appears to have a rock-solid alibi. Difficult to see any motive he might have for getting rid of Gallen but, until we know otherwise, we keep an open mind. And the same goes for another dad, Clive Marsh, father of Chloe. Archie's interview notes are on the file and you'll see from them that there was indeed a row between him and Gallen, one that Marsh deeply regrets. When asked about his previous charge for possession of cocaine he claimed to have kicked the habit long ago, though Archie's sense is that he's probably still on it. He owned up to a terrible relationship with his daughters ever since his wife left him. Especially with Chloe, the older one, whose promiscuous behaviour he's finding difficult to cope with. That's what he said triggered the row. Along with the coke perhaps. So, yes, you could say he had some kind of motive, but if he were guilty it's unlikely he'd have been so upfront about the row and his helplessness in wanting to protect his daughter. He also has a solid alibi. So, not out of the frame, but looking like an outsider. There's more though on the Italian parents. Garibaldi?'

Garibaldi got to his feet and moved to the front of the room.

'Right,' he said. 'Thanks to Milly we've discovered that Sam Bannister's been lying about her reasons for giving up tutoring the Rivetti daughter. And it appears that's not the only lie she's told, or at least not the only truth she's been keeping to herself. I don't know how we missed this. Whoever was looking at the parents of the kids Gallen was tutoring might want to reflect on it.' Garibaldi cast a glance in the direction of DCs Hodson and McLean. 'Maybe it's because this is an international thing and we didn't look that far – though given that the deceased had recently been working for an Italian family in Italy maybe we should have been a bit smarter. But anyway, it seems that the Rivettis had an interesting summer. They were in the habit of throwing parties at their Tuscan villa. Quite well connected, the Rivettis – they attracted all sorts to these bashes. Anyway, there was one particular party this summer where an unfortunate event occurred. The morning after the party a young woman, Antonella Bruno, was found dead in the Rivettis' swimming pool. Excess alcohol in her blood. Also cocaine.'

Garibaldi paused and looked round the room.

'How does this relate to Sam Bannister? As you know, she was working for the Rivettis over the summer, along with Giles Gallen. They were both there on the night of the party, not *at* the party as such, they weren't invited guests or anything, but they were hanging out together in their accommodation. They had access to the party booze, and they stayed up late, listening to the party going on around them. They drank and they chatted until the early hours. There was no point doing anything else while the party was going on, so they stayed up until it seemed to have ended. And then to clear their heads, they decided to go for a walk round the gardens. And when I say gardens, we're talking Capability Brown here, not your average back garden. They were heading towards one end of the gardens when they heard voices. Women's voices. They were coming from behind a hedge. They crept closer, keeping out of sight, crouching down next to the hedge. One of the voices they recognised. It was Maria Rivetti's. But they didn't recognise the other. They were both speaking Italian and neither Sam nor Giles could pick up on what they were saying. As they were listening the women's voices grew louder and it seemed their conversation had turned into some kind of row. Before they knew it they were listening to Maria Rivetti in full rage. They'd both seen her temper before and they knew what she sounded like when she lost it. That's what they were listening to here, after the party, in a corner of the villa's gardens – Maria Rivetti shouting and raging at this other woman. Sam and Giles waited until her rage had passed and they heard the two women walking away. They made their way back to the villa. By then it had all been tidied up by the staff and the place was quiet. Sam Bannister reckons it was probably about three in the morning.'

Gardner raised a hand. Garibaldi gave her a nod.

'Was anything going on between Sam Bannister and Giles Gallen?'

'Going on?' said Garibaldi. 'You mean something sexual? Sam Bannister says not. She says this was the night when they came close to it but she's insistent that nothing happened between them.'

'So,' said Gardner, 'they were getting intimate on this particular evening. That's why they went for this walk together?'

'She didn't give any particular reason for this walk. If they wanted to have sex I'm sure they'd have stayed in their rooms. Unless, of course, Gallen had this thing about al fresco copulation. Maybe he likes doing it in gardens. Tuscan villas. The Red Lion. I don't see how this—'

Gardner held up her hand in apology. 'Maybe it's not relevant.'

Garibaldi nodded his agreement. 'So they headed back to the villa. By now the staff had gone to bed. It was quiet. But as they walked back to their rooms, Sam and Giles heard voices. It was the women again. They were beside the pool. Again, they ducked out of sight. Another hedge apparently. Seems this villa was full of them and I know all this overhearing makes it seem like some Shakespearean comedy, but this is what she says happened. They could see the women now. It was Maria Rivetti and a woman they didn't know. They assumed she was a party guest. They were standing close to each other and they were standing by the pool. This other woman, apparently, seemed very unsteady on her feet. She was swaying. They looked at them and listened for a while but decided to head back to their rooms. So, keeping out of sight they crept back behind the hedge. When they got back to their rooms, they speculated about what had happened. And that's when Giles told Sam what he'd seen. As they had walked away he'd seen someone standing in the shadows looking at the pool. Giles turned in his direction and the person turned in his. Giles was in no doubt who it was. It was Luigi Rivetti. And Luigi Rivetti had recognised him.'

'OK,' said Deighton. 'And where does this take us?'

'When Giles and Sam saw a picture of Antonella Bruno in an Italian newspaper report on her death they recognised her immediately as the woman who had been arguing with Maria Rivetti, the woman standing by the pool. I've been in touch with the Italian police. Despite my surname, my Italian's not great, so it's just as well they spoke good English. It seems that Sam and Giles weren't questioned by the police and they were too shocked and frightened to volunteer information. It also seems that nothing's sticking on Rivetti. Who knows why? Could be all kinds of reasons. But the story is, Bruno, under the influence of alcohol and cocaine, fell into the pool and drowned.'

'So,' said Deighton, 'it's possible that Maria Rivetti was involved in her death?'

'Who knows?' said Garibaldi.

'It's also possible,' said Gardner,' that Luigi Rivetti, who seems to have been watching them both beside the pool, knew about it as well.'

'It's possible.'

'And is it possible,' said Deighton, 'that Rivetti saw Giles at the side of the pool, thought he knew what was going on and killed him to keep him quiet?'

'Possible,' said Garibaldi, 'but if both Giles and Sam saw it, why didn't he kill Sam as well? It could be that he only saw Giles.'

'We need to bring Rivetti in,' said Deighton. 'Check again with the Italian police about what they know, but bring him in and see what he comes up with. On a different front we've had the DNA results back for Simon Prest and

Roddy Ireland. The DNA found on Ireland matches the DNA on Emily Francis and Sam Bannister, but there's no evidence of the same DNA on Simon Prest. I'm not sure where this leaves us. We know this isn't the killer's DNA. We know the same man attacked Francis and Bannister – it's also confirmed by CCTV. We know that same man attacked Ireland. The question is – is there any reason why we didn't find the same DNA on Prest? The lab's looking at it again – there's a possibility it could be the fabric of Prest's Barbour, or it could be that there was less physical contact in that attack. Although we, as ever, assume nothing, I think for the moment we should still treat the attack on Prest as part of the series.'

'What if these attacks on Forum carry on?' said Gardner.

'Who knows?' said Deighton. 'Forum have warned all their tutors to be on the alert, to take care of themselves and to report anything at all suspicious.'

'So what do we do?' asked Gardner.

Deighton turned to look at the board behind her. 'I think we should talk to Signor Rivetti again.'

43

Garibaldi looked at Luigi Rivetti across the desk of his Lonsdale Road study. The Italian looked cool and unflappable in his expensively tailored suit.

'Mr Rivetti, on July 18th this year Antonella Bruno was found dead at your villa in Tuscany. Is that correct?'

'You know that is correct.'

'The post-mortem showed alcohol and cocaine present in her blood. Is that correct?'

'Again, you know this. Why are you asking me?'

'Mr Rivetti, were you aware of the consumption of drugs at your party?'

'I've answered these questions already, Inspector. I've answered them many times. You are wasting my time here. And your time. All of this has already been explored.'

'I've spoken to the Italian police and I'm familiar with the details of their investigation. It appears they were very thorough. They questioned a lot of people who were at the party that night, Mr Rivetti, but it seems they didn't question everyone.'

'What do you mean?'

'Your staff.'

'Of course not. What would the cook or the maids know?'

'Or your tutors?'

'My tutors?'

'Giles Gallen and Sam Bannister. Sam says they saw some interesting things that night.'

'Interesting things?'

'In the early hours of the morning, when the party was over, they saw your wife in an argument with another woman.'

'I know nothing about this.'

'Shortly after that, Sam saw the two women together by the pool and Giles saw you standing nearby.'

'They may have seen these things, Inspector, but I don't see how they are of any relevance.'

'The relevance may well be that the woman they heard your wife arguing with, who they saw standing with your wife next to the pool, was Antonella Bruno.'

'Are you suggesting that my wife and I are in some way connected to the unfortunate death of Antonella Bruno?'

'I'm telling you what Sam says she and Giles saw and heard.'

'I have nothing more to add to what I have told the Italian police, and they are not treating it as anything other than an unfortunate accident.'

'How did you know Antonella Bruno?'

'She was a business associate. I had worked with her for many years.'

'And your wife knew her as well?'

'We both knew her. She had been to our villa many times before.'

'Mr Rivetti, did Giles say anything to you after the death of Antonella Bruno?'

'We were all shocked, but I can't remember any conversation with Giles. Or with Sam.'

'Are you aware of the series of assaults on private tutors?'

'I am, yes.'

'Do you have any idea why they are being attacked?'

'No. Should I?'

'Do you have any idea of how these attacks might be connected?'

'What is this? Some game? A test? Yes, I know what connects them. They all work for Forum Tutors.'

'You're right. But some of them, most of them, also worked for you. The murdered man, Giles Gallen. Sam Bannister, who was in your villa on the night of that party. And Simon Prest may not have worked for you but you had just interviewed him for a job as a possible replacement for Giles.'

'But what about the other one? She didn't work for me, did she? And what about Roddy Ireland?'

'The thing is, Mr Rivetti, these people weren't just attacked. They were threatened and warned. And the warnings were to keep their mouths shut, to keep in line, to remember what happened to Giles Gallen.'

'What are you suggesting?'

'I'm suggesting that Giles Gallen may have known something about the circumstances of Antonella's death and that was why he was murdered. To keep what he knew a secret.'

'Are you suggesting that I killed him?'

'I'm suggesting nothing, but out of interest where were you on the night of Giles's murder?'

'Which night was that?'

'Saturday 13th September.'

Luigi Rivetti took out his phone and consulted his calendar.

'I was at home in Lonsdale Road with my wife and

children. We had a takeaway and watched a movie in our basement cinema. They can confirm it. So can the staff.'

'I'm sure they can.'

Garibaldi leaned forward. 'What do you know about Forum?'

'We got some of our tutors through them. That's all I know.'

'Can you think of any reason why anyone might want to assault and threaten their tutors?'

'None at all.'

Garibaldi didn't like the way it was going. Rivetti was too smooth, too assured.

'How well did you get to know Giles and Sam, Mr Rivetti?'

'As well as I know most of my staff. No, maybe a bit better than that. Tutors are different.'

'Really? How's that?'

Rivetti shrugged. 'They're doing a different job. They're not cooking a meal or cleaning or driving. They're educating your children.'

'I understand that Sam Bannister recently left your employment. Do you know why that was?'

'I don't know the details. I understand she found a job.'

'That's what she told you, but it's not the truth. She didn't have another job at all.'

'That's her concern. What does that have to do with me?'

'Do you think it's possible that Sam Bannister stopped working for you because she was worried about what happened in the summer and thought she might be in danger?'

'How can I say? She may well have been worried by the tragic events in the summer. But to suggest that is why she stopped working for us is nothing more than speculation.'

'One more thing, Mr Rivetti.'

'Of course.' Rivetti spread his arms wide and smiled. He looked confident, as if he thought he was winning.

'Giles sent a message to Sam before he was killed saying that you had made him an offer.'

'Me personally?'

'You, the Rivettis.'

'You've asked us about this already.'

'I'm asking again.'

'My wife asked him to consider taking over Sam's tutoring of our daughter.'

'Nothing more.'

'She also offered him the chance to live in.'

'To live in?'

'We have a small self-contained apartment in the house. If he took on tutoring both kids it might have suited him to be with us the way he had been in the summer.'

'Why didn't you say this earlier?'

'Is it important? Is it relevant?'

'It could be. I'm just puzzled why you didn't mention it.'

Rivetti's shrug suggested he didn't think it important.

'And my worry is that you might have made other offers to Giles Gallen that you haven't told us about.'

'No other offers, Inspector. Just tutoring.'

'Can we get back to Forum Tutors, Mr Rivetti? Were you pleased with the service they provided?'

'Very pleased. Giles will be difficult to replace, but this man they sent a few days ago – he seemed a good prospect.'

'That would be Simon Prest, the man who was attacked and threatened after he left your house. When did you find out about that attack, Mr Rivetti?'

'My wife told me.'

'And how did she hear?'

'Roddy Ireland rang her to let her know. Poor man. Now he's been threatened as well.'

'Mr Rivetti,' said Garibaldi, 'do we have your permission to take a DNA sample. For the purposes of elimination?'

'Am I under any obligation?'

'No, but it would help us, and, of course, help you.'

'I understand,' said Rivetti, 'and I am more than happy to do so. Anything that helps find the killer.'

'Thank you,' said Garibaldi, getting up to leave.

Luigi Rivetti's confidence had irritated him enormously.

44

'Boss?'

DS Gardner stood in front of Garibaldi's desk.

'We've just had a call from a Beth Austin.'

Garibaldi raised his eyebrows. The name meant nothing.

'She was Giles Gallen's girlfriend for a while. They broke up earlier this year.'

Shit. He remembered now. Gallen's grief-stricken parents had told them about her. Why hadn't they followed it up?

'What is it?'

'She didn't say. She lives in Chiswick and I said we'd call round this evening.'

'OK. So—'

'And I've been thinking . . .'

Garibaldi looked at his sergeant, suppressing the instinct to make a joke.

'I've been thinking about how unlikely the whole Rivetti thing is. If he killed Gallen then why would he only warn Sam Bannister? Why not kill her as well? And why would he attack and threaten the others? I mean, Emily Francis hasn't got any connection to them, has she? Nor has Simon Prest.'

'Whereas they do work for Forum.'

'Exactly. There is one other possibility, though.'

'What's that?'

'We keep thinking Luigi Rivetti, but what about his wife? She's the volatile one, the one with the temper, the one who was arguing with Antonella Bruno. What if she'd found out that Bruno was having an affair with her husband? Maybe that's what the row was about. Maybe that's why . . .'

'But why would that make her kill Gallen? How would she know he heard them and saw them?'

'Maybe Luigi told her.'

'Why would he do that?' Garibaldi scratched his head. 'Not getting any easier, is it? You know what we need?'

'Yeah. Some kind of breakthrough.'

'I was thinking more of a stop-off at Gail's on our way to Beth Austin's.'

Gardner smiled. 'You're on.'

Beth Austin's Chiswick flat reminded Garibaldi of his own first rented property, the one-bed flat in North Kensington he had been so keen to make his own. He could still remember the hours he had spent selecting the prints for the walls and arranging his bookshelves and CDs in an attempt to give the impression that he may have been a policeman but he wasn't without a brain or immune to good taste. Glancing round the bookless room, Garibaldi sensed Beth Austin hadn't felt the need to try quite so hard.

'Thanks for getting in touch,' he said as he sat down with Gardner. 'We'd very much like to hear anything you think might be of relevance.'

'Look,' said Beth, 'I still can't believe this has happened to Giles. I can't imagine it happening to anyone I know, but Giles? The thing is, I went out with Giles for about eight months. We were at Cambridge together. Our paths crossed a few times because we had some friends in common but we didn't know each other well there. Then, about a year ago, we met at a party and started seeing each other. He was tutoring and I was working for a PR firm. Look, I have no idea whether this is of any relevance, but I thought I should get in touch. I was devastated when I heard the news about Giles. It made me think about our time together and whenever I did I kept coming back to the same thing. It may be completely unimportant, but I . . .'

'You did the right thing,' said Garibaldi. 'Sometimes the tiniest detail, something that seems insignificant, can turn out to be the most important.'

Beth Austin smiled and nodded, as if reassured. 'The thing is Giles seemed to change during the time I was going out with him.'

'In what way?' said Gardner.

'It's difficult to describe, but I guess the best word I can think of is troubled. Yeah, that's probably it. He was troubled, as if something was preying on his mind.'

'When did this change happen?' said Garibaldi.

'It was a gradual thing. I don't think it happened suddenly, but looking back on it I think it may have started when he got this job tutoring an Italian kid and he went abroad with them. When he came back from that first trip abroad he seemed, I don't know, much less sure about things. It's difficult to be specific but one thing he started talking about was the whole tutoring thing. I think being exposed to the super-rich made him question what he was doing. We spoke about it and I can remember him saying that maybe it wasn't the kind of thing he wanted to do, maybe he should be doing a bit more good.'

'Do you think something happened when he was away?' said Garibaldi.

'He didn't mention anything and as I say the change wasn't dramatic. And when I say do good I don't think it was some kind of road to Damascus moment. Something was niggling away at him. The thing is, this all happened at a time when we'd been sort of drifting apart and it had come to the point where I thought it would be best if we stopped seeing each other. And when I told him I wanted to finish with him he said a few things which I didn't think much of at the time, but now . . . I mean, I was mainly concerned with ending it all in as friendly a way as I could. I didn't want to hurt his feelings, so I was treading carefully, maybe not taking in all of what he was saying. But when I heard the news I thought of what he said again and . . .'

Garibaldi leaned forward. 'What did he say, Beth?'

'I'd expected him to put up some kind of resistance, or to argue a case for us carrying on, but he didn't. What he said was that I was right to stop going out with him. "I'm not a good person, Beth. You're better off without me". That's what he said. As break-ups go, it was pretty close to "it's not you, it's me" but that's usually the line of the one who's doing the dumping. But it was weird that he came out with it because the thing about Giles was how nice he was, how decent. But he said he wasn't a good person and he followed it up with something else. He said "I've done a terrible thing and I need to come clean. I can't live with it any longer." Looking back on it, I should have asked him what it was, but I was so relieved that I'd told him and that he'd accepted it I didn't ask. Then when I heard the news I just wondered if it was significant . . .'

'So,' said Garibaldi, 'he gave no hint at all about the terrible thing he'd done?'

Beth Austin shook her head.

'Do you think,' said Gardner, 'that it might have been something to do with his work as a tutor?'

'He didn't say. All he said was that he thought tutoring might not be the thing for him, or at least not the type of tutoring he was doing.'

Garibaldi thought of Devon Furlong and Gallen's pro bono work at Hillside.

'And let's get this straight,' said Gardner. 'He said that after his first stint abroad with the Rivettis?'

'That's right.'

'So could it be,' said Garibaldi, 'that the terrible thing he did and his disillusionment with working as a private tutor might be connected to something that happened then?'

'As I said, I didn't ask. It could be, I suppose. I mean, that's when he first started talking about it but he didn't mention this terrible thing until I broke up with him.'

'You've definitely done the right thing,' said Garibaldi. 'But I'm a bit puzzled as to why it's taken you so long?'

'I've been away on holiday and didn't find out until I got back.'

'Nobody let you know?'

Beth shook her head. 'Maybe everyone thought I would have found out. Maybe some who knew thought they didn't want to ruin my holiday. I mean we went out together and everything, but—'

'None of his friends got in touch?'

'His friends? No. It was funny, but I never really got to know any of his friends.'

'Why was that?'

'I don't know. There were one or two from Cambridge he saw now and then but he mostly seemed to hang out with his schoolmates. I found it a bit weird. I mean, he'd been to uni and everything and started working – or whatever version of working you call being a tutor – but it was his school friends he saw most of. I don't know if that's usual – it's certainly not the case with me– or whether it's a public school thing. They all seem a bit like that, as if they're clinging on to it in a funny kind of way.'

Garibaldi had seen it himself, right down to the way they still called each other by ridiculous names. Stonker. Biffy. Todge.

'Any friends in particular he saw a lot of?'

'There were two in particular. Simon and Hugo.'

'That would be Simon Prest. He was also working as a tutor. Stand-up comedian as well, apparently.'

'That's the one. And I can't remember what Hugo does. I think he's in the City.'

'And did you get to meet them at all?'

'No, never. Whenever Giles met up with them it seemed very much boys only. You know the kind of thing.'

Garibaldi nodded. He knew it only too well.

'They seemed very close. I even heard him give them a nickname.'

'A nickname?'

'Yeah. The Three Musketeers. I mean, fucking ridiculous, right?'

Stonker. Biffy. Todge..

'Yeah,' said Garibaldi. 'Totally.'

45

Simon Prest kept touching his hand, as if to remind Garibaldi and Gardner of what he had recently been through.

'We have a few more questions for you, Simon,' said Garibaldi.

'I can't believe there's anything more I can tell you. I hope you're getting close to finding Giles's killer.'

'We're very close,' said Garibaldi. 'Very close indeed.'

'Good,' said Prest. 'This whole thing. It's been a nightmare.'

'Did you ever meet Giles's girlfriend, Beth Austin?'

Prest shook his head. 'No, I don't think so. I knew they were going out together but we never got to meet.'

'The thing is, we've just spoken to her and she came up with a couple of things we thought we'd follow up. The first thing she said was that Giles felt uneasy about his work as a private tutor.'

Prest laughed. 'That's hardly news, is it? I think most people who do it feel exactly the same. I mean I'm only—'

'You're only doing it,' cut in Garibaldi, 'until you're onstage at Hammersmith Apollo. I know.'

'What I mean,' said Prest, 'is—'

'I know what you mean. Beth Austin says he started to talk about this when he came back from his first stint abroad with the Rivettis. Did he say anything to you?'

Prest shook his head. 'Of all the tutors I know, Giles seemed the least troubled by it. Unlike the rest of us there wasn't something else he really wanted to do. And he was good at it.'

'So he never expressed any reservations about it after he started working for the Rivettis?'

'Not reservations. All he did was play it down all the time, make out it wasn't the cushy number it clearly was.'

'Beth Austin suggested that he was getting fed up with his work. She says he said he wanted to do some good.'

'That sounds like Giles, all right. I think he's always been a bit like that.'

'If he's always been like that, isn't it a bit strange that he should end up doing his kind of work?'

Prest gave a shrug. 'Maybe. But then he did do his pro bono work, which is more than I ever did.'

'So he never said anything to you about stopping tutoring?'

'Nothing specific.'

'Because it appears he told some of the kids he tutored just before he was killed that he'd be stopping his lessons with them.'

'Well, that's news to me.'

Prest felt his hand again and grimaced.

'Giles also said something to Beth that's interesting. When she was breaking up he told her that she was doing the right thing because he wasn't a good person.'

'Giles not a good person?'

'That's what he said. And he said more. He said that he had done something terrible. He said he'd done a terrible thing and he needed to come clean. Do you have any idea what he might have been talking about?'

Prest turned down the corners of his mouth and gave a slow shake of his head. 'I have no idea, none at all. I mean, maybe . . . no I'm sure that's not the case.'

'What's that?'

'Maybe something *did* happen when he started working for the Rivettis? Maybe that's where his disillusionment came from.'

'But he never mentioned anything?'

'Nothing.'

'Beth Austin was surprised when he came out with it. She said she got the sense that Giles was troubled by something. That's the word she used. Troubled. And Giles also told her he wanted to come clean. Like he was guilty.'

'I'm sorry, Inspector, I can't think of anything he might be talking about. As I say, he never mentioned anything.'

'OK,' said Garibaldi. He took out his notebook and flicked through some pages. 'One other quick question. We've been through Giles's phone records and it seems the last call he received on the night he was murdered was at 10.42. That call was from your mobile.'

'Was it?'

'It was. Can you remember what you called him about?'

Prest screwed up his eyes. 'I can, yes. I called him because I couldn't find my scarf in the pub and wondered whether he'd picked it up by mistake.'

'And had he?'

'No.'

'So you never found your scarf?'

'I never had it in the first place.' Prest chuckled. 'It was at home all the time. That's what happens when you have too much to drink. You start imagining things.'

'I know what you mean,' said Garibaldi. 'I do it even when I'm not drinking.'

'Tell me, Inspector, are we any closer to finding Giles's killer?'

Garibaldi got up to leave. 'Very close, Simon, very close indeed.'

As he headed for the door he wondered how he found the lie so easy.

Garibaldi sat at his desk trying to make connections.

He had spent half an hour entering Giles Gallen in a Google search and pairing it with a range of other names – the kids he tutored, the parents he worked for, the friends he had. The results were as expected – nothing emerged that was new or of significant interest.

It was only when he paired Gallen and Simon Prest that the search engine threw up something that intrigued him.

School photos showed Gallen and Prest together in sports teams (Prest, Garibaldi noted, was captain in all of them) and in a couple of dramatic productions. Their names also appeared together in several articles, mostly sports reports and reviews. They also showed up together in lists and photos taken at school reunions.

It was these reunion photos that piqued his interest.

In most of them Gallen and Prest appeared in large groups, bottles of lager in hand in some City bar, arms round each other's shoulders, smiling at camera. There were, though, two photos of them in a group of three, Prest in the middle with Gallen to his right and the same man on his left.

Garibaldi kept coming back to these pictures. There was something about them, and he couldn't work out what it was.

He enlarged each of them, moving in close looking for details that might explain his strange feeling. He couldn't place it, but he sensed it was more about this third man previously unknown to him, than it was about the other two.

He called Gardner over and pointed at the screen.

'Look at this. It's a photo of Gallen and Prest at a Radley reunion.' He pointed at the third man. 'And this bloke's a contemporary of theirs. I keep looking at him and thinking there's something odd. Do you see anything?'

Gardner narrowed her eyes and leaned close to the screen. 'What's his name?'

'I don't know.'

'How did you find this?'

'I just Googled Giles Gallen and Simon Prest and this came up.'

'And you've no idea who this other guy is?'

Garibaldi shook his head.

'Let me have a look.'

Garibaldi leaned back, thinking Gardner wanted to bring her eyes even nearer to the screen, realising only when she walked back to her own desk, sat down and started tapping at her keyboard that she had another kind of look in mind.

Five minutes later Gardner was back.

'The third guy in that picture's called Hugo Mountford.'

'Did you say Hugo?'

'Yeah. Hugo Mountford.'

Gallen. Prest. Mountford. The Three Musketeers.

'How did you find that out?'

'Prest's social media. That picture was up there and Mountford was tagged.'

'Ah, yes,' said Garibaldi. 'I was just about to look at social media myself.'

He knew it was a lie, and so did Gardner. Googling was

about as far as Garibaldi went in these matters – and he was chuffed it had got him as far as it had.

'There's more up there of that same reunion,' said Gardner. 'More photos but I've also found a couple of videos.'

'Videos? Of what?'

'One of him dancing with Gallen and Prest.'

'Dancing?'

'Yeah, a sort of joke dance.'

'And what's the other one?'

'One of him walking in and waving.'

It confirmed all Garibaldi's reservations about social media. Who was interested in this kind of crap?

'Come and have a look.'

Garibaldi followed Gardner back to her desk. She leaned over and pressed a couple of keys.

On screen the three Radleians, clearly drunk, were dancing and singing and playing with a cap which they kept putting on each other's heads. It was a drunken game in a drunken dance. Garibaldi had no idea what song they were dancing to but he knew it wasn't Johnny Cash.

'They're pretty pissed,' said Gardner. 'But they seem to be having a good time, bless them.'

'Yeah,' said Garibaldi. 'Bless them.'

Garibaldi looked at them, Gallen wearing the hat and making a face close to the camera, then taking it off and putting it on Prest's head, Prest pulling a silly face before taking off the cap and putting it on Mountford's head. Hugo Mountford followed suit. A silly face. A silly dance and then off with the hat.

'Stop it,' said Garibaldi. 'Go back.'

'How far?' said Gardner.

'To the beginning. And freeze it when I tell you.'

Gardner pressed the keyboard. The video ran again.

When Prest put the hat on Mountford's head, Garibaldi shouted, 'Freeze!'

He peered closely at the image.

'What is it?' said Gardner.

'Have you got the other video? Of Mountford walking in.'

'Sure.'

Another film started. Hugo Mountford walked into the reunion, smiling and waving at the camera, as if he was a movie star on a red carpet. He was wearing the cap handed round in the video.

This time Garibaldi didn't need to freeze it.

He'd seen enough.

'We need to find out all we can about Hugo Mountford,' he said. 'Everything.'

'I'm on it boss,' said Gardner, heading back to her desk.

Ten minutes later Gardner was back again.

'I don't know how significant this is but I've just discovered something about Hugo Mountford.'

Garibaldi raised his eyebrows.

'Yeah,' said Gardner. 'He's worked for an investment bank since graduating from Bristol. And working for this bank is someone we know.'

Gardner paused, looking as if she was enjoying the thrill of withholding vital information and extending the delay – like a TV presenter announcing the winner.

'Are you going to tell me?' said Garibaldi, after Gardner had kept silent for several seconds. 'Or are you going to stand there looking like you're in some gurning competition?'

Gardner snapped out of it. 'He works for the same bank as Luigi Rivetti.'

*

Felicia Ireland thought nothing could shock her more than the murder of Giles Gallen but recent events had come close. Emily Francis attacked. Sam Bannister attacked. Simon Prest attacked. Emily Francis's articles and the *Mail* feature. Then, to cap it all, Roddy himself attacked.

The assault on Roddy confirmed, beyond dispute, that someone was after Forum. It also confirmed her belief that Forum were unlikely to emerge from all of this unscathed. Everything – the murder, the assaults, the press coverage – had tarnished the Forum name so deeply that it was unlikely the taint could ever be removed. They were the talk of London middle-class dinner tables, and the talk was not good.

What the hell was going on? Who was behind it all? And where would it all end?

She'd spent hours going over things in her head. Probably more than that bunch of useless detectives. Especially that short one with the Italian name. He seemed to have no idea. She couldn't believe he'd spent as many sleepless nights as she had going through the possibilities.

And whenever she went through possibilities she always came back to the same one.

The Rivettis.

Wealthy and powerful and, she was convinced, not as clean as they seemed. She'd heard stories about them. Nothing specific but a sense that they weren't to be trusted, that they might have things to hide.

Should she have told the police? Maybe. But on the other hand the Rivettis were clients and she felt some sense of loyalty. Besides, if she spoke up about every client about whom she had suspicions she'd be speaking for a long time.

She was terrified. Whenever she left the house she tried

to make sure she was with someone else and she'd stopped going out after dark some time ago.

And she was worried about Roddy. Felicia had always sensed that there were dark emotions lurking beneath his cool, easy-going charm but they had, over the years, remained very much out of sight. Roddy was good at keeping his feelings in check, keeping things hidden and it had been rare to see him lose his temper or show real anger. But since the murder of Giles Gallen she had seen more of Roddy's anger than she had in all their time together, and it frightened her.

She thought she knew her husband well, but in those sleepless nights when she was going through everything in her mind, she had begun to wonder whether she really did.

46

Garibaldi was sandwiched between DCI Deighton and DS Gardner.

Others used the term sandwich metaphorically, joking about the way he was the filling between the two women – Deighton above and Gardner below – but now it felt almost literal. To one side of the desk was his boss, peering over his shoulder at the computer screen. To the other side, leaning forwards to work the keyboard, was his sergeant.

'OK,' said Garibaldi, 'here's the footage of the man following Emily Francis before her assault.'

They looked at the grainy images of the man walking along the Lower Richmond Road.

'Can you freeze it?'

Gardner pressed a key.

'Look closely,' said Garibaldi. 'Look at that jacket. Puffa jacket, isn't that what we call them? Sort of quilted.'

'Yes, that's a puffa jacket,' said Deighton from his left.

'Quite small quilts,' said Gardner from his right.

'Right,' said Garibaldi. 'And bright blue – well not very bright given the time of day and the camera quality, but a light blue. And with a hood up.' He turned to Gardner. 'Now show us the other picture.'

Gardner's fingers worked the keyboard.

On the screen came another picture.

'Does that look to you like the same jacket?'

'Similar,' said Deighton, 'but—

'Same colour?' said Garibaldi.

'Yes, but—'

'Same size quilts.'

'As far as we can tell, yes.'

'Hang on,' said Garibaldi. He turned to Gardner. 'Now go back to the earlier bit.'

The screen changed. It now showed the same figure on the same night walking along the Lower Richmond Road. The hood of the jacket was down.

'Freeze,' said Garibaldi. 'Here he is a few seconds earlier. No hood. But he's wearing a cap.'

'Right,' said Deighton. 'He pulls the hood up before the assault.'

'Can we go as close as we can on the cap?'

Gardner zoomed in.

'Look at this.' Garibaldi pointed his finger at the screen. It hovered over the front of the cap. 'See that logo? What's it look like to you?'

Deighton peered at where Garibaldi's finger was pointing. 'Looks like, I don't know, the head of an animal, a lion's head perhaps.'

'Exactly. Now look at this.'

He nodded to Gardner who clicked through to another photo.

'Move in on the cap.'

Gardner zoomed. Garibaldi pointed his finger again. 'What does that look like to you?'

'OK,' said Deighton. 'I get what you're saying.'

'A lion's head, right?'

'But there are loads of caps like that,' said Deighton. 'And loads of jackets like that as well.'

'Bit of a coincidence, though, isn't it?' said Garibaldi.

'This is hardly evidence,' said Deighton. 'Nothing more than fanciful speculation.'

'And isn't it a bit of a coincidence that he works at the same bank as Luigi Rivetti?'

'It may be,' said Deighton, 'but we—'

'We assume nothing,' said Garibaldi. 'Yeah, but we also see what he has to say.'

Crossing the Thames from the south, even cycling across Hammersmith Bridge from Barnes, made Garibaldi shudder. Heading further away from the river towards the city's northern heights often brought on nausea. That was the joke he liked to crack about North London but now, as he and Gardner flashed their warrant cards and introduced themselves at the door of Hugo Mountford's Islington flat, he felt a slight dizziness and a knot of unease in his stomach and wondered whether truth might have caught up with his fiction.

'Hugo Mountford? We'd like to ask you a few questions about Giles Gallen.'

'Giles? What's happened?'

He already looked uncomfortable.

'He was murdered. Didn't you know?'

'No, I know that. It's just. I thought—'

'Can we come in?' said Garibaldi.

Mountford opened the door wide and stepped back. 'I'm sorry, it's a bit of a mess,' he said, leading them into a sparsely furnished room, dominated by a large-screen TV and huge sound system. It looked like a single man's home. Mountford picked up newspapers from a couple of chairs and brushed them down.

'Poor Giles,' he said, offering the seats. 'I still can't believe it.'

Garibaldi took out his notebook as he sat down. 'Tell me, how did you know Giles?'

'We were at school together. Radley.'

'With Simon Prest?'

'That's right. We were all in the same . . .'

'Social?'

Mountford nodded, surprised at Garibaldi's mastery of the school language.

'And you kept in touch.'

'With Giles? Yeah, we'd meet up every now and then for a drink.'

'With Simon as well?'

'Yeah, it would usually be the three of us.'

'I see.' Garibaldi made a show of consulting his notebook. 'And you work in banking?'

'Yeah, for my sins.'

'Sorry to drag you away from work.'

'No problem. You've actually done me a favour. It's long hours and even weekends so it's good to be home before nine or ten. Needing to see the police was a pretty good getaway.'

Garibaldi looked at his notebook and turned a few pages.

'I understand that you work for the same bank as Luigi Rivetti.'

'That's right, I do. I'm very junior, of course, and he's Mr Big, Mr Very Big, so it's not as though we see much of each other.'

'Bit of a coincidence that Giles Gallen should end up tutoring his kids, isn't it?'

Mountford chuckled. 'Yeah, it is.'

'Did you mention it to Mr Rivetti?'

'I didn't have to. He mentioned it to me. He actually came to find me to say that he'd just taken on an old friend of mine. I was impressed. I mean, he didn't have to do that, someone as important as him.'

'So you spoke about Giles?'

'Yeah, we had a chat. He was interested in him.'

'Interested? What did he want to know?'

'Not interested that way. I mean, he wasn't asking questions about him or anything. He wasn't checking him out, he just said that he knew we were old friends and that he was pleased to have taken him on. He said Giles was a nice bloke and a good tutor, that his son liked him.'

'When was this?'

'I can't remember exactly, but I think it was shortly after he'd hired him.'

'So before Giles went to Italy with them for the first time?'

'I think so, yeah. He went away at Easter, right? This was way before that.'

'And did you and Luigi Rivetti talk any more about Giles?'

'Whenever we passed each other or were in the lift together or something he'd strike up a conversation or make some reference. I have to be honest it didn't do my reputation much harm. I think there were some who were a bit, you know, envious that Rivetti knew who I was and was speaking to me.'

'So you spoke often?'

'Don't get me wrong, it wasn't as though he was seeking me out or anything or that we had long one-to-ones. But he might pass me and say something like, "Here's the friend of my son's tutor. The one who's going to get him into St Mark's". You know what these alpha male bankers are like.'

Garibaldi nodded. He saw enough of them in Barnes on Saturday mornings.

'Did you tell Giles about this?'

'I told him, yeah.'

'And how did Giles react?'

Mountford shrugged. 'He was pleased, I guess. To be honest, I don't really remember.'

'Did Luigi Rivetti talk to you after Giles's murder?'

Mountford nodded. 'He came to find me.'

'When was that? The Monday morning after he was found?'

'No. It was Tuesday, I think. Yes, it was Tuesday. I only found out myself on the Monday.'

'How did you find out, Mr Mountford?'

Mountford hesitated, as if thrown by the question. 'How did I find out? Simon told me. He called.'

'Simon Prest?'

'Yeah. He was devastated. In a real state of shock.'

'And now he himself has been attacked. Have you spoken to him about it?'

'Yeah. He's shocked, frightened. Can't understand it.'

'Did he say anything to you about who he thought might be behind it?'

'Nothing more than anyone would think.'

'And what would anyone think?'

'As I understand it, those attacked have been other tutors working for the same firm. What's it called? Forum?'

'That's right. And there's also been an attack on one of the owners of Forum.'

'Are you saying they're involved in these . . . incidents?'

'I'm not saying anything.'

'But if there's this link to Forum—?'

'You're right, Mr Mountford, these attacks have been on

people connected with Forum but many of the victims have had another connection. The Rivettis.'

'Of course. And Simon had just been interviewed as a replacement for Giles.'

'How do you know that?'

Mountford looked surprised. 'He told me. Simon told me.'

'Did he think it was relevant?'

'I don't know. He just told me.'

'Tell me, has Luigi Rivetti said anything to you about these assaults?'

Mountford shook his head.

'Does he know that Simon Prest was a friend of yours and Giles?'

'I'm sure he would have known from the interview, but we haven't spoken since the assault.'

Garibaldi paused, head down in his notebook.

'Mr Mountford, where were you when those attacks occurred?'

'Why do you need to know? You can't possibly think—?'

'We're thinking nothing. We'd just like to eliminate you from our enquiries.'

'Eliminate me? I—'

'I have the dates written down here,' said Gardner, reaching out to him with a sheet of paper.

Mountford looked at the dates and shook his head. 'You can't possibly think—' He looked up at Garibaldi. 'Look. I can cover all of these. I can tell you exactly where I was on each of these evenings.'

'That would be very helpful,' said Garibaldi. 'And while you're checking those dates perhaps you could also check where you were on the night of Saturday 13th September?'

'Saturday 13th? You mean—?'

'The night of Giles Gallen's murder.'

'Are you serious?'

'Absolutely.'

'But that's ridiculous!'

'Perhaps you could just tell us where you were.'

Mountford braced himself, as if he had just found new confidence. 'Well I can tell you that straight away. I was at a restaurant round the corner with friends. They'll vouch for me, so will the restaurant. They know me there. I booked the table. Look, this is ridiculous! Do you seriously think I have anything to do with any of this?'

'And the other dates, Mr Mountford, where were you then?'

'I can't tell you off the top of my head. I'll have to check my diary.'

'I'm happy to wait, Mr Mountford. Where's your diary? Are you like me —' Garibaldi reached into the inside pocket of his jacket and pulled out a black Moleskine, 'or are you . . . digital?'

'It's on my phone,' said Mountford. He patted his pockets searching for it. 'Which is in the bedroom. I'll just go and get it.'

Mountford got up and walked to a door.

'Do you have a wardrobe in your bedroom?' said Garibaldi.

Mountford stopped, his hand on the door handle. 'Yes. Why?'

'Maybe while you're in the bedroom you could have a look at your clothes and see if, amongst them, is a blue puffa jacket and a baseball cap with a lion's head on it?'

'What are you talking about?'

'A blue puffa jacket and a baseball cap with a lion's head on it.'

Mountford looked puzzled, as if he couldn't imagine such clothes, let alone be in possession of them.

'No. I don't have anything like that.'

'Are you sure? You wore both to a recent reunion with your Radley chums.'

'I don't understand. I—'

'We can show you the photo if you want. We can also show you some other interesting footage in which you seem to be wearing exactly the same gear. Doesn't say much for your intelligence, does it? All that money thrown away on an expensive education and you make a mistake like that.'

'This is fucking ridiculous!'

'Your bedroom's in there, is it, Mr Mountford?' said Garibaldi, getting up from his seat and walking towards it. 'If we were to have a look in your wardrobe and go through your clothes can you swear we wouldn't find a jacket and cap just like those?'

'You can't do that!'

Garibaldi stopped and turned. 'I know we can't. Don't have a warrant, do we? So why don't we just wait here until you come up with some explanation of where you were on those dates.' He pointed at the sheet in Mountford's hand.

'As I said, let me get my phone. I can cover all of them – I can let you know exactly where I was.'

Mountford walked past Garibaldi to the bedroom door.

'That would be very helpful, Hugo. As you can imagine, we're very concerned about these attacks.'

Mountford reached for the door handle but stopped himself and turned, trying to look defiant but unable to hide his panic.

'They're nothing to do with me,' said Mountford. 'I didn't do them. And I definitely didn't kill Giles!'

Garibaldi let the words sink in and said nothing, fixing

Mountford with an evaluative gaze. The words were still spinning through his head as he walked towards Mountford and stopped in front of him.

'Hugo Mountford, I am arresting you on suspicion of assault, threats to kill and carrying a bladed article in public. You do not have to say anything, but it may harm your defence if you do not mention when questioned, something which you later rely on in court. Anything you do say may be given in evidence.'

Mountford straightened himself. 'I don't believe this. I want a solicitor.'

'You'll get a solicitor,' said Garibaldi, 'don't worry about that. You might also need that phone.'

47

Garibaldi waited for Deighton to finish reading the notes. She turned over the page, hooked her glasses off her nose and smiled.

'It may come as no surprise to learn that Luigi Rivetti's DNA doesn't match the DNA found on Giles Gallen.'

'No surprise at all,' said Garibaldi. 'People like Rivetti keep their hands clean. If they want something done they pay someone to do it for them.'

'But there is some good news,' said Deighton. 'Hugo Mountford's DNA matches the samples found on Emily Francis, Sam Bannister, and Roddy Ireland.'

'So we've got him,' said Garibaldi.

Deighton leaned back in her chair and sighed. 'Looks like it.'

'Still big questions, though. Like who killed Gallen? Like why did Mountford attack and threaten those people? If Mountford's DNA was over Gallen as well as the others we'd have an answer. He killed Gallen and he wanted to warn all those people, wanted them to keep quiet, not to give any sense that he killed him.'

'But none of those attacked claimed to know anything at all about who killed Gallen.'

'If we believe them, that is.'

'But if they all knew, why wouldn't they tell us? Why would they lie?'

'I don't believe they did know. If they did, at least one of them would have revealed it.'

'There's one other possibility we haven't considered,' said Deighton. 'Just because Mountford's DNA isn't on Gallen doesn't mean he wasn't involved in his murder. It doesn't mean he wasn't *there*.'

'Yeah. I've thought the same myself. Problem is he says he was at a restaurant with friends. And his alibi sticks. The restaurant confirms a booking in his name and his friends have confirmed it.'

'OK,' said Deighton, 'so looks like he wasn't there after all.'

'On the other hand,' said Garibaldi, 'Mountford gave us alibis for the nights of the attacks and it was pretty easy to blow them apart. He doesn't need to know that this one checks out, does he?'

'What are you saying?'

'I'm saying that if we forget the alibi and if we tell Mountford we think he might have been there . . .'

'I didn't hear that, Jim. I really didn't.'

Garibaldi got up and grinned. 'And I didn't say it either.'

There was a knock on the door. They both turned.

'I've found something,' said DS Gardner.

Deighton waved her in, offering her the chair next to Garibaldi.

Gardner sat down. 'It's to do with a couple of statements,' she said. 'Emily Francis's and Simon Prest's. I've looked at them again and I've gone back over CCTV evidence and it doesn't all add up. What you see on CCTV doesn't support what they've said.'

Garibaldi looked at his sergeant, impressed.

'It's to do with when they left the Red Lion on the night of Gallen's murder. Gallen left the pub at 10.32. CCTV shows that. And CCTV also shows both Francis and Prest leaving together at 10.36, four minutes after Gallen. So if that's the case, why did Prest say they left about half an hour afterwards? Could be faulty memory, I suppose. Could be that he'd had a bit too much to drink and it's all a bit vague. But the thing is Emily Francis said that they left very soon after Giles.'

Gardner took out her notebook and flicked over a few pages. 'She was quite specific. She said she fancied another drink but Simon was in some kind of hurry.'

'So the question is,' said Deighton, 'why would Prest lie about his time of leaving?'

'Exactly,' said Garibaldi, 'especially as he left with Francis, who would tell a different story. And why would Francis say that Prest was in a hurry? Where did he have to get to? He said he went home, which is just at the other end of Barnes. Why would he be in a hurry?'

'When did Gallen get that call from Prest?' said Garibaldi.

'10.42,' said Gardner.

'Right,' said Garibaldi, 'so we now know that Gallen at 10.42 wasn't at the Red Lion. He may have been on his way home. He may even have been on his way to the Old Cemetery. And Prest, who was also now no longer at the pub, calls him to ask if he'd picked up his scarf by mistake.'

Garibaldi looked at DCI Deighton, the word *narrative* flashing in his head.

Deighton smiled at Gardner. 'That's good work. How did we miss it?'

'I think the attacks kind of took our eye off the ball, took us away from basics. You know, check everything . . .'

'We need to talk to Prest,' said Deighton.

'We do,' said Garibaldi. 'But first I think we need to talk to Hugo Mountford.'

In Interview Room 2 Hugo Mountford sat beside his solicitor opposite Garibaldi and Gardner. The tape was running.

'Mr Mountford,' said Garibaldi, 'we have just received the results of the DNA swabs we took when you came in and the results are interesting.'

He looked across the table at Mountford, and let a silence develop. Silence often worked better than words.

'Your DNA matches the DNA traces found on the clothing of Emily Francis, Sam Bannister, and Roddy Ireland, all of whom were assaulted at knifepoint and threatened. We're running more checks on Simon Prest's clothing.'

Mountford turned to his solicitor who leaned towards him and spoke quietly in his ear.

'This DNA evidence,' continued Garibaldi, 'together with the CCTV footage suggests that you are the man who assaulted the aforementioned people on the nights in question.'

Garibaldi paused and held the gaze of the man opposite.

'We would also like to know where you were on the night of Giles Gallen's murder, the night of September 13th?'

'I've told you,' said Mountford. 'I was at dinner with friends.'

'Do you expect us to believe that? You gave alibis for each of those four attacks and none of those checked out. What's different about this one?'

'It's true.'

DS Gardner leaned forward, elbows on desk. 'Mr Mountford, did you attack those people to frighten them into silence, to make them keep quiet about Giles Gallen's murder?'

'I didn't murder Giles Gallen.'

'But that doesn't mean,' said Garibaldi, 'that you weren't there.'

Mountford looked surprised. 'I wasn't there.'

'But,' said Gardner, 'you were there on the nights those people were assaulted. We have the evidence.'

Mountford's eyes darted uncertainly from one to the other.

'Can I remind you of something you said when we interviewed you earlier,' said Garibaldi. 'When asked about the attacks and the murder you said, and I quote,' Garibaldi consulted his notebook, '"I didn't do it and I definitely didn't murder Giles Gallen." Does that statement strike you as odd in any way?'

Mountford gave a slow shake of his head.

'"I didn't do it and I *definitely* didn't murder Giles Gallen". Why didn't you say "I *definitely* didn't do the attacks? You made it sound like you didn't kill Gallen but you weren't so sure about those assaults.'

'That's ridiculous. And, anyway, I don't remember saying that.'

Garibaldi pointed at his notebook. 'You did. I wrote it down.'

'If I said it, I didn't think about it,' said Mountford. 'It just came out.'

'Which makes it all the more revealing, doesn't it?' said Garibaldi.

'I don't know what you're talking about. They're just words.'

'I'm not sure about that. When you added that "definitely", I think you also suggested something else – that you definitely know who was behind the murder of Giles Gallen.'

'This is absurd,' said Mountford. 'You're reading too much into it. One word doesn't prove anything. I didn't mean anything. A slip of the tongue. Like I said, it's only words.'

'As the Bee Gees once sang.'

'What?'

'It's only words. But, as the song goes on to say, words are all we have. Or maybe it was all *I* have. Can't remember. But then memory's a strange thing, isn't it? Plays tricks with us, don't you think?'

Another silence.

'DNA evidence confirms that you were that man in the puffa jacket hoodie and the lion baseball cap, the hoodie and cap we have removed from your bedroom wardrobe this morning. The game's up, Hugo. So why don't you give us some more words. You were there on the night of Giles Gallen's murder, weren't you?'

'I've told you. I was at dinner with friends.'

'We're not convinced you were.'

'Check it out. The restaurant. My friends. They'll tell you.'

'I think you were in Barnes Old Cemetery on the night of Gallen's murder. You may not have killed Gallen yourself but you definitely – and I use that word advisedly – you definitely know who did.'

'I've told you. I wasn't there.'

Garibaldi put his elbows on the table and leaned forward, speaking softly. 'The thing is, Hugo, there's a difference between assault at knifepoint and murder. A huge difference. Threatening with a weapon will get you anything between six months and four years. Murder will get you . . . well, you know what murder will get you, don't you? Of course, if you help us by telling us everything you know it will help your case enormously.'

Garibaldi leaned back in his chair. 'Think about it. That promising career at the bank. The bank that made Luigi Rivetti a very rich man. Think of that future.'

'We're trying to help you, Hugo,' said Gardner, 'trying to give you a chance to make it easier for yourself. Why don't you tell us why, if you didn't kill Gallen, you assaulted those four people and told them to keep quiet, reminding them of what happened to him?'

'All of those attacked are connected, aren't they?' said Garibaldi. 'Some work for Forum, one owns Forum. Some are also connected to the Rivettis. So tell us why you attacked them.'

'I didn't attack them.'

'Remember,' said Garibaldi. 'Whoever killed Giles Gallen is looking at something life-changing, something from which they might never recover. Someone, on the other hand, who owns up to what they have done, who tells us what they know . . .'

'I didn't do it.'

Mountford looked up to the ceiling. Was he praying? Was he making some final decision?

'But I did attack those people.'

Garibaldi's body relaxed. He shot a glance at Gardner who returned a smile.

'And why did you do that?' said Garibaldi.

'I shouldn't have done it. Once Giles was killed that was it. I shouldn't have said yes.'

'What do you mean? Did someone ask you?'

Mountford froze, checking himself. Was he about to change his mind?

He shook his head. 'You wouldn't understand.'

'Try me.'

Mountford held his head in his hands. 'I never thought I'd do this. I don't believe it. Everything. I can't do it. I'm sorry, I can't do this.'

'Hugo,' said Gardner, 'we want to know why you attacked those people and we want to know how that is connected to the murder of Giles Gallen. Do you know why Giles Gallen was murdered?'

Mountford bowed his head again.

'Was it because of his work for the Rivettis?' said Garibaldi.

His head was still down.

'Was it connected to something he knew about them? Was it to do with something that happened when he was working for them in the summer?'

Mountford's head came up slowly.

'I don't know why I did it. I felt I had to.'

Garibaldi and Gardner exchanged looks.

'Someone made you attack those people?'

Mountford looked from one to the other. Garibaldi looked at his eyes. They were blank and distant. Something had gone.

'I wasn't the one behind Gallen's murder. It was him.'

'Him?' said Garibaldi, leaning forward and looking into Mountford's eyes, trying to connect with them. 'Are you saying that Luigi Rivetti is responsible for the murder of Giles Gallen?'

Mountford continued to turn between Garibaldi and Gardner, a cornered animal, wide-eyed in its search for escape.

'You don't understand,' he said, 'He had got himself into such a mess. He needed my help. I didn't want to let him down.'

Mountford was staring into space, addressing no-one in particular. He was talking as if in a dream. Garibaldi wondered what was happening to him. Did he need to call a doctor?

'Can we get this straight, Hugo?' said Gardner. 'Luigi Rivetti had Giles Gallen killed and asked you to attack and threaten Emily Francis, Sam Bannister, Simon Prest and Roddy Ireland. Is that correct?'

Mountford's gaze was still distant, fixed just above eye level. It was as if he was in a trance.

'Just tell us, Hugo,' said Garibaldi. 'Tell us and we can get this thing done. If you tell the whole truth it'll be easier for you.'

Still nothing. If anything, Mountford seemed even more removed from reality.

'Tell us about Luigi Rivetti, Hugo. Tell us what he did.'

Still no response. Mountford's mouth dropped open but no words came.

'Tell us why you attacked those people,' said Gardner. 'Was it because they knew Mr Rivetti had murdered Giles Gallen?'

'He didn't murder him,' said Mountford, his eyes still fixed ahead, his face still frozen.

'So he didn't do it himself,' said Garibaldi, 'but he got someone to do it for him. Is that right? Is that what happened? Tell us what you know, Hugo.'

'You don't understand.'

Garibaldi leaned across the table, his head down, looking up at Mountford, trying to make contact, trying to bring him back from wherever he had gone.

'Hugo, tell us about Luigi Rivetti.'

Suddenly Mountford's body jolted and his face came back to life. He looked around, as if he'd just woken up from a disturbing dream.

He turned his eyes to Garibaldi.

'Luigi Rivetti?' he said. 'Luigi Rivetti's got nothing to do with it.'

'What do you mean?' said Garibaldi. 'You said—'

'It wasn't him. It wasn't Rivetti. One of us had gone and the other, the other . . .'

Garibaldi looked away and in the corner of the interview room he saw his mother again, bent over his jumper, sewing a label into its neck. He was eleven again, about to start at grammar school. A new school. New friends. New challenges. And there was his mother stitching in his identity with no sense of what lay ahead, of how his schooldays would be marred by tragedy.

Garibaldi blinked.

His mother was gone.

He turned back to Mountford. His last words echoed in his head. One of us had gone. And the other . . .

Garibaldi suddenly saw something else.

He leaned forward again. 'Hugo,' he said softly, 'tell me about the Three Musketeers.'

Mountford's face flushed. He looked at Garibaldi through narrowed eyes, pained, puzzled.

'What? How—?'

'The Three Musketeers. Tell me about them.'

'I don't see how—'

Mountford bowed his head. When he raised it, he looked as if he had shrunk, as if he was a little boy again, a tearful, frightened schoolboy.

'Strange thing to call yourselves, isn't it? I mean, had any of you read it? But then I guess it wasn't the chivalry, was it? It was more the motto, that little saying, wasn't it?'

'Look,' said Mountford, 'it's not what you think. I—'

'What do I think, Hugo? Tell me.'

Mountford rested his head on his hands.

'One of the strangest things about Giles Gallen's murder,' said Garibaldi, 'was the way we identified him. Do you know how we did that, Hugo?'

Mountford kept his head down.

'We did it from his clothes, Hugo. From his jumper. He was wearing a jumper with his name tag sewn into the back of the neck. You know – the kind of jumper you wear when you're at school. And in this case it *was* the jumper Giles wore at school. At Radley. So tell me about the Three Musketeers, Hugo.'

'I didn't kill him.'

'I know you didn't, Hugo. But I now know who did. So tell me.'

Mountford looked up. He said nothing for a while, his eyes darting round the room, his lips tight. Then, in a quiet voice, he started to speak.

'There's this cemetery. We used to go there, the three of us . . .'

Garibaldi leaned forward and listened.

48

DCI Deighton shook her head in disbelief.

'So you're telling me it's all because they were at school together?'

'Looks like it,' said Garibaldi. 'That's where they met. That's where their friendship started.'

'Taking the old school tie thing a bit far, isn't it?'

'Funny term, isn't it? Old School Tie. I mean, I've always got the reference to the thing you wear round your neck, but "tie" has other meanings, doesn't it? It's a connection, a link, but it's also something that binds you, restricts you.'

Deighton gave a puzzled look. 'Was it something sexual?'

Garibaldi wondered whether she thought he was suggesting some kind of bondage.

'Who knows? No evidence that it was, or that it carried on. At the moment it doesn't seem relevant. What is relevant is that.' Garibaldi pointed at the print-out on Deighton's desk. She picked it up.

'I still find it difficult to believe,' said Deighton.

'Which bit? That they did it, or that they managed to get away with it?'

'All of it.'

'Mountford made it sound plausible enough. Three

Sixth From public schoolboys allowed out into Oxford one Sunday afternoon. They get booze from an off-licence, and they head off to their favourite place – Holywell Cemetery, a little out of the centre on the way to St Catherine's. A hidden gem, according to Google. And they stay there all afternoon, drinking and smoking weed if they'd managed to get hold of some. Then they'd head back to school and hope no-one would sense what they'd been up to. According to Mountford hardly anyone came into that cemetery and if they did the chances were they wouldn't see the three of them. They had their favourite spot in a corner, very much out of sight. But on this particular day some bloke appeared. A "chav". I think that's the word Mountford used. He was young, about their age, maybe a bit older. He stood in front of the three of them, pulled out a knife and asked for their money. They said they didn't have any. He said he didn't believe them and started waving the knife in front of them. And then Simon Prest stood up. He was the athlete, the strong man. He stood up and went towards the youth. He grabbed the arm holding the knife and kicked him in the groin and soon the youth was on the ground. Then Prest was on him, punching and kicking and he called for Gallen and Mountford to join in. And they did. All three of them, kicking and punching this bloke in the corner of an Oxford cemetery.'

'Could it be seen as self-defence?'

'Who knows? I guess that's one for the lawyers. The problem the three of them had was when they saw the next day's *Oxford Mail*.' Garibaldi pointed at the papers in front of Deighton. She leafed through the pile and picked up a sheet.

'Youth found beaten to death in cemetery,' she read.

'What were they going to do? It was obviously the bloke with the knife who'd asked for their money. It was obviously the bloke all three of them had attacked. It was obvious they'd killed him. They were in a real state. And they were divided. Gallen thought they should come clean and own up. Prest thought the opposite. Mountford couldn't decide. They talked about it at length but eventually they decided. They'd keep quiet. They'd hope the police would find nothing connecting them to the death. How could they? They'd taken the bloke's knife and thrown it in the canal on the way back and they'd cleared up all the cans and bottles. They were pretty sure no-one would have seen them so they thought they might get away with it. So they decided to keep quiet. And they made a pact. They would never mention it. They would always be there for each other. They would never let each other down.'

'The Three Musketeers.'

'Exactly. And it seemed they'd got away with it. No-one came to the school asking questions. No-one mentioned it. The case of the youth beaten to death in the Oxford cemetery remained unsolved.'

'Did Thames Valley have anything to say about it?'

'Happy to open up the case again in the light of new evidence.'

'And all of this – you got it from Mountford?'

Garibaldi nodded. 'And the rest. Giles Gallen had always been the one most uneasy about it. Who knows what was going on in his head over the years? Maybe it had been preying on him, nagging at his conscience. What we do know is that, for whatever reason, he decided he had to own up. He was going to come clean. But he knew he had to tell Prest and Mountford about his decision. He told Prest first. And he told him on the night of the Forum party, the night he was murdered.'

'All this from Mountford?'

'All from Mountford. We don't know when, exactly, Gallen told him that evening, but Prest was fuming. Absolutely beside himself. He left the Red Lion a few minutes after Gallen, not half an hour after as he said, and he gave Gallen a call at 10.42. And we know that wasn't to ask about a missing scarf. He said they needed to meet to talk about it, to think things through. And he asked to meet at Barnes Old Cemetery. According to Mountford they used to hang out there a lot when they were home from Radley. Maybe it's where they met regularly. Whether they met there after beating a man to death in another cemetery I have no idea. Maybe Prest will be able to inform us. Maybe Prest thought it was a good place to remind Gallen of what they had done and of what was at stake.'

'So where did Prest get the murder weapon?'

'My guess is he went to the Old Cemetery via his house and picked up the knife there. He told Mountford he had no intention of using it, but he was angry, and he wanted to show how angry he was, to make his threats more threatening. So they met at the cemetery and they argued. Prest was insisting that Gallen kept his mouth shut. What was the point of mentioning something that happened years ago? They'd got away with it. Why ruin things now? But Gallen was adamant. Prest never meant to use the knife. But he lost his temper and he took it out and waved it in front of Gallen. They grappled and Prest stabbed him. Once. Couldn't believe what he'd done. Panicked. Took Gallen's phone and wallet and presumably got rid of them with the knife. They're probably somewhere in Beverley Brook.'

Deighton gave a slow nod, as if things were falling into place.

'So why did Prest tell Mountford all this?'

'Because he was in a state of absolute panic and didn't know what to do. So he turned to his old friend, one of the gang of three.'

'The Three Musketeers.'

'Exactly.'

'How could one of them have killed another? It didn't make sense. They had been so close. How could this have happened? Prest couldn't believe what he'd done. He asked for Mountford's help, pleaded with him. So they met – Prest and Mountford. Mountford couldn't believe it. He had no idea what to do, what to suggest. He tried to persuade Prest to hand himself in, but Prest would have none of it. He thought of telling the police himself but he couldn't bring himself to do it, couldn't snitch on his old schoolmate, the Musketeer. So, instead, they hatched the plan. It wouldn't necessarily get Prest off but it would complicate things by implicating so many more and lead the investigation in different directions.'

'But why?' said Deighton. 'Why would he do that? Why would anyone do that?'

'I look to the L's and all I can see is a distorted, warped version of Love and a hefty dose of Lunacy. Mountford couldn't believe that one old friend, one of the three schoolboys, all in the same Soci – house had killed another, couldn't believe that the friendship they had all shared, the love they had for one another, could have ended so tragically. Like Prest, he panicked, and between them they came up with the scheme. First Mountford attacked Emily Francis, a friend of Gallen's and another Forum tutor. Turn the attention towards Forum. Then Sam Bannister. She worked with Gallen for the Rivettis, so turn the attention on them. Then back to Forum. Why not attack one of the owners, Roddy Ireland? Mountford did all of these. The same method. The same threats. Took a lot of work, finding out where these people would be. Emily Francis was easy enough – Prest knew her regular tutoring commitments. He also knew about Roddy Ireland's late-night dog-walking habit. He'd told him about it several times and Prest lives near him in Barnes and was able to check it out. Mountford came down to stay at Prest's house for both. Sam Bannister needed more work, but, as I've discovered, you can find out a lot from social media. Mountford hung around the Hampstead party on the off chance and struck lucky. All to take the pressure of Prest, to get the finger of suspicion pointing elsewhere.'

'And what about the attack on Prest himself?'

'What better way to get us looking elsewhere? Prest worked for Forum as well and if he was attacked on his way back from an interview with the Rivettis that would keep them in the spotlight as well. But they didn't think this one through. Prest faked it all. The story and the knife wound on his hand. But there was no actual attack. No DNA on his clothes. He rolled around on the path near the nature reserve to get stuff on his clothes, to make it seem he'd been pinned to the ground. But no DNA. Mountford wasn't there. He gave himself the knife cut.'

'So,' said Deighton, 'the attacks were carried out not by the man who murdered Gallen but *for* the man who murdered Gallen.'

'Exactly,' said Garibaldi.

Deighton's phone rang. She picked it up.

'DCI Deighton.'

She nodded as she listened to the voice on the other end.

'That's great,' she said. 'Thank you.'

She hung up and smiled at Garibaldi.

‘It’s a match. Prest’s DNA matches the DNA found on Gallen.’

Garibaldi sighed with relief. ‘Let’s see what he has to say about that, shall we?’

He got up, bracing himself for the interview to come.

‘One thing I don’t get,’ said Deighton, ‘is why Mountford’s told you all this.’

‘He saw the game was up, I guess, and he weighed up the consequences. He’d tried to help his friend but he’d been found out. He couldn’t wriggle out of the attacks, so what was he going to do? He was in trouble but not as much trouble as his old school friend. So he landed him in it. He knew he’d be done for the assaults and everything that went with them. And he knew he’d be questioned about the youth in the Oxford cemetery, but he saw no point in carrying on. Prest had killed one of them. The whole thing had been blown to pieces so why carry on the pretence. So much for the Old School Tie, eh?’

‘So Forum are in the clear, then?’

‘It seems so, though I still think there’s something shifty about them.’

‘And the Rivettis?’

‘I’ll speak to the Italian police. They might want to talk to Sam Bannister, but what’s the Italian for Teflon? I’m pretty sure nothing will stick.’

‘And the kids Gallen was tutoring and their parents?’

Garibaldi shook his head. ‘Nothing. And the same goes for Devon Furlong and White City. Absolutely no connection.’

‘Funny, isn’t it? Gallen was up there simply doing something good. Difficult to grasp, isn’t it? That someone so decent could have done something so wrong.’

‘We’re all capable of it,’ said Garibaldi. ‘The problem

is, if you do something bad that's what gets remembered. The evil men do lives after them; the good is interred with their bones.'

'Larkin?'

'Shakespeare,' said Garibaldi. 'As so often, he nailed it.'

'Let's do the same with Prest.'

49

The Evening Standard

TUTOR AGENCY SPEAKS OF RELIEF

Forum Tutors, the elite tutoring agency that employed Giles Gallen, the 27-year-old found stabbed to death in Barnes, have spoken of their relief after a man was yesterday charged with his murder. They have also spoken of their shock at discovering that the man charged was also employed as a Forum tutor.

Giles Gallen, 27, who had been working as a private tutor since graduating from Cambridge, died from knife wounds after being attacked in Barnes Old Cemetery on September 13th.

The man charged with his murder is 27-year-old Simon Prest, of Barnes, who was also employed as a tutor by Forum.

In their investigation of Gallen's murder, Metropolitan Police detectives looked closely at Gallen's tutoring activities and the firm he worked for. Forum Tutors insisted that they knew nothing about what might have led to his murder and saw no connection with his work for the agency.

Yesterday Felicia Ireland, who runs the Forum Agency with her husband Roddy, gave her reaction to the recent developments. 'First of all, I am relieved that the police have been able to charge a man with Giles's murder. I sincerely hope that whoever is responsible is brought to justice and we are able to draw a line under this horrendous event. My sympathy and my best wishes go out to Giles Gallen's family who must still be going through such unbearable pain.'

When asked about Forum's employment of the man charged with Gallen's murder, Felica Ireland said it came as a horrible shock. 'We had absolutely no idea. We are meticulous in our checking of references and in our safeguarding checks and are as surprised as everyone else. All we know is that both Giles Gallen and Simon Prest came to us with excellent references from the school they attended together and from their universities.'

Another man was charged yesterday with offences believed to be related to Gallen's murder.

Hugo Mountford, of Finsbury Park, was charged with assault, threats to kill and carrying a bladed article in public. Three of the victims of his assaults also worked as Forum tutors.

When questioned about this, Felicia Ireland said, 'We will leave it to the police to discover the reasons for the attacks. All I would like to say is that Forum tutors and those using our tutoring services should now go about their business confident that they are safe. For Forum it is now very much business as usual.'

Giles Gallen, Simon Prest and Hugo Mountford were all pupils together at Radley College.

Radley College were unavailable for comment.

WILL PRIVATE TUTORING EVER RECOVER?

EMILY FRANCIS *gives her reaction to yesterday's events.*

It is a huge relief to learn that the police have arrested and charged a man with the murder of Giles Gallen. But it is a huge shock to discover that the charged man was also working as a private tutor.

Ever since Giles Gallen was found murdered the spotlight has been thrown on the whole tutoring enterprise. When tutors were attacked and threatened, London's affluent tutor-employing classes started to ask themselves serious questions. Who are these people they let into their homes? Who are they trusting with such intimate access to their children? What risks are they taking? In short – is it worth it?

It's certainly worth it to firms like Forum who make huge amounts of money, feeding off parental anxiety and the ultra-competitive nature of London schools. They may parade their charitable initiatives (Forum, for example, engage in pro bono work in inner city state schools) but that is no more than a sop to their conscience and a smooth PR gesture.

I am still employed as a tutor. I knew Giles Gallen. I was one of those assaulted in the wake of his murder.

But these events have left me in no doubt that now is the time to stop. I don't know what I will do next to bring in money (though a career in journalism still remains my ultimate goal) but I don't think I can carry on working as a tutor.

DCI Deighton raised her glass. 'Cheers, Jim.'

Garibaldi clinked his glass against hers. 'Cheers!'

'I think it's safe to call me Karen, don't you?'

Garibaldi smiled. 'OK. Cheers, Karen.'

He looked round the bar. Discreet and sophisticated and Deighton's choice. He wasn't sure why this surprised him, but then he wasn't sure about so many things when it came to his boss.

'We haven't come here to talk about work,' said Deighton, 'so let's get the Gallen case out of the way first, shall we?'

'Sure,' said Garibaldi. 'Though I'm not sure what to say. Let's hope we can get Prest and Mountford. As to what they did to that boy in the cemetery, who knows what will happen?'

'Good to think that justice might be done.'

'A long way to go.'

'Yeah, but enough of that. Let's talk about you.'

Garibaldi felt he was blushing. So many years of feeling he didn't really know his boss and now an evening of intimate revelation. He wasn't sure he was up to it.

'Sometimes,' said Deighton, 'I get the sense you don't

really want to be a cop at all. Then at others I think you're one of the best I've ever seen. I don't get it.'

'Nor do I,' said Garibaldi. 'Some days I love the challenge, the desire to solve the puzzle. Other days I want to chuck it all in.'

'What would you do if you chucked it in?'

'I've always wanted to go to university.'

'So you'd go as a mature student?'

'Yeah. Philosophy maybe. Or History. Maybe Italian, though I don't think I'm up to that.'

'Maybe you should do it.'

'Are you trying to get rid of me?'

'Why would I want to do that? You're a good egg, Jim.'

A good egg? He couldn't remember ever having been called that before. He wasn't even sure what it meant. Typical Deighton.

'There's one question I've always wanted to ask you, Jim, and I guess now might be the right time.'

Garibaldi braced himself. What was coming?

'Go on,' he said. 'Ask me and I'll promise you an honest answer.'

'Does that mean I only get one honest answer all evening?'

'We'll have to see.'

Deighton took a sip of her drink. Her face had lost the pastoral care look it had worn earlier in the evening. She seemed a different person.

'OK,' she said. 'I know you don't drive. Everyone knows that. It's one of your, how shall I put it, charming eccentricities, along with your habit of quoting writers and making references that leave people baffled—'

'Maybe it's what makes me a good egg.'

'Maybe it is. But my question is *why* don't you drive?'

Garibaldi paused. Should he tell her?

'I mean, is it because you tried to learn but couldn't? Is it because you never learned? The only reason I ask is that nearly everyone drives and . . .'

'OK,' said Garibaldi. 'It's like this.'

He took a breath and told her. How he lost his parents and how whenever he sat behind a wheel the flashbacks came and panic overwhelmed him. How it only happened when he held the wheel, not when he was a passenger.

When he had finished Deighton nodded as if she understood. 'I had no idea,' she said.

'Why would you?' said Garibaldi. 'And now it's my turn. One question and an honest answer.'

'I'm all yours.'

'Before we swap notes on what it's like to live with a teacher, I want to know all about yours. So, tell me. What's she like?'

50

Garibaldi sat beside Emmylou Harris. Her head was bent over her guitar but her eyes were turned to him. He looked down at the guitar in his hands.

He still didn't know what to do. Emmylou was being very sweet but her understanding smile was making little difference.

He could have a thousand private lessons with her and he still wouldn't be able to play the damned thing.

'Jim?'

Emmylou was speaking.

'Jim? You OK?'

'I'm fine, Emmylou. I just can't—'

'Jim?'

He heard the ring of a phone and opened his eyes. He had fallen asleep. The *Standard* lay on his chest and his phone was vibrating in his pocket.

He fished it out and looked at the screen.

Alfie.

'Hi, Dad, it's me.'

'Alfie, how are you?'

'I'm OK, thanks. About this game on Saturday.'

'Yeah. Preston. Always a season highlight.'

'The thing is . . .'

Garibaldi tensed. Was it another refusal? Was it another sign of what was to come?

'I was just wondering if I could come down Friday night and stay over?'

'Sure. What is it? Another party?'

Alfie laughed. 'No, there's no party. Just thought I'd hang out.'

'Hang out?'

'Are you still busy on the case?'

'Not so busy, no. Looks like I've done all I can.'

'Great. So maybe a takeaway curry or something?'

'Sure,' said Garibaldi. 'See you then.'

He hung up and smiled.

'Who was that?' said Rachel coming out of the kitchen.

'Alfie. Wants to stay on Friday night. Is that OK with you?'

'OK with me? Of course it is.'

Rachel picked up the remote and pointed it at the speakers.

First Aid Kit started to sing 'Emmylou'.

'You OK, Jim? You've been asleep.'

Garibaldi rubbed his eyes. 'Yeah, just dropped off.'

Rachel pointed at the newspaper lying on his chest. 'Interesting stuff.'

'Yeah. A real shot in the arm for private tutoring.'

'And public schools.'

'Or, as I like to call them, private schools.'

Garibaldi hauled himself up and sat on the edge of the sofa. He looked up at Rachel. 'You've got to get it in perspective, though, don't you?'

'Of course you do,' said Rachel. 'I'm all in favour of a bit of perspective.'

'I mean not all private lessons are bad, are they?'

'Do you have any particular ones in mind?'

'Yes I do.'

'And are you going to tell me which ones they are?'

'They're the ones I always enjoy, the ones I'll never tire of.'

'Tell me more.'

'They're the ones with you, miss.'

He hauled himself off the couch and took Rachel's hands.

First Aid Kit continued to sing. Garibaldi led Rachel to the bedroom ready to be Johnny Cash to her June and Gram Parsons to her Emmylou.

Acknowledgements

Thanks to: Laura Macdougall and Olivia Davies at United Agents, Kate Beal and Sarah Beal at Muswell Press, Fiona Brownlee, Laura McFarlane, Graham Bartlett, Barnes Bookshop. Special thanks, as ever, to Jo and Rory.

Simon Mullholland banker

Giles Gallen tutor

pupils: Paulo Rivetti

Briony Ainsworth [1]

76

99 Jade Murray

82 Freddie Barker [2]

{ Amy Marsh

91 { Chloe Marsh

Penny + Jeremy

Lucia + Luigi

Hilary + Vince X

Ginny + Phil X

Laura

Helen + Clive X coke row